PARTY LINE

Peter A. Luber

Sageous
New York
2009

Sageous
Amsterdam, NY 12010

First published in 2009
By
Sageous
Copyright © Peter A. Luber, 2009
All rights reserved
Publisher's Note
This is a work of fiction. Names, characters, places, and incidents either are the
product of the author's imagination or are used fictitiously, and any resemblance
to
actual persons, living or dead, business establishments, events or locales
is entirely coincidental.

Party Line / Peter A. Luber
ISBN: 978-0-578-03593-2

Printed in the United States of America

CONTENTS

Lou

Ashley

Howard

Alice

Phillip

Gloria

Ted

Lou 1

His thin cheese raft did not inspire Lou's confidence, but it was enough, in a soft sort of way. Though the craft lay motionless on the calm surface of the scenic lake, his bare feet felt motion. Lou could not see the clear water that suspended the soft white craft high above the lakebed. Lichen-covered boulders crowded below him, with small red fish darting between them. Wary of the melted Swiss seeping between his toes, he dove off the tasty raft.

Lou plunged headlong into the chilly water. He shut his eyes and kept them tightly sealed, wary of startling the little red fish. One of the creatures stopped inches from him and tipped its bowler to his consideration. Lou smiled and reached to shake the friendly fish's fin. Just as his fingers approached the extended fin, a fishhook snagged the happy creature and hoisted it out of sight. Time to go back to work, Lou thought. Lou swam for the surface, his eyes still shut tight. He broke into warm air and slapped the hard area encircling him for a purchase. His hands slid uselessly across the smooth surface that impeded his exit. He shook off his ire at his pointless effort, and used the steps on which he was standing to wade from the kiddie pool. He cleared the still pool comfortably dry. And, he noticed that his eyes were still closed.

He cursed those sealed lids when an object that confined his left foot halted his progress through the playground. He pried them open and stifled his objections with a paternal sigh. The kids don't need to hear that kind of language, he thought. Of course the darlings likely heard nothing, save their own uproarious laughter. A glance down with unlidded eyes told him why all the students in his classroom were so amused: he had stepped into the metal wastebasket again. They tossed their ancient math books in the air in delight. The books capitalized by climbing out of reach in a violent flurry of paper wings. The flock of texts escaped through the open classroom windows and disappeared into the overcast night sky. The students yelped with joy and chased their texts, darting as a chattering unit through the windows.

Lou strolled the empty aisles. Years of bic-tooled etchings immortalized each wooden desk. Third row center: `Eddie loves Allie.' Fifth row front: `Jim Morrison lives.' First row, back seat: a flawless reproduction of Da Vinci's Mona Lisa, with sunglasses added and robe removed.

The walls of his classroom were green blackboards littered with unsolvable equations, blank papers with gold stars, and awards from the noblest of institutions. Lou smiled, turned halfway around to face an assembly of his formerly esteemed colleagues. They had convened behind an importantly long cardboard table, careful to position all of their metal folding chairs on one side of the formidable object. That way they could avoid conversation with anyone but him. They did not applaud his presence, as their hands were occupied with the concealment of either their mouth, ears or eyes. Lou paid their hopelessly cliché no heed. The panel of his peers would always be there, expecting nothing, so he gave them nothing. Nothing but peanuts. Lou grabbed a few handfuls from the leather peanut pouch on his belt. He tossed them to the scientists. They held their mute positions. The long words Lou had tossed bounced harmlessly off their oversized foreheads, their black caps shattering on impact, lost forever. Lou threw up his arms in disgust, wishing the vermin gone from his sight.

He laughed. They were.

The wind from his guffaw blew the papers on his desk into the air, inciting a snowfall in his kitchen.

"Well shit," Lou swore. He absently triggered the microwave. Leaving the open oven to the task of melting the snow, Lou settled back down to Tuesday night poker with the boys.

The boys were discouraged that Lou would consent to allowing a woman to play. He shrugged off their grimaces. He had never met this smartly dressed woman before, but if she wanted to risk her sizeable pile of chips against them, why, Lou didn't mind one bit. Poker was poker.

Lou bet all his blue chips on a pair of threes. The thin woman puffed her cigarette thoughtfully, brushed back a lock of perfectly styled and colored blond hair, and called without speaking. When Lou showed them his fine hand, the boys grew suspicious and dropped out. The confident woman stayed in.

He bet a red chip. The woman grinned and sent her own in after it. Her greedy blue chip won a plastic wrestling match on the thick green cloth, then devoured the carcass of Lou's poor dead bet. Lou didn't appreciate that type of play, but the rules demanded that he wager again.

The wily woman folded under Lou's three chip ante (though he did manage to pull one back with a piece of sticky bacon without her noticing). Lou won. She threw her hand on the table in disgust. One of her five kings rose up and hurled itself at Lou. Lou reviewed his high school thesis on vector analysis and caught the card as it emerged from the back of his neck. Not wishing another near-death experience, Lou stood, gathered his chips, and turned to leave the game.

His first step fell unfinished into blue sky. He followed. He screamed. He gobbled the Fritos in his hands so that he could free them to flail in a desperate struggle for a handhold. He reached behind him and painfully discovered that an unseen cliff loomed inches behind him. He spread his fingers to grab a convenient outcropping on the granite face. When they found one, he dug his fingernails into the rock. They miraculously held. Lou jerked violently to a stop on the cliff wall. His breath shallow, his heart breaking ribs, Lou hung suspended above an abyss he dared not survey. He waited. In time, he regained his composure and dropped ten inches to the ground below him. Grunting noises on the red prairie to his left attracted him.

A large maple tree on the horizon caught his attention, probably due to the boy lodged in its thick lower branches. Beneath him, a small yellow dinosaur of the stereotypical cartoon T-rex variety jumped in the air repeatedly. Its smiling jaws slammed shut at the apex of each short flight. It was trying to lodge its long white teeth into the boy's dangling sneaker. Its short forelegs waved menacing, useless talons. The dinosaur snapped them in frustration with each failed attempt to snare lunch. The boy spotted Lou. Their eyes met. Lou knew the boy, or at least understood his plight.

"Mister," the boy whispered, "You gotta help me. This thing escaped when my fish bowl fell off the dresser. It ate my whole family."

"What am I supposed to do, Howie?" Lou called up, hands forming a megaphone over his mouth.

"Just talk. It'll be attracted to you. See?"

Lou didn't see. He was busy trying to escape the attacking little beast. He was doing well, concentrating on staying to the green gravel path that the heavy dinosaur would sink into. As luck would have it, a red traffic light forced him to stop to wait for the green. Lou faced the red light, arms folded. He tapped his foot lightly, rolled his eyes. He did not dare to look over his shoulder at the cause of the hairs tingling on the back of his neck. He wished the light commanding the empty crossroads would change, so he could escape with his life.

It finally did, and Lou crossed the crowded street to enter the safety of the movie theater. The building had no doors, just an open wall into darkness. Lou hustled in, attempting to disguise his troubled gait with an Irish jig. He stood in front of the rows of empty red chairs, at the foot of the screen. The curtain opened, the house lights dimmed. Pre-feature footage rolled. The absent audience cheered. Alice was next to him, resplendent in her blue sequined evening gown.

"Isn't it amazing how much they get away with in films these days?" she asked as she studied the refreshment stand ad. Lou was surprised that popcorn and soft drinks dancing across the screen could be so enticing. When the Milk Duds started their routine, he had to turn away, unable to face the twelve-dollar candy.

Thousands of cheering fans applauded for him.

"Lou! Lou!" they chanted. It sounded like Boo! Boo!

Lou waved to them, pleased with the attention he felt he deserved. With a gesture from Alice (the graceful removal of her gown), the audience was silent. She handed Lou a scrap of chalk. Lou addressed the blackboard, his finger pinching his lip. He scanned the unfinished equation filling the green surface. He shook his head, sensing that little pictures of teddy bears did not belong in the denominator position of the solution. He selected a peanut butter and jelly sandwich from the chalk tray.

"That'll do," he said aloud. He tried to wipe the board, succeeding only in smearing jelly on the equation. Furious, Lou tore the board from the wall and flipped it at the innocent students seated attentively at their desks in the sunny classroom. The solemn kids craned their necks to prepare for death. Lou shed a tear. He knew that soon the ragged slab of slate would reach his class, severing all their precious little necks. He attempted a rescue, but the vector analysis papers he threw at it only flocked together and escaped through those windows.

Little Howie, free of his Jurassic nemesis, stood up in front of the hurtling blade. His furious, glowing red eyes did not leave Lou as he whipped his hand above him. He caught the knife and tossed it to the ground.

"Thanks," Lou shouted, unfulfilled by Howie's success.

"No problem, mister," Howie replied, "But I only stopped it cause I got something more to show you."

"What?"

"Oh, you already know."

Howard smiled and raised a burly arm behind his large head as if to scratch behind his ear. Instead, he grasped the handle of a large brass zipper sewn into his neck. Howard pulled it. He worked the metal fastener over his head, dividing his thinning scalp. He moved the noisy zipper over his pasty furrowed brow, then down his face. He split his false grin. He continued, unzipping his wrinkled neck and barrel chest. The zipper's track followed the man's six-foot frame to his groin, where it met the fly of his faded Levis. Howard was ready to shed his skin.

Lou was fascinated, but annoyed by the independent action. He would get no more information out of little Howie. Lou lost interest in the undisciplined spectacle. Howard froze in space. He then began to lose resolution, disintegrating into black sand crystals that floated lazily to the grass. Howard had become an uncased hourglass.   Lou was uneasy, deeply, empathetically, disturbed. He felt as though Howard's rapid decay was happening to him. He looked down.

It was.

After his high-top sneakers had dissolved, Lou felt a soft tickle in his toes. The grey fog that surrounded him was nipping at his bare feet, eager to dig in. When his feet became part of that fog, the tickle became pain; deliberate, nauseating pain. He panicked, and by the time his knees joined the soft mist, he thought to look away from the carnage.

The change in perspective did not halt his dissolution. Lou had no need to imagine the agony as his thighs vaporized. He glanced down again. The decay made him seem immersed to his crotch in the thick smoke that surrounded him. There was nothing, Lou knew too well, to dip in the mist.

He swung his locked hands below his hips, passing them through the former location of his legs. He suspected now that the grey cloud was him. He realized the cost of his experiment after his hands came back before his face as hazy outlines, mere images of their former substance.

Lou screamed, swatting at the fog with his stumps. He watched his hips slowly disappear. The cloud of his dissolved parts inched up his stomach, toward his chest. Lou was about to die. He was not interested in the sensation, but was without recourse. He could only tremble and wait for his dust to fill his open mouth.

"Relax," a female voice hidden behind him casually whispered.

Lou turned around to face a muscular, sun-stained woman perched atop an ancient John Deere farm tractor. Alice. The farm implement dieseled quietly, slowly crossing the freshly plowed field. It lumbered toward the county fair that shimmered in the distance. Alice was still speaking.

"It's not going to bite, and neither will I," she smiled, reaching a hand down to help him up, "Now climb onboard, or we'll never get to the fair in time for the chicken fest."

Lou took her hand. Alice hauled him up and tossed him onto the soft hood of the tractor. She worked the shifter, ground some gears, and the red convertible launched into the desert sunset, heading for the distant New York skyline that only slightly marred the flat horizon.

Lou paused to admire the stranger beside him. She was a good farmer, but overqualified for the job. He studied her almond eyes, feebly concealed behind rose tinted sunglasses. They were glassy, as though Alice was damming a river of tears. They betrayed her otherwise cheerful demeanor.

Alice sensed his gaze, and nervously ran manicured fingers through her natural blond hair. As they drew to a stop in traffic on the crowded avenue, she cast a questioning glance at him.

"Do I know you?" she asked.

"I certainly hope so, Alice," Lou said, "We just drove 2,000 miles together."

"Good point."

"Besides, you know I needed a ride to the city today, so we must know each other, right?"

"Right. So let's go into the bank to catch the chicken fest," Alice concluded.

They gave the car to a passerby and climbed the steps of the Stock Exchange. Once inside, ripe human stench was first to greet them from the smoky gloom. Lou crossed the empty marble vestibule to the main trading hall. He entered in time to watch the last few moments of frenzied corn pecking before the final bell.

He paused near the door, enjoying the spectacle of little yellow talons scampering among the fallen bits of paper and droppings. The peckers gathered in tight groups, wherever some corn remained, heads bobbing at the floor as often as at each other. They argued fiercely, thrusting paper scraps into each other's faces, and then bobbed frenetically for more corn. Their suits were immaculate, however, guaranteeing no betrayal of their activities when they boarded their trains later.

Lou sprang into the air at the clamor of a fire alarm bell above his head. It clanged a half dozen times, directing all activity on the floor to cease. Almost all of the peckers complied. Well-groomed gentlemen dropped their remaining bits of paper, spat out partly chewed kernels. In the orderly fashion of polite society, they quietly donned London Fog raincoats and left.

One disturbance defied the recess. A group of traders huddled in a far corner of the giant room. They shouted obscenities and pecked maliciously at a trader crouched in their midst. Lou turned to them. He grabbed the nearest offender by his Armani shoulder pads and hurled him out the majestic double doors. The others took no notice. They continued their abuse.

The dark figure in the center saw Lou and stood up. He towered above the peckers, and casually shoved a couple aside as he stepped toward Lou. He took Lou's hand, shook it vigorously with both of his. Lou felt displaced relief when his hand reemerged from inside the man's grasp intact.

"Thank God you're here, mister," the forlorn trader spoke in a soft tenor that denied his bulk, "I was sure these guys were going to tear me apart. They've been after me for days."

"You look okay to me," Lou responded, "Why didn't you just walk away, Phillip? You are Phillip, right?"

The glaze of fear left Phillip's deep set eyes while he scanned Lou. He started to mouth a question, but his peril interrupted. He tried to grab Lou's hand again, missed, put a hand on his shoulder instead.

"You don't understand, mister," Phillip said, trying to steady his voice, "They've been after me, trying to get me. I didn't realize when I ducked into this place that I was walking right into their lair."

They were alone in a high school gymnasium, safe. Phillip brushed dust from his blue suit and adjusted the football jersey beneath it. Lou curbed his personal disgust long enough to admire the physique of the young man. Phillip's build nearly burst the suit jacket. His neck was bigger than Lou's thigh. His abdomen stretched the blue, numbered shirt with every breath. Like the rest of the peckers, his feet ended in the same poultry talons.

"Maybe they just want you to belong, Phillip," Lou observed.

"No. No, this is not where I go. Oh, no," Phillip's last exclamation was blurred by his movement away from Lou, toward the far goal posts. He broke into a dead run when the peckers arrived on the field. Their striped ties flapped like red tongues behind them as they took up the chase. Wall Street Journal banners waved from the steel poles they shouldered. Lou watched the parade disappear over the desert horizon. When the action subsided, and the horizon was again a pencil line, he turned around.

He stumbled down unlit basement stairs, crashing into musty steamer trunks stacked at their base. He rolled over, rubbing his bruised head. Though he dreaded to raise his eyes toward the shadowy cellar, he did. A single incandescent bulb clutched by a frayed wire nailed to the floor joist above poorly lit the cluttered room. Directly under the bulb was a tired old armchair, burdened with the quivering body of a slim young woman. Her thick dark hair hung damply against her scalp and face. Her long, sinuous legs were bare, and a panting teenaged boy in a flannel shirt held her frail ankles firmly and far apart. Three more youths of equal size and hygienic abandonment crowded closely, cajoling the aggressor into frenzy. The battered girl's body shook with revulsion, her face was wet with tears and sweat, but her cold eyes never left her assailant's.

The group took no notice of Lou, as the soft yellow light could touch little more than their own sweating faces. He scrabbled around in the dark for his feet, items he was inexplicably pleased to find, and set them flat on the dusty floor. This didn't help, for, even poised for heroics, his limbs would not respond. The scene continued unhindered, an arm's length away.

"Gloria!" Lou shouted, panicking. He heard his shout, felt his chest contract, his throat burn with the effort. The players ignored him.

The first monster was finished. He gasped that gasp, wiped sweaty drool from his chin, and handed twitching ankles over to the next eager user. Gloria had ceased to struggle. Her only movement was the heaving of her exposed chest. Her eyes, though half lidded, still remained focused, frozen, and far from empty.

Lou quit his futile rescue attempts. A subtle change in the nature of the cellar encounter had rendered his aid unnecessary. The second assailant repeated the actions of the first, but the ambiance of the event had changed. Lou felt at ease, pleased at the imminent outcome. He reclined on silk pillows and confidently witnessed the true rape take shape.

Gloria held a dark oblong object in her hand. The dim bulb did not allow Lou to identify it. When Gloria raised her arm to the level of the current attacker's head, he was able to see a small power tool: a saw, he decided, with a thin, silently spinning circular blade. Like something used in an autopsy, he supposed.

With no dramatic warning, Gloria placed the whining saw against the youth, scribing a bloody line into his temple. The youth did not react as she continued her cut across the top of his head. He pumped as if she were still docile. Indeed, he seemed to aid her surgery by keeping his head steady, tilting it towards her to facilitate the brutal surgery.

The other monsters overlooked Gloria's activity even after she had removed the bloody cookie jar lid she had created from her ignorant assailant. What finally tore their attention away from their sexual mayhem was the shimmering spectacle contained in the current ravager's skull.

Gloria tossed the scalp and saw aside. She reached her gloved hand into the open head. The boys closed in for a better look as she scooped out a handful of cut, glittering diamonds. She took advantage of their awed delay to reach in for a second helping. She placed her booty into a cloth pouch, tied it shut, and dislodged herself from her attacker before the thugs moved in for their own piece of the new action.

They fell to the floor with the opened attacker, burying their grimy arms in his head, thrilled by the warm grey matter they pulled out. They held it, dripping, to the light, inspecting it with unveiled greed before shoving it deep in their pockets. Even the victim was partaking. He reached up unsteadily, dipping his hands into his head; mining his own brains. Gloria stepped away, nonplussed. She pulled her black leather outfit back on, and squatted next to Lou.

"Hey mister," she said, moonlight glistening on her raven hair, "What are you doing on my roof?"

"Your roof?" Lou asked, hands in his pockets. He tried not to stand as near to her as he wished to.

"Yeah. My roof," Gloria said. She cut a striking figure against the lights of the city behind her. She stood as tall as Lou did, but her defiance and the brick cornice bent his neck. One thin white hand rested on her hip, the other spun a small crowbar like a baton.

"I staked this place out months ago," she hissed, "Did my research, all the groundwork. This is my job. Now get off my roof!"

"Hey," Lou said, turning, "No problem, Gloria. "He was unable to hear her last query.

Lou straightened the pencils again. He had three, but only two fit at a time in the slot at the top of his slanted school desk. One clattered to the floor of the silent classroom, causing the teacher to glance up from her desk at the front of the class. She couldn't locate the sound. Lou dropped his eyes back down to his test paper to avoid capture. He returned to the task of filling in the little multiple-choice dots on his answer sheet. Lou wished someone gave him a test sheet in order to verify the correctness of his answers. Oh well, he thought, they're always right anyway.

A chorus of flatulent exposition disrupted his work. The fat boy to his left, Ted, was squeezing his hands together repeatedly, taking innocent delight in the obnoxious sounds he generated. The teacher took notice. She stood up and banged her ruler, trying to appear angry.

"Now you stop that, mister Pantagone," she said, stifling a giggle.

Ted did not respond, nor did he stop. Instead, he concentrated on his successful disruption, increasing the volume until the riot echoed off the blackboard.

The whole class was involved. Ted's display delighted all 40 of them, but they managed to quell their laughter to avoid Teacher's wrath. When Ted lifted one cheek to coincide with his palm squeezing, adding a melodramatic sigh of relief with each effect, the class could no longer contain itself. The children burst into uncontrolled laughter. They rolled in the aisles, slapped each other silly with joy. Lou was mildly disgusted, but understood their wild amusement. He turned his attention back to the progenitor of the adolescent entertainment.

Ted had aged twenty years since last seen. His vast bulk was jammed tightly into his desk, bending it. He continued to produce the sounds. The class continued its hysteria, but Ted was no longer amused.   His eyes, two ink dots behind great puffy cheeks, were moist. He was trying to shout over the din; trying to shout at the children, at his teacher, to stop laughing.   Lou reviewed the class.   The children still celebrated, some did handsprings. No one was going to stop. Lou turned back to Ted, feeling pity swell within him.

Ted had swelled as well, doubling his size since Lou's last glance. He still sat at his desk, though it was hard to see. His girth had shoved the other desks in his row several feet away from him. Fat, still tightly wrapped in a green surgical gown, drooped to the floor in the aisles on either side. Ted's eyes were lost behind ballooning mounds of pink flesh. Tears squirted from two of the folds, and Ted continued his silent shouting.

He also continued to grow. His head had reached the ceiling, blubber from his cheeks forming buttresses on his shoulders to support the weight. The other children, still raging with laughter, streamed from the room. The teacher ushered the last of them out, then left with them. Suppressing a giggle, she closed the door behind her.

A handsome woman in wrinkled business attire approached Ted from her unaffected seat at the front of the class. Her tweed skirt puffed out in the fury of Ted's flatulence. She opened a three-foot diaper pin, brandished it before Ted.

"This is for you, Ted," she shouted, tears streaming. Ted seemed to breathe a sigh of relief, but it was hard to tell since fat had sealed all his orifices.

She hefted the round end of the open pin, carefully aimed the point at Ted, and ran at him with the lance.

Ashley 1

Casual pressure from Ashley's slim-fingered grip dimpled the skyscraper window's metal sill. She liked the view. Sculpted buildings ranged below, each of their myriad lights aglow against a twilight gray sky. Ashley floated high above a sea of grandeur, her hungry eyes filled with countless testaments to success.

Her office window was propped open. She leaned out to peer into the concrete abyss that disappeared beneath her lofty perch. The rabble scurried far below her, visible only as ants in little red ties or blue skirts. She was above all that, throned in the clouds, locked safely in Bill's old office. Poor Bill. He was out west, skydiving, missing everything. Everything. She smiled, patted the neatly packed parachute on her new desk. Poor Bill.

A cold breeze crept into her spartan workplace. Icy fingers of soot threatened the careful purity of Ashley's bare legs. She didn't mind. A little grime never hurt anyone, she thought, especially when it's subservient. She scraped it off with one of Bill's ties, careful to leave the grimy cloth in a corner, where it could lie untouched by harmful wind. She ran a hand across her ivory desk, pausing for an extra rub of her rhino horn penholder. She always took special delight in her special luxuries.

A memo from the executive boardroom requesting her return to the strip poker game interrupted her reverie. She acceded, allowing herself once more to lower herself to her superiors' level. All in the name of success, she decided. She wondered why the men would want her back in the game after she had already laid them bare. I guess it makes sense, she thought.

Ashley rocked in a high-backed leather chair, across the round green table from the new, fully clothed, dealer. He did not share the awe that the fleshy pink executives held for her, and that disturbed her. It wasn't right. She tried to get up, go back to her office to demand that someone research the turn of events, but the stranger had already begun dealing. Ashley remained, preparing herself for the critical round of five-card draw by lighting a fat cigar.

She chose not to pick up her cards; they were handling the play functions quite well on their own. They shuffled about on the table, grunting a little, and then set themselves in the desired order. Three kings and two jacks, face up. They all mugged at her, seeking to attract her approving glance.

Ashley ignored the hormone driven antics. She studied instead their poker value, carefully planning the use of each paper royal. Three kings and two jacks. She thought that might be a good hand, but perhaps not good enough. She checked her purse. Two kings, unaware, were scaling her cluttered handbag's satin lining. The thin royals had raided her untouched sewing kit for threads, climbing rope, and safety pin pitons.

She plucked them from their heroic endeavor, pocketed their climbing gear, and slid them into her hand, where they needed to be. She touched the inadequate jacks with the glowing end of her cigar, sending them quickly into deserved flame. The knaves' tortured cries of pain and humiliation subsided before the dealer noticed. As a precaution, however, she dropped the errant flaming cards to the floor, snuffed them under her foot. She lifted her head to face her opponents.

The dealer had chased out her flabby poker buddies with a gutsy one chip bet. Ashley's chips lifted off the felt table and flew into the pot, seeing and raising him. She admired their fortitude, for poker chips.

Suddenly her kings erupted into battle against each other, locked as they were into an inevitable heated contest for her favors. Two noble warriors fell, leaving her with just three of a kind. Ashley cast a furtive glance at the dealer. He was waiting, confident. He would win, she knew. She folded, furiously hurling her impotent kings at the dealer. He showed her his hand. She had lost to a pair of threes. The game was out of her control. She had sacrificed perfectly good chips to a pair of threes.

Ashley felt herself sweating, squirming. This isn't right, she thought. The dealer had won. The dealer can never win,

unless she, Ashley, held the deck. Ashley shook uncontrollably.
She wanted to run away from the dealer, the troublemaker. Yet
she was his. She was at his mercy, and he was oblivious to his
awesome power. This is wrong, she thought, pounding her fist on
the table. It was her office! Her victories! The ignorant asshole
had to be there for Fuck's-sake, or be gone!

The smoky room shook for her, its grimy mahogany walls
fading to a uniform shade of dull gray. The man abruptly jerked to
his feet and threw himself out Ashley's window. He left an empty
metal folding chair behind, fallen on its side. It rocked a few
times, and then melted rapidly into the tile floor. After it had
vanished, her office walls regained their beige pastel hue, defining
lines and windows returned. Her bathrobed colleagues also
resumed their positions, ready for more abuse. The play
continued. Ashley reached for the phone to take Bill off hold,
changed her mind. Another time, she thought; maybe when he
lands. Poor Bill.

Satisfied, Ashley gathered all the chips on the table and left
the game. She crossed the carpeted hall, shoved open the door to
the supermarket selling floor. She strode the baked goods aisle,
pleased with her ability to ignore all the fattening foods. She
hurried past the checkout clerks who watched her with poorly
veiled envy. One, Sharon from the old days, hustled around the
candy display to greet her. Dogged respect littered her puffy eyes.
Touched, Ashley swatted Sharon out of the way with extra care.
Sharon seemed to appreciate the extra attention. She positively
glowed as she headed for the cleanup on aisle four. Ashley was
pleased that peasants from her past had come out to welcome her.

The old world, however, was not where she wanted to be.
She pressed on, strolling through the automatic door that
whispered her name as she crossed its rubber threshold into the
crowded mall. The mallies, in their uniforms of shorts and silk-
screened t-shirts, reverently broke ranks to allow her passage. She
stood six feet above them all, and was impressed by her ability to
avoid stepping on them.

Ashley paused to admire her altruism in sparing the little
people before, for Image's sake, she squashed a young couple
happily pushing a stroller built for twins. She had to chase the two

babies around in several circles before her Gucci pump found them. Its sensible heel landed squarely on their diapered rumps, squeezing tiny squeals from their fat pink mouths. Squeals of glee, of course.

Ashley burst through the mall's front exit doors. Her two-handed thrust launched the heavy glass panels into a row of the parked cars that filled the vast parking lot. When a crowded blue Chevy minivan blew up, its pyrotechnic demise drew a gasp of appreciation from Ashley. After the smoke cleared and she could survey the destruction, she nodded in satisfaction. Cars and body parts were scattered widely, lending a pleasant seasoning to the boiling asphalt. Emergency vehicles arrived on the scene too late; tar rendered them immobile and useless.

Serves them right, she thought, for parking so close to the mall, making me have to use a handicap spot. She stepped over some flaming rubble to her car. The overpriced German luxury coupe was idling in the handicapped-only spot, left front wheel parked on a flattened wheelchair. A man with no legs struggled nearby, failing to make headway through the hot tar. He turned angrily at the approach of Ashley's clicking heals. She paused before she strode over him, and waited. His pale features softened.

"Oh, its you, Ashley," the crippled sot said from somewhere below her skirt, "Then I guess it's okay that you parked your fine car in my spot, 'cause you deserve to."

Ashley smiled down at the poor fool, sensing that she had once known him. She dismissed the thought and the image of pity that the man projected, and stepped into her car. Her $80,000 car, with every option. Of course the sorry cripple respected her; she had made it.

Before she could find her keys, the passenger-side door of her car opened for her. Ashley ceased her search and threw herself through the driver's side glass to save time. She crawled across the wide leather seats to the opened door. She stepped out of the car, careful to display ample leg before she stood. Cameras clicked while rabid fans cheered her talented exit. She scanned the crowd, ready to meet the glance of every onlooker, every empty, hopeful loser. Ashley would show them that someone – that she – cares. She would look them right in the eyes with her practiced droopy gaze.

Just one set of eyes returned her majestic gaze. The rest were cast down at her presence. That single pair was plenty. They were tired eyes, regarding her from a world away: trying not to stare, embarrassed by what they saw, yet unable to look away. Angry at being shaken by those eyes, Ashley dismissed them, made them go away. And away they went. Her power renewed, she stepped through the brass lobby doors, past the leering jeers cast by small groups of lingering admirers. She stopped, peered down the great marble hall that coldly welcomed her, as she did every morning.

That morning it was especially unappealing. Black moss carpeted the stone wainscoting. A foul-smelling blood red liquid, thick enough to support a dead security guard, flowed like a noxious river into each of the banks of elevators at the center of the hall.

"Hey," Ashley said, "I have to get upstairs."

The river, of course, parted for her.

Ashley stepped over a drying red rivulet and into an empty elevator car, mindful to maintain the volume of her clicking heels. She pushed her button, the top one, and waited for the stragglers to jump in before the doors closed. She hated that, when the stragglers would try to get a ride in the last instant before the elevator doors closed. Often she would push the 'door close' button as well as her own top floor button to cut those tardy interlopers in half as they crossed the collapsing threshold.

This time she magnanimously broke her rule and left the door of the empty car open as long as possible, hoping for some company during the long ride to the top button. No one came. The steel doors slammed shut.

Ashley put on her elevator face anyway. She watched the lights flash across the overhead display...2, 3, 17, 44, 212. The gleaming doors opened, and Ashley stepped out into filtered yellow sunshine to face her unruly seventh grade math class. They were chattering, playing games, singing, and being happy. Not one of them was looking her way.

She dropped a potted geranium on the big desk near the blackboard, its resonant thud drawing no attention from the children arranged in neat rows before her. Though her classmates were generally smarter than she was, Ashley was obliged to teach them. Someone, after all, had to teach them, or at least take down the names of the talkers.

The lowlife children, in between nose-picking, whispering, and coughing, were busy poring over the test on their desks; one of those institutional tests that define how smart children are. Half the students were trying to fill in their answer sheet circles with naked bananas. Smart. The kids were quiet, showing respect for Ashley and all the institutionalized tests she had taken. She sighed, pleased that her superiority had won over these mindless urchins that she called friends.

The behavior of that damned kid, Theodore subverted her authority like a fire alarm. Theodore was her first husband, or a guy just like him. He was trying to be a class clown again, following all the rules proscribed in his book. He was making obnoxious noises through his clenched, chubby little fists, and then looking up at the ceiling in apparent innocence. He had completely abandoned his test. His banana was eaten, its peel placed carefully on the floor, awaiting an unsuspecting passerby.

Ashley ignored his silent cry for attention. She looked back down at her budgets, as if nothing had happened. The printout columns swam before her. Numbers jumped off the sheets and square danced away, confounding her attempts to make any sense of her important job. Ashley was confused, lost, and decided to abandon her budgets and go back to something she knew: her classmates, and getting them in trouble.

Her inattention benefited Theodore, whose antics had rallied the class, winning their laughter, applause, and undying loyalty. Ashley, vomiting at this thought, took charge by slamming her clever laser pointer on her desk, seeking the class's audience. She was pleased at their obedient response, and took advantage of her political victory over Theodore immediately. She wanted to laugh out loud, but knew that that would not be fitting. Instead, she raised a finger at the miscreant, and conjured her best authoritarian persona.

"Now you stop that, mister Pantagone," she shouted. Her anger seemed to excite Theodore. He squeezed harder, pneumatically pumping himself up to unavoidable proportion.

Ashley left the classroom. Outclassed for the moment, she vowed to return with a special weapon to deflate Theodore's dangerous ego.

She sat near the back of the plane, in the seat that disaster movie had noted was the safest of all. A sweaty man shivered beside her, clutching a large briefcase. The case ticked, intriguing Ashley. She was sure that briefcases don't tick. Not even in the airplane movies where they blow up.

Blow up.

Ashley panicked. She juggled the hot case between her hands.

A stewardess, neatly clad in a flowery blue housedress, stopped at her seat.

"Would you like some tea, Miss Ashley?" the stewardess asked, proffering an open can of yellow latex paint.

"No thanks. Would you like this bomb? The man in the next seat just gave it to me."

"What man?" the stewardess asked politely, indicating the large hole in the plane where the man's seat once was. Clouds and chickens whisked across a grey sky backdrop.

"Well, he was there," Ashley corrected herself, "And he did leave this case. Maybe I should give it to you."

"But it's ticking, Miss Ashley," the stewardess laughed.

"Of course it is," Ashley smiled, "Bombs do that. Now, can I give this to you or will I have to defuse it myself?"

"Sorry Miss Ashley. Airline rules say we cannot collect bombs on board," she leaned down and pinched Ashley's cheek, "Now why don't you just keep it as a souvenir? Now, please remember to fasten your seatbelt dear. Ta ta."

"Fine, I'll handle it myself, as usual. Bitch."

Ashley unlatched the case and lifted the lid. A rush of air filled the vacuum inside. She winced. Nothing happened. She peered into the open briefcase. It was empty, except for a peeled banana and a large diaper pin. She shoved the banana whole into her mouth and swallowed. She then snatched the pin, and tossed the briefcase out the hole. Once it was outside and clear of the plane it exploded. The blast caused a rain of confetti to fall on the pretzel vendors in the street below.

Ashley unbuckled her seatbelt hastily. She was late again. She had overslept during the long flight and, and now feared she would never make school by the homeroom bell. She went straight to the front of the plane and accosted the cab driver, demanding that he pull over.

"But lady, we got three blocks to go yet, and there ain't no traffic."

"I don't care. We need to land now. I'm late for my institutionalized test."

"Oh. In that case, Miss Ashley, I'll pull right over, and don't worry about the fare."

The cab pulled onto the sidewalk and Ashley's door flew open. She felt a twinge of guilt about the fare and threw the wretch a nickel, then burst through the brass doors of her school.

She reentered her class, relieved to see that she was not too late. Theodore was larger but, like her second husband, he still hadn't released yet. She waved a shotgun at the lesser children to encourage them out of the classroom. They left in a hurry, glad to be free. Only Theodore and a dark child wearing a dealer's visor remained. Close enough. She approached Theodore, pin ready.

Theodore released. His obnoxious noises filled the room, almost knocking her down. Ashley was bigger than that. She would take her pin and pop Theodore, before he ruined her school. She could do it. She was the only one. Sadly, she could make no headway against his wind. Theodore filled the room. Ashley looked at her pin. It seemed very small. Theodore was large. Hopelessly large. Hopelessly. Ashley could do nothing.

Theodore blew up. Ashley screamed, in anger.

Howard 1

Howard kicked a pebble, encouraging it to precede his trudge up the grey, dusty hill. He was lost again. His mother was nowhere in sight. Nothing was in sight; just a lump of a hill, a gnarled old oak tree standing sentry at the top, and the road he followed, switch-backing its way up the smooth shallow incline.

Howard predicted that the yellow monster from the meat department was on the other side of the hill. Why not? It wasn't anywhere else. He thought he had thwarted it back at the bank, but instead it took all his cookies and left him alone.

Alone. So alone.

Howard made a fist in anger, accidentally squeezing too hard the hand of his companion. She yelped in pain. Howard slowed his gait enough to turn to Claire, to see that she was all right.

She seemed fine, though a lot younger than she should have been. Since they were on their way to school, he decided that was proper. Howard tried to murmur an apology to Claire for crushing her hand. She did not hear him. She just presented him with a baby-tooth grin and continued walking along the straight road. She swung Howard's arm playfully with each step. Howard turned away, fearing the worst from the yellow monster over the hill. As long as it's just Claire with me, he thought, I can handle things.

"Of course it's not just Claire, Howard," a deep voice sounded from over and somewhat above his shoulder. His father caught up to them, swinging his lanky frame in easy cadence with Howard's short steps. He continued, "You know we wouldn't leave you be at a time like this."

"I wish you had," Howard shouted, "Now I have to protect all of you from the yellow monster!"

His family ignored him. They resumed their stroll up the hill. All his brothers, his parents, and several relatives he failed to recognize strode abreast on the narrow path. Howard shook his head, continued walking. He was not getting to school on time.

As they neared the crest of the hill, Howard's hopes swelled. After all, he thought, it is the family, even if they aren't wearing the clothes I bought them. And they were all heavily armed.

His brothers wielded a silver tea service with open malice, and his father and mother each hefted open cans of green house paint. The three strange women at the rear carried extra rolls of paper towels. Howard admired their diligence.

Over the hill the sun was rising, gilding thick green grass. Bears frolicked, birds sang. Howard was pleased. He intentionally squeezed the palm of his bride, and screamed when his fingers closed tight on themselves.

Howard dropped to the grey gravel road with a thud. He sat cross-legged where he landed, adjusted the cuffs on his dungarees, and tried to make it all go away. It was too late. The yellow monster had already snatched Claire into its roomy jaws and waddled away. The family chased the creature down the hill, the way they had come. Howard wished to get up to rescue his doomed family, but his legs would not uncross. He sat still as the beast dove, little arms first, into the horizon. It was followed, in fine style, by his family.

His world was quiet. Howard remained seated, nursing unwarranted optimistic anticipation. Maybe the family rescued Claire, he thought. Maybe I won't find her in the meat section this time. Maybe I'll get to keep my cookies. Maybe everything will be happy again.

Howard's small thoughts were interrupted by a steady slow thumping in the distance. He would have hoped that it was his Dad thrashing the monster. But, he was accustomed to the worst, and waited for it.

Beginning at the tree, a wide crimson shadow swept down the hillside, passed Howard with a liquid whoosh, and disappeared into the horizon. The road on which Howard was planted remained grey, as did the oak's ancient trunk. Its leaves, and all else in Howard's universe, were bloodied.

The thumping grew faster.   Howard's legs uncrossed themselves, bounced him to his feet.   He spotted a police car parked in the red field to his left.   He hesitated, remembering the rule about bringing police into the play.   Howard decided he had no option.   He dashed across the field, skipping happily over short pink grass and crimson hay bales.

The car's windows were closed and fogged.   Howard tapped the glass nearest the driver's seat, desperate to get the officers' attention.   The window shattered, revealing the gaping maw of the yellow beast just before its hand-sized teeth snapped together, scraping flesh from Howard's nose.   He shrieked in terror, overturned the police car with a gesture, and sprinted to the tree.   He looked over his shoulder as he ran, keeping a close eye on the monster's progress.

It had burst through the bottom of the dropped birthday cake, and was brushing off great chunks of vanilla icing.   It roared piteously at its plight, casting its glassy eyes about for Howard.   It had terrible vision.   He guessed that he might have enough time to make it to the tree before the beast noticed him.

He was right.   His gaze connected with the beast's marble stare one step before his arrival at the base of the tree.   The chase stopped while the opponents considered each other.   The monster winked.   Howard turned his attention to the tree.   Its first branch was too high.   Far higher than the monster, or Howard, could reach.   Howard had no choice.   He began twirling his arms in windup for his daring leap.

The yellow monster was at the tree when he jumped. Howard pressed the ground with great force, unleashing all his tightly sprung energy at once, and flew.   He swept straight through the beast's tiny outstretched forelegs, landing safely on the first branch.

The monster was little now, far below him.   It roared in anger.   It tried to copy Howard's flight, but failed.   He was safe. Miserably safe.

Howard waited in the tree, as he always did, for the monster to go away.   It always did, never to be found again.   His family, especially Claire, always disappeared.   Never to be found again.

Something changed on the ground far below him. The monster remained, snarling and trying to be ferocious. The tree was the same. The breeze still carried crimson ripples across the fields. There was a new silhouette on the ground near the monster.

Howard brightened at the gratefully unexpected development. This man'll help, he said to himself, I'm sure of it. He might even bring back Claire. Howard searched himself for something to say, something smart and adult that would keep the man there with him. He drew a deep breath.

"Mister," he shouted, cupping his hands, "You gotta help me. This thing escaped when my fish bowl fell off the dresser. It ate Claire. It scared off my whole family." Howard was angered at his words, certain that was not what he wanted to say. The man on the ground noticed Howard, but said nothing. Howard tried to get his attention again, this time not expecting a response:

"Mister, just talk to me for a second. I need you to pay attention to me," Howard said. Moved by a suspicious warm feeling for the man, he called down an addendum to his plea:

"Forget that! Don't say a thing! It'll be attracted to you if you talk, and I don't want that to happen. Run now, mister, before it sees you!"

Howard saw that his message was understood by the silent stranger. The man turned and raced down the hill, the yellow monster nipping at his heels. Howard was relieved, certain that the man would be able to escape the monster with ease. He also felt good because he could safely drop to the ground just below his dangling feet and continue his search for Claire. He followed the branch away from the trunk to its end, and stepped off.

Howard landed squarely on the grass, his sneakers digging two cube-shaped dents in the ground where he had touched down. He stepped out of them, and ran to the market to warn Claire.

Claire wasn't in the meat department. No one was. The butcher's counter was empty. No meat, no sausage, not even any blood. The place was scrubbed clean, glistening under the bare fluorescent bulb. Howard was ready to despair when he remembered school. Elated at his memory, he turned and ran up the steps to his math class.

Class was already in progress when he arrived, panting, and sat at his desk. He wasn't in trouble, though, as the teacher was preoccupied with the man at the blackboard. He was trying to add three and four, but couldn't seem to draw the line at the bottom of the equation.

The teacher encouraged the man, as did the rest of the students in the crowded classroom, but the poor fellow was making no headway. He was becoming more frustrated as well, grabbing the clipboard from the strange teacher's arm and hurling it at the class.

Howard enjoyed the comical diversion. He snatched the clipboard out of the air. The man was relieved that he had caught the teacher's clipboard, and waved his thanks before returning to his difficult math problem.

"No, that's not the right problem, mister," Howard shouted, trying to keep the man's attention without disturbing the teacher, "But as long as you've stopped, I've got something to show you. It's the yellow monster."

The man was not paying attention. Before he could continue, Howard felt a distant memory nudge him; a memory that included the man, the yellow monster, and a tree. He slapped his forehead in recognition.

"Oh, that's right. I don't need to tell you. You already know. In that case then, follow me. You've got to help me save Claire." Howard turned around, elated that the man had joined ranks with him and his family. He rolled over to slap the back of his new partner.

And connected only with the empty sheets of his lonely waking bed.

Alice 1

Alice shook her head violently. She wished for a change in her vacant surroundings. Light avoided her wide eyes, denying her opportunity to fill her world. She needed light. Illumination was exit, freedom from emptiness. Light was substance, comfort. She banged her head on the hard slab behind it, but could not even produce stars to aid her vision.

Alice refused to concede to the persistence of darkness. She pried herself from the sheet of ice that clutched her in a frosty embrace. She swung her legs over an edge she could not see, and let her feet fall until they contacted a rough floor. She stood, hoping for a high ceiling. When safely erect, she extended her arms into the ink. Her elbow had barely unfolded before her hand shattered a pane of black glass. A deeper sob of delight overshadowed her instinctual cry of pain. The blackness had broken with the pane. Illumination was present. Not much, but enough slivers of silver moonlight had disrupted the equalizing ebony air to thaw her heart, and her bed.

She gingerly traversed the broken glass littering the weathered wooden floor, able to avoid both splinters and loose boards lit by the moon's shattered reflection. The narrow hallway she traveled was damp, dim, and lacked a destination. The dark was unwilling to surrender to the weak light. Its long shadows lunged, wrapping their icy, unfelt talons around her. They wrung life from her shivering limbs.

Alice was nervous, but trusted her resilience. She sought the way out, the glowing exit signs she knew hung over each of the countless doors that must line the shadow walls. She could not find them. She was unable to turn her head, or to coax her own eyes into movement, cooperation. Undaunted by her growing terror, Alice pressed on. The priority of comfort was overwhelming. She needed to escape the nightmare, to return to the soft realm of warm satin sheets.

Alice spied a glimmer at the end of the infinite hall. Her body twitched to the distraction. She felt her face flush. Fresh morning sunlight enticed her from beyond a pinhole in ancient lath and wallpaper. It could not invade the gloom of the hall. Alice was glad it had failed, saving both levels of purity from corruption. The brilliant light did not require intrusion to lure her to its warmth, to encourage her reluctant body into action. When she moved, she was impressed with her power and focused decisive action.

Alice reached the beacon in one stride. The hole was large enough to allow easy egress. Its thick rim pulsed with warm pink blood. It exuded a subtle scent of lilac. Alice hesitated, transfixed by the beauty of the undulating doorway.

"This is very cool," she said aloud. Her ear-piercing words broke her trance, allowed her to notice a change in the living hole.

The fleshy exit was closing, fast. Soft cilia wriggled at its edges in anticipation of joining their approaching mates. Remembering the darkness she occupied, Alice sprang into the shrinking diaphragm. At its threshold, she decided to retreat. She feared that she would not fit. She was too late. Her legs had already hurled her into the tightened opening. Alice held her breath and ducked her head away from warm wet plaster.

The viscous iris tickled her thighs as it closed around them. She giggled at the sensation, and then laughed in victory as her ankles popped through the orifice. As a last gesture of benevolence or maybe indigestion, the orifice launched her to freedom, to light. She could not look back at the unknown creature that had almost consumed her. She concentrated instead on the landscape spread before her.

Alice sank ankle deep into soft, caressing red grass. Giant oaks, whose lowest branches sprouted twenty yards overhead, shaded her from the oval sun. Their dead leaves, larger than her, fluttered to the dirt path she followed. Though they were pleasant to observe in motion, Alice was annoyed that she was obliged to stop repeatedly to drag fallen leaves out of her way. The hard work impeded her progress toward comfort.

The path led her through a grove of singing pines. The tall trees were harmonizing a Hank Williams tune. She hummed along with them as she ambled by. The path provided a world of distractions: enchanted squirrels; tattered beggars dancing at bonfires; a baby shrouded in snakes; pink pastures that flowed in a shallow arc to the city in the distance. All of them demanded her attention, but she shook them off. All but the city. There was comfort there. In the distance.

She needed the city. She wanted to explore its canyons, to bask on its quiet shores. Sadly, it was far away, well beyond the range of her bloody feet. She searched her environs for a means to reach the city. The best journey tools Alice could discover were the path and her legs. She chose not to believe that meager fact, and forced her reluctant eyes to make an extra effort. It stung her temples, but a careful peripheral glance to her right revealed transportation. She rolled her soft, strained blue eyes. It was right beside her.

"I knew it," she said softly.

It was her car, from before. Long, red, open, it rested serene at the side of the road, inches from her. She lifted the door latch near her wrist. It moved too easily. The car was locked. She had no pockets in the t-shirt she wore, so she had no keys to get into the convertible. Undaunted, she took a few steps back, breathed deeply. At the crack of the starter's pistol, she sprinted at the door, hurdling it at just the right moment. The open space of the convertible was not that easily entered, however. Her leap did carry her into the air, but not into the car. Clear, breathable molasses suspended her in the air above the door, outside the car.

Enraged, Alice summoned unknown reserves within her to push through the thick air. Her body shook with strain as it struggled to move through the empty space. The sole reward for Alice's effort was a throbbing headache. The red vinyl upholstery still lay empty an arm's length away.

"Dammit," she said as she surrendered to the heavy air, "Isn't it amazing how much abuse I take? They left the car, my getaway, right there, but kept it out of reach. The bastards. Oh, to hell with it."

Alice felt her frustration ride her words away from her. She was relaxing, releasing tension, and, she thought not coincidentally, breaking her unseen bonds. She fell from the air into the driver's seat. She sat in quiet, mild surprise before pulling her chrome key from the gold chain at her neck. After a few unsuccessful attempts, she inserted it in the ignition. She turned the key. Nothing happened.

"Fine," she said, "will my problems ever stop? These shitty days are driving me nuts. Come on car, cut me a break." Alice finished her plea with a sentimental peck on the steering wheel. The car sputtered to life. Alice rolled her eyes and smiled. She revved the engine of her retired ticket, nodded. The comfort of the city was not far. She moved the shift lever to 'R', and pointed the hood ornament toward the city on the horizon. Freedom filled her, and she liked that.

When she stopped for a red light at a silent crossroads, she noticed a man crouched in the sandy grey shoulder beside her. His panic-stricken attitude disturbed Alice. His arms swung frantically, fending off an unseen demon. Though his slim torso twisted violently, his legs were folded, limp. The soft features of his face were also passive, though his mute mouth was open wide. He faced away from her, and his consumption of quiet terror had precluded awareness that she idled beside him. This guy's really got a problem, Alice thought.

The light changed to green. Alice automatically lifted her foot from the brake, but a strong feeling prevented her from releasing the clutch. She looked back at the man. His condition had deteriorated. Alice was alarmed and ready to flee before she laughed at her own foolishness. Hell, she thought, shouldn't I be giving this guy a leg up too? She spoke, welcoming the man to her car.

"Relax, mister," she said. Her words ricocheted off the man's head, tousling his black hair, and returned to her. They were a cold slap of wind in her face, ineffective. She tried again, easing her effort.

"Relax."

The man heard her. His frenzy ceased. He slowly turned to face her. His bright, bottomless eyes regarded her amicably.

She saw that he wished to go with her. She gestured through molasses air for him to get in the car, but he was hesitant. She smiled.

"It's okay mister. This is my car, my old one. It's not going to bite, and neither will I. Trust me."

The man was getting her message. He had to have been, as only a few of her words were blowing back at her. She stretched across the car to the other door, opened it. She had to push mightily with her legs to move it through the stubborn air.

"There," she said, "I wasn't sure you knew I was here. But I am. Always. Now, climb on board, or we'll never get to the city in time."

The man acquiesced, entered the car. His ability to move easily through the thick air impressed Alice. He sat straight in his seat, left the seatbelt unbuckled. He regarded her quietly, respectfully. She liked that, too.

They cruised the wide empty avenue. Skyscrapers leaned in from above, taunting her old car with their silent threats of crumbling in its path. The canyon walls held their breath, however, and the red convertible was able to pass unhindered through the mighty gauntlet.

Alice parked at the foot of the largest granite sentinel on the narrow street – a looming grey edifice that invited no one. While studying the building, she noticed the man in her passenger seat. His presence startled her, but she held her defenses at bay. The stranger regarded her with knowing, caring grey eyes that denied danger, promised hope. She self-consciously fixed her hair, smiled at him.

"Excuse me fella," she asked, "But do I know you?" The man seemed surprised at her question.

"We just drove 2,000 miles together," he said, his voice soft, familiar, right. Alice considered his compact response. She wondered what he meant.

"That's a good point," she found herself saying, "I guess we both need to get to the beach today, huh?" Huh for real, she thought.

"No," the man contradicted, "I needed a ride to the city today." Fine. Alice thought, I guess maybe I don't know this guy after all. She gestured to the crimson door of the ugly building beside them.

"I suppose you're right," she said, resigning herself to his wishes, "So let's forget about the beach. You go ahead into that bank that seems to be more important than our comfort, and I'll catch what's left of the city's peace."

The man smiled and turned to his door. Almost in response to his gesture, the city vaporized, leaving her to drift in white emptiness.

Alice waited impatiently for her world to return. The rapidly enveloping blackness was of no concern to her. This darkness, though quickly complete, contained no shadow, and it was warm. Her world, her comfort, was coming; it was just a little late. She sighed when it silently lifted its pink pasture up against the soles of her bare feet. She found a sandy path and followed it through hazy sunshine to the beach.

Alice heard the muffled thunder of distant breakers. She ached to taste the sea's salt once more. She stood on a wet grey boardwalk. Calliope music whistled behind her. A glass railing at her waist prevented her spontaneous leap to the cherished sand below.

A little girl played beside her, carefully removing the arms from her special dolly. Alice smiled down at the girl, tugged one of her pigtails. The adorable child looked up at her with cartoon-sized black eyes, listlessly acknowledged Alice's presence, and then returned her attentions to her doll. She hugged the doll, eliciting a moan of affection from Alice. Then the child opened her little mouth wide and tore into her dolly's chest with scythian teeth. She ripped cloth and stuffing out with abandon, spitting it onto the beach. Plastic blood spurted, soaking the boardwalk with crimson pain.

Easily turning from the child, Alice faced a cotton candy vendor. The ancient Italian man in a black and white striped shirt handed her a tuft of rich pink fluff. As the vendor cackled, she staggered under her treat's great weight. It quickly overwhelmed her grasp, slipping free. It snapped the guardrail and fluttered toward the beach.

Alice seized opportunity by clinging to the paper cone. She tumbled to the beach with the purple tuft. The candy reached the sand first. She landed on it, allowing its sticky sweet tendrils to break her fall. She did not need to clean the mess: the animated confection crawled off on its own when she stood.

Alice wiggled her toes in the soft cool sand of the beach she had finally achieved. Its velveteen texture caressed her bare feet, drawing a moan of pleasure from her. She was at the beach, the place of comfort. She reveled in her personal triumph as she walked toward the water. Before she completed three light steps, the beach rejected her intrusion.

It thrust sandy talons blindly into the space around her paralyzed feet. The beach was intent on pulling her beneath its luxurious surface. Its sandpaper grip scratched her, burned her, engulfing her slender limbs. She fought, striking with clenched fists, biting when the sand reached her chin. Her fierce defense loosened the sand, facilitating her descent into the angry shore. Regardless, she fought on, forestalling despair until slick silicon shadows dimmed her eyesight. There're those shadows, she thought grimly.

After it fully confined her in its gritty midst, the sand eased its grip. It held her gently, rubbed her softly in a sensually effective manner. It was trying to comfort her, but not in the way she had expected. Alice found terror in the new, tender, embrace. She needed to hide from it, to go home; back to hard safety.

She understood. Seconds passed, resolve set in. Like a drowning victim she calmed, realizing her inevitable fate. Alice waited for the blackness to come at last. She smiled, feeling her cheeks displace warm sand. It would be over soon. Something powerful wrapped itself around her hair and plucked her like a carrot from the sand to safety.

She turned to face the smooth chest of her rescuer, a beautiful man who stood over her, smiling casually. Alice gasped. His majestic, dark features would have sent Michelangelo back to the marble. In relief, she reached her arms around his neck and stood on her toes to kiss him. His lips stretched into a thin grin. The pleasant gesture continued as she approached, beyond natural bounds. His grin spread to his ears, disappeared behind hairy lobes. Her hero separated those lips, revealing rows of uneven pointed teeth. A green forked tongue darted from between them.

Alice gasped and recoiled, but the violent face closed in, filling her vision. Blue eyes to torn red eyes, the couple regarded each other. Alice felt scaled hands closing on her neck, a cold vice careful not to throttle, just control. She felt leather lips touch hers.

They kissed, and the embrace did not disgust her. She did not hate the creature. They kissed again. That tongue entered her mouth. Its whipping motion excited her. This isn't so bad, she thought, I could be happy with this monster. She opened her eyes for a less biased view of the man. His lidless red eyes concentrated on her pleasure, not her fear. That was good.

A distant tolling moistened the broken eyes of her dead lover. He dropped her, returned to his original form, and ran away. She landed with a thud on the breaking waves. She felt no need to swim. Rolling over in soft comfort, she saw the naked back of a man lounging on a satin beach towel nearby. He was reaching for the source of the tolling, grasping at empty air.

The toll.

Alice realized her world. Her existence was renewed. She woke quickly, happy to arrive home. She slapped her husband's bare ass.

"Ed, you'd never believe the dream I just had," She said, rubbing her eyes and pushing a strand of sweaty blond hair from her eyes, "It scared the shit out of me."

"Try me," Ed said, rolling over to face her. His motion caused Alice to slide into a trough with him. The warmth was nice, Alice admitted, but she still had trouble with the insistent pressure from the new waterbed to push Ed against her. She wedged her arm between them.

"Um, let me think," she said, and paused, trying to remember what had so recently been the most important event of her life.

"No use," she said at last, "It's gone now. But I tell you, it was really something. Oh well. Never mind. It mustn't have been important enough to remember."

"Guess not," Ed responded with a yawn, "What time is it, anyway?"

Alice glanced at the battered alarm clock on the side table.

"Oh shit," she said, sitting up, wide awake, "It's late! We have to get to work. It's past time to feed the chickens."

"I was hoping you wouldn't notice," Ed smiled, rubbing her breast. She politely pushed his hand away. He sighed and got up, strolled naked into the bathroom. Alice admired his build as he walked across the bedroom. She did that every morning, but this time with a special interest in his upper torso. Ed smiled at her before he entered the bathroom, uncharacteristically locking the door behind him. She dismissed his action before she heard the hiss of the shower a moment later. She yawned and studied the ceiling, feigning an effort to remember her dream in order to linger in bed another minute. Then she sat up and struggled over the high rail of the waterbed, cursing softly at the distraction. Well, she thought, buying it was my idea. Besides, it was good for their backs, and Ed's sex life. She summoned the strength to leave it.

Alice stood, wincing as her feet contacted the cold parquet floor. Her right foot touched something else as well.

A shard of glass.

She swore at the cut on her foot, checked for blood.

Then, she remembered.

Alice cried out and scrambled for the bed. As her fingers slid off warm satin sheets, the floor became fluid. She fell into darkness; smothered in frigid, liquid wood.

Phillip 1

Run. Don't stop. Keep exhausted legs pumping. Clutch tight the checkered bundle. Don't wear out. Don't eat. Don't stop. Just run.

One step ahead is the goal. One step. Turn left, sprint the dark alley. Maybe that will shake them. Glance over left shoulder, see if they're shook. Forget looking back; there is no need. What's coming comes, regardless. Don't stop. Just run.

Master the steps of the Exchange, two at a time. They won't go in there. They never do. Can't follow. Don't look back. Climb the steps, two at a time.

Stop. Wait.

No.

The steps lead the wrong way. No Running allowed at the exchange. Only trading, stealing, and chickens. Why run to the Exchange? Because. Because it's the place. The right place, the secure place. A place they dare not tread. A place they avoid. A place where they can't follow.

A place to be avoided.

Bound down the last five steps into the living room. Father's there, with his pipe. He takes notice, nods in acknowledgement, then resumes ignition of the mouse in his bowl. The mouse squeals, but its smoke is savory and well worth the minor complaints. Father stands, closes the front door. He's a small man. He has to reach up to the doorknob. He sports a red satin smoking jacket. The house as always is warm, big, secure.

Father is walking down the long carpeted hall, toward the kitchen. He gestures for company. He pauses at the stock ticker, an antique, near the phone. It's working. He picks it up, carries it to the trophy case farther down the hall. The towering case is full of rusty football trophies. They're not working. They're rotting. Father is laughing; mottled teeth vibrate in his open mouth. The burning mouse seizes opportunity and escapes.

Father pitches the ticker at the case, smashing protective glass. The tiny football heroes leap from their tin towers, weather the rain of glass and ticker tape. They descend mighty pine shelves to the floor, working in perfect synchronization: each figurine forming part of a living ladder that the next could climb down. The last fugitive, a tiny Pop Warner star, is caught handily by his athletic comrades. A tiny cheer goes up.

The glory is premature.

The ticker tape machine still ticks. Paper tape had flowed to the floor, landing in small fluffy piles until the chickens formed. A fine group of birds they are, resplendent in double-breasted blue suits and smart red ties. The trophy gang stoically faces the new threat. They huddle, discuss their play options in squeaky little voices. The chickens capitalize on the delay and peck the players. The golden huddle, and remaining trophies, are consumed.

Just run.

Run through the kitchen, past mother to the back door. Flee the hungry chickens. Don't stop. Just run.

Fling open the back door. Leap over the wooden threshold. Fall onto the sturdy carpet of the Exchange. Get up quickly. Slip on canary printout, fall down again. The chickens are still hungry. Get up!

Too late. They are speedy chickens; clever poultry. They are already here. Hovering, just above, attempting to snicker through lipless beaks. Try to stand. Try to run. Fall down. Think: hell, let them peck. There are worse fates in life...

No. Don't stop. Father's on the balcony, watching. Chortling that jovial, ugly, practiced chortle. He stuffs another mouse. He lights up. Squeal, squeal, squeal. Chortle, chortle, chortle.

Just get up.

The pecks don't stop. One chicken at a time. Perfect order. Hands over face, protection. Maybe that will help make it all go away. A pinch, somewhere, claims otherwise.

Get up.

A feather sprouts, left forearm. Another pokes through spandex thigh. Shit. Don't panic. Just get up. Just run.

Can't get up. Scraping talons can't find a purchase on the floor. No purchase, no getting up. Think: oh well. Everyone must accept certain sacrifices in life. Running would have been nice.

One chicken clucks. An odd cluck. Beady eyes wide, it surges into the air, out of the fray. It plunges into the waiting jaws of a wolf. Seems hungrier than the chickens. The others notice, annoyed that order has been disrupted. Annoyed but smart. They cease their pecking. They step aside. Get up. Stand. Got up, good.

Now. Just Run.

No. Not yet. Thank the grey beast, pet its soft fur. Thank it. Say:

"Thank God you're here mister. I was sure these guys were going to tear me apart. They've been after me for days. I was ready to join them one more time. Be secure."

The wolf growls. A friendly growl, like a purr. Don't tell the wolf it purred. Big mistake. Instead, let it make its statement, then disagree. Best to disagree with friendly strangers, then run. Like Father always said.

The wolf stands tall on its, his, haunches, forepaws folded over his chest. Now, say it. Don't let him interfere with perilous security. With the chickens. Understand. Shake this dog off, it only wants to help:

"No. No, this is not where I go. This isn't where you go, either. I've lost enough time as it is, time from security. Oh, no. Excuse me, now mister; I've got to make this down."

Just run.

The chickens, regrouped, plucky, hungry, approach. Prepare. One last chance to run. Fix the shoulder pads. Tuck in the blue jersey. Tighten grip on the ball. Head low. Squat into position. Launch, and run.

Run like hell.

Out of the barn, onto the field. Long field. Hash marks are many yards apart. No matter. Just run. Downfield the grass is greener, taller, more threatening. Slow high stepping legs. Make the tall stuff take longer to arrive.

Too late. Its here. Underfoot. Slicing cleats. Forget stopping. Besides, the chickens are still behind, as hungry as ever. Just run.

Jump.

Try to leap over the tall grass. It nips Nikes with a venomous snap, slows progress. Pedal legs, and hang on. Almost there. Progress adds height; the grass has eaten the chickens, and the goal is in sight.

Fly.

Clear the tall grass, land. Dig cleats into fresh Yale Bowl sod, spring damp and smelly. Cross the goal line, spike the ball.

Stop spiked ball from ricocheting through living room. Fail. The mindless ball bounces wildly, breaks the Steuben pig on the mantle, shatters the glass frame entombing the first share Father ever traded. It heads for father. Stupid, stupid ball. Father catches it, stuffs it in his pipe, and lights it. The ball squeals, Father chortles. That practiced chortle.

The house is the same. The stock ticker is larger, shinier. The run is over, the change was short. But Father is pleased. Always pleased.

"Just run, son. That's all I ask. Just run."

Gloria 1

"This is it," she whispered, "This is it."

Everything had gone according to plan. After scaling the sheer face of the office tower wall, Gloria clung to the right floor, the designated window. She didn't need to reference the blueprints to verify her position. The grey full moon spotlighted in silver tones the door set in the skyscraper's flank. Gloria turned the wrought-iron knob, gave the thick oak door a medium tug. It broke off its hinges. Gloria held it in the air, checked below her, and then dropped it cautiously to the grass. When it touched the ground, Gloria took a chance and pushed the door over onto the lawn. She winced when it landed with a solid thud. She was aware that there might be people in the empty house.

She waited silently until she was satisfied that nobody had witnessed her clumsiness. She breathed again, checked her equipment, then crossed the tattered wooden threshold. She wriggled through the rusty casement and dropped into a dank basement. The painted pane that had allowed her entry flapped shut behind her. Its rattle echoed through the cellar.

"Watch the noise!" she scolded herself. Gloria's vision was not impaired by the dark cellar. She was, after all, a cat burglar. She snickered at her clever thought, then began her foray.

Leftovers from the Victorian mansion sprawling above her littered the cement floor: old furniture draped in billowing sheets; a well maintained pool table, rack of balls set for breaking; a small group of rats quietly playing craps in a corner, eyeing her suspiciously over their little grey shoulders; a stack of dry lumber near the stairs, covered in dust and termites whose chewing she could hear.

The room brightened abruptly, lit by an incandescent bulb suspended directly over her head. Gloria instinctively froze. She had not triggered the light. She moved her eyes, searching the cellar for an appropriate hiding place. There was no chance to attempt an exit without a speedy capture.

"Who's down there?" a cracking adolescent male voice called from the top of the unpainted wooden stairway. Gloria didn't answer, didn't move. She just clenched her fists, and shook with anger. She wanted to scream. She had worked for months on the job, and it had been ruined by some bastard who had switched on the light.

The light.

Gloria smiled. That was the key. The light. All she had to do was turn off the light and the voice upstairs would go away. She stretched to where the bare bulb fixture swung from a frayed cloth wire. She tried unscrewing the bulb. It wouldn't turn in its rusted socket, but it was hot enough to melt her flesh. She pried loose the fingers that remained stuck to it after she retreated from the stubborn bulb. She was surprised that it did not hurt to leave so much of herself attached to the hot yellow bulb. She felt for a switch above its glare. She found a small knob and twisted it. The knob turned, clicking loudly, repeatedly. The light stayed on, burning brighter with each click. She tried pulling instead of turning, deducing that it was one of those special three-way lights. The knob did not dislodge until she had extracted more than a foot of rigid plastic shaft from the socket. She hefted her prize, happy to pack the extra weapon. The bulb was still glowing. She carefully sewed the small saber to her already well-stocked tool belt. Abandoning her initial plan, she stood silent, still, and hoped the caller was just checking that all was secure.

"Who's down there?" another voice shouted down the dusty wooden steps. Equally adolescent, but deeper, bigger. Gloria's heart stopped. Her taught mind was swept bare. It was Them. Again. Dammit, she thought, I should have recognized this basement!

She transformed her paralyzing shock into panicked, excessive action. She snatched a ball-peen hammer from her belt, and swung it at the condemning bulb. It was a frustrating endeavor. With every true whack with her hammer, the bulb would sail, unsmashed, across the room. It bounced off a wall, knocked books off a shelf, and then reset itself above her for the next try. Gloria endured the torment for three swings before she submitted to its resilience.

She dropped the hammer, her only weapon, and hastily searched the room for a possible escape. There was no outlet. Someone had bricked in the small window she had wriggled through to gain entry earlier. Crapshooting rats already occupied all the possible hiding spots in the shadows, and she had no interest in disturbing their games. She decided that, instead of trying to run, she might behave as if she belonged there. Maybe it wasn't really Them, she thought, and I'll just have to explain my presence to a suspicious homeowner.

She went to the pool table and grabbed a cue. It bent flaccidly when she picked it up, its tip flopping lazily to the floor. She discarded it and picked another, this time one not made of rubber. She lined up the cue ball with the rack, took a couple of practice strokes, and shot hard, determined to sink all the balls in one break. If she did, she could prove that she belonged there.

She scratched, missing the cue ball entirely. Unchecked force sent the cue stick across the room, where it impaled itself in the concrete wall. She selected another and tried again, with similar results. She grabbed a third cue stick, bent over the table with determination. She concentrated on her shot, keeping her eyes open for it. That made all the difference.

Gloria discovered that her strokes had been true. The timid cue ball was rolling out of harm's way each time a cue tip approached it. She heard its timid screech when the stick approached, followed by a sigh after all was clear. Gloria put her hand to her mouth, embarrassed that she could be so callous in her actions as to let a helpless cue ball become a victim of the hard wooden stick. She dropped the cue and picked up the warm little ball. She caressed the shaking orb. She was surprised at how soft it was. She wondered how, being so fleshy itself, it could manage a career of knocking all the other balls around.

A subtle air current disturbed her. Gloria cocked her head up in time to see a green cinderblock hurtling slowly toward her. She screamed, and threw the cue ball at the block. The ball wailed pitifully in flight, but succeeded in its purpose. The cinderblock and ball exploded into a thick cloud of popcorn on impact. When the air cleared, Gloria was still in peril. Her ruckus had summoned the boys into the cellar. They hovered less than a yard away, sneering, leering, munching popcorn. They wanted more, and again Gloria was unable to escape.

She tried anyway, fruitlessly running around the pool table, facing a member of the greasy gang of sophomore toughs with every turn. They blocked her way, let her turn and run some more, then blocked her way again. Their leader, an especially well-oiled brute in self-torn Wrangler jeans and green flannel shirt, eventually tired of the game and blocked her path permanently. He grabbed her arm, preventing her from turning. He drew his pitted, oily face to hers until their noses touched. He stared at her, his black eyes boiling with rage.

"Who's down there?" he whispered hoarsely. His cold spittle landed on her lips.

"No one" Gloria tried, "No one at all."

"Oh," the leader said, releasing her. He and his three buddies looked at each other, puzzled.

"Hey, man, don't look at me," the tall one in back said, "I just said I thought I heard something. Don't mean I did!"

"Yer an asshole, Norman," the leader sniped, "Let's get outta here." They turned and headed for the stairs. Gloria tittered with delight at the unexpected success of her ploy.

The boys stopped as a unit upon hearing her quiet laughter. They kept their backs to her while they exchanged glances, realizing that Norman wasn't such an asshole after all. Gloria's stomach shrank into a tight knot. She rolled her eyes. She couldn't believe her reckless stupidity. I'm stuck now, she thought, I'll have to deal with the inevitable again, and make the best of the situation.

The leader was in her face. He bent over and snatched up her ankles. Laughing, he hoisted her feet into the air. She back-flipped gracelessly into an old overstuffed chair.

Pinned in the musty chair, her world tilted and half blocked by its tattered wings, Gloria grew confident that she was in the right place. She had been there before, countless times. It had been a long time since They had accompanied her, but she understood the necessity of Their presence. She braced herself for Their attack. She had to let Them; They were about to make the best of her situation for her. Gloria suppressed laughter at the sick irony.

When one of them ripped her panties away, she felt her body fight the violation without instructions. It valiantly worked itself into a sweat, struggling to keep its legs crossed. She distantly felt her thigh muscles surrender, one at a time, under the untenable pressure of the evil adolescent force controlling them. She felt her body's shudder of revulsion as the panting youth broke into her. The boy feigned haughty laughter to signify his empty victory. Her sensibility's treason frustrated her, but Gloria accepted it. The plan called for self-deception.

She paused her review of her rape, fulfilling an unexpected impulse to check the dark corners of the room with refined peripheral vision. She felt the presence of a voyeur lurking in the corner, near the rats. She could not see him in the shadows, but he was there, ready to interfere. She wanted to turn to him, tell him to get the hell out, that this was her score, not his. That unseen man had interfered before. She was unable to react to his presence. Any attention garnished on him and his rude intrusion would scare off the brute working her crotch. If the attacker withdrew too soon then all her planning, her career, would amount to nothing. Her moment of panic was assuaged, however, as the man proved unable to act as well. He cowered in the shadows with the rats. She smiled, proud that her destiny could outmaneuver the man.

Her pleasure was an interior facet, as her body was occupied, enduring the pain and humiliation of the moment. She let it continue, unwilling to raise suspicion in Them with an unexpected movement. She saw that her primary assailant had managed to destroy most of her once tidy pink polyester outfit. The speed of his pumping indicated that there was an end in sight. His empty black eyes clouded with anguish over the inevitable finish. He jerked twice and stopped, panting, still inside her heroically uncooperative body. Gloria thought she heard a cry from the man in the shadows. She decided that it was time to finish her job. She relaxed her body, asking its forgiveness for the submission. Only her bare chest moved, uncontrolled as it heaved in air to forestall the shock. The leader withdrew, used one hand to wipe the sweat from his chin. She let him back off. The blueprints had indicated that he was not the right one. She needed the worm with the red flannel shirt.

She quietly rejoiced when the leader passed her ankles to that very shirt. Another greasy child with no mirrors at home, but an object of perfect beauty to Gloria. She forced her body to let him in, and felt its cold reaction to her betrayal. He did enter, though, and Gloria set to her task.

Per the plan, her tool belt had all the necessary tools within easy access. She took control of her arms and reached to her waist. Careful not to relay her actions to the mindless young fool humping her, she eased a grease pencil from the belt, twisted the knob at its top, and raised the exposed point to the boy's forehead. Pushing lightly to avoid detection, she scribed a straight line across the top of his forehead, extending each end to a point just above his ears. Red Flannel failed to notice. She sighed, relieved at her initial success. The scoring had gone according to plan. She shed any remaining doubts, confident that the effort was worth the revival. Ian would continue his perfect record.

She returned the grease pencil to its place in her belt, and felt a little to the left for the mini circular saw. It was there. She pulled it out, tested the trigger. The blade spun, releasing the high-pitched whir of a well-tuned machine. She touched the spinning saw to the guideline on the boy's forehead, chose the best starting point. She couldn't hesitate. His sweat was already causing her score to run. Gloria sliced into the acne-ridden flesh without incident or blood. He didn't notice. His approaching climax assisted her by steadying his head as he concentrated on his final moment. His groaning accomplices, including the leader, paid no heed to her surgery. Gloria's only concern was that the interloper would try to cut in on her action. He didn't, still bound by whatever ties or fear held him in the shadows. She paid as little attention to him as possible, her concentration consumed by the score of her life.

The saw's pitch rose as it came to the final millimeter of uncut scalp at the back of the boy's head. She gripped a clump of his matted hair in her gloved fist and removed his lid. She tossed it to the floor, mindless of the reaction it might provoke in the onlookers.

The moment was hers. The diamonds were hers. As Ian had predicted, the head of the red flannel shirted deviant was indeed the repository for thousands of her sparkling stones. A glittering cache of perfectly cut stones commanded the meager light. None were less than a carat, some more than three. Gloria allowed herself no more time for awe. She thrust a hand into Red Flannel's head, scooping as many diamonds as she could hold without making her fist too big to retract. She deposited her new wealth in a small sack drawn from her belt.

Time was running out. She noticed that the audience had quieted. They were aware that the game had changed. Red Flannel, who had climaxed dramatically before she finished the cut, caught their stares. He lost interest in his recent dominance and cast his eyes upward. He wanted to see what his partners were gawking at.

Gloria took advantage of the diversion generated by the gang's recognition of new treasure and thrust her hand in for another helping. The second catch was larger, and her greedy fist was stuck in the confines of Red Flannel's skull. She shook her head at her carelessness and yanked hard. With much abrasion but no loss of diamonds, Gloria's closed hand cleared the boy's head. The attentive audience responded to the discernable pop by moving in for a closer look.

Gloria tied shut her pouch, returned it to her belt, and dislodged herself from the remains of her nightmare. She fell out of the chair, hitting the dusty floor squarely with her face. She heard the commotion above her as the boys dug in for a share of Red Flannel's treasure. She rolled unnoticed to safety. She dismissed a tug of guilt for subjecting her body to the torture again with a pat of the bulging pouch at her waste.

"Hell, it would have happened anyway," she said, "Always does. I might as well cash in." She saw a tattered, empty doorframe in the cinderblock wall. An indigo night sky beckoned from beyond the peeling frame. She asked her body's forgiveness once more before she leapt through the narrow opening.

Her primordial relief at escaping the boys was immediately eclipsed by fear from the same source as she left the safety of the office tower and plummeted toward a dim rooftop twenty stories below. Her childish fear was short lived, as pride in her recent heist would not allow her to fall to her death. She wanted to enjoy the sparkling stones in her pouch, to live the life they promised. She turned her palms into the rushing air, forming the same airfoils that she had once, long ago, made out the window of her parents' station wagon. The ersatz wings caught the wind, worked it effectively. Her fall slowed to a brief, gentle descent. She touched her leather boot heels down on the roof. Her knees bent on her landing, but her new skill had protected her. She resolved that next time she should think her operation through to the escape so she wouldn't have to learn to fly.

She adjusted her leathers, checked her tools and her pouch. All were in order. She performed a quick scan of the dark Park Avenue roof, and was startled to observe that she wasn't alone. A grey-eyed man was squatting a few feet away, watching her.

She studied him. He obviously wasn't a resident, judging by his simple dress, humble demeanor, and blatant lack of fear. A wave of jealous anger broke against her. Gloria's body and her mind, again one, both shook. She summoned strength unknown for the massive personal effort necessary to prevent herself from either attacking the quiet man or jumping off the roof. She didn't want to hurt him, or learn how to fly, so she held her ground. She straightened and spread her feet to appear intimidating. And a little taller.

"Hey mister," she thought she shouted, unable to hear her voice, "What are you doing on my roof?"

"Your roof?" the man responded. His question thundered through her, echoing out into the empty night sky beyond the roof. The blast nearly leveled Gloria, but she clenched her toes and remained standing. She focused her strength, drew a deep empty breath, and projected her words with all the force she could muster at the man standing meekly a dozen paces away.

"Yeah, my roof," she bellowed. Gloria still could not hear her words, but sensed that he had. She removed her crowbar from her belt, hefted it in what she hoped was a threatening manner.

"I was here first. I knew where the diamonds would be tonight. I let these guys rape me after school. I staked this place out months ago. I did my research. I paid my dues. This is my job, and I don't think you have a right to it, mister. Now get off my roof." She gasped for breath, nearly rendered unconscious by the last sentence. Still, she had to look defiant, protect her wealth.

The man allowed her little time to prepare for his response.

"Hey," he boomed, hands in his pockets, "No problem, Gloria."

He turned his back to her, disappeared into a bright room filled with children, and then was gone. So was the room.

Gloria's weak knees failed. She collapsed to the liquid surface of the roof. She submerged into warm, confining black tar. Her face floated above the hot liquid. She felt no fear. It was her roof. With little else to do, she gazed up at the night sky, watched the moon race from horizon to horizon and back.

She was at peace. She had her booty. The man was gone. The goons were gone. Her parents' station wagon was gone. Only she remained. Just her and her tar blanket in her own bed on the tenement roof. She rolled on her side, fluffed her pillow, and pulled the sticky blanket up tight around her head. Content.

T_{ed} 1

They gathered in a circle around him. All dressed in nurses' outfits: starched white, pressed, and far too roomy for their skinny boy bodies.

The evil little shits were laughing at him again. They giggled at his size, whispered about his failures, wrote on the boys' room walls about his eating habits. And the pictures they drew on the blackboards: horrible pictures that chased themselves around the room. Fat ink monsters gobbling chilidogs and candy bars. French-fries screaming in terror at the approach of a horribly outsize flabby hand groping for more. The pictures jumped off the boards and joined the delinquents in their chant.

"Theodore Patagonia,
The thing that ate Romania.
He's so fat it hurts to look,
Don't get to close or you he'll Cook!

Theodore Patagonia,
The creature from Slobonia.
Eats and eats, just won't quit,
Except for when he needs to shit!"

He zipped his fly, choosing to hold it again, and covered his ears. Oh, how he hated these boys! How he wanted them to be his friends.

Covering his ears with flabby hands made the noise go away, and allowed him to acknowledge the group of children who had been silently line dancing before him. Curtsying, flapping their white skirts like can-can girls. He laughed, hard enough to need his hands on his belly. Hard enough to pee his pants.

They were back, and they saw the stain:

> "Theodore Patagonia,
> Huger than Arizonia.
> Drank up all the seven seas,
> Used his pants to catch his pees!"

"Look guys," Bobby, the sixth grader, said, "We got a new john in the john. 'Cept this one's name is Teddy. Take your best shot. He's hard to miss."

He tried to step out of the way of their little fountains, but he had made dents in the tile floor from standing in the same place too long, and tripped. He landed on his back. The vermin gathered above him, their pricks out and hanging almost to the floor.

Golden fountains bloomed above him, the splashes and his protests unheard over the laughter of the minute monsters. He burst into tears, rolled over on his belly. It sank another dent in the floor. He cried, begged them to stop. Instead, they sang on:

> "Theodore Patagonia,
> Stinkier than a swampia.
> Loves to eat and drink and kiss,
> Now he's swimming in our piss!"

The warm torrent wasn't going to stop. He pulled himself from his hole, crept toward the door. His chubby hands gained little purchase on the slimy floor, but he was moving. He pulled harder, out of the showers, toward the exit. The safety of the monitored hallway lay beyond it. A hundred yards away.

The dirty green door whipped open, startling the boys behind him. They all zipped up quick, one of them too fast. He had zipped right through his prick, and was regarding it silently as it lay limp on the floor, still peeing.

Sister Mary Regina filled the open doorway, glowering behind wire-rimmed glasses. She stormed into the boys' room and stood above him, glaring as only a wimpled nun can glare at the urchins.

"How dare you little beasts attack this young man," she shouted. From where he was lying, he could see right up her skirts. He could see her underwear! It looked just like the white parts of her habit. Sister Mary Regina continued browbeating the pukers.

"You know Teddy can't help his size, and you shouldn't tease him about it. How would you feel if you had some horrible disease and he came and sat on you? Hmm?" The abusers hung their heads in mock shame, waited for their punishment to end.

"Now," Sister Mary Regina continued, her mouth foaming, "You go back to your classrooms this instant, and think about what you have done. I will expect a five hundred-word essay about it from each of you. Your mothers can help."

The young deviants lined up, head behind head, and left the boys' room, leaving him alone with Sister Mary Regina. She backed up to the doorway, regarded him for a cold, dark moment. Her thin lips parted, yellow crooked teeth trying to improve the smile, and she sang:

"Theodore Patagonia,
Bigger than Bulgaria.
Ate Father Brown's old sick mule,
Now the kids just stare at you!"

Sister Mary Regina burst into a torrent of unbridled cackling, knocking her wimple right off her withered scalp. She turned and left the boys' room. The door slammed behind her. The echoes of her cackles lingered, taunting him even after he was finally left alone. He covered his ears again, cursing every Twinkie he ever ate, swearing that he would get those monsters someday. Someday.

His body jerked him awake, causing him to sit up noisily in his desk. Whoa, he thought, it was just a dream, from that time at St. Mary's. I gotta stop eating so much at lunch. Not only is it knocking me out during institutionalized tests, now its giving me crazy dreams.

He picked up his pencil, honestly to start filling in circles to the answer sheet. Instead, he decided to peel the pencil and munch on the banana that lurked beneath the thin layer of yellow paint. It tasted like wood, which was okay, because bananas come with entertainment. He carefully set the peel on the floor at his side and waited for the teacher to make her cheater rounds. It would be great. The class would love it.

She did not make her rounds. The teacher, who was a stranger, probably a substitute, cowered behind her desk up front. He decided that he should switch to audio distractions to amuse the kids. He put his palms together, then pulled them apart. Pleased at the disgusting sound he produced, he continued in rapid repetition. The kids failed to notice; their eyes would not leave their tests. The substitute teacher was a lost cause, completely oblivious to him. The eyes of the big kid to his right occupied her.

He tried harder, slamming his hands together until they burned, frightened that these damn classmates of his would go the whole test without enjoying one of his stunts. Without paying one moment of attention to him. He gave up on his hands, which had done no more than burn themselves to the bone, juicy with wasted sweat. He leaned over a bit, clearing a passage for the real thing, and squeezed.

No reaction. The test consumed his audience. Filling in dots in random patterns on the answer sheets had taken priority to his clever antics. He squeezed again, harder, but still got no reaction. He looked down, sniffed, and realized why. There was nothing coming out! Nothing at all. No wonder they didn't notice. Better try the old faithful.

He lifted the top of his desk, revealing in the compartment below all the treasures of his life. Twinkies, Scooter Pies, Oreos, ice cream, boxes of Jell-O mix: a trough of wonderful goodies, waiting for a rainy day. He looked outside. Yes, it was raining. He started stuffing prepackaged food down his throat. Right over his teeth; chewing wasted time. He unwrapped only the ice cream, to keep it cold. He started to get larger. It was their favorite floorshow.

They continued to overlook him. He grew impatient, felt betrayed, and ate more. He gobbled Twinkies by the handful, Oreos by the box. He expanded, stretching his desk. Still, they didn't laugh. The teacher rudely left the room. This tactic wasn't working, either. He would have to get their attention some other way. So he ate more, and shouted at them. He tried to think of a good test joke to break the ice, but none came to mind. So he ate more.

His tiny desk burst, flattening beneath him. He hoped the thunderclap from his landing would draw their attention, but they continued to take their tests, oblivious to his presence. They mindlessly continued crafting pretty dot patterns on their answer sheets.

He tried to rest his head in his hands, but could not find them. He felt tears pooling in the layers under his eyes. His vision blurred. He had failed, again. And he was getting bigger. He longed for the safety pin his mother once threatened him with, to prevent his binges. Though he had gorged with purpose, he was nothing but huge. Huge and unpopular. And growing huger.

And more unpopular. The kids left, their test complete. He filled the room, unable to get out. So he ate some more. His head touched the ceiling. His stomach rumbled. No, not now, he thought, as his insides squirmed. There's no one to enjoy it.

Regardless of his silent protests coupled with a prodigious effort to keep the valves closed, he released.

His flatulence blew him out of the school, tearing the roof off the building. He soared into the sky, shedding his weight as he soared, trailing a long tail of wrapped Twinkies, Scooter Pies and Oreos in a streaming matrix of vanilla ice cream.

When his momentum and food supply depleted, he ceased his climb and slowly tumbled back to the ground. As the schoolyard passed under him with each tumble, he was able to catch a glimpse of a crowd of children gathered to watch him. They were animated; waving at him, laughing hysterically, cheering.

Ted smiled.

Lou 2

The family reunion at the summer cottage was going well. Everybody acted happy. No one noticed the wall missing from the south wing. Grandma Georgina, dead 30 years that month, was enjoying a TV broadcast of 'Jeopardy' in the living room. Lou reclined on the dark hardwood floor beside her rocker. He admired her ability to shout out the questions before Alex Trebec revealed the answers. Many children, some of whom were family members, violently ranged the living room, jumping on furniture and lobbing hot coffee pots at each other.

Outside, by the front porch, Lou's siblings were arguing about when the decaying retreat would finally crumble. Freddy, one fleshy hand hanging flaccidly over the shoulder of his latest spouse, the other gripping a beer bottle tightly enough to form it into an hourglass, was postulating a convincing argument.

"I'm telling you," he said, slapping a rusty auto fender that littered the lawn, "These old Buicks were built tough. They'd last forever as long as you changed engine fluid regularly." Lorie and Lucie, Lou's obnoxious twin sisters, stood together, facing away from Freddy, arms folded, actively ignoring him.

"Freddy!" Lorie and Lucie shouted over their shoulders, high oriental cheeks touching, jaws moving in sync, "Be serious. The house is ready to fall tomorrow. Look at the porch. It needs paint." They pointed together to the lake that shimmered in the distance.

Lou wanted to interject with an argument about the south wing, but thought it wise to keep his counsel: they weren't really his sisters, who were both much taller and blond. Lou was smug with his bit of superior knowledge. However, the young nude Asian girls did present a convincing thesis of their own. When

Freddy responded, a mouthful of beer garbled his wise words. Both sisters nodded their agreement to his nonsense.

Three emergency vehicles turned the corner at the end of the tree-lined street distracting Lou. The ambulance and hook & ladder negotiated the turn flawlessly, but the backhoe driver misjudged his speed and rounded the turn with his vehicle's left tractor tread high in the air. The fifty-ton machine landed safely, sacrificing a stop sign and two small children playing jacks. The group of vehicles pulled up to the curb by the cottage. Lou was intrigued. There was no fire or other important distress. What, he thought, do emergency people care about a wall or two falling down?

He left Freddy's argument, inclined to partake in a little pedestrian rubbernecking. He sidled up to the backhoe before its siren ceased wailing. A single firefighter was on board, fooling with a tangle of hoses that interfered with the operation of the myriad levers in the cab. The big man, frustrated by complication, jumped from his steel cage. His landing displaced a wave in the asphalt whose gravel crest launched Lou into the air.

"Sorry about that, mister," the man below him said. He deftly caught Lou and stood him up. He tied Lou's sneakers, zipped his fly, straightened, and stepped out of his hole.

The fidgety man stood a head taller than Lou did. His hairy hands wrung a yellow hardhat nervously as he spoke.

"Mister," he said in uneven baritone gasps, "I'm here to save a lady, and I was sure she wouldn't be here."

"Then why are you here, Howard?"

"Cause she is too."

"Oh. Well, then I'd bet you'll find her in the house, near one of the crumbly parts."

"Thanks mister," Howard said, clasping Lou's hand and violently shaking it. Lou, vibrating like a tuning fork, watched Howard turn the corner of the house. He put his hands on his hips, shook his head, and sighed. He had sent the great man on the wrong crusade.

When the C-sharp hum faded to a heavy passionate whisper, Lou heard a muffled plea rise from the road at his feet. He stepped back, startled, and saw that he had misled Howard. Gloria was right there, in the hole Howard just exited, buried to her shoulders in the tar. Her hands, with pale fingers adorned with inch-long sharpened fingernails, waved from above planted wrists. Lou bent over, his hands on his knees, for a closer look.

Gloria squinted up at him from the shallow depths of the dinosaur footprint. Brachiosaur, or something larger. A puff of mist blew softly across the ditch. Perhaps from the dinosaur's breath, Lou thought. The image he conjured of a gentle beast with very large feet and a stuffy nose stirred instinctive adrenaline in spite of its cuteness. When the cloud obscured Gloria, Lou suffered unavoidable concern for her safety. Eager to act, he hastily took a breath and blew it at the fog. It cleared for him, but he feared that Gloria would be gone when it did. He was almost right.

Gloria did reappear, buried to her nose in the old asphalt. It produced little puffs of dust when she breathed, eventually making nostril-sized dents in the rising road surface. Shying from that hauntingly familiar scene, Lou shifted his attention to her eyes. They were more interesting than her busy snout, and much angrier. Lou stared, stunned, as they sank. Adolescent passion, summoned by the hate her dark orbs radiated, surged in his veins. Finally, black road consumed the eyes, lids still raised. The asphalt surface was smooth and hard again.

Lou did not accept her elimination. He dropped to the road, wedging his chest between the legs of the chalk forensic outline. He thrust his arm deep into the soupy road, rooted around until he found Gloria's submerged hair. He wrapped his fingers around a fistful of the thick stuff and yanked. A crowd of onlookers in tin rain slickers mocked his effort. Lou tried to ignore them, to focus on retrieving his hidden victim.

Nothing happened. Lou pulled harder. He squatted for a better purchase, planted his feet carefully. He arched his back, groaned, and concentrated on his lofty task. He was nearly erect before something below the grade gave with a sickening organic snap. The sudden release of tension hurled him through the iron rack of empty slickers. He landed hard on his back, a rabbit skin clenched in his sweaty fist. He remained prone on the bowling alley floor, trying to reflect upon what had happened.

Lou wept, lamenting the unforgivable mistake of leaving Gloria stranded in the road. The guilt gnawed at him until he realized that it had all been just a dream; Gloria was fine and no doubt subject to Howard's imminent rescue. Besides, he had never met the girl, never even heard of her. He was glad to be awake and rid of the responsibility of that dream.

A warning shout from behind disrupted his morning reverie. Lou lifted his head from the oiled hardwood floor, saw his old friend Jane waving her arms at him from the end of the alley. She still had bloody gauze on her face from her fatal suicide attempt after college. He couldn't hear what she was saying over the rumble of the watermelon she had just bowled down the alley. He assumed she suggested he avoid it. In life she did so care for him. Though he tried to oblige, Lou was helpless, unable to gain a purchase on the slippery alley. Each attempt brought him closer to the watermelon as it tumbled slowly toward him.

He resigned himself to being splattered by the massive fruit, in spite of shouts of encouragement from faceless family members clustered around the ball return. They were jumping up and down, waving at him, drinking beers, laughing, and playing horseshoes. He waited, prone, for the juicy finale.

The watermelon twirled on its axis, dominating Lou's field of vision. The big fruit conjured images of famous actors and high school teachers on its spinning striped rind. It touched him, then stopped approaching. The edible nickelodeon continued to rotate madly an inch from his nose.

Lou was enjoying a clear green impression of Jimmy Stewart as George Bailey when the picture segued to his tenth grade math teacher, Sister Mary Dante. Lou gasped. He was not pleased at seeing a torturer from his past, a sure harbinger of doom. The spinning watermelon was a weapon, poised to end his life the moment it splattered on him. Lou wanted to close his eyes and say a prayer, but he lacked the nerve and proper canto. He summoned easier panic. He was able to cry out, to release a tattered, airless scream that no one would hear. Sister Mary Dante tittered with delight. The teacher's green tongue shot out to lick Lou's nose with each watermelon revolution. By her third sticky lap, butter coated Lou's nose

The math teacher's mouth gaped open, stretching to absurd limits. An abyss formed behind the circle of appetizing watermelon flesh. Lou was nonchalant until the pit grew large enough to swallow him, and he knew it meant to suck him into the fruity maw. He tried to postpone his demise by clinging to an edge of the watermelon. The slick green hide rejected his desperate fingers. He let go, dropping obediently toward empty death.

Warmth wrapped itself around Lou's wrist before his descent commenced. He growled in anger when he was drawn to safety from Sister Mary Dante's mouth. The watermelon rolled harmlessly in the black dirt, knocking into a stand of corn three plow furrows away. The corn exploded into white flame, delighting the throng of cheering fans warping the green guardrail of a nearby overpass. Able to read by the ample firelight, they passed out books and newspapers. Lou took pride in his assistance, but at the same time his immobility annoyed him.

He inspected the hand that still shackled his wrist. A woman's hand; rough, callused; sporting a manicure, gold rings, and a Cartier watch. He followed the tan, slim arm to its ivory source, passed some wispy blond hair, finally stalling his scan at a familiar, yet alien face.

"Alice."

"That's right mister," Alice responded, looking beyond Lou to the burning apartment complex, "Pulled you out of another one, and I still don't know who the hell you are."

"Story of my life," Lou responded, wiping soot from his overalls, "Thanks for your help. I would never have made it out of that blaze without you."

"Seems to be what I'm here for, doesn't it? You're the only thing I manage to get right."

"Seems to be what I'm here for, Alice," Lou retorted, "Is there somewhere else you'll be taking me now? How about a ride?"

"Not now mister," Alice said, bowing her head, "I still got eggs on the fire, and I can't do nothing until those damn eggs finish their hatching."

Lou understood. He reached to turn off the TV set, on whose screen Alice wrestled in a black and white perfect kitchen with Bud, Cathy, and Robert Young. His frank tears clouded his vision. He tripped over the leaky vinyl beanbag chair that he had thrown out years earlier. Hell of a time for that to show up, Lou thought. Out of control, he stumbled down the short flight of concrete steps between his porch and the quiet street. He flailed comically enough to laugh. His arms spun like helicopter blades. The proven cartoon tactic worked. Lou was able to steady himself in the air. He hovered, arms blurred as they chopped beside him, then settled at the base of the steps. He rubbed red sand from his eyes and admired the monument he had just negotiated.

The stair rose above him, a marble wonder sweeping steeply to meet the great white office building that held it in thrall as a humble pedestal. The building was a glass Parthenon. Its crystal columns glittered in the hazy sunshine. Shading his eyes from the mild green glare, Lou could see silhouettes of people walking among the columns and standing in tense groups on the vast landing high above. He focused on one group that had separated itself from the building. It consisted of five people: two men and a woman in office attire, and two security guards. One man and the woman were shouting at the second man, who had a brown cardboard produce box in his arms and stood one step below the rest of the group. Lou climbed two steps so he could clearly see and hear the action. The bleached blond woman was poking a finger cruelly into the lower man's chest. Tear streams ruined her carefully overapplied makeup and attitude.

"That's right," she hissed, her arrogant voice and actions revealing none of the heavy grief her tears betrayed, "You're outta hear, Carmine. You have got to accept that we simply can't have your type working here."

She pushed Carmine down two more steps. Carmine stumbled smartly into a handstand. He caught the cardboard box between the outstretched soles of his work boots.

"What did I do?" Carmine asked, commendably maintaining his dignity. Ashley laughed.

"You hired me, you fool," she said. She made a subtle hand gesture to the two gorillas. They tossed aside their bananas and approached Carmine. He valiantly gripped the smooth marble, not taking his eyes off his mutinous employee. One gorilla picked him up in its hairy arms, tossed him to the other. They played catch with him, treating Carmine like a rag doll. When they tired of the diversion, they flung him down the steps. Lou caught the doll, held it at arm's length. It was a simple cloth doll with orange yarn hair, deadpan face painted on a flat white head. Its faded eyes regarded him coldly.

"Let me down, or I'll bite your face off!" the rag doll demanded.

Lou tried to comfort the doll, holding it close to his chest. The doll snapped at his throat with vicious incisors. Lou parried, shoving the cardboard box filled with cash into its bloody pink mouth. The jaws closed on the box. Its ignorant teeth worked feverishly at the paper meal. Disgusted by the doll's greed, Lou threw it into the pool behind him before it finished chewing. It thrashed for a moment, then swam toward a group of bathers in the shallow end. Lou turned back to Ashley.

He leapt to the safety of the meridian in time to simply be sideswiped by a black limousine. He stood in tall grass near the shoulder, watched the car drive to the nearest crossing on the empty highway. It slowed, carefully executed a safe 'U' turn across the grassy meridian to the oncoming traffic lanes, and sped past him in the other direction. Lou watched it until it rounded a curve, brake lights flashing. It was then lost behind a stand of birch trees.

"They'll be back, mister," Phillip panted, steadying himself with a hand on Lou's shoulder, "They always come back for a second try."

"Who are they?" Lou asked, brushing Phillip off his shoulder, absently knocking the powerful man to the ground.

"Agents, all of them," Phillip said, catching his breath. He stood and tore off remaining shreds of the fine business suit that had once hung perfectly from his wide shoulders. Phillip relaxed, forced a smile. Then his eyes darted toward the road, and he began to sweat. He continued, clutching Lou's robe, "They're a great bunch of guys. Really well meaning. I've been trying to shake them forever. I could go on about them all day, but I gotta move now, before they catch me...can't let them catch me." Phillip wanted to say more, but he had spied the car again. It was accelerating toward them, its regal horn blaring. The driver's door was open. A faceless man leaned out, waving a handful of papers.

Phillip shrieked and bolted down the highway, sobbing. He outpaced the town car, scaling the nearest hill before the vehicle reached its foot. Lou followed the pair of dots as they rose and fell on the rolling foothills. They moved fast enough to force the road to wrinkle into a wave behind them, whipping tiny cars and semis into the countryside as it took up the chase.

A larger dot, white, obscured the action, angering Lou. It flattened the hills, stretched the interstate like a ribbon as it sped toward him, filling the lane Lou occupied. The certainty of a collision angered him more, so he slammed his fist down on the top of the TV set.

The impact launched the ambulance into the air. It barrel-rolled twice before landing on its wheels. The back door opened, and a fat man in a white dress stepped out. One hand was on his hip, the other twirled a stethoscope.

"Now what did you do that for, mister? Can't you see I've got an emergency to get to? People need me!"

Lou did not respond to Ted. It was more important to step into the back of the ambulance and ride with him to the emergency.

The medical office inside was well appointed. A small reception area with faux-wood panel walls and plastic couches greeted him. So did a pretty nurse, from behind a half closed frosted glass partition in the far wall.

"Can I help you sir?" she asked, honey dripping from the crease of her fleshy lips. Real honey.

"No," Lou said, incensed that she interrupted his perusal of National Geographic. The magazine featured an intriguing pictorial studying naked pigmies on lawn tractors.

"That's fine, sir," the nurse replied cheerfully, "The doctor's not in anyway. He thinks he's out on a call."

"Yes I know," Lou said, "Now leave me alone." But it was too late. The channel had changed, and he was struggling through a strip of Gufus and Gallant at the beach. He lobbed the outdated magazine at the nurse. The periodical caught her squarely in her face, throwing her through the ambulance windshield. Ted turned on the wipers to clear the mess. He continued to ignore Lou, intent on his emergency call. He honked his horn, blew a kazoo, and blinked a table lamp on and off to urge traffic from his path. Ted was in heaven.

Lou struggled with the back door of the ambulance. He could work the latch, proving to himself at least that it was not locked. The door, however, held fast against his straining shoulder. He pushed until his limbs shivered, hit it with a sledgehammer, even ran back into the house for a coffee pot to pound on it. It would not open. He was trapped.

Ted's face appeared in, or rather filled, the rear window of the ambulance. The orange cross painted on Lou's side of the glass slid off. It drifted like an autumn leaf to the floor. Ted was grim. Lou heard a click, and the door slid open. Ted, who still failed to notice him, was an impassable barrier. Lou was still trapped in the Pinto. In an effort aimed more at getting attention than hurting the fat man, Lou pounded vigorously on Ted's chest. His fists sank wrist deep into soft polyester-shrouded flesh with each thrust. Lou was furious at the apathy of the passersby. They ambled listlessly beside his scene without noticing him. All of them, he thought.

Without even noticing.

Lou smiled.

He reclined in the rusting cargo area and waited. Sure enough, Ted was merely reaching for his bedpan. He lumbered out of Lou's way after he retrieved it.

Lou threw himself from the ambulance, landing on Gloria. She was buried to her waist in cold tar. Her black leather shirt was clean. Gloria casually tossed Lou off her, saluting him with her middle finger as he floated to the curb. She turned away from Lou, redirecting her attention to the backhoe bucket that swung mightily down at her. Lou sat back, picked a blade of grass and tried to whistle through it.

The massive rusty shovel crunched onto Gloria, pounding her under the grade. The ignorant machine continued to dig the trench it had started. Howard deftly worked the levers, dredging a half ton of tar and dirt with every haphazard stroke. His concentration on the task was unhindered by Lou's attempts to blow the grass. Gloria swung from the airborne bucket's teeth, presenting a victorious raised fist to her rescuer. She then let go, waved to Howard as she dropped to the ground, and resumed her argument with Freddy and the sisters. Lou groaned, certain that no one would ever realize that the house was falling. Except Grandma Georgina, but she was dead.

Howard 2

Howard crushed the ringing phone into a cold black plastic snowball. He hefted it, felt its frigid essence ooze between his fingers. When it rang again, he hurled it through his office window.

He watched it pinball through the unfinished foundation outside. It left the site to roll up the nearest utility pole, then out on a wire. The frightened phone followed the wire at light speed, seeking asylum as far from Howard as it could get.

Howard smiled, satisfied. He hated that damn phone, and was glad to hear it stop ringing. He stood, flipped his cluttered desk, and crossed the office to the doorway of the trailer. Someone had swiped the door. White daylight poured in. Howard squinted.

Two small human shapes marred the brilliant flow. They were the dark sides of his kids. The sons Howard and Claire had never found time to make. They stepped across the office threshold, out of the shadowy glare, and adopted forms that Howard could recognize. Two fine boys, both best resembling Claire. Figures, Howard thought, rubbing his chin.

The smaller boy stepped forward, took Howard's hand in both of his. The gesture sickened him, but Howard allowed it. The child, a toddler, arched his tiny neck. Claire's eyes met Howard's.

"Daddy," his son chimed, "We can only stay for a second. We shouldn't be here at all, I think. We need to warn you."

"About what, Nathan?"

"About a change. An accident, maybe. I'm not real sure."

"Is that all you can tell me? Nick, can you tell me more?" Nicholas stepped forward. Claire's eyes studied Howard once more.

"No, Daddy, I guess not," the elder boy chanted, "Except maybe that Mommy's been wondering where you are. Waiting for you to turn up." Howard let go of Nathan, and the boy left. Howard crouched low, took hold of Nicholas's shoulders.

"What do you know, Nick?" he asked, gently shaking the boy's flimsy shoulders, careful not to crush them, "Do you know where Claire went after the supermarket?"

"No Daddy," the boy said, fear in his/her eyes, "All I know is that she's afraid of it too, even though it'll bring you to her."

"Of what?"

"That's what!" Nicholas shouted. He broke from his father's grip and ran outside to play with his brother. Howard tried to follow. The bright sunshine hindered his pursuit, miring him in its warm rays. His children returned unscathed to wherever they had come from. He would always wonder where.

He emerged from the supermarket, his blood-soaked T-shirt and jeans clinging to his skin. He had given up the chase, traded it in for the wait.

He paced the sidewalk in front of automatic doors, attempting to find meaning in his sons' new message. If only I could remember who the kids were, he thought, or what they said.

With each measured pass he made, the automatic doors swung open, inviting him in. He ignored them as best he could. He also ignored a legless teen's incessant pitch for a fifty-dollar candy bar, but felt guilty for not buying it.

Tired of pacing, he stepped off the sidewalk. He kicked up dust as he crossed the busy construction site.

Howard was building a new prison. The biggest, securest penitentiary ever built. Anger eclipsed his pride when he remembered that his prison would remain empty long after it was completed. He shoved his hands in his pockets, lowered his head, strode purposefully back to his sanctuary, his office trailer. Something was in his pocket. Something else new.

It was a brochure that fat salesman from Indiana had left. A glossy photo of their latest product, his latest purchase: a Caterpillar backhoe. One of the big ones. He had bought it one year earlier, for a major and formerly important project. Right after Claire left.

Howard threw the brochure skyward. He then jumped out of the way, landing face down in the dirt. He grabbed a pillow to shield his head.

Nine tons of digging power landed a few feet from him, bounced gently on its steel treads once before settling to the ground. Its running engine chattered softly. Howard climbed into the cab, sat in the leather seat. The Cat's engine stopped. What the hell, Howard thought, the damn thing's brand new; it shouldn't stop yet. He kicked the dash in an attempt at restart, failed.

He scanned the complicated instrument panel, crowded with gauges and dials, but the multitude of mechanical bits intimidated long before it explained. Strange levers, pipes and wires were everywhere. The tangle confused Howard, a twenty year veteran of heavy machinery operation.

Driven by the new priority of moving the machine, Howard pushed all the buttons, pulled all the levers. Nothing happened. Frustrated, Howard kicked the steel dashboard again, causing two frayed wires to drop from the yellow ceiling. They dangled before him, enticing him with lively blue sparks.

Holding his breath, Howard clasped the thin leads, twisted them together and waited. With a preamble electric wine and clattering gears, the Cat roared to life. Labels appeared on all the switches.

Delighted, Howard dropped from the cab to the road below. He landed beside his tread, bumping into a man who occupied his point of touchdown. Knocked off balance, the man fell into Howard's arms. Howard helped the man back to his feet.

"Sorry about that, mister," he said to the man, brushing off his clothes. He thought he recognized the stranger he was cleaning, but dismissed the notion before it matured. He continued:

"Didn't mean to bang you like that. Guess I should have watched where I was going."

The man remained silent, but attentive. Perhaps, Howard thought, he's still a little stunned at my initial impact. Or maybe he knows something and is keeping it to himself, Howard surmised.

"Mister, I'm sure you don't know shit, and I'm not expecting you to, but I'm here to save a lady. And she's my wife, if you must know. Can you help? Probably not, huh? Hell, that's okay. I was sure she wouldn't be here anyway."

"Then why are you here, Howard?" the man asked, his intensity startling Howard. Howard was relieved that the man spoke.

"Cause she is too," he answered, strengthened by his own response. The stranger paused a moment before he gestured to the apartments behind him.

"I'd bet you'll find her in the house, near one of the crumbly parts," the man said.

"Thanks mister," Howard said, shaking the man's hand, "You got no idea what this new information means to me." He started toward the apartment complex, but didn't see the house the man had mentioned.

He did recognize the block of garden apartments that he had built on speculation in the 70's. Did pretty well by them, too, he acknowledged.

Howard slapped his forehead, remembering.

"Of course!" he shouted, "I knocked down an old house to build these. The guy must have meant that house."

Inspired, he boarded his backhoe, which idled quietly beside him, and skillfully piloted it to the nearest wall of the apartments. He wished he had brought a bulldozer instead, but made due.

He thrust the bucket into the wall. It lifted the brick face away intact and Howard set the wall carefully aside. A woman, caught showering in her bathing suit inside the exposed dwelling, put her hands on her hips to punctuate the indignity of his intrusion. She jumped out of the way before his next thrust.

"Now look what you've done, you buffoon!" she screamed, "You've made me lose my shower cap!" She scurried off in search of it.

He broke through another apartment, found nothing. A party was in progress in the third, ground floor apartment. He broke it up, sending furniture, munchies, beer, and pieces of people into the air around his cab.

He disregarded the mayhem, furious that the man had lied. His building, now leveled, had revealed nothing. Not wanting to squander his efforts, he swung the backhoe around. Maybe the guy meant the foundation of the old house, he thought, I buried it out here in the street.

He let the bucket fall into the pavement, then drew it back. He and the backhoe scraped a deep channel of asphalt into the bucket. Howard relaxed. He always did enjoy digging with the backhoe, and was often ashamed at himself for having risen above it.

On his next pass he scooped up fresh black dirt and a thin young woman clothed only in a tattered fishing vest. A child's doll in the same scanty outfit swung from a lock of the woman's long dark hair, its little plastic fingers struggling not to lose their grip.

The woman, though she seemed grateful, was not Claire. Howard sighed. He swung the Cat around and emptied the bucket of dirt onto the nearby field.

Howard separated the wires, silencing the backhoe. He kicked open the cab door, crossed back to his desk, sat behind it. He once again began to sift through the clutter. The notes. The police reports. Those awful pictures.

Everything was as it was the previous thousand times he studied the mess. No new clue. He stopped, put his head in his hands. A sharp knock sounded on the red door to his office. He wanted to answer it, but the door was bolted and locked. And he had lost the key.

Gloria 2

Gloria crouched low, concealing herself behind a low hedge. She was unnaturally wary that the occupants of her father's house might spot her. She checked her equipment: glasscutter, rope, two knives, toothbrush, Barbie doll, crowbar. Confident that she was properly equipped to break back in, she wriggled through the thorn bushes and ran across the high grass to the front porch. Cursing herself for wearing black in broad daylight, she hoped it would be typically dim inside.

When she reached the whitewashed latticework under the porch, Gloria removed the coil of thin rope from her shoulder. She chose a suitable brick from the pile on the ground and secured an end of the line to it. She then tossed the brick straight up, high enough to cross the porch rail far above her head. The brick snagged on the first try. Gloria pulled the line taut and began to climb.

She hauled herself hand over hand up the rope, ascending its fifty-foot length quickly. Her exhaustive efforts brought her no closer to the rail. The house was again denying her entry. Beaten, hands bleeding, she straightened her legs to stand on the worn dirt that bordered the old structure. Knees shaking, she hugged the porch rail for support. She felt herself sobbing again, disregarded the tiresome emotion, and sought an alternate entry. She searched the yard for tools, rejecting both the small bulldozer her father used in his landscaping business and the red door near the porch that swung loose on rusty hinges. She felt a light tug at her hip.

A little raven-haired girl had joined her. The child stood beside her, clutching a Barbie doll like hers, except with newer clothes. Gloria smiled at the child, who returned the gesture with an expression of innocent pleasure at Gloria's attentions. Gloria lifted the little girl and hugged her. She held her close and tight, not wishing to release her again. The child was talking, but Gloria's enveloping chest muffled her. Gloria felt the small vibration of the girl's words. She loosened her grip to hear the child's prattle.

"...oming. I mean it, you gotta run," the girl said, her tiny voice unable to lend substance to her warning. Gloria chose to ignore the gibberish, hugged the child close again. She held on tight, fully absorbed in the warmth of the moment. She inferred that the struggle at her bosom was returned affection, and hugged harder.

Something about the embrace had changed. The girl was becoming too easy to clutch. Gloria gasped, tried to let go. The child was dissolving into a thick liquid. The ravenous cancer held the child's original shape until its entire victim had succumbed to it. The girl's wide eyes remained, lidless and moist. They showed no fear, and stayed focused on Gloria until they were absorbed as well. The lukewarm shadow squirted from Gloria's tight grasp. It flowed like black quicksilver down her leather-clad chest. She tried to grab what she could of the viscous girl, but the child's slippery remains drained though her spread fingers, leaving not even a stain on her hands.

Gloria sank to the ground, heard herself sobbing again. She wanted to join in, but had to silently witness her distant misery. Participation was taboo. Instead she sat on the lawn, watching the last of the dark juice seep into the loose dirt beneath the porch. She played in it with the two Barbie dolls in her possession, banging them together in a pretend fight until one fell. The remaining Barbie, the one Gloria had included in her equipment inventory, crouched by her fallen sister, touched her forehead, closed her painted eyes. She dug a hole by her sister's side. When it was big enough, the tiny doll slid the dead Barbie into the neat little grave. She tossed a micro handful of dirt in after the deceased doll, then jumped back onto Gloria's utility vest.

Gloria, touched by the gesture, slid loose sand into the hole until it was piled into the typical mound that every freshly buried body demands. She found a plastic Dairy Queen spoon nearby, and jabbed it in moist soil to mark the grave. During the obligatory moment of silence, Gloria reviewed what she had done, then clapped her hands and shrieked with glee.

"What a fool I've been," she cried, "Trying to climb into the house, when all along I was supposed to dig my way under it. Into the basement. I should have known."

Energized by her new discovery, Gloria rose to her hands and knees. She burrowed into the ground. The first thing she excavated was Barbie's grave. She tossed the doll over her shoulder and dug deeper. She reached into the hole with two hands, pulled out black dirt, then shoved it back between her legs. She dug with vigor, setting aside the items that came out with the dirt—an old shoe, a live mouse, a faded toy dinosaur that ran away when she set it down, a wadded five dollar bill, and a Matchbox car—until she pulled out a cinderblock. She hefted the block. One side was painted dark green, signifying that it was part of the basement wall. Gloria stopped digging, threw the block back into the hole and dove in after it.

She crawled down the tunnel, deep into the Earth. When the tunnel's granite ceiling was high enough to allow her to stand, her progress was not eased: the gloom had faded to inky blackness. She felt the pockets on her vest for her flashlight, and then realized with a sardonic laugh that she had forgotten it. Figures, she thought. Her negligence was moot, however, as her groping hand found a light switch on the wall nearby. She flipped it on. A single light bulb suspended from the ceiling by its frayed power cord bathed the tunnel in soft yellow glow.

The illuminated, empty dirt chamber sparked in Gloria a sudden desire to return to the dark. She tried turning the wall switch in the opposite direction. Nothing happened. She felt small hairs standing on her neck. She shivered violently. Gloria did not like being in the tunnel anymore. She had forgotten why she had burrowed it in the first place, and stopped fighting eternal sourceless pressure to get out. Panic had set in, and Gloria was ill equipped and perhaps unwilling to fight it. She twirled on her left heel, revolved on that axis repeatedly in search of a way out. She pushed with her right foot to accelerate her spin.

A steel ladder shot by with each rotation. Initially she paid it no heed, as someone had hung an official looking sign that read "DO NOT USE" on a lower rung. Finally, seeing no other route from the hole, she stopped spinning and approached the ladder. Before touching its iron rail, she snatched the tin sign to inspect it.

She snapped the rusty chain that secured it. She flipped the sign over, saw that it had an officially stenciled message on the back as well. "JUST KIDDING," it read. She laughed, and climbed.

She was at the top of the ladder in three rungs, bumping her head on an unseen rafter. She peered down into the basement. The ladder rails reached their vanishing point long before they touched the distant dirt floor. She sighed, seeing that she had narrowly achieved safety. The boys on the floor below were gathering at the base of the ladder, looking up.

Gloria abandoned her false security. Since the leader's ears were smoking, they were trying to devise a plan to capture her. One of the others raised his hand, silencing the mindless banter his babbling buddies exchanged. He wrapped a filthy fist around a rail and jarred the ladder. A wave of bent metal worked its way up to Gloria, nearly shaking her off when it passed.

Her complacency erased by the attack, she withdrew the crowbar from her vest. She scraped its tip on the ceiling in search of a crack, a loose board; anything that would help her break into the floor above. She looked down again. The boys had started climbing. She decided not to look down anymore.

Her crowbar suddenly slid into a crack in the floorboards. Gloria's trained reaction was swift. She tugged frantically, spreading the slim opportunity into a fissure wide enough to allow her tight passage. She reached her hands up to the daylight above, grabbed onto a hot, hard surface, and hoisted herself out of her hole. She managed to pull her head and shoulders into daylight. The rest of her was still trapped below. She slapped unyielding asphalt.

"This is real fair," she snarled. She had dug herself into a new, unfamiliar, hole. A shallow dent, a paved pothole pressed into the surface of an old urban street. She thought she saw a man standing directly above her, talking to unseen others as if he were coordinating some emergency operation. She tried to reach up to him, but the asphalt trapped her hands. The man looked down, noticed her. He bent to her.

Before she could ask for help, Gloria felt a mighty tug on her ankles. They had her. She looked down, and was able to see through the gap between her cleavage and the tar that the boys stood in a circle directly beneath her. Three of them controlled her legs while the fourth worked loose her belt, smacking his lips in delight at the easy prey. Gloria looked up again, to beseech the aid of her father. He stood aloof on the porch above her. The porch, whose clean painted planks she could no longer tread.

"Daddy," she cried out to him, "Please!"

He shook his grey head slowly, silently transmitted his regrets, turned and left his porch, entered his house. He pulled the front door closed behind him. She could hear its locks tumble into place before the thick oak door vanished into white clapboard.

Another tug.

Gloria shot an imprudent glance down in time to catch one of the monsters waltzing around the cellar with her jeans. Another was fondling her exposed crotch while the two with her legs counted to three and yanked. Gloria surrendered another foot of her temporary freedom to their adolescent energy. Her nose touched the road. Gloria was barely able to keep her face on the better side of the cellar's ceiling. Breathing grew difficult. Her eyes' final taste of freedom was the image of the man in the road reaching for her. His spread, empty fingers were the last things she saw before she fell down into the darkness below.

She thought she felt his touch. For a blissful instant she was safe, different. Then she was on the dusty floor, surrounded by misguided youth.

The attack had already begun, and Gloria could not fight the ritual. She relaxed, deciding to accept their aggression. Her father had turned away and the strange rescuer was useless; so what was the point of fighting?

She felt a subtle change in her abuse. The pain had changed to pleasure. A sensual caress of her breasts was drawing her back into the fray. One of her molesters had changed. It was Ian.

Her mentor was bending over her, gently kissing her cheek, running nimble fingers through her hair. He embraced her, held her tightly while the shortest thug was having his turn between her battered thighs. Ian looked into her eyes. Gloria focused only on him, keeping his image steady while her body jerked back and forth. His head was bowed, his eyes wet. When they met Gloria's, a tear slipped free from one. Gloria gently wiped it with a clean tissue.

"Gloria," he said, his satin voice filling her head, "Is this how I taught you? If you're in a tight spot, look around you. Use what's available. Improvise. Don't disappoint me." Gloria did not hear him well, but his message calmed her. She lifted her head to kiss his cheek, only to have a vomit soaked tongue thrust in her mouth. Ian was gone.

Gloria twisted away from the unwashed face. She obediently studied the cave she had excavated. It was empty, freshly dug. She tried to find a tool that would aid her, but located nothing except a family of rabbits that had moved into the tunnel. Well, she thought, Ian said I've got to make the best of my surroundings, and God knows he's always right.

She withdrew a loaf of sliced bread from one of the pockets of her utility vest. She ripped off the plastic wrap with her free hands. The boys did not notice her break the loaf into bite-sized pieces. They let her sprinkle the shreds on them. One of them snickered, calling the bitch kinky, but they otherwise ignored her tactic.

Her attackers missed it, but the rabbits caught on immediately. The entire horde of fluffy critters hopped on them to gobble the bread. The greasy youths still failed to acknowledge them until the voracious bunnies finished the bread and started on flesh. Theirs. Then they screamed as countless cute little mouths chewed at their feet, their hands, their faces. Gloria crept out from under the rabbits' wiggling pink noses unscathed. She found the ladder again. The rungs were wooden, carpeted in fresh linen to ease her flight. She left the carnage behind her, careful not to look back.

Three rungs brought her to the roof of the cave. Soft dirt fell on her as she clawed through it to safety. She remembered the exhumed Barbie, and wished that she had left it safely in its final resting place. She poked her hand through the moist earth, felt the warm air above. She tugged her hand and a final armload of dirt back down, leaving a hole big enough to get most of her body through. She extricated herself halfway out of the hole. She once again faced the man that had failed to aid her last escape. Not this asshole again, she thought as she presented her middle finger to him in response to his approach. Gloria looked around for another source of assistance.

She found one in the form of a massive cold jaw that passed over her head, brushing her hair. She grabbed for it. She missed once before she managed to get her hands around one of its teeth on its next pass.

The yellow machine whisked her through the air in a graceful arch. It deposited her gently on a mossy knoll nearby. She turned to thank the driver for his trouble, but the backhoe was silent, empty, and very rusty. It had sunk over time into the road it once devoured, dead. Gloria's throat tightened. She lowered her head in sorrow at her loss. She strode past the Cat, trying to read her watch. She was certain that she had overslept again. Ian would be furious.

Alice 2

Gold, dusty wheat. Head-high. Security. Delicate prison bars, confining her in their empty organic embrace. Comforting in their life, damning in their consistency.

Alice put her hands together before her, as if in prayer. She recited a Hail Mary and pushed her wedge of fingers between two stalks. She separated her palms. The stalks crumbled to dust at her distant hands' light pressure. Two more stalks closed in the fresh void. Alice made the same motion, got the same results. She tried once more. And again. Always, more bars of the food she grew were waiting for her. Fully grown, ready for harvesting. Easy to knock down, to turn to dust. Messy dust that hung in the air, invaded her eyes, her nose, her self. Always more bars.

Alice dropped to the soggy ground, leaden, surrounded by tall shoots of gold, dusty wheat. Gold, dusty wheat. Perfect in its creation. Sinister in its abundance. She shook her head and wondered what to make for dinner.

A familiar noise caught her attention. She stood, craning her neck and ears to the racket. A riot of clacking valves and grinding gears subdued the sounds of violent and wholesale destruction of her wheat. She looked to her left, spotted the farm's tractor crashing through the stalks, clearing a path wide enough for her to navigate her red convertible through. If she hadn't traded it in for a minivan. It shuttered to a stop in front of her. The cab door flew off, spinning recklessly into distant grain. Ed leaned out, along with all six of their kids.

Her family stayed on the tractor, firmly attached to its rusting body parts: Ed, bolted to the roof, Ed Jr. to the hood, the twins wrapped securely onto the hitch with stout chain, and the three young ones riveted to the rusty fenders. They all smiled at her, waved if they could, but said nothing. Alice waved back, tried to shout up to Ed a word of thanks for the road, but found none. She shrugged, turned away from the tractor, her kids, Ed, and the wheat.

A dilapidated bridge rested in the distance, its towers soaring high above the empty prairie. Suspension. Old, rusty, with many frayed or broken cables. Elated, Alice bounded down the green hillside toward it. She climbed over a rubber guardrail to mount the freshly paved approach road. When she stopped to catch her breath, she saw that the bridge was reduced to a tiny red silhouette, nearly negated by distance. Alice frowned, angry at her lapse in concentration and movement, and started forward again. Her determined pace brought the old bridge close immediately.

She saw that the bridge crossed a wide white river before it touched the base of tiny round mountains that rolled into the horizon. She lowered her head and dashed to the crumbling span, eager to test its meager strength.

Alice backpedaled comically, skidding to a halt before she could traverse the first corroded expansion joint. She had nearly tumbled into a giant pothole that punctured the bridge, corrupted its purpose. She could see the river rushing beneath it. White water flowed swiftly, carrying debris, a yellow house with screaming children, and small crying animals with it on its swift wet journey. The river had eaten everything, and the pothole promised her passage into the deep rapids. Undaunted, she stepped back, and sprinted to the hole.

"It's just another long jump," she said, puffing, "I can handle it. I have to handle it." She executed a perfect launch, flew nicely, but the pothole moved with her as she passed over the bridge.

Alice didn't panic. Her planned response to the emergency would work. And if it didn't, she knew how to swim. She spread her legs apart in a wide split, shredding her faded Levis. As she had hoped, her bare toes caught the soft tar at the pothole's edges. She brought her thighs together, thankful for their solid strength. The road clung to her toes, stretched with them. The hole was closed, the road was new again. The bridge gleamed overhead. Cars, backed up for miles on the expressway behind her, honked their horns in appreciation. Alice waved modestly to them, directed the first car to cross the bridge, then dove off the side to swim to the other side.

The river was warm, placid. Alice scooped a mouthful of fresh water, savored its sugary taste. She reached the grassy bank, but felt reluctant to climb it. She faced the river again, its bridge now a distant broken smile. A car spotted her wistful gaze and hurled itself off the bridge and into the river after her. Alice scrambled up the bank, out of the water scant seconds before a man-sized silver barracuda snapped at her from the waves. She laughed at its attempt, and the fish laughed back. It was clearly the victor, though still hungry. Alice climbed the soft bank, dry, content, not minding her missing jeans.

The small rolling hills were knee-high, and rolled slowly enough for Alice to step gingerly in the passing valleys to make headway. She was careful not to trample any of the tiny villages that dotted the countryside at her ankles. The hills stopped rolling where they met a familiar dirt footpath that led through pink pastures and under oak trees that dwarfed the bridge she just fixed. Alice followed the path, walking slowly enough to enjoy the pleasant pink park, fast enough to stay ahead of its disintegration into white haze behind her.

She stopped at a fork in the path, pondered the significance of her two new choices. Both options were identical, except that the path that disappeared to the right had deep red footprints embedded in it. Fresh footprints, she surmised, as the blood that filled them had not yet dried. She chose the marred route, eager to meet the troubled soul able to imprint her path so vividly. She matched her steps to the footprints, splashing a bare foot into each warm crimson puddle. Small mobile weeds with barracuda buds that grew in the cracks between each crooked slab of the ancient suburban sidewalk snapped at her. Alice was glad the deep footprints she followed avoided the cracks so she wouldn't be bitten, or have to break her mother's back.

The footprints ended. Alice was left standing alone on the sidewalk, next to an unkempt vacant lot. The lot was not totally vacant: three figures crouched around a small blaze they had set in a rusty fifty gallon drum. Intrigued and hopeful that the step maker might be among them, Alice left her path. She crossed the flowery meadow to the group. The sun set before she reached them, but the crackling campfire illuminated its users' faces. She picked up a stout twig with a hot dog already attached and sat with the solemn group.

Her father greeted her with a forced smile. He appeared as she had left him a lifetime before, in his gray three-piece suit, watch fob complementing the gentle flames. She knew he would have no words for her, and was relieved. She wondered at his presence, feeling the incongruity of their meeting transcend the reality of the moment. Her father shared her thought, but said nothing. He took another bite of his hot dog, eating his twig with it, then averted his face from the fire light to chew.

The bonfire's orange flames deemed to shed their gentle light on the second camper. Alice's heart fluttered. It was Mike. From before. Her first and only. He smiled at her. He would attend to her, she knew, as soon as he finished eating. He always did, warming her with his comforting embrace, touching her tired soul with his devoted gaze. He never asked for an explanation, never an apology, never for more.

Mike coughed up fragments of hot dog, smiled at her through shattered teeth. Porcelain splinters in a broken doll. He made no sound beyond the gurgle in his clogged throat. Alice stepped back, repulsed by his wrong response to her presence. She shook her head, confused, wishing Mike away from her. He remained, in heated struggle with the third firewatcher. The bonfire did not reveal the new figure's identity. Its misguided flames did reflect occasionally off a wet foul weather suit that wrestled with Mike, but the illumination merely compounded the miserable mystery.

The bout did not last long. The shadowy slicker hefted Mike, still mute and broken, above it. It spun Mike once, then flipped him into the bonfire. Mike executed a skillful somersault before falling, still mute, into the white flames. Alice tried to scream, failed, and attacked the shadowy fisherman. She bent her leg and whipped it forward, kicking the raincoat square in its back. It flapped away, releasing the long scream of pain and terror that Alice had wished to emit herself.

Alice returned to the fire, spreading its flames apart with her hands, searching for Mike. She whispered another pointless Hail Mary. His blackened face peered up at her for a moment, looking again like it had in eons past.   Then the cold flames absorbed it.   Alice sat back, relieved that she would not have to face him again, after what she had done to him.   She finished her hot dog before throwing sand on the fire.   Her father had taught her always to throw sand on the fire before leaving it.

A hand shot out of the dying flames.   Its smoking fingers wriggled, groping for a handhold.   Alice cursed herself for not throwing the sand soon enough.   She inspected the flexing fingers. It was not Mike's hand that sought her attentions.

"Fine," she said, "Now I have to rescue a stranger from a damned barbecue pit."

The hand slid back into the fire.   Alice followed it with her own.   She extended her arm into the flames, fished around for the unseen hand.   She felt fingers, followed them down to a wrist, set her grip and hauled the dead weight.   A man, tall, familiar, completely out of shadow, burst from the flames, landed on his feet beside her.   He regarded her silently for a brutally long instant, then smiled.

"Alice," he said, his calm, deeply passionate voice thrilling her.

"That's right, mister," Alice responded, checking the bonfire for the light source that illuminated the man.   The fire emitted the same peaceful orange flames, incapable of generating such brilliance.   Alice accepted the illusion, deciding that the man must have extra batteries.   She did appreciate the added light, however.   It helped her to recognize the familiar stranger.   She continued:

"You again.   How come you keep turning up?   Where's Mike?   Oh never mind.   But I guess I pulled you out of another one, huh?   At least that's the feeling I get.   And I still don't know who the hell you are."   Alice caught herself rambling, struggling to say everything in the short time that the stranger would be in her presence.   She stopped to allow him to speak.

"Story of my life," the man responded.   His unchecked volume rattled her bones.   He straightened his perfect blue suit, saying, "Thanks for your help.   I would never have made it out of that blaze without you."

"Seems to be what I'm here for, doesn't it?   You're the only thing I manage to get right."

"Seems to be what I'm here for, Alice." His words warmed her. She was glad she pulled him out instead of Mike. The man was still speaking.

"Is there somewhere else you'll be taking me now? How about a ride?"

Alice considered his offer. She knew that she still had obligations at the fire. She needed to extinguish it, to remove its warm glow from her horizon. She cast her eyes from the man. She wanted to stay with him, to take him somewhere, but the steady tug on her paisley print apron was too strong. Unheard commands, unfinished chores beckoned her return to the house.

"Not now mister. I have still got to put some sand on the fire. I can't help it if there's still eggs cooking on it. They'll have too be covered too, once they're done cooking. But in the meantime, what can I do?" she paused, confused, angry at her shackling words, "Nothing. Until those damned eggs hatch."

She turned away from the man, shaking in anger, quivering in fear at what she knew she would face once he was behind her. Sure enough, the man was gone. The fire was gone. Mike was gone. Her father was gone. The bridge, the path, the car; all gone. The grain was back. Tall, fragile bars, surrounding her in a dry, brown crescent. In front of her was the tractor, lying helpless on its side. Her family swarmed it, lost, searching for some way to get it back on its wheels. When they as a group noticed her arrival, they cheered. Yes, Alice thought, I'm here again. To help.

She approached the tractor, arms folded on her swollen maternal belly. Her family parted for her, allowing her to touch the foundered tractor. She patted her belly, spoke to it.

"Don't worry," she said, "This won't hurt a bit. Not you, anyway."

Alice reached a hand under the frame of the tractor. With a gesture she flipped it back onto its wheels. Her family gleefully reattached itself to their machine and clattered away. Without a word of thanks, or encouragement. They had left Alice alone in a silent circle of tall wheat.

Gold, dusty bars. Home.

Ashley 2

The company cafeteria was drearier than usual. The sputtering torch flames that lined the pastel walls allowed only dim echoes of illumination. Ashley had to squint to identify the diners at her table. Her pursed eyelids framed the images of her father, mother, and three brothers, compressing them into focus. They were dressed in their Sunday best; embarrassingly shabby ensembles in Ashley's environment. She was confused when she scanned their peaceful visages, unable to understand their imbecilic posturing. She did not trouble herself with the strange child that sat directly across the table from her, happily munching live sugarcoated lizards from that new breakfast cereal for which Ashley had once done an excellent spread.

"What are you people doing here?" Ashley asked, masterfully tempering her voice so as not to sound angry. She still might, after all, need them for something. Her mother, wearing that awful violet flower print dress with live blossoms sprouting from it, looked up from her beef potpie. She frowned, wiped brown scum from her cheek, and stared at Ashley with empty eyes. Clear, hard, crystal: no whites, pupils, or blood. Empty.

"We came to visit, princess, just to see that there's nothing you might want from us," she droned, reading from a script propped against her plate. Ashley cringed at the response, chose not to speak to her anymore. She also looked away from her. The woman's blank eyes were nauseating her. She turned to her father, who rivaled his wife's taste with his sky blue polyester pinstripe suit. He was nodding solemnly behind the same empty eyes. Her brothers, whose names she could never remember, regarded her with equal crystalline severity.

Ashley shivered, faced the blonde child across the table. The child's eyes were normal. Blue. Kind of pretty. The girl, seeing she had Ashley's attention, politely spat out the remaining, front, half of the lizard she chewed. The lizard escaped, gamely waving a talon at Ashley before dragging itself over the edge of the table.

"Mrs. Friedman, we need to talk," the child whispered, her cheerful demeanor masking the panicked tone of her voice. Ashley bristled at the use of her last husband's name.

"Who the hell are you to call me that? I don't know you. Where's your mother?"

"Mrs. Friedman, you have to listen to me. See, there's this yellow monster, and…"

"Monster!" Ashley screamed, "Monster! Do you think I was born yesterday, you little shit? There's no such thing as a yellow monster. I'm too old for monsters. Too important!"

"But Mrs. Friedman…"

"And quit calling me that, you pint-sized bitch. My name is Ashley. Ashley… um," Ashley paused, groped for her current surname, surrendered, "Well, it's Ashley, and that's enough for you. Now get out of my face."

Ashley dispatched the child by flipping the long table onto her. It hovered long enough to allow their lunches to drop comically on each of her family members' heads, then landed upside down, flat on the plaid tile floor. To Ashley's mild disappointment, her action had also trapped them with the little girl. Each pair of their legs protruded from under the steel slab, twitching grotesquely. Ashley rolled her eyes at their plight.

"Maybe if you people were a little stronger, this wouldn't have happened," she said softly before turning away from them. She hooked elbows with Carmine, her old boss, and Mr. Green, her new boss, and resumed descending the steps outside her office building. It was a wonderful day. The sun was shining, the air was warm, and she was firing Carmine and taking his place in the same action. Ashley was euphoric.

Carmine was speaking, rushing his words, "…this to me, Ashley? I brought you in, took a risk in fact, when I hired you. I trained you myself, taught you everything you know. How can you discard me, with no justification?"

"Of course it's justified, Carmine. You don't properly fit in anymore.   Right Reggie?" she said sweetly, her hand gently rubbing her new boss's unzipped fly.

"That's right, gorgeous. Carmine, I'm sorry to say that the firm simply cannot use your services anymore. Your fifteen years are greatly appreciated, of course, but Ashley here will do a far superior job."

"That's right, I will. So you're outta here Carmine. I'm real sorry, but you have got to accept the fact that we simply can't have your type working here anymore."   The words Ashley watched herself speak thrilled her.

"But Reg, on what grounds are you letting me go? I've always been the best. You said so yourself. What did I do?"

"You hired me, you fool," Ashley proclaimed for Mr. Green. She gestured to two security guards stationed three steps below. When they approached, she instructed them nonverbally to take the fine man, her accomplished mentor, out of her sight. She was annoyed when she couldn't overlook the guards' crystalline stares. Their glassy eyes depreciated the glory of the moment. The glory of watching perhaps her best friend thrown bodily to the wet sidewalk.

Ashley grinned.

The scene around her shifted, blurred by her tears. She was enveloped in a haze, then mired in darkness.

She cursed the bathroom light for failing again, and stepped dripping out of the shower, risking a chill, to switch it back on. The wall switch fell off in her hand, and the light remained off. She worked a wad of saliva and toilet paper in her mouth until she could no longer contain it, then spat the mixture at the errant light. It met its target.   The projectile's slimy impact compelled the fixture to flicker back to life.   The slick green residue from her improvised mortar round slid down over the mirror below.

Ashley stepped back into the shower, anxious to finish washing her hair. She was late for work. She plucked the tube of shampoo from its shelf. She squeezed the tube, mindless of the cap that was still screwed on tight. The shampoo would not pour through the cap.

"Come on, cut the shit," she said, squeezing the tube harder. Her extra exertion freed the cap, launching it through the pink marble shower stall wall. The bottle's contents, the best dandruff shampoo made, followed it through the hole in a creamy white stream. She attempted to disrupt the flow, but the bottle held its position even after she let it go. When it was empty, it fell to the floor with a plastic thud. The spent bottle bounced a couple of times before it disappeared down the drain.

Ashley slumped to the floor of the shower as well, drawn by the vortex of the hungry drain. Her desperate grip on the orange daisies she had pasted on the stall floor a week earlier prevented her from sharing the bottle's fate. Ashley knew she was supposed to cry, to lose her sanity to the bizarre and powerful drain, but she did not. She was in control, sure that the disaster wouldn't make her late. Because someone needed to be disciplined that day, her arrival at the office was preordained.

"But I can't go to work with dirty hair," Ashley groaned, "No way." She looked around for a solution. The bathroom was empty; even the sink had been torn from the wall. Her hair, too dirty to touch, began falling out, landing on the orange daisies in wispy clumps. Ashley stood, still harboring the confidence necessary to resolve the situation. A blonde child she had missed earlier perched on the toilet, playing with the back half of a lizard. Ashley numbly sensed that the child was there to help.

"Right," she sneered over the girl's head, "Like I need help from a snot-nosed puppy. Beat it kid, you don't deserve to be here." When she presented her silky, perfectly tanned back to the well-meaning child, she faced the fist-sized hole that her shampoo blasted through the marble tile.

"Well, duh," Ashley said, shaking her head at her own naivety, "Must be all this pressure. Yeah, that's what it is." She reached into the dark hole to retrieve her shampoo.

Her hand slipped into the wall followed inexorably by her wrist, her arm, and most of her shoulder. Ashley stopped reaching. She had no interest in entering the wall for the sake of some shampoo.

"At least not yet, anyway."

She extracted her arm. Ashley was delighted to discover that it was frothy with fresh, white lather. She peered into the hole, saw that it opened on her kitchen. She hated her kitchen, never used it. She was disappointed, and almost abandoned the hole without registering the trail of shampoo lather that bisected the kitchen. She did, however, and followed the smoking scar it had etched in her hired-hand polished hardwood floor to the kitchen table. The table was bare, except for a wooden bowl laden with rotting fruit. White lather oozed in the bowl.

"Of course," Ashley said, replacing her hand in the hole.

She deposited her arm in until her cheek contacted the wet wall, ruining her makeup. She waved her unseen hand in circles, back and forth, up and down, felt nothing. She tried standing on her toes, though she was worried that her leather-soled pumps would slip despite the orange daisies.

The stretch proved worth the risk. On her toes, Ashley was able to scratch the edge of the bowl. Of course she didn't, seeing no sense in ruining a perfectly good manicure. Unable to close her fingers on the thin wood, Ashley chose to slam its rim, flipping the bowl over. She yanked her arm out of the hole and squatted an instant before the fruit smashed against the other side of the wall, loosening the tiles above her head. One piece of fruit passed through the hole, dropped to the shower floor in front of her. An overripe banana.

Ashley reached for it, but an orange daisy had it safely in its grasp before she could pick it up. She grabbed the banana anyway.

"Oh no you don't, you practical ornament!" she shouted at the rebellious daisy, "I stuck you there, and I'm in charge of what you protect. Understand?" The orange daisy, being a plasticized paper label, did not understand, and held on.

Ashley wrapped her other hand around the banana, bored a spiked heel into the porcelain floor, arched her back and pulled. She was careful not to squeeze the banana and its precious contents too hard.

After a commendable struggle, the orange daisy lost. Unwilling to release the banana, it unwittingly allowed Ashley to rip it from the floor. Helpless, the orange daisy let go of the banana. It orbited the shower drain a few times, trapped in the whirlpool, before being flushed to its doom. Ashley heard its quiet wail of grief at betrayal, but shrugged off the guilt.

"Hey," she said to the drain, "I've got better things to do than worry about the drowning of a damn orange daisy. I've got to wash my hair."

She stood, wet her hair again, and held the banana at arms length, not sure how to open it. The blond child, balancing on the porcelain rim of the toilet, spotted the banana.

"No!" she shrieked, "Don't open it! That banana is not for you to peel!"

"Nonsense," Ashley said, "But before you go, thanks for your helpful hint on getting the shampoo out." The child tried to shout more silly warnings at Ashley, but she dispatched the young prophet by casually leaning forward and flushing the toilet. The child lost her footing and fell in. Oddly, the sweet little thing was laughing at her fate.

"Well, bitch," the child said, offering her middle finger as she twirled in the blue water, "Don't say I didn't warn you."

"Okay I won't," Ashley retorted, dropping the toilet lid over the empty bowl. She shook her head in distaste, wet her hair once more, and peeled the banana.

The fruit inside, though a bit ripe, seemed harmless enough. Ashley discarded the peel, squished the banana in her fingers. She kneaded it to a liquid consistency, and put it in her hair.

It felt good; clean, comforting. Ashley rinsed her face while she was still lathering, opened her eyes.

The shower stall was full of heavy yellow lather that reeked of sulfur, rot. Ashley waded through the gut-wrenching bog until she was under the showerhead. The feeble trickle of brown water failed to rinse the mess from her dry hair. Ashley fumbled for the faucet handle, found it and tore it from the wall. The water stopped flowing. The bog lapped at her thighs.

Frustrated by the inconvenience, Ashley stepped out of the shower stall. The waste-high bog was too thick to spill out, but some did cling to her clothes.

"Mother of God," Ashley said, "I just had this pantsuit cleaned. Now it's ruined." Her designer outfit, picked specifically for the landmark day, was indeed different. The scarlet shade she had so forcefully demanded had faded to sickly mustard, and the outfit reeked of rotten eggs. Oh well, she thought, trying to control her temper, I can always change. She glanced in the mirror to see how well the shampoo had cleaned her majestic mane.

She screamed.

Her reflection was yellow, round, and hairless. She opened her mouth in terror, pressed gnarled broken hands to her cheeks and screamed again. Her shriek allowed the scaly dry crack that was her mouth to spit a dozen rotted teeth into the mirror, shattering it. Ashley threw herself through her small bathroom window without hesitation.

She landed on the marble steps, on her feet and two steps above Carmine, who was still pleading his case. Ashley shook her head, checked her hair (all there - and clean!), her smooth hands. She sighed, relieved that it was all a dream, and held open arms to Carmine. Openly relieved, he stepped up to her.

When he was close enough, she seized the opportunity and pushed Carmine's chest hard, with both hands. He tumbled down the mountain of steps to the street below. Before he could stand erect, a bus hit him, erasing him.

Ashley laughed.

Phillip 2

Keep moving. One step ahead. Can't see them. They are there. Back there. In a car. Best to get off the road. Feet can't always beat wheels.

No choice. Stay on the bridge or jump over the rail, into the cold Hudson. Take the bridge. The bridge ends, still no exit. Building-sized New Jersey barriers protect Fort Lee.

The Meadowlands rise up on the dirty horizon, coaxing, cajoling, poised for attendance. For participation. It would be good there. Lucrative. Healthy.

Wrong.

Rotate. Turn back. Head the other way. Back to the City, where green is measured on Big Boards, not gridirons. Spy an exit ramp, to the left. Run down it. Keep moving. The car, carrying the pursuers that missed the turn, passes harmlessly above. Headed for Newark. Don't relax. Keep up the escape.

The exit ramp ends at a red light. No traffic, no crossroad. Another highway. A long, empty, foreign highway. Parallel concrete strips scribed in green grass stretch until joined at the edge of the world. In the near lanes is Mother, setting breakfast on the dining room table. Not the kitchen. Must be a special occasion.

The light changes to green. Cross the pavement to Mother's small world. Food. The dining room table. Sit in the available chair. The others are taken: one by Father, one, though still empty, by Mother, and the fourth by a child. There is no Sister, never was. Allay suspicions; this is family. Sit. Mother smiles, takes her own seat across from Father, who spits his chaw to make room for the morning fare.

Sharp yellow fingers of sunlight reflect off the nearest, empty plate. Father's, mother's, young Sister's are heaped with oak leaves and meatballs. They politely wait until all are served. Don't confuse them. Please them. Eat the sunlight. Catch yellow glimmer in the silver spoon, swallow it quick. Smile. Nod. Enjoy the bite, though it burns inside. The family smiles back. All but Sister. Sister stares, blue eyes wide behind overgrown blond bangs. She speaks. No sounds are heard. Concentrate. Draw sounds from her tiny moving mouth.

"...keep moving. You know that. You have to go back to work, to the city. They're not the only ones after you, Phillip. There's another. And this one does not want to make your life better."

Stare politely. Say:

"Who is it?"

The words emerge garbled, barely audible. No matter. Sister is gone, place setting and all. Don't question Mother about her exit. Don't question her presence. After all, there never was a sister. Question her words, still echoing. Another. One with no papers, no promises. One to truly fear. Another reason to keep moving. Keep moving.

Get up. No. Stay seated. Mother and Father are together, eating, happy. Stay. Enjoy the waxed beans heaped on a greasy plate, though they do burn. Mother smiles, eyes closed. Like the last time, long ago. In the long mahogany box.

Father throws his cleared plate over his shoulder, leaving it to roll to freedom down the empty highway. He leans back in his chair, pulls his favorite pipe and a long wooden match from his breast pocket. He strikes the match on Mother, accidentally setting her hair aflame. He laughs raucously at his folly. Mother smiles, meek. She douses the fire by pouring the pitcher of orange juice on her head. This is Family. Keep moving.

Leave it. Make an excuse. Say:

"I must go now, to the Market. Yes, the Market."

Mother frowns.

Stand up. Ivy is already halfway up the tailored suit. Peel the noble weed off. Leave the table. Leave the family. They'll be happier that way. Walk away.

Down the road, too far to see, distant tires whine their protest at unwarranted misuse. Turn to the sound of a revving engine. See the Checker Cab emerge from the horizon, swelling like a yellow wart on the road until its bumper blocks all else. Jump left, quick, far. Flesh shoulder hits gravel shoulder hard. Padding protects. The blue jersey is ruined again. See the dining room table, dinner, Mother, Father and his pipe be obliterated by the Taxi. It's gone now, the strange Taxi. The new harbinger for the usual pursuers? Or absent Sister's warning realized? Keep moving.

A new shape rises from the busy horizon. Black, familiar, approaching at a safe, sensible velocity. No time to run. Hide in the uncut patch of meridian grass. Duck. Now. Peer through reeds at the car as it quietly passes, tinted windows closed. Roll out of the way to allow a familiar stranger to land his medium sized bulk. Fallen from the sky, from nowhere. Don't question the stranger, use him. Like a crutch, a trainer.

Stand at the shoulder, waiting for the knees to function. Look both ways. The car is gone again, lost down the horizon of the empty road. Need to keep moving. First, regard the stranger. Say:

"They'll be back, mister," The words are clear. Odd. Say more: "They always come back. They need me. They want to get me in for a second try."

The man responds, revealing benevolent eyes, an open smile as he casually tosses you across the road. Relax bunching muscles. Don't react. Give the man a chance.

"Who are they?" the stranger whispers, brushing grass stains off his clean T-shirt. Say:

"Agents, all of them. They've been after me for years. Ever since college. Even before."

The man does not believe, starts to turn away. Grab him. Hold the potential for protection tight. Keep talking.

He can hear. His attention may be held as well. Say:

"They're a great bunch of guys, really. I know them. I've had lunch with them. They're well meaning, but simply don't understand the rules. I try to run, usually. I've been trying to shake them forever. I couldn't convince them to stop."

The man does not hear. Or won't. His eyes sweep slowly the empty surroundings. Keep talking. Get the stranger back. Change the subject. To what? There are no other thoughts. Think. Search. Say:

"I could go on about them all day, mister, but I'm sure you don't want to hear about it," The words are still easy, but the subject is changed. Over the man's shoulder, the car reappears. The black one. Dark, closed, inviting. A window opens. One of them leans out, waving that so desired contract.

Move. Back to the Market. Keep moving. The man's eyes return. He is waiting for an explanation. No time left for words, for him. Say:

"Sorry mister, no more time for words. I gotta move now. Before they catch me. I can't let them catch me."

Turn. Leave the man. Keep moving. Pump the legs, bury cleats in soft tar. Pump, pump, pump. Acceleration wets eyesight, the road passes underfoot, a blur of kinetic pavement.

Spy the signpost ahead. Small, green, hopeful. 'Wall Street,' it reads, in dull white letters. Relax, slow down. Turn right, onto this street. It is home. They might not be able to make the turn. Look back, see the black car miss the turn, disappear behind grey marble. Turn again, to the Market. Dodge children on bicycles. Shrug off street vendors and their carts of apples, strawberries, meat pies. Find the steps. The steps, covered with plump chickens for sale. Keep moving, up the steps, crushing the occasional fowl. No matter. This is the Market. The security place. The dirty, unforgiving place. The required place, for a permanent roof. Keep moving.

At the top of the stair the Four Horsemen crouch. Each touches muddy fingertips to the floor. Golden helmets gleam. No matter. This is the Market. Tradition runs strong here.

Strong enough to break this line.

Lower head. Tuck attaché tight under right arm. Protected. Secure. Bound the last of the steps, three at a time. Take the line head on. Knock the Irish from their perch to the street below. Laugh as they land in a watermelon cart, sending the angry farmer's wares down the canyon floor.

Cross the threshold to safety. Through the great doors, into the gloom. Turn back. One more look out the doors to bright daylight, blue skies. The platinum portcullis drops. The world outside the grid reverts to the cold grey haze that it must be. Find the Floor, and all will be well. As Father always said. Keep moving.

Long, cold marble corridors, wider than the street outside, are the way. Controlled steps on tattered carpeting shorten vast distance to the second, gold, and opening portcullis ahead. Pass. Hear it slam, behind. The Floor lies here. Empty, dangerous. Crowded with empty dangerous figures. Stop moving.

T ed 2

Shopping with Mother, he happily pushed the heavy steel cart, half filled with colorful food and tasty surprises. He had no control of the cart he labored to propel. He was not able to stop it at his favorite spots. Mother's chubby, spotted hand was doing the real work; tugging the mobile cornucopia behind her while she ignored his pleas for fudgesicles.

She paused in the cookie aisle. He spotted a previously sampled package of Oreos. He watched with glee as his hand stole one, the telltale rustle of cellophane barely audible. A shadow loomed over him before he was able to separate the chocolate cookie outsides. For a terrifying instant, Mother's forearm filled his vision. The Oreos were gone and the cart was already down the aisle when he finished cowering from the expected blow.

He sat, resigning himself to studying the awful tile pattern of the floor on which he reclined. Mother was gone. Lost. Retired to another aisle, leaving him alone and helpless in the bright place. Still, he was hungry, and it was a food place.

He rolled over, onto his back. He gazed in wonder at the towering city of staples. He wondered how much of it required cooking before it could be safely eaten. A particular skyscraper drew his attention; an ominous, slightly swaying edifice built from Campbell's soup cans. Their motion cast thin but complete shadows in the bright aisle. As he watched, the tower groaned like a great ship toppling into a trough. The carefully stacked cans began their descent. Shoppers ran for cover.

He rolled over, found his feet and dashed down the aisle after the distant large and small globs of color that were Mother and the shopping cart. He caught up, grabbing the wire cart cage to assist his braking. He orbited the cart and his annoyed parent once, then landed on the ugly floor beside them. He climbed aboard the shelf on which mother usually put Butch's dog food. Of course, Ol' Butch didn't need any food that week, or any week, since he went to visit Doggie Heaven.

The cart remained stationary long enough to tempt him with a glimpse of a special surprise. He brushed a blond lock out of his eyes with a pudgy finger. Yes. There, on the bottom clean white supermarket shelf was a handful of Cocoa Puffs. Precious Cocoa Puffs. He trilled at the discovered treasure, the real reason for enduring the tortures of food shopping. He scooped up the handful, ate every last puff.

And spit the dog food out with overzealous disgust. He looked at his hands. They were painted with gooey, half-eaten dog food. He rubbed them vigorously on his Easter suit with no effect. No effect on his hands—the suit changed hues from light blue to dark brown. His actions were disturbed by movement nearby.

Mary Grace, the nosy kid who volunteers to take names of talkers when Teacher leaves the class, grabbed his forearm with two equally grubby hands.

"Ted," she panted, brown eyes wet, "You gotta go, gotta run! The yellow monster's coming back again!"

He laughed at her silliness.

"That's crazy, Mary Grace. There's no yellow monster. Or green. Or brown."

Still, as a precaution, he leaped through a classroom window, soared effortlessly over two mountain ranges, and landed on his feet in the schoolyard below.

The sunless sky was bright. In the distance, some kids were playing dodge ball on the cold grainy asphalt. He longed to join them, but he wouldn't have been picked even if he were there when they had started playing. He sat on the fresh cut grass to watch, playing with a carefully chosen blade. After several vigorous rubs, it unfolded into a tasty carnation. Strawberry, he decided, chewing thoughtfully.

The great yellow monster, thankfully the only thing in the neighborhood bigger than him, rounded the Goldberg's house. Its roars vibrated the ground, rattled picture windows. His neighbors ducked into their homes for cover. Some of the cowards crashed through closed doors in panic. He stood his ground bravely, deciphering the presence of the beast. In time, he snapped his fingers and headed for his Pinto. There was a life to be saved! He was elated, hoping for another drowning victim, close to death. Real hero stuff. What he needed.

He was prepared. He ceremoniously unfolded the green surgical gown he stowed in the black leather pouch tied to his waist. It didn't fit, and he was forced to don the nurse's outfit stashed at the bottom of the pouch. At least it was white. And Union. He squeezed into his car and sped after the yellow monster, siren wailing.

It had left the block. He was not concerned. He easily tracked the monster by following its watermelon droppings. His car bounced violently over the obstacles, crushing them into a mouthwatering pink pulp. He retained control and followed the droppings along the sandy shore of a polluted lake. He could see very little contaminated water, however, as the lake was filled with gray fishing boats. They were lying against each other at all possible angles. A dozen fishermen working two rods each lined the boats' rails. They were reeling in thousands of fish, piling them high behind them. The overloaded craft settled deep in the sick water. Whenever a fisherman dropped in a line, another fish would bite. The frenzied activity angered the crews, inconvenienced by the bounty the lake provided.

He too was not pleased with the scene. It made him hungry. He plucked a passing watermelon and shoved it in his mouth. There was no time for chewing, so he ground the fruit in his practiced jaws only once, and swallowed. Happily, the watermelon tasted like fish and satisfied him. He resumed the chase.

He rounded a corner in a quiet suburban neighborhood he did not recognize. He narrowly avoided two small children digging holes in the road. He shouted at them. They waved back.

One boy's raised hand grew to enormous proportions, bigger than the Pinto, and slammed into the passenger door. The Pinto flew into the air, but he was able to bring it to a safe landing on the road. Fearing that the gas tank might explode if he used his door, he climbed out the back hatch.

A man blocked his exit. He failed to recognize the brooding stranger, but was aware that the man had something to do with the yellow monster, and with getting the boy to swat his car. He felt that the man did those things with intent, to inhibit his pursuit.

"Now what did you do that for, mister?" he asked, easily maintaining his professional composure, "Can't you see I've got an emergency to get to? People need me. They want my help. I think someone might even be almost dead and only I can revive them. Isn't that great?" The man did not respond. Instead, the stranger retreated to the rear of the car and climbed into the hatchback compartment.

His new passenger remained silent, neck craned forward, looking through the windshield at where the car was headed. He wedged himself into his moving car, switched on the siren and warning lights, and returned to the trail of watermelons.

They were shrinking, first to rotten cantaloupes, then raisins, which were eaten by a flock of ravenous pigeons. He drove aimlessly, wondering if he should feel guilty about losing the trail. When he stopped at a crossroads ruled by a broken traffic signal, he spotted more raisins.

The telltale fruit left the intersection in three directions, and no one was there to tell him which one had taken the correct route. He pounded his fist on the steering wheel, shattering it. He swore to himself, angry at yet another delay. He retrieved a fresh wheel from the glove compartment and slid it into position. He sped straight across the intersection.

He had picked the right trail. Fresh watermelon blanketed the road. The light thumps as the Pinto rolled over them were music to his ears. He smiled, hummed the Battle Hymn of the Republic, and skidded his car to a halt next to a recently demolished old farmhouse. He passively noticed that he had driven through a stone wall onto the front lawn. He hoisted himself from the car and sprinted to the back of it. He lifted the glass hatch. He rooted around in the sea of empty beer and soda cans awaiting recycling until he found his black doctor's bag. In his haste to attend the emergency, he left the hatch raised behind him and burst through another section of stone wall in front of him without slowing.

He jogged down a narrow tar path, past nicely landscaped gardens to the ruined apartment complex ahead. He tried to hurry when he saw plenty of injured victims scattered on the lawn, but his vast bulk would not allow him to accelerate. With each attempt, he simply pounded his white shoes deeper into the asphalt path.

In a few steps he reached the smoldering apartments. No injured remained. Only a man and a woman he thought he should know stood near the wreckage, quite healthy. He could discern a line of ambulances disappearing in the distance. He sat on the remaining apartment building and tried to cry, to be naturally upset at his predicament. It didn't work. He realized that he could not be, and should simply wait for his next chance, when someone else is near death. Then maybe he would have another chance to be a medical hero. He stood and headed across the burnt field to the A&P in the distance, hungry for Cocoa Puffs.

Lou 3

Lou opened his eyes. Closed them. Opened them. Closed them. He fluttered his lashes and lost track of their position. It did not matter; his world remained the same. Gray closed, gray open.

"Shit," he swore softly, "It's going to be another boring ride. Ah, well, might as well make the best of it." He determined that his eyes were open when he spotted his nose with one. He then refrained from blinking to keep things straight.

He was floating in a vast, empty expanse. His world was gray, clear, and dull. He had assumed he was aloft in a desolate winter sky until his lower lip lightly scraped a warm wet surface. He stuck out his tongue to probe the new sensation. It slapped against a hard wetness. He caught some, pulled his tongue back in. Water. Briny water. He was held firmly by water. Not ice, because he was told that salt water doesn't freeze. Salt water. Must be the ocean, he thought.

Lou was unable to look straight down to survey his trap. He tried to open his mouth, but the water restrained his chin. His ability to tread water without disturbing its steel surface awed him. When he twisted around, he winced as the water's edge scratched his throat. His pain was poorly sacrificed: the emptiness he had turned from still faced him. He was in the middle of a motionless gray sea that did not change when he left it. Empty, blank, endless, and dull. Lou was not even afforded the small entertainment of a horizon. The sky, just a shade paler than the sea, blended too well for him to target a division.

Lou thought. He was alone. No sound, no ships, no fish. He couldn't feel his body, hidden beneath the surface. He guessed it was moving, treading water without a ripple. Lou didn't fear. Instead, he felt isolated, abandoned, with an entire lifeless sea to explore. To explore. To explore if he could move. Lou shook his head, lacerating his throat again.

"Explore what?" he said through the constricting water. There was nothing, nothing anywhere. Nobody to find, nobody to care. He was left alone, to watch nothing. The absence of something or someone to watch angered him, made him wish to risk injury and cry out.

While aimlessly surveying his surroundings, Lou spotted his reflection on the wet mirror. He smiled, watched himself smile back. He winked, and the gesture's amicable return lightened him. He laughed aloud, squirting more blood from his throat. The pooling red fluid chased away his reflection. Lou despaired. Seeking proper effect, he tried to weep, succeeding to release not a stunning tear but a large crystal pear from the corner of his eye. Steuben, maybe.

The glass fruit rolled off his cheek and into the sea. It broke through gray steel on impact, leaving a small jagged hole that allowed Lou visual access to the vibrant depths below. Lou rallied his emotions, driven by his pear's descent into another world. He was encouraged by change, by the prospect of passage to the comfort of others. To purpose. He had to act fast, however. The hole's rim was shrinking, concealing the moving shadows and dancing colors below. If only he could move. Move.

Experimentally, Lou tried raising his arms above his head. His hands immediately passed through the surface without causing a ripple. Delighted, Lou clapped his hands together, making no sound. He wanted to think up a new Zen koan about the quiet of two hands clapping, but chose instead to adopt his new priority. He was out of the water to his armpits, positioned well to attempt escape to the depths below.

He pounded fiercely on the surface with his freed fists. What the sad crystal fruit had ruptured effortlessly would not yield to his desperate impacts. Lou tried pressing his hands against the water to force himself out. He suspected he made some progress, but when he stopped to watch his hands, he noticed they could not gain a solid purchase on the clear smooth glass. The hard water directed his pressure sideways, and the altitude he thought he achieved was merely his hands sliding from his sides. He tried to break the surface once more, repeatedly thrusting both arms in the air as if signaling a touchdown, then slamming them with all the strength his depressed psyche could muster onto the resilient barrier. And, repeatedly, his mighty thrusts were first slowed by thick air, then bounced off the water's surface harmlessly. Without a ripple.

Lou grew restive. He tried closing his eyes, but the backs of their lids still mimicked the somber hue of the sea. He held them open, wondering in tired fascination at the hopeless new laws he faced. An empty gray world where failure was the norm, capping a crowded, vivid sea. He tilted his head forward until it rested on the water, drummed his fingers silently, pensive. Suddenly Lou straightened and burst into laughter. He pounded his forehead with both palms and shouted:

"Of course! What an asshole I was! All I need to do is hold my breath!"

Lou couldn't hear his words, but clearly understood what he was saying. Still feeling a bit sheepish, he rolled his eyes, took a deep breath and didn't let it out. He slid into the sea, beneath the grim surface. Where he belonged. Lou was elated.

He idled in the brilliant blue water, sucking the sweet liquid deep into his lungs. He kept his refreshing pause brief, for there was much to explore in the interesting place. He didn't have to search hard. He recognized everything. All was as the narrator on PBS had described it: schools of colorful fish, hungry sharks, sea turtles, whales, undulating kelp, and two women in bathrobes engaged in intense argument under a giant brain coral.

His curiosity piqued, Lou made his way to them. The going wasn't easy. He was forced to walk because he had forgotten how to swim, and his upright position was encouraging schools of small brown minnows to push him back one step in the water for every two he made toward the women. He wasn't angered at the minnows' waylay. Each fish carried an irresistible expression of exuberant joy that prevented Lou from finding fault in the school's activities.

While he struggled to reach them, the shorter of the two women snatched a small turtle trying to swim past her. With no warning - the other woman was still speaking - she unclipped a little brass clapper and gonged the turtle's ornate shell three times. On cue, a trap door swung open beneath the other hapless debater.

Alice tumbled into a large dark hole in the ocean floor, serving her opponent a look of abject disgust that made Lou shiver.

The hatch thudded shut, and the Trident sub the victorious woman straddled rose from the ocean bottom. Once enough debris had been scattered, a second, round, hatch swung open on the submarine's steel deck. A plume of bubbles erupted from the open silo. Lou felt the urge to duck and cover but stood his ground. A crescendo of bubbles erupted, followed by Alice, who was still in her robe. She clasped her hands gracefully above her head, reminding Lou of Esther Williams. She continued talking as she accelerated out of the hole. She shot to the surface far overhead and was gone. The hatch slammed shut.

Ashley laughed, her gaze following Alice's trajectory until she was out of sight. Then her face paled. She waved both arms up at the bubble stream frantically, then dove through the screen door in the sub's conning tower. Lou cynically noted the screen and felt that Ashley was going nowhere in that faulty ship. He was right. The sub lifted out of the silt of the ocean bottom, wandered aimlessly around the lagoon, then drew to a stop in front of him. He sighed at the tragic loss, plucked the sub from the sea and dropped it into his pocket. Tired of useless behavior, Lou pushed off the concrete bottom and rose to the surface of the pool. He turned his attention back to the barbecue.

The lounge chair he sat in was being infuriatingly unhelpful. Each time he got himself settled, the chair would fold up on him, forcing him into a fetal position and spilling his iced tar on the fresh cut purple grass. He really wanted the iced tar, too, but the chair got the best of him. By the sixth or seventh fold, the glass was empty, clean.

Lou stood and threw his glass at the chair, hitting it squarely on the frayed yellow plastic webbing. The chair yelped in pain, turned and galloped away. It disappeared into the distance, folding and unfolding in a staccato, annoying clatter. Lou shook his head and crossed to the group of people standing on the fur patio, to mingle. Lou hoped his host wouldn't notice the missing chair until after the party. Whoever his host was.

He didn't recognize any of the guests. Of course, he thought, I don't have many faces to pick from. Though there were about twenty people attending the occasion, they all shared the same two sets of features. The men were tall, of average build, with dark hair and olive skin. The women were a bit less tall, of average build, all with fair complexions and blond hair stretched into tight buns. Feeling a need to be sociable, Lou attempted light conversation but couldn't break in. Everyone was talking at once, engrossed in an animated conversation that he failed to comprehend. He listened more closely and found they were all discussing the same topic, in excited tones. No amount of concentration could translate their mysterious language. He would have to learn it himself. On a hunch, he grabbed the nearest woman's wrist and drew her to him. She met his stare with twinkling eyes, smiled. He leaned toward her until his nose was inches from hers.

"What are you saying?" he shouted, "I need to know."

"Rutabagas," the woman responded pleasantly, sipping her iced tar.

"What?"

"Rutabagas," she repeated. She paused, smiled knowingly, and waved her index finger at him. She continued happily, "Rutabagas rutabagas rutabagas. Rutabagas, rutabagas rutabagas."

"Oh," Lou said, "Thanks." He tenderly grasped her shoulders, turned her around, and pushed her back into the crowd. Now that he knew, Lou could hear the chant of 'Rutabagas' being uttered by all. He lost all interest in the silly extras, choosing rather to admire his host's surroundings.

The grounds were lush, well trimmed, and splashed with evenly spaced fluorescent orange trees. The purple lawn ended at a brass hedge a few yards away. The glittering hedge blocked out the rest of his host's neighborhood, as desired. The house was impressive as well. Old, Tudor, he guessed, as it sported day-glo green timbers on its outside walls. Lou wondered what the heating bill was like for a mansion with no glass in any of its window openings.

Movement beside a far wall caught his attention, and Lou rounded the side of the house to investigate. A backhoe labored on the front face of the house, its bucket positioned near the sill of an upstairs window. A raven-haired woman in black leather crouched in the Cat's bucket. Her attention was fixed on the pane of glass the bucket was about to pass through. Without looking down, she waved hand signals to the operator in the backhoe's cab. The driver expertly inched the bucket into the glass, its enormous mass bending the pane slightly. Lou was curious.

"Hey you! Whatcha doin' up there?" he shouted, hands cupped to his mouth. The woman flashed doe eyes at him, and ducked into the bucket. Lou waited. In time, her fingers curled over the steel rim of her shelter, followed by the cautious set of dark almond eyes. They had lost their fear, but did slit with anger when she noticed Lou. She stood in the still moving bucket, hands remaining on its edge for support.

"What the hell are you doing here, asshole?" she shouted down at him.

"Huh?"

"You heard me! This is my job, not yours! I already told you. Now get your ass out of my face before I..."

Lou didn't witness her threat. The bucket had worked the glass free during her speech, pushing the thick pane in one piece into the house. The sudden release of tension launched both bucket and burglar beyond the open window, into the mansion. Fine, Lou thought, shaking his head slowly, another perfect crime and once more I'm an onlooker. He was checking his pockets for loose change when a shout thundered from the Caterpillar's cab.

"Hey you," the operator said, "Outa there! You want to get yourself killed?" Lou jumped to the edge of the ditch as the backhoe bit a small hill of black dirt from the spot he had vacated. A hand grabbed his collar and yanked him off the ground. He flew in a half circle, landing on his feet in front of Howard's belt buckle. The great man, easily eight feet tall, beamed down at him.

"Now you be careful next time big fella," Howard said, his baritone voice patronizing, "I've got a ditch to dig here and can't be flattening onlookers."

"Yes sir," Lou said, hands buried deep in his pockets. His face warming, he backed off a few paces before raising his head. When he did, he had to squint from the sunlight reflecting off the virgin strand before him.

Lou smiled, rubbing his bare belly. He loved beaches, and this stretch was most inviting. It was adorned with the purest white sand, no tourists, and a calm blue ocean beyond that glistened in the noonday sun. Lou ripped off his loafers and sweat socks in preparation for a jog on the beach. Just to stand near the water for a time, curl his toes in the cool wet sand. Maybe a dip in the water, if it was warm enough. Of course it'll be warm enough, he thought with a grin.

A hammer blow on his right shin interrupted his first step. Lou stopped, grabbed it and hopped about like a fool until he saw what hindered his passage. Then he hopped some more. It was the brass hedge, rising nearly to his knees. Lou didn't appreciate a barrier erected to prevent him from reaching the beach. He clenched his fists into angry balls, retreated twenty paces, and charged the hedge, screaming TV Indian war whoops.

After a sluggish start, he wondered if he would clear the foreboding obstacle. He didn't allow his confidence to falter, however, and was rewarded by the discovery that he moved faster when he bellowed the whoops. Encouraged, he released some more, pushing his chest with his hands for more volume. The wind from his acceleration drew vision-blurring tears. He checked his watch to see how fast he was moving and was not surprised to see the needle edging past sixty.

The hedge was approaching fast. Lou prepared to make his leap, checked his knees for proper shock absorption, flapped his arms. On his last step before launching over the hedge failure threatened. Lou found extra strength in one last mighty whoop.

He cleared the hedge, and the beach. He soared at an altitude of twenty feet above calm blue water, then green ocean. He had leapt too hard, and had failed to land. He reviewed all the calculations he could think of to reason himself back to the beach. Unfortunately, any solution was moot. He had forgotten how to fly. Without aviary skills, he could neither turn around nor land in the water below. Lou sighed. His only option was to wait for landfall and hope for a tree to grab. He put his arms out in front of him in correct superhero form and waited for the flight to end. Lou hoped it was the Atlantic he traversed, or a Great Lake.

Land loomed sooner than expected. He had just passed over the thin blue stripe of the equator when he spotted Atlantic City rising above the waves. The casinos were unlit. Their windows were boarded, doors chained. Good, Lou thought, I can do without them anyway. The boardwalk was his concern, its steel rail approaching at about his waist level. He hoped it too hadn't decayed.

The cold steel, solid in Lou's grasp, provided ample support as he pivoted over it, his flight concluded when his face slammed onto the weathered boardwalk. He sat up, rubbed splinters from his eyes. When they cleared, he faced a young girl in a cute pink dress. She smiled at him mischievously.

"Hi, mister. Nice landing," she said sweetly.

"Hello, little girl. Are you here all by yourself?"

"You want some nice cotton candy?" The girl offered him a bale of pink cotton candy, larger than Lou. He reached for it, but couldn't get his fingers around the paper cone and the candy fell to the ground. The girl screamed, stomped her foot.

"Now look what you've done, you stinkin' bastard! Look at my candy! Pick it up, now, you ugly mother!"

"Okay, okay," Lou said sheepishly. He bent to where it had landed near his bare feet. He wrapped both his hands around the cone, getting a good grip. He pulled, but the cone was stuck.

"Pick it up, asshole, before I get my gun!" the sweet child prompted, smiling coyly.

Lou screwed his eyes shut, bent down low, let out a heroic TV Indian war whoop and stood, heaving. His muscles shuddered, his lungs ached, but the cotton candy was moving. However, the floor tempered Lou's triumph. It flexed in unison with his movements, nearly knocking him off his feet.

"Now cut that out!" Lou heard a nasal shout, opened his eyes. The girl was gone, the boardwalk was gone, the cotton candy was gone. An inner tube of fat from Ted's gut had replaced them, and Lou needed it to stay afloat: Ted was careening down a booming set of rapids, and Lou didn't wish to fall into the frigid white water.

"Sorry Ted," Lou shouted, mindful of his tight grip, "One can't be too careful you know."

"What do you mean, 'too careful'? I got you, mister. You're safe. It's what I'm trained for," Ted said, lifting his head high enough to make eye contact with Lou, "Now stop pinching me."

Lou obediently released Ted's blubber. It briefly retained the shape he had formed with his clenched fingers, then puffed back out to complete Ted's smooth belly. Lou was unable to maintain his perch on Ted through the next set of fast rapids. Ted did his best to provide a stable platform, but the waterfall ahead was promising to soak Lou. Remembering that he had forgotten how to swim and fly, Lou didn't bother to ponder an easy solution to his plight. He waited instead for a rescue to present itself to him. The wait was thankfully short.

He spotted a convenient branch stretched across the river, just before the water dropped out of sight. The stick waved to him, unaware that it already had his attention. He jumped for the outstretched tree as Ted passed under it. Ted, his head already past rescue, failed to notice Lou's exit and passed over the falls without further comment.

Alice pulled Lou into her convertible in a graceful arc. She deposited him in the passenger seat, not allowing him to interfere with her concentration on piloting the car.

"Hey, mister," Alice said, "You know it isn't safe to hitchhike." She turned to him as she spoke, her familiar appearance unsettling Lou. Her clear blue eyes probed him, saw through him. Crows feet at their ages implied her amusement at him. Lou felt his spine tingle at her scan. He tried to remain calm, touching her wrist where it rested on the gearshift.

"Well thanks for picking me up all the same, Alice. You've been real helpful lately."

"S'what I'm here for, mister," she pointed with her thumb over her shoulder, "Picked this guy up hours ago, and he hasn't said a word yet. You know him?"

Lou turned to the back seat. A large man in a blue football jersey and helmet sat sideways in the confined rear passenger area. His hands rested, frozen, on a computer keyboard. He stared, unblinking, at the blank green screen before him. Lou turned his attention back to Alice.

"He does look familiar, but I'm not sure. Did you ask him?"

"Yeah, but he didn't tell me shit. I'm a little bugged by him. Don't even know when to let him off."

Lou rotated his head to ask the passenger again, but knew at a glance that he would get nothing from the athlete. He turned back around to see where they were headed. Not much help there, he thought, as the car was passing through a dense white cloud bank. Alice didn't notice.

"Mister," she said, "You wouldn't believe the day I had. First some she-bitch wastes my kid, then I pick up Mr. Excitement back there, now you throw yourself on me. What's going on? Will I ever be alone again?" She was livid, her face bright red, blond hair standing on end. Lou empathized, but had no easy solutions. He looked around for one as he spoke to her.

"I know what you mean, Alice. People keep turning up... people like you. You're not supposed to be here, but you are. Weird world, Huh? Wait, I think I see up ahead where you can unload our passenger. See the strip mall up on the right?"

"The one floating at about 2:00? Doesn't look like much parking there mister."

"We won't be staying. Just pull in by that sporting goods store and watch what happens."

They did. Alice dropped the car with a metallic thud on the sidewalk. Lou checked the back seat. Phillip was still frozen at his terminal. Alice checked her mirror, frowned, put the car back in gear. Lou held her wrist.

"No. Wait for it."

"Wait for what?"

"Don't know, but wait."

"Fine."

Lou looked through the glass front of the store. It was crowded with patrons, all wearing blue warm up suits. One of them, leaving the store with a package, spotted Phillip. The fan dropped his package and, eyes wide, pointed at the back seat.

"There he is!" the fan screamed.

Everyone in the store rushed the windows for their share of the spectacle. They recognized Phillip, and demanded the walls be raised. The windows opened like Lou's garage door at home, and thousands of fans stormed the car.

Phillip did not react until fifty pairs of hands reached over the sill of the car and snatched him by his Armani shoulder pads. His fans dragged the limp hero, whose shock left him silent, from the car. They carried him on their shoulders into the store. The windows slammed shut behind them. After the building spat Phillip's computer onto the sidewalk, the store was still, its asphalt parking lot vacant. Lou released Alice's thin wrist.

"Now we can go," he said.

"I guess. Thanks mister," Alice said, "But what about you?"

"Damn good question, Alice. What about me? Why do these things keep happening to me?"

"Don't know. Don't even know who the heck you are."

"Well in that case, I'm out of here. Let me off at the next stop."

"There are no stops."

"Okay, then just pull over."

"Can't. No road."

She was right. Lou peered over the door, down to the white emptiness below, and above. He was getting tired of emptiness.

"I see," he sighed, "Can I get out right here?"

"I don't care, mister."

"Okay, bye." Lou turned away from Alice and opened the wooden door.

He stepped out onto his back porch, happy to see that the floodwaters had receded. He could make out some green patches of grass pushing through the mud. His neighbor Ed's powerboat lay grounded on one, its engine still running. Ed didn't seem to mind. He continued to steer and rock back and forth as if he were at speed. He spotted Lou and waved, the wind ruffling his long black hair.

Now this is more like it, Lou thought as he waved back.

Gloria 3

Gloria leaned over the rail of one of the real reasons for taking things: floating above the suburbs with Ian in a giant, silent balloon, descending peacefully onto the night's target. Gloria lived to drift with her mentor above the well guarded, alarm system ridden estates of rich people she knew she hated. All in preparation for the true thrill: getting in. When she saw her mark, a great white house that sprawled below them, she grabbed Ian's wrist.

"That's it," she whispered to Ian.

"You sure?" he asked.

"Definitely. I can tell by the hedge. Only gold one around. Let me out here."

"Okay. You're the boss."

"Yup. That's me. The boss," Gloria said. She cupped his cheeks with her gloved hands and kissed him on the mouth. He tasted like sandpaper and sawdust. Gloria stood on the balloon basket's iron rail, waved, and hopped over the side.

The small drop basket Ian had designed was a success. Originally a three-quart saucepan, it caught her leather-clad buttocks smartly, gripping firmly. Gloria kicked her feet as the basket lowered her to the mansion below, enjoying the ride. As planned, the basket stopped its descent inches from the large darkened second story window she had cased earlier.

She popped open her little black toolbox, suspended by a string beside her, and set to work dismantling the window frame. She expected the foray to go well until she pried a rusty casement nail too hard, snapping it free into the air. Not wishing to betray her activity, she lunged for the errant nail. It deftly evaded her grasp and fell out of reach. She tracked its slow spiral to the ground, where it landed next to a familiar man clad in wet jeans and a T-shirt.

The stranger had his hands cupped to his face. His mouth was moving, but he said nothing. What a dick, Gloria thought. Maybe so, but he was a witness. It'd be best to get rid of him.

"So what the hell do you think you're doing here, asshole?" she shouted. He was less than ten feet below her, but she shouted anyway.

The man did not respond.

"C'mon mister. You know you heard me. Now we've been through this before, haven't we? This is my job. I scoped the place out, not you! I know I already told you this, and I'm not repeating myself now. So get your ass out of my face before I give in and come with you."

Gloria heard her speech but paid no attention to her words. The real priority was the window, not the stranger, and while she wasted time speaking, it had swung open, surrendering to her skills. It also was never locked. Gloria forgot about the intruder the instant she passed through the open window and landed squarely on the dirty wooden floor inside.

The Camp Yellow Eagle great room was damp, mildewed. Persistent rain had fallen for so many days that its moisture had permeated everything. Wetness was not a problem that night, however. Like everyone else in the room, Gloria was anxious. Two more camp counselors came in out of the rain, dripping wet and despondent. The head counselor met them at the rickety screen door.

"Any luck?" Mrs. Grayson asked, wringing her worm-covered hands. Earthworms. Little pink ones.

"None," the young man said. He showed no visible concern for his soaked and shivering self, only anguish over the missing child.

"We searched everywhere. Even places nobody thought of, but we just can't find little Sarah anywhere. And we also can't find Mrs. Baker."

"It's okay," Mrs. Grayson stammered, "We'll find her. We have to. Mrs. Baker, the dear soul, must still be out there searching for Sarah." She bent to the floor, anxiously picked a dusty throw rug up off the floor, wrapped it around herself, and left the cabin to venture out into the gray downpour to begin her fruitless search. Gloria watched her leave, saw the counselors exchange poorly masked looks of concern. Her mood blackened further. There was no hope.

When Gloria bent down to hitch up her knee socks, she spied the small door that led to the cabin's basement. On a hunch, she pushed the rotted wooden door until it creaked fully open, and stepped down three slick steps to the cramped, musty basement floor. It was dirt, dry, with puddles of black water scattered randomly. Shadows dominated, cloaking the already dim space with patches of empty darkness. The room was small, wet, barren, and occupied.

A little girl emerged from a gloom-ridden corner. A shadow cast by her wispy, wet black hair concealed her face until the rest of the child had emerged. Gloria wanted to retreat, to escape back up the sagging steps. Back up to the comfort of the great room. She had no interest in seeing this girl's face. Still, she had to. Rules were rules.

The young girl raised her head. Gloria retreated one step, instinctively drawing the foot she left behind in quickly. The child looked at Gloria, her hands innocently stashed in her jumpsuit pockets. She was wet, dripping, as if she had just come in out of the...

"You," Gloria whispered, "You know. You know where Sarah is. Don't you?"

The child did not speak, but she did reply. She replied with a smile. A lipless black psychotic smile. Gloria gasped. The child knew.

It's more than that, Gloria thought. In response to her suspicion, the little girl's smile grew. From ear to ear it spread, still thin but revealing pointed rows of teeth that glistened with moist drool.

Gloria froze: it was her. The little girl had killed Sarah, hidden her away somewhere. The little girl from the shadows had everyone in the camp risking their lives to find poor dead Sarah. And God yes, she thought, there was Mrs. Baker. The monster had killed, brutally killed sweet Mrs. Baker. As she stood, exposed, before the child, Gloria sought desperately to deny the truths she had realized. She could not. Worse, she knew the next truth: the child could not let her go. It took a childish, tentative step toward her, still smiling. Still drooling.

Screaming, Gloria ran from the cellar back into the great room. She stopped in front of the cheerful fire that crackled in its worn stone hearth, and turned to pass her warning to the counselors gathered in a frantic circle around her. She tried to speak, to convey her panicked message, but failed. The little girl had followed her and stood in the shadows near the stairs, still dripping wet; dripping evil. Smiling. Gloria choked back her words. She would be next if she uttered a word about the child's obvious guilt. She would surely be the victim of the bloody carving knife the young girl wielded. Firelight glinted off it in flashes of silver and crimson.

Gloria, unable to help the counselors or herself, terrified of the tiny killer, tried to wake up. She shook her head, screamed, even pinched herself, but nothing happened. She was trapped. The counselors seemed concerned. The child laughed, soundless. Gloria fled. She jumped from where she stood near the hearth and did not put her feet down again until she stood safely in the mud outside the white mansion.

She didn't mind the drenching rain. She was clean and back at work, and that was all that mattered. As she climbed the ivied lattice to the second floor, she did feel a twinge of guilt about something. As if she had abandoned a puppy. She suppressed the feeling...Guilt is for jellyfish.

She passed through the open French windows without incident. She thought she saw a small figure disappear into the shadows of the dark bedroom, but paid it no heed... Fear is for sissies.

The bedroom was remarkably clean, but promising. Though furnished lavishly with bureaus, tables, and cabinets, none of the flat surfaces held an object except the nightstand on the far side of the big four-poster. A single key rested on its polished surface. Gloria picked it up, examined it with gloved fingers. Cheap, she thought as she replaced it... Cheap is for amateurs.

She went to work, deciding to start at the large armoire near the door. Its doors were stuck, either jammed or locked. Having forgotten her crowbar, Gloria abandoned it for the large bureau. Its drawers didn't open either. They were more than jammed, too.

She had pulled hard enough to break off the brass handles. This angered her. They were just drawers. Drawers don't lock. A closer inspection revealed no seam between drawer and dresser. Maintaining composure, she crossed to the smaller drawer chest near the bed. She got the same results. The room was a complete failure. The blankets wouldn't even turn down on the bed. Furious, she crossed to one of two closet doors. She twisted its crystal knob, expecting nothing. The knob functioned. It wasn't locked. Gloria focused her anger on the unlatched door and pulled.

It whipped open, offering no resistance. Gloria stuck her head in the dark, saw nothing. No light entered from the bedroom. She pulled her flashlight from its holster, flipped it on and aimed into the closet. The halogen beam couldn't pierce the darkness. She passed her hand through the beam, verifying that it functioned properly. It did. In fact, it continued to shine on her hand when she experimentally moved that into the closet. Pleased with the hint of progress, Gloria stepped into the closet, using yellow light playing on her outstretched hand as a beacon.

Her idea worked well until a dark frigid shadow broke the beam. It wrapped around her wrist, clenched, and shook Gloria's hand like a rag. Gloria screamed, silently dropped the flashlight on the dirt floor, still on. The landing fixed the light. Its yellow beam illuminated Gloria and her assailant from below. The weak glow cast long shadows up the little girl's smiling face. Gloria tried to scream to someone, anyone, for help, but could produce no sound. The little girl snickered. Others snickered back. Others. Unseen.

That's it, Gloria thought, I'm out of here. With the same aerobic concentration that got the door open, she kicked her flashlight away, further into the empty, crowded closet. It went out. The cold clamp at her wrist released. Gloria backed out, fast, and slammed the door. The knob shattered, and the door bounced open. Two yellow eyes glowed in the darkness, watching her. Gloria didn't see but sensed those lips. That knowing, moist smile.

Gloria slammed the door again, jamming it closed by wedging her leather jacket into the crack near the floor. The door stayed shut. She caught her breath, feigned ignorance of the quiet scratching behind the door. One closet remained. Gloria circled the bed to reach it, tested the brass handle. It twisted freely.

Gloria was relieved. At least the venture wasn't a total waste, she thought.

She pulled the door open. It was a difficult task; the door was massive. Like it had been cast from a solid block of lead. Could be a good sign, she thought. She had to dig in and pull with all her might to induce it to swing open. Her heels carved holes in the floor, her powerful biceps twitched. Nevertheless, it would move, and that was what mattered. Once it started, she had only to jump out of its way, allowing it to travel on its own inertia. It swung its full arc, thudding gently against one of the bedposts. Gloria looked inside, squealed, and gave the air high-fives.

The closet, as big as her entire apartment, offered all she sought: overfilled jewelry boxes sagged gilded shelves that lined the walls; a safe, open, rested on the floor near her feet, wads of cash spilling from it; a Rolex watch display case rotated quietly in a corner; from a bar stretching thirty feet hung scores of furs from more endangered species than Gloria could name. She was afraid she was going to soil her pants. Gloria looked around for any unseen visitors, grabbed an extra pillowcase from the bed, and stepped in the closet. As her foot crossed the threshold, it all went away.

Not just the treasure, the furs, the light. Even the dark was gone. Gloria was surrounded by nothing.

Nothing. Not a whisper. Her own heartbeat abandoned her. Gloria tried to scream, and forgot how. Forgot. She forgot where she was, who she was, what she was. She had become a shapeless mass, unknown, unnamed, and unheard.

For an eternal instant Gloria was dead, and knew it.

A heavy metal thud, a whoosh of cold dry air, and Gloria was back in the bedroom, facing the closed closet door, well aware this time of its contents. She turned away from that closet door in time to notice the other had opened a crack. Little fingers emerged, curling around damp wood. One yellow eye glowed in the thin dark opening.

Gloria shrieked, launched herself across the bed, and slammed the door shut. Three light plops followed its thud. Gloria looked at the floor, watched as three dismembered pink fingers slithered under the door.

Gloria stepped back, put her jacket on and resigned herself to hoping that the door would stay closed. Her thoughts worked well; the closet remained closed. She sat on the hard bed, relieved but careful to keep her attention on the door. As she tried to catch her breath, she heard a noise behind her – a typical cinematic old door sort of creak. She turned. The other closet door was inching open, cracked enough already to reveal the poorly hidden treasures inside.

"Everything else is sealed! Everything! Why can't you stay shut?" Gloria ranted as she threw herself across the bed. The door was heavier than before. She had to lean her back into it. She used her heels to dig footholds again. One heel snapped. She felt stomach and thigh muscles rip but knew it was worth the effort. After all, she thought, I am at death's door.

"Death's Door!" she shouted, bursting into uncontrolled laughter at her awful pun. She wasn't particularly amused, but did feel better when she heard the mechanical thud of heavy tumblers as the door slid home.

She stepped gingerly to the foot of the bed, waited. She had lost all interest in looting the place, did not want to remove her eyes from either door. Looking elsewhere was academic anyway, since those were the only two portals in the room.

This needs to end," Gloria said, arms folded tight, "It has to. I can't deal with much more."

In response, both doors simultaneously creaked. Gloria's entire body spasmed in its inability to choose which door to hold shut. Unwilling to admit defeat, Gloria ran in circles around the room, arms still folded on her chest.

"No. No, no. No no no no no no no no..." she chanted, circling faster. The room blurred as she raced through it. Colors, shapes, materials were homologated by her speed into a single brown and green blur. Only the hearth and the two doors, still slowly opening, remained static, clear.

The hearth?

Gloria acknowledged its presence for the first time: a stout marble fireplace with a pleasant fire crackling within. It floated in viscous air with the two opening doors, finishing a triangle around her.

"Of course!" Gloria cried. She stopped running. The room stayed blurred, the two doors flew open behind her, and the fire welcomed her.

Without looking back at the doors or their emerging contents, Gloria crossed the fuzzy brown floor to the fireplace. She pulled out the three burning logs as a unit, relieved that they burned coolly. Must be some new Duraflame, she thought.

She stepped into the fireplace and climbed the narrow stairs lining the chimney without hesitation. Then she stopped, slapped her forehead, and started back down.

"Well shit," she said, "How stupid can I be?" Back on the hearth, she reached out through the tiny fireplace opening, grabbed the bottom log, and pulled the fire back in.

"Awe now come on! That's not fair!" a child cried from the far side of the flames. Gloria thought she heard more, but the words had changed to indecipherable moans of frozen anguish. Gloria didn't hang around: fingers of blue frost were already enveloping the logs. She re-entered the chimney, climbed its stone steps to the outlet on the roof.

"Thank God this house had a stairway in the chimney," she said to the starry night sky above, "They don't build 'em that way anymore."

She spotted a shadow crossing the sky, dodging twinkling stars. Gloria waved at Ian, trying to draw his attention.

Either he didn't see her or had lost control, Gloria wasn't sure, but the balloon was going to pass right by. She couldn't believe Ian had overlooked her. The balloon was close enough to touch. Indeed, she had to duck back into the chimney to avoid it. Gloria realized her mistake a moment too late, and missed the straw basket when she jumped for it. The drop basket clubbed her head as it swung by, knocking her off the roof. Ian, shrugging, waved to her as she tumbled down the terra cotta tiles. Gloria was pleased at least to enjoy a fleeting glance of Ian and his vanishing airship before she left the roof. She landed in a half-empty swimming pool. The murky warm water was deep, forcing her to tread it. She was relieved that she remembered how to swim.

"Why the hell would I forget?" she said aloud. She felt a small object rub her leg. Then another. Gloria didn't panic. After all, she thought, this can't be worse than being at Death's Door.

She sniggered, not noticing the objects surfacing around her until a dozen or so surrounded her.   They were little toy submarines. Intricately built, she noticed, with little sailors in the conning towers and tiny, yet functional missile hatches. She giggled.

"Oh how cute!" she said, "And they must be valuable. I have to grab a couple."

She started towards one, but saw that the diminutive warships had their own agenda.

Tiny Polaris missiles, toothpicks really, began emerging from the open silos.   Equally minute hissing yellow flames propelled them as they arced en masse toward her. Gloria gasped, fearing she was about to be nuked, and tried to remember how big a bomb has to be to really hurt. She dropped the thought, however, since her only alternative was ducking into the murky stagnant pool water, and she had no intention of doing so. Its darkness raised a distant memory that she didn't care to review.

The missiles fizzed past her anyway, landing instead on the toy subs themselves. They all blew up at once. The fine display of tiny mushroom clouds delighted Gloria. She clapped after several obligatory ooh's and ahh's, then waded to the patio. Bobby, Ian's porter, greeted her with a fluffy white towel. She thanked him and settled in her lounge chair to sip her tall glass of iced tar.

Howard 3

The phone, overwhelming the Louis XIV sideboard that strained to support it, rang. Its clangor was a fire alarm, demanding attention. Howard did not wish to answer it.

But he would. And did. He dove for the terrible machine before the third ring sounded. He crushed the receiver in his haste. Stiff wires inside kept the mouth and earpieces properly spaced. He waited, bearing no desire to be the first to speak.

"Hello?" he said.

"Howard? Howard is that you?" a weak voice murmured, clothed in thick whispers of terror. She repeated herself, gurgling as if an air hole had been punched into her throat.

"Howard? Howard is that you?"

"Yes," Howard shouted back, his voice toppling the sideboard, "It's me."

"Howard. It's Claire."

"Claire. Where are you? Tell me!"

"I can't," she said, her meager voice trembling, distant, as if her precious lips were far from her mouthpiece.

"What do you mean?" Howard demanded, "I paid. I did everything like they said. Tell me where you are!"

"Howard. I can't." Almost no sound.

"What can you say?"

"Howard. They said to say good-bye." Click.

Howard's tears graciously blurred the contents of the meat freezer. Hands shaking, he numbly dropped the lid closed.

"That her?" Officer Brown repeated.

"Yes, and she appreciates your outstanding efforts, Officer Brown." Howard wrapped his hands around Officer Brown's neck. He hoisted the suburban flunky in the air, pulled his face close.

"Or would you like her to thank you personally?" Howard said before hurling Office Brown into the dairy case.

The useless policeman shattered rows of plastic milk cartons, unleashing a white rain shower. Howard turned the worn collar of his trench coat up against the weather and trudged on down the grey sidewalk.

"I can't give up the search," he said aloud, laughing at his trite statement.

He had gotten a tip, apparently reliable. Unfortunately, he had written it on the inside of his trousers, and was unable to capitalize on the revelation. He scratched his thigh in disgust.

"I hate it when that happens," he mumbled.

He was cursing his absent-mindedness for forgetting an umbrella again. He had tried holding a crying child over his head but the fidgety youngster was too small to offer any cover from the rain. So he gave the boy a glass of water and sent him to bed.

Howard was beginning to regret that decision as well. The kid could have at least kept his hair dry. Well, he thought, a little rain is better than I deserve. Now where did I put Claire?

His best dozer idled at the curb where he'd left it. Its engine clattered softly, impatient for work. As he leaped from the soggy curb toward the steel tread, a tiny reflection in a curbside puddle halted his progress.

He squinted, focusing on the pale glow. He grew impatient, waiting for the vital reflection to come into focus. It seemed to take longer every time. Finally, the words came into view. The words. The clue. Words burned into his inseam by a flame long since extinguished.

Howard started to read, but accidentally urinated, obliterating the message. Words gone, his leap concluded. Two steel tread links bent when is feet, supporting inhuman weight, contacted them. He sat in the cab, cradled his cheeks in his hands.

"How could I do that?" he admonished himself, "How could I be so stupid?" He revved the cat's loud engine to avoid a response. He checked his pocket organizer to verify the piece of the message he had managed to jot down:

Claire OK.
Buried alive.
In...

Well, he thought, at least she's okay for now. But he had no notion of where she was buried, or how alive she might be. He did have the dozer, though. And the will to dig.

He worked the machine through its gears, getting up to speed. Then he eased back on the right stick and began circling clockwise, searching through the rain for a spot to dig. He circled and circled, found no clues. Undaunted, he circled some more.

Howard had not noticed that before he began his circling he had failed to raise the blade. His negligence forced him to stop. There was little searching to be done from the bottom of the canyon his mindless wandering had formed.

"Damn," he said, "Now I'll have to start all over again." He lowered the blade, gunned the engine and accelerated straight down the canyon. He charged recklessly, attaining blistering velocity. He was confident that he had enough inertia to easily crash through the far end of the furrow and start searching for another spot to dig.

Some man in jeans and sneakers, who nonchalantly stood in the furrow like nobody's business, suddenly blocked his path. Howard was surprised to see that the man paid him no heed. The stranger was scanning the far wall of the canyon. Howard heaved both control levers back, simultaneously raising the blade. He was able to slam into the dirt wall slowly, burying the blade, but not the man or dozer.

"Hey you!" he shouted, "Get out of there! Do you want to get yourself killed?"

The man heeded Howard's belated warning and jumped to safety. He smiled up at Howard, said nothing. Howard had to admire the stranger's resilience. He had to; there was no other option. Prompted by his newfound admiration, Howard stepped out of his Cat.

It was time to do more than holler at the naive traveler. He reached down and lifted the man by the scruff of his neck. He carefully set the man on the relative safety of the steel treads. He brushed some loose dirt off the man's cheap blue shirt, said:

"Now you be careful next time you're near a construction site, big fella. I've got a ditch to dig my way out of here, and it's important work. Very important. I can't be responsible for flattening unsuspecting onlookers. Understand?"

"Yes sir," the man said sheepishly, head bowed.

"Good. Now off with you, mister, you're putting me behind schedule," Howard said.

The man obediently backed away. Howard, feeling magnanimous, decided to help the traveler on his way. He shoved the stranger into the nearest dirt wall. He did not remove his hands until the hard clay fully engulfed the man. Howard smiled, happy to be of assistance. He brushed off his suit, paid the driver.

"Keep the change, buddy," he said.

"Thanks Mac," the marine answered, pulling the cab door closed from inside after Howard had stepped onto the curb.

The FBI building loomed before him. Steel, concrete, and marble. Not much glass. Permanent, solid, as immortal as he once felt.

Heavy chains secured the row of steel revolving doors leading to the sensible lobby. The barrier did not impress or frustrate Howard. It was the sign crudely taped over the 'For Sale' notice that solicited true anger:

> SHE'S
> NOT
> HERE

Howard lifted the detonation plunger and pushed it back down. An electric whir, then a turbine whine, followed by a terrific crash as his private jet flew into the fifth floor.

Howard allowed himself to be distracted as the punctured building deflating, bouncing around the Phoenix skyline. When it settled in the desert, a great flaccid chunk of rubble, he returned to his hopeless and forgotten task.

Forgotten.

He rapped his forehead with two sets of white knuckles.

"How could I forget?" he asked the child buying ice cream from the mailman at the corner, "How?"

"Don't know," the child responded, wide dark eyes peaking up between popsicle licks. So innocent. So adorable.

Howard angrily snatched her up with one hand, held her near his face. The child dropped her treat, watched it fall until it landed on Howard's feet.

"Don't know, huh?" he shouted at her, "And what is it exactly you don't know? Tell me!"

The child looked back at Howard. Her eyes shrank to little black, dull dots.

"No, Mr. Barlowe," the child said quietly, "What I don't know would take centuries to relate. I won't tell you that. Why don't I tell you what I do know?"

"Fine," Howard said, still angry, "Go."

"What I do know is that you made me drop my pink popsicle and I'm very, very angry. And..."

"And?"

"And I also know that in a second or two you'll be putting me down so I can play with my only friend. I don't have to tell you another thing."

"Oh," Howard said. He let the child fall into the swirling water of the rain-swollen gutter below. She paddled about for a bit, then found rescue in a hairless, jaundiced rat that stopped to offer a ride.

Howard left them to each other.

"Serves them right," he shouted. He glanced around the deserted street, seeking clues revealing his purpose. He found that purpose on the Palace Theater marquis. In bright lights and red letters:

LOOK IN HERE

Howard rooted in his pockets, found nothing smaller than a hundred. He hoped he could gain admission with such a large bill.

No one attended the art deco ticket booth, so he slipped the hundred under the closed theater door. He heard a click, watched a $94 bill and a slip of green paper emerge from the crack under the door. He retrieved both, pushed open the leather door.

He handed the ticket to the cop stationed inside, and entered the theater. The house lights were still up. Good, he thought, I'm not late. He took a seat near the edge of the water that filled the deep end of the theater. He waited.

The house lights stayed on. Nobody else came in. Just as well, he thought, since his was the only lounge chair on the beach. He squinted in the bright sunlight. It bothered him that he had forgotten to put on his sunglasses.

He picked up Claire's straw beach bag that was resting in the sand beside him. He only had to root around in it for a moment before he found them. Claire always kept them in the same place. Sure enough, there they were at the bottom of the bag, next to the Sucrets tin filled with aspirins.

Howard cast an admiring glance over to his organized wife. She smiled back. Her lips didn't align properly. Howard put down the bag, donned his Ray Bans, and took his beloved spouse's cold hand in his.

With the glare gone, Howard was more able to admire his beautiful wife: her pasty violet skin tone; those lovely dry blue eyes (one eye anyway. The other was missing); her perfect body, limbs joined together again with hastily stitched fishing line; that supple wide-open neck; that lovely toothless smile.

The smile. It reminded him.

Claire.

He found her.

Howard was careful to gently lay his slaughtered wife's hand back on her bare (skinless) knee before he stood on his chair, doffed and threw aside his Ray-Bans, and executed a swan dive into the sand. Back to the hell of consciousness.

T ed 3

"This is the worst movie," he said aloud, his voice fording the load of popcorn and Milk Duds he processed in his mouth. Each hand mined its own bucket: left for popcorn (buttered, salted, and oiled), right for Milk Duds. Soda was buried safely in the folds of his naked thighs, and two packs of Sweet Tarts were cleverly tucked in his armpits.

The movie preempted total contentment. Once his favorite, Godzilla had lost its charm. The veteran monster's impervious hide had taken on a sickly shade of mustard, and a glistening, giggling Pillsbury Doughboy was beating it to humiliation. He watched in anger as the Doughboy wrestled an enfeebled Godzilla down a hill, off a cliff, and into the movie-set ocean. The monsters fought on, with large-scale fisticuffs in the water. A tidal wave generated by the fray hit the beach, initiating a horrible, model-busting earthquake. When he turned his attention back to the offshore struggle, he noted that the Doughboy was winning.

"That's it!" he cried. He flipped the barrels of food off his lap, burying fellow viewers. They didn't mind, of course. He stood, charged the screen. The rows of seats before him were not an obstacle: one leap propelled him over the next four rows and into the screen. With Olympic poise he executed a classic swan dive into the roiling ocean, displacing nary a wave. He swam under the battling monsters, then employed his natural buoyancy to float up to a position just beneath the battling behemoths. Careful to first spit out any remaining popcorn, he opened his mouth, tilted his head back, and sucked. Forming a whirlpool around the action was simple, tasty.

The monsters took notice of his offensive too late. The Pillsbury Doughboy's struggle was futile, and it slid between his lips easily. One chew silenced the giggling. Unfortunately,

Godzilla tumbled into the vortex as well, man-arms flailing as his maelstrom engulfed it. He hesitated, unwilling to sacrifice any morsel of nourishment. Admiring his sense of sacrifice, he regurgitated Godzilla onto the shimmering surface. The great monster with the tiny brain, green again, waved a paw in thanks and swam away, toward Monster Island.

He bobbed about on the surface of the quiet lagoon. No emergencies, no ugly, spiteful thin people. Afloat, peaceful in the tropical sunshine. Thoughts about his next meal darkened his bliss. His last meal, store-bought biscuits, was already coursing through his lymphatic system. He felt his stomach rumble, lifted his head to admire it.

His stomach was not the source of the sound. Instead, a man balanced there, gripping a small flap of his smooth soft skin for support. A little man, eyes closed, familiar, apparently in trouble; an annoying thin person causing substantial discomfort with his bony hands.

"Now cut that out, mister!" he shouted. The man heard the command, opened his eyes, didn't let go. The stranger did respond.

"...Too careful..."

"What do you mean? Too careful? You're being nasty and painful," he explained, "You don't have to be. See, you're safe with me. It's what I'm trained for. Now just hold on."

Saving lives. Ten years of medical training. Surely he was competent, able to keep the imperiled man afloat. He could certainly float. The man perched up there did not seem to share his confidence. A wave of pain stemming from the man's nervous fingers rippled across his vast canopy of flab.

"Stop pinching me!" he cried. The man complied, releasing the steadying handhold he had created. A moment of intense concentration was needed to reshape the freed flap of swollen skin. The man tried to stand on his own, but faced poor footing on his flexing bulk. Without trained help, the man's stay on the dry safe belly would be short indeed. He began to play his stomach muscles with great skill, summoning all his talents to maintain a level surface for the interloper.

The stranger fell off a few seconds later, thankfully taking to the air instead of the rushing stream. He looked upstream at the man, who hung in the safety of a parachute. His attention on the man was overspent; when he did finally turn his head back downstream there was no stream to see. It ended abruptly, with a roar. He realized his fate too late; his fault entirely. He accepted his plunge toward the green spot a mile below with admirably stoic resignation.

He floated alongside the falling white water. He touched it, felt it move through his fingers. It was falling faster than he was. His girth apparently acted as a parachute, preventing acceleration. He landed lightly on his back, floating gently on the warm smooth surface of the small pond in his back yard. Before he could relax again, he noticed that a large praying mantis had lighted atop his belly. He remembered that the praying mantis, even if it was as big as his arm, was endangered. Kill one and it's jail for sure. So he was gentle as could be. Careful to watch, not touch, like mother always said. He watched. The mantis ignored him, concerned only with its own grooming and the position of its intimidating forelimbs.

Something disturbed the water nearby, interrupting his reverie. Ripples ranged the stagnant water. A mosaic of concentric circles surrounded him. It was a small, geometrically fascinating disturbance, but he knew it was not a scene to admire. Rather, it was an event to inspire terror, a danger to shrink from.

To shrink! Ha!

The ripples became hundreds of tiny wakes. The empty apex of each wake was on a collision course with him. He tried to move, but the placid water offered no mobility. He tried to scream, remembering belatedly that one rightfully can't scream until the pain begins, like mother always said.

The nearest wakes disappeared as the first arrivals ducked beneath the surface. He felt a nibble on his lower back. He screamed mightily.

More bites came. He recognized his assailants even before they started leaping from the water for his tastier dry bits. Boxes of Thin Mints, Trefoils, Do-Si-Dos, and Samoas. They were all there, voracious empty Girl Scout cookie cartons, back for more: more meat, more blood, more revenge. They sought payback for his years of terrible, terrible abuse.

They swam below him, leaped over him, and bit. Bit, chewed, gorged, tore flesh and bone with abandon. The situation was destined to get worse. He knew. Except, except that this time he had help. The mantis was still nearby, casually watching the meal. He cried out to it, beseeching its assistance. After all he had, for fear of criminal punishment, saved its life.

The creature seemed to respond. It turned in circles on his belly, then climbed down his mauled left hip, stopped near the water. The insect surveyed the carnage with empty black eyes, paused, then removed a toy skyscraper that was strapped to its left hind leg. It flipped the tower over, turned its base like a pepper mill. A legion of tiny living gingerbread men swarmed from the office tower to his skin, all too near the waterline.

The panicked morsels attracted the marauding boxes to them as they struggled fruitlessly to scale his slick belly's slope to safety. The boxes went into a frenzy, swallowing handfuls of screaming gingerbread men along with great chunks of flesh.

He screamed again, and screamed and screamed.

The pain, though still intense with each bite from those nasty resealing tops, was replaced by anguish. The sight of all those years of development being ripped away like so much bloody cotton candy paralyzed him with sorrow. He screamed.

The mantis flitted away.

He tried to squeeze his eyes shut, but a Samoa sampler had devoured their lids. He knew his ribs were beginning to surface through exposed gore. The swarming cookie boxes had made a mess of his flesh. He could not identify most of what floated before him, and some pieces were missing.

Then, perhaps sated, the boxes swam away.

He was alone again. Home again. No more pain. At peace in his oversized tub. Until, with all his extra flotation stolen, he sank into grimy bathwater. He thrashed about, tried to grab the iron rim of the tub, but was in too deep. He merely scraped the porcelain, slid back down. He did not give up, however. He was not trained to surrender to silly fate.

Reward came swiftly: when one of his futile slaps met the closing jaws of an iron vise. That vise yanked him clear of the tub.

His rescuer was not the expected metal crane but a small, athletic, woman. She set him down gently on the soft muddy field.

   "Thanks lady," was all he could muster.   He self-consciously wiped gallons of bath water from his restored body. Smooth volume again. The woman saw his pleasure, smiled.

   "Hey no problem, big guy. It's what I'm here for."

   "You too?"

Alice 3

Warm, perfumed water flowed from the wide, gilt faucet. Alice held her manicured toes under the most fabulous of luxuries: bubble bath straight from the tap. Though her marble tub was full, she dared not turn off the soothing flow. The bubbles would be gone if she allowed the fresh bathwater to stop pouring. She had little choice; there was no spigot. Besides, the tub did not overflow. Alice slid deeper into the marble basin, chased away any thoughts that might disturb her.

With the thoughts went the bathroom. She didn't notice the walls' departure until a silver fawn bounded over the tub. She marveled at the chromium deer's grace, but it was gone before she could focus her camera. She dropped her Polaroid in disgust and it was gone too.

Gone.

Alice noticed. Everything was gone. Black, empty space surrounded her tub. She could see nothing, not even a star. She did spot her toothbrush for an instant, where the sink used to be, but then it too was gone. It wasn't that darkness had invaded her bathroom. She could sense a great depth to the emptiness. It expanded around her forever. Nothing was there. Nothing was anywhere, everywhere. Her tub, however, remained. It enveloped her; warm, bright, and still spouting bubble bath. All else was nullified.

Good, she thought, spreading her toes under the gilt faucet again, I didn't have anyone to talk to just now anyway. She stretched, careful not to allow her fingers to break the plane of the tub walls, lest they too be nothing. She closed her eyes, rocking the marble tub gently in the empty space.

Alice hummed a tune whose title escaped her. A peaceful tune, long forgotten by the restless, crowded world. She hoped the bath was eternal, its warm soapy water filling her, encasing her in unknown, perhaps forbidden luxury. The warm comfort of an empty world. Perfect in its lack of intrusions, interruptions, and responsibilities. No kids to feed, no strangers to save.

"Now what made me think that?" Alice wondered aloud, forgetting the question as she phrased it. The beauty of the words disappearing into empty space was overwhelming. She smiled, closed her eyes, and forgot.

A door slammed behind her, shattering her nothing. Alice opened her eyes, tentative. She wished to continue seeing nothing.

"No," she said.

Her bathroom was back, cluttered, complete. A small woman with very big hair stood in the center of the miserable wood paneled room. Her hands were on her hips. Her face was plastic; a Barbie doll's. It could not move or create any expression, much less speak. However, Alice sensed that the woman was angry. Not allowing the minor irritation to ruin her solitude, Alice shrugged, returned to her bubbles.

Their soft caressing texture had changed to a clinging slime. Warm greasy slime, all too familiar. Alice succumbed to irritation, and blamed the intrusive toy for her misfortune. She cast a stern glance at the doll, and tried to enjoy what was left of her bath.

The doll, proportionally perfect and dressed in the best of natural fibers, crossed the shabby tile to the lip of Alice's chipped iron tub. Alice ignored her, hoping the creature would go away on her own. The doll leaned forward stiffly and did disappear behind the tub wall, but a well-tanned arm remained. It hovered over Alice, swaying like a rattled cobra, then plunged fingers first into her water. Alice watched passively, curious, as the arm writhed between her thighs. It was warm, recently shaven, so Alice didn't mind its presence. As long as it didn't do anything wrong, she was willing to share her diminished bath.

Without warning, the arm suddenly punched through the bottom of the tub. Fine, Alice thought, and we have a running faucet with no spigot. The room's going to fill to the ceiling... I'd best break out the towels.

By the time she stood, the water level inside and outside the tub matched. It was over her head before she reached the towel rack. She grabbed a towel, and, out of guilt, pulled off a second for her plastic guest. Her unwanted bathmate had floated to the ceiling and was struggling in the water. Odd, Alice thought. She tapped a tiny kicking ankle, passed up the extra towel. The doll took it, floated down to the floor. She offered no thanks, as if Alice was its servant. Such arrogance put Alice off and, once she dried off, she spoke her piece through the water:

"You're welcome," Alice said, sardonic. Barbie failed to respond. Alice didn't care.

"Now, young lady," she snapped, "Why did you make all this water come out? It'll take hours to dry. My house might be ruined." Her censure seemed to vex the vacu-formed woman. Alice was pleased, but still a little nervous. There was something right about the perfect young woman, something that made her belong, like the other interlopers. Alice hated the thought, but recognized her crosses and bore them.

"Look," she said, accepting fate, "I know you're supposed to be here. At least I think I do. You need me for something, but this is my house!"

Alice was awarded no response from the woman. Perturbed, she searched for something to prove that the place was hers. She spotted three of her kids lined up near the door, waiting for their brother, Josh, to finish brushing his teeth. Alice pointed to them, said:

"Look over there. That proves it. Now listen to me."

The doll didn't listen. Instead, she snatched Josh, rolled him into a ball and tossed him through the medicine cabinet. Josh shattered the mirror, releasing a peal of innocent terror that shook Alice to her foundation. She forgot about aiding the Barbie doll and swam through the mirror frame after her son. She was confused by her efforts. Josh, after all, wasn't supposed to need any help. Alice shook her head in consternation as she passed through the broken mirror into the rusty white darkness of the medicine cabinet. She bumped the mirror frame during her passage, accidentally setting it ajar. She casually reached out to adjust it.

Before she aligned the mirror properly, she angled it down to check the back seat. Her passenger was still with her, as immobile and boring as ever.

The hefty young man just sat there, staring at a football. Occasionally he would pick it up and bounce it around in his hands. Then he'd put it down and stare at it again. Boring. Alice re-adjusted her mirror in time to spot a hand waving frantically from a large puddle she had just splashed through. She skidded to a stop, threw the car into reverse and backed up, splashing through the puddle again. She stopped, pushed open the passenger side door. With chin and both hands on the edge of the passenger seat, she peered over its edge to the activity in the muddy puddle below.

A man's hand frantically groped the air at her doorsill, fingers opening and closing. A man's hand. Familiar. Fearing it would sink back into the puddle, she leaned out and grabbed the swaying wrist. She pulled a little, and a head and shoulders appeared. Relieved, she hoisted the man by his wet denim collar and set him in the passenger seat. She put the car back in gear and drove on.

After a few quiet desert miles, she decided to pass the time with the familiar stranger.

"Hey mister," she said, "You know it isn't safe to hitchhike." She looked over at him, dropping her rose sunglasses to the end of her nose. He stared back, his ancient gray eyes wet with emotion. Or puddle water; she wasn't sure. He probed her, saw her as she was. Alice liked that. So rare in a man. She brushed his hand when she shifted. He spoke.

"Well, thanks for picking me up all the same, Alice. You've been real helpful lately."

"It's what I'm here for, mister," she pronounced, happy to admit her curse to the stranger. She then remembered her other passenger, and checked her mirror to see if the excitement had disturbed him. Of course, it didn't. He still studied his football, occasionally kneading it with his fingers. She gestured with her thumb to the passive occupant, said:

"Picked this guy up hours ago, and he hasn't said a word yet. You know him?"

The man cast an obliging glance over his left shoulder. When he faced forward again, he shrugged.

"He does look familiar, but I'm not sure. Did you ask him?"

"Yeah, but he didn't tell me shit," Alice said. She glanced in the mirror, hoping for a reaction. None. She continued, "I'm a little bugged by him. Don't even know when to let him off."

"Mister, you wouldn't believe the day I had. First, some Barbie doll wastes Josh, then I pick up Mr. Excitement back there, and now you throw yourself on me. What's going on? When will I ever be alone again?" Alice didn't really mean what she was saying; alone was right outside the car, waiting for her. No, these people were supposed to be there with her, in her car, cruising the lonely desert highway. A field of rusting, discarded bathtubs in the distance did elicit a quiet pang for solitude lost. The man was watching her reflect, and a tear escaped his right eye. He bowed his head as if to hide it. That's nice, Alice thought. The man looked up and spoke again, in a soft clean voice, as grey as his eyes. His lips barely moved.

"I know what you mean, Alice," he said, "People keep turning up. People like you. You're not supposed to be here. But you are. Weird world, Huh? Wait. I think I can see up ahead where you can unload our passenger. See? That strip mall, up on the right."

Alice scanned the horizon. She saw nothing but red rocks, cacti, and old women. She drew a breath to say so, but refrained from comment. She didn't want to deny any observation this man made. Her hesitation paid off. An image caught her peripheral vision. She looked right, and up, and spotted his drop off point.

A monolithic rectangle of dirt and rock loomed overhead. A long low building, barely visible, topped the angular mound, which was suspended in the sky by cables from a balloon of magnificent colors and proportion. On the balloon, a hundred-foot-tall blue neon sign flashed 'Galleria.' Oh, she thought, happy that she wasn't humiliated by not noticing the obtrusive place.

"The one floating at about 2:00?" she said nonchalantly, "Doesn't look like much parking there, mister."

He smiled. Awesome.

"We won't be staying," he said, "Just pull in by that sporting goods store and watch what happens."

Alice flashed her 'up' turn signal and pulled onto the meager strip of asphalt outside the building, careful not to bump any suspension cables (which she found, to her satisfaction, were formed by thick strands of bright yarn). She inched past storefronts until spotting one with tennis rackets and roast chickens in the window. She parked, waited with the engine running for the young man in back to pick up his football and leave. Hearing no sound, Alice repositioned her rear view mirror, aiming it at the rear seat. You never know, she thought, he is quiet.

The kid was still there, concentrating fiercely on his football. Occasionally pressing it. Caressing it. Alice, disgusted and a little bewildered by the man's false instruction, reached for the gearshift. He intercepted her, gently touching her fingers with his. She looked up. He was watching her, with quintessential sincerity. She tingled. He spoke. Grey words.

"No, wait for it," he said. She obliged, letting his luxurious touch linger.

"Wait for what?" was all she could muster. He let his fingers linger, but looked toward the store again. She relaxed.

"Don't know," he said, not turning, "But wait."

"Fine," Alice acquiesced, trying to be confident that a change would come. A new event that would get this loser out of the back of her car. As soon as she felt sure something would happen, she saw movement behind the glass storefront.

People milled about inside. They were dressed alike, in blue football uniforms, pads and all, that were fresh versions of the torn rags worn by the kid in back. One of the shoppers, exiting through automatic doors, did a cartoon double take when his dull eyes spotted Alice's car, particularly its back seat - those same eyes suddenly turned bright red and burst from their sockets. An antique horn blared. The shopper, a young man, pointed at her passenger.

"There he is!" the youth shouted over his shoulder. His call brought a swarm of equally red pairs of eyes to the storefront. They pressed against each other, fighting for position against the heavy glass. Some demanded with their fists that the windows be opened. Others had tantrums, pounding fists and feet until someone let them out. Alice wondered why they didn't just use the automatic doors. Her question was answered when the entire glass wall lifted as a unit, allowing the boisterous mass of people to flow onto the sidewalk towards her car. Hundreds of them, shaking the sidewalk, vibrating the yarn cables, threatening disaster. They swarmed around her car, countless heads, but only one face between them. A mean face; dark, intense, with red eyes and a swollen nose.

Then they were gone, the glass doors had shut and all was quiet once more. The man's light touch stopped. Her tingling, which she had forgotten, stopped as well. She missed it. The man regarded her warmly.

"Now we can go," he said, looking straight ahead. Alice glanced in her mirror. Except for a thick black extension cord, any sign of her rear passenger had been erased.

"I guess," she said, "Thanks mister." She prepared to move on, but paused when she felt an alien twinge of fear. She looked at the man.

"But what about you?" she asked.

"Damn good question, Alice," the man said, "What about me? Why do these things keep happening to me?" Alice thought she saw him fade slightly, becoming nearly translucent. Best to keep talking, she thought.

"Don't know. Don't even know who the heck you are."

He refilled his space. Alice smiled at her effect. The man was not returning her pleasant gesture. Instead, he shook his head unhappily, appearing oddly confused. He faced her again. His face, though still opaque, had again lost some of its definition.

"Well," he sighed, his tone subtly changing from gray to slate, "In that case, I'm out of here. Let me off at the next stop."

"There are no stops," Alice tried again, hoping he didn't notice the Ramada they just passed.

"Okay. Then just pull over."

"Can't," Alice said, "No road." She watched him peer over his doorsill, nod. She couldn't believe her luck. This guy is so agreeable, she thought. Unfortunately, he was also almost unrecognizable. A gossamer human shape now, barely distinct from the storm clouds behind him. She wouldn't be able to hold him much longer, regardless of what she said.

"I see. Can't I get out right here?" the man asked, barely audible. Alice, suddenly stabbed by sharp empathy, gave up.

"I don't care, mister," she lied. She pulled over to the curb on a quiet side street. She was careful to stop under the shade of one of the ancient elms lining the street. The man would surely disappear if he were to be directly exposed to the bright sun overhead.

"Okay, bye," the man said. With no further ado, he pushed open his door and stepped into his house. During the instant she could follow his speedy passage, or escape, Alice saw that he had regained his fine form. She patted herself on the back as she pulled away.

She spotted the familiar arches of a McDonald's restaurant. Alice wasn't hungry and the arches were blue, but, seeing as it was the only place in sight on the empty desert road, she pulled in for a bite. She stopped at the talking drive-thru sign, but could not read the empty plastic menu. That's not right, she thought. Of all places, McDonald's always has a menu. The sign didn't speak to her, either. Frowning, she continued around the building to have her suspicions confirmed.

Her further inspection revealed that it wasn't a McDonald's. It was a construction site for a different, inferior restaurant. Its clever concealment under a McDonald's shaped tent had fooled her. She saw the truth in the form of a tiny site office-trailer surrounded by bricks, wood, and some free-formed concrete. Someone had tried to build a frame earlier, but had apparently forgotten nails: a rickety wooden structure swayed back and forth in a light breeze that ruffled the vinyl roof. They must have abandoned the project after their first failure, Alice thought. She sensed no activity on the lot. She walked under the haphazard structure toward the trailer door, careful not to step on any dropped worms that had been used in lieu of nails. She climbed cinderblock steps to the trailer door. She tested the aluminum knob. It was locked. She put her hands against the plastic window, peered inside. A shadowy figure materialized behind the filthy window. A familiar figure. Alice smiled, put her hands on her hips.

"Well, I'll be damned if it isn't Barbie," she said.

Either Barbie was too big or the trailer too small, Alice couldn't tell, but the plastic woman inside occupied a disproportionate amount of space in the small field office. Alice really didn't care and was about to leave when the woman came to the window, noticed her. Her face had become malleable, though it was still fettered with far too much make-up. The woman spoke, barely audible.

"Lady," she cried, eyes widened by primal panic, "Give me a hand! I've got to get out!" Alice was repulsed by the helpless woman's overbearing tone. She paused, feeling a decision coming on.

"Sorry, no can do," she said.

Alice was turning to leave with that thought when the stricken woman released a tirade that made staying well worth Alice's time. She cocked her ear to the window.

"I must get out of this office!" the woman screamed through the plastic pane in a garbled whisper, "You don't know what I did to it! It wants to kill me!" Alice looked in at the woman. The obnoxious plastic bitch had grown taller, more massive, grotesquely filling the room. Alice understood the trailer's plight. She patted its blue plywood skin.

"I don't blame it," Alice said to the woman, "What with you abandoning it, the only job you were qualified for. What was that job, anyway? Office temp?"

"Damn you! I was a secretary!" the woman retorted. Her doomed eyes were filled with anger. No desperation, no humility, just stupid anger. Alice folded her arms, smiled.

"And a good one, too," she said, "Oh well..." She turned to initiate a dramatic exit.

"Wait," the woman called after her. Her cry was so pure, so needful, that it compelled Alice to turn. Unfortunately, the window had shrunk to the dimensions of a playing card. Alice resisted a force that tugged at her from the trailer. Rightfully so, she thought, but the situation does need a speech.

"I told you, Ashley," she said in her best patronizing tone, "I said you needed help. Well, you didn't listen, and look; now the window's too small anyway." Alice wanted to laugh at the silly little big woman, but the best she could do was turn away, drawn by the whitecaps forming on a nearby puddle. Tiny waves were already breaking on her bare toes.

Hands on her knees, she bent low for a closer look. A round man was struggling in the frothy Lilliputian sea, desperately fending off a discarded box of Girl Scout cookies that bobbed nearby. He was going down for the third time. Alice giggled, put four fingers over her mouth to stifle her mirth. She reached a finger down to the struggling victim. He either didn't notice her, or was too far gone to care. Choosing not to take a chance, she caught the fat man's chubby little arm between her thumb and forefinger, yanked him out.

Alice was nearly overcome by the onslaught of flesh that resulted from her tiny gesture. She ducked her head, waiting to be smothered by the great wall of soft pink skin that had swollen from the puddle. Instead, she found herself standing before a sadly globular man in a white dress and matching sensible shoes. Somewhere in the folds of flesh that guarded his face, she sensed a smile. Then the face moved, like designer pantyhose filled with jelly.

"Thank you ma'am," he said. His voice was amiable and distantly familiar. Fine, Alice thought, another one. She returned his smile, waited to speak until he was through wringing a small sea of excess water from his uniform.

"Hey no problem big guy. It's what I'm here for," she said, releasing his wrist. She wondered at how she had managed to grasp the ham-sized appendage until she glanced down at her own hand. It was larger than a tennis racket. Oh, she thought. Upon his release, the fat man appeared puzzled.

"You too?" he asked.

Alice didn't respond. She simply turned, climbed back into the John Deere, and set about finishing her furrows before the sun rose to ruin everything.

Phillip 3

Tap...Tap...Tap Tap Tap. Hunt and peck, hunt and peck. Find the right keys. Push them. Look at the green screen. Carefully scrutinize nothing. Tap...Tap...Tap some more.

Hunt and peck, hunt and peck. Watch the blank green screen. Be enthralled by the green screen. Wait for a change. A sure thing. Enjoy no difference. Tap...Tap...Tap Tap Tap.

The phone, in free-fall as well, rings. No separation, just one steady mechanical bell. Reach for it, floating out there in space. Try to grab the elusive receiver. The ringing phone parries, falls faster, almost out of reach. Still ringing. Grab handle of office chair, under the seat.

Pump it, lower the chair. Grab the phone, say:

"Hello?"

Hang up.

Watch a little parachute bloom above the quiet phone. It is safe. Tap...Tap...Tap the keys again. Scan for results on the blank green screen. Enjoy no difference. Move closer to the blank green screen. Spot a detail. A mere byte, tucked down in the lower right corner of the green screen. Lean closer. Need a closer look. There; better. Clearer. Blank green screen is big now; too big. It is everything, everywhere, green solid lines of resolution. Impassive, not oppressive. But there is a dot.

A dot that grows.

Watch it grow. Follow the red rectangle. It ascends. Ascends from the lower right corner of the blank green screen. Ascends and grows. Grows until it is no longer red, not just red but red and white, with details. Try not to pee in joyous celebration at the new found information. Be careful, it could be a trap.

A trap.

Scramble. Pedal legs, hard. Try to crank office chair up and away. Chair's gone, floating away into the blank green screen. A little parachute carries it to safety.

Naugahyde hits hand. Screen's gone. Blank green is replaced. Replaced by blue sky. Fluffy white clouds. Pink, soothing wind ruffles the driver's blond tresses.

No.

Wrong. Blue sky is wrong, clouds, wind, all wrong. Free fall is gone, flight now under control. Wrongly under control, through fluffy white clouds and blue sky. Wrong, wrong, wrong.

A remedy is needed. The green screen is needed. It is a Cure-all, the green screen.

No screen is handy. Only Naugahyde, metal, glass, and two heads up front. Find the green screen. Search pockets. Pull out all liners. Find the green screen. Last pocket, jacket, inside, proves empty save for three tic-tacs and string. Look around, still no green screen. Just blue sky, pink wind, and fluffy white clouds.

One more pocket appears, to be searched. Vest pocket, for watches. Vacant now, because Sears sells no fobs. Vacant but bulging. Say:

"Hmm."

Investigate bulge. Pat outside of pocket. Tap...Tap...Tap, it sounds off in response.

There is a God.

Dig thumb into pocket. It's all that fits, but is enough to hook the tiny keyboard cord. The umbilical to the green screen. Once hooked, pull the cord. A little tension. The green screen resists, then pops like a champagne cork onto the Naugahyde.

Waste no time. Tap...Tap...Tap Tap Tap. Hunt and peck. Hunt and peck. Search the green screen. Analyze no information. The blank green screen is alive once more. Mechanical peace, it is yet surrounded by Naugahyde. Still encased in strange control, moving with direction through blue skies and fluffy white clouds. A pink wind still tousles the driver's blond tresses.

Tap...Tap...Tap tap tap. Hunt and peck. Scrutinize blank screen. Scour lines of resolution for a positive resolution for free fall. The blank green screen remains bright, blank. No new information.

There is a God.

The blank screen envelops Naugahyde. Blue is green, clouds are snow, and blond tresses are now on end from static, not pink wind.

Relief is short. The blank green screen wavers, loses its perfect shape. Tiny lines of resolution become light and dark green waves, then separate.

Tap...Tap...Tap tap tap. Hunt and peck, hunt and peck. Search the not so blank green screen. Hunt and peck. Curse lousy typing teacher. Tap...Tap...Tap no more.

Too late.

The fingers move. Not animated, really, but alive. Alive and perilously friendly. They reach out, thousands of them. Thousands of them reach out. Blindly groping, clenching, then, not so blindly.

They touch. They hold on to the best in natural fibers with startling tenacity. All green is gone. All color is gone. Everything is gray fingers. Unmanicured. Touching, groping, holding on tight.

Fight, try to fight. Wriggle, jiggle, spit, pee. No success, only more ugly gray fingers guiding. Guiding more surely, more accurately than the Naugahyde and blond tresses. No easy answers this time; no more pockets, no keyboard, no tapping.

No green.

Sigh, say:

"Fine. Take me."

And be taken. Led surely through glass doors, concrete halls, odorous locker rooms. Led from the abyss of order, ease, to the well-groomed hell of success, aspiration.

Fight. Reach through hands, open lockers, dig in tiles for the blank green screen. Under benches, inside cheerleaders, anywhere warm truth might hide.

No green.

Just gray. Gray walls, gray floors, gray fingers.

Tap...Tap...Tap tap tap. The taps are there. Reassuring. Hopeful. But where? Clear sound, but no keyboard. No green. Wait. Force gray fingers still.

Tap...Ta...

Move once more, led by gray through gray.

Tap...Tap...Tap tap tap.

Stop.

Tap...Ta...

Go.

Tap...Tap...Tap tap tap.

Repeat to be sure, then scan down to source.   There. Attached to strong ankles, walk black shoes.   Black shoes with unseen little metal fingers.   Tapping.   Reassuring, informative. Gray fingers lose their grasp.

Keep moving.   Maintain the tap.   Gray, gray and gray ends ahead, abruptly.   An open door.   Framing, yes, green.   An expanse of green at the tapping shoes' beckoning.   White lines of resolution laid out clearly.   Lush green.   Secure green.   Step on green.

Tap...Ta...

Say:

"Uh oh."

Stamp feet, press lush green with shaking fingers.   Fall on green.   No sound.   No security.

Wrong.   Wrong.   Wrong.

Lie still.   Green, lush green is at eye level, stretches forever.   At the edge of forever, a flash of red.   Red, with blond tresses blowing in pink wind!

Stand.   Jump.   Land.   Shout.   Wave.   Pee.   Shout.   All fail. The red byte, the abandoned vehicle of salvation, moves aimlessly in a tight, steady circle around the green.   Not, of course, in it.

Charge.   Run.   Chase chase chase.   Blond tresses and, yes, Naugahyde come no closer.   Always, always at far end of field.

Stop.   Wait.   Red ticket to freedom, steel jump from the hell of fate and wisdom contradicting, and those blond tresses continue to circle.   Say:

"What?   What do I need to cut this grass?"

Wait for reply.   Wait.   Listen.   Listen.   Wait.   No reply, of course.   The red ride fades.   Fades until all is green.

All but a spot.   A spot there, just a few short yards away. Dive to it.   Grab the spot.   The gray, plastic spot littered with dots. Dots filled with letters.

Pick it up.   Hold it.   Nestle it.

Tap it.

Tap...Tap...Tap tap tap.   Hunt and peck, hunt and peck. Watch the lush green sharpen into countless, relentless lines of resolution. Lines grow thin, close. Green is encased. Adjust the office chair, sigh placidly in familiar free fall.

Blank green screen inches away. Wait for a change. Say: "Next time."

And wonder why.

Ashley 3

"Where is the damn controller?" Ashley demanded, running a hand through her luxuriously soft hair. She was alone in her living room, and annoyed that she received no response. She scanned her apartment, recognizing nothing, especially the TV remote. Her chic pastel decor had been replaced by Early American Farmer Brown pine and cloth. Nauseatingly simple, common. And no controller.

"Shit," she said, "Now I'm going to miss the Wheel." In anger, she kicked over the 50's vintage TV. The sturdy machine bounced on the tattered carpet, unbroken. Her 60-inch flat screen would have crumbled; a proper finish to a perfect tantrum. Ashley stormed out of the living room. She bumped into a wall that wasn't supposed to be there before turning the corner into the kitchen.

It was wrong, too. Old and greasy, as though someone had actually been cooking in it. Ashley's stomach twisted at the thought. It turned again when she spotted a woman bathing in her sink. Not simply washing her hands, but fully immersed in bubbles, enjoying a Calgon getaway. In my sink, Ashley thought, my sink. I think not. She put her hands to her hips and freshened the evil in her glare.

"What are you doing here?" she snapped, marveling at her refined stern tone. The woman appeared not to notice.

"What are you doing here?" Ashley tried again. The woman sponged her shoulder, oblivious.

"What are you doing here?" Ashley yelled, shaken by the rage her shrill voice projected. The woman glanced up, as if by accident, and acknowledged Ashley's presence with a nod. The nerve, Ashley thought.

"Dammit, bitch, what are you doing in my sink?" she screamed. The woman stared blankly at Ashley, as if she couldn't hear.

"Oh, you're a shrewd one, aren't you? Making believe you can't hear. Well listen bitch, I wrote the book, so you can't fool me."

The woman shrugged, shook her head slowly. Her blue eyes were slits, clearly telegraphing irritation. That broke Ashley. She took off her rings, rolled up her silk sleeve and thrust her hand into the warm dishwater. She felt around the sink, careful not to rub the woman's thighs, until she found the chain holding the rubber stopper. She gathered it in her fingers, smiled sweetly at the woman, and pulled. After she stepped away, a torrent of warm greasy water spewed between the woman's knees. The kitchen was deluged with the stuff, filled to its beamed ceiling in seconds.

The woman frowned. Cheeks puffed, she rose from the sink and floated across to the pantry door. She looked again at Ashley, then pulled the door open and ducked inside. When the woman disappeared, Ashley realized that she was under water and couldn't breathe. She thrashed, struggled, then swam to the ceiling, but found no air. Before she needed to panic, she felt a tap on her ankle, looked down. The woman was back, robed in a yellow rain slicker. A second raincoat hung over her arm. She passed it to Ashley without much urgency. Ashley snatched it and donned it quickly. She zipped it closed, and breathed. She floated back down to the woman.

"Well." Ashley said, "It's about time you came back with these. I nearly ran out of breath."

"You're welcome," the woman smiled. Her weathered face hardened when she continued, "Now, young lady, why did you make all this water come out? It'll take hours to dry, my house might be ruined."

"Your house?" Ashley snapped, "The hell it is! This is my apartment."

"Look," the woman said, rolling her eyes, "I know you're supposed to be here. At least I think I do. You need me for something. But, this is my house!"

"It is not! And no I don't!"

"Look over there," the woman said, pointing, at a 'Home Sweet Home' sign embroidered into the front door, "That proves it. Now listen to me..."

"Fine," Ashley interrupted, "It was your house. Now it's my apartment." She snatched the largest iron frying pan from the group hanging over the range. She sought a likely target behind the woman, found it over the sink. A window, she thought, perfect. She swung the pan into the window, smashing it with rewarding effect. First glass shattered outward, then water followed it into the sunny painted backdrop outside.

The room drained quickly. The vortex draining dishwater always creates was substantial, and the woman was positioned too near its source. Ashley pointed a lazy finger behind the woman, but chose not to warn her. The drain sucked the unsuspecting woman from the kitchen. She shot through its small opening, leaving Ashley with a pathetic expression of anger and loss that delighted her.

The stream slowed, and Ashley's kitchen began to dry. She remained focused on the window. A cartoon sun glowed outside, smiling at her. The woman was gone. Ashley looked around her strange kitchen: the empty ceramic sink, the pot on the floor, the awful paisley wallpaper. The woman was right: everything was wrong. It was her place, not Ashley's. The unthinkable had occurred: Ashley was wrong. She was wrong, and headed for a setback. A major setback, she thought, and all because of this place. She didn't want to be there anymore. She wanted to be with the woman. Even though Ashley wanted for nothing, she needed the woman's help. So she threw herself through the kitchen window.

"Wait for me, lady!" she shouted.

Ashley landed on her feet atop a large malformed rubber raft. The raft floated placidly in a muddy lagoon. Everything seemed peaceful, safe for the moment. Her apartment was gone, the woman was gone, and a real sun glowed above her. She relaxed, forcing composure to return. She smiled, forgot the woman and felt good about herself again. She was out of her screwed up apartment and in control, even if the raft had no paddle. The piranhas did, however, make her nervous.

The little fish swarmed around the raft in a silver cloud thick enough for Ashley to walk on, if not for all the teeth. They didn't notice her, but voraciously attacked the raft. Hundreds of them took little bites of flesh from it, swam away, and hundreds more immediately took their place. Spreading blood formed a crimson fog in the water. At the rate they chewed, the raft would not be afloat for long, and she would be swimming with the fish. Not good. Ashley needed a solution, a way to get herself to a bank.

Ashley noted that the raft bellowed in agony each time a little fish tore a chunk of flesh from it. The rubber boat was clearly alive, and suffering terribly from the attack. This might be of some use, she thought. She felt she could take advantage of its pain if she got all the piranhas to eat one side only. She decided that would make the other side shudder from pain, thus acting as a paddle and propelling raft toward shore. Before the fish ate everything, she hoped.

She retrieved her can of mace from her purse and carefully sprayed the raft's wounds on one side. The raft reacted with fresh screams. Really very pitiful, Ashley thought. She smiled. The tactic had, however, worked. The piranhas, repulsed by the taste of mace, were swarming to the other side. The raft released another anguished cry, which Ashley was easily able to ignore. There were, after all, priorities. She was progressing toward a grassy bank at a fair pace. She hoped that the raft would hold out until she could step off. As if inspired by her need, the land was suddenly a few short feet away. As she stepped off it, the raft let out one final wail; an appeal for help. Ashley blamed the raft's plight on its own stupidity and, once disembarked, slammed the door behind her.

Assuming she should be exhausted from her adventures, Ashley slumped into the cloth chair behind the metal desk. An IBM Selectric typewriter hummed quietly at her side. She turned to it, started typing a perfect memo at great speed. When she typed her initials in lower case at the bottom of the page, it occurred to her where she was, what she was doing.

Ashley leapt to her feet in alarm. She picked up her typewriter with one hand and hurled it into a wall. It crushed like a watermelon on impact, layering the office walls and floor with its inky guts and keys. Ashley tried to leave, but could not reach the door. Each time she neared it a fresh sheet of pink message paper appeared on her desk, demanding her attention. She turned to it instinctively, then realized her mistake and tried to reach the door again. The cycle continued until she found herself circling her desk at high velocity. It wasn't working. Nothing was working for her. Things actually were functioning in concert against her. Against her. Ashley skidded to a stop. A major setback. She had never had one before, at least not one she couldn't pass onto a close friend. How could she cope? Would there be time to?

Ashley wiped a thick layer of sweat and makeup from her forehead, crumbled onto the desk in a ball. It had become too small to support her, and collapsed under the oppressive mass of her trim figure. Puzzled, Ashley inspected the rest of her empty first office. It was smaller as well: the ceiling or floor was closer, the walls seemed nearer, and the door and open window were not their usual size.

The window, Ashley thought. She bolted to it, put her hands on the sill. She could feel the frame contracting under her fingers, but the window was open. There was time. When Ashley started to climb through the opening, she found her passage blocked. Blocked by another woman. The tired young face looked familiar to Ashley, but she couldn't identify her right away and didn't care to try. Ashley had no time to waste. She had to use the woman immediately, to take her chances on a hasty plan.

"Lady," she shouted, trying to control the panic in her voice, "Back your face out of the window and give me a hand. I've got to get out of this office."

The woman clapped, beaming at her joke.

"Sorry. No can do," she chimed.

"What! Are you nuts?" Ashley lost control, "I must get out of here! This is my first office, you don't know what I did to leave it behind. It wants to stop me!"

"I don't blame it, what with you abandoning it, the only job you were qualified for. What was that job anyway? Office temp?"

"Of course not, damn you! I was an Executive Assistant."

"And a good one, too. Oh, well," the woman said softly. She turned away, to leave.

"No. Wait," Ashley cried. The woman responded by facing her again. She glowed with simple purity. Her wet eyes betrayed her comprehension of Ashley's plight.

"I told you, Ashley," she purred, "I said you needed me, and I needed you. Well, you didn't listen. And look... now the window's too small anyway." She laughed, though her exhausted features bore no humor. Ashley watched her through the tiny window. Watched her cross the company grounds to the massive ugly marble fountain near the road. Watched her pull a bloody fat man from the fountain. Watched the fat man wipe off gallons of blood before hugging the woman. Watched the woman point to her. Watched him cheer, her weep. And, finally, watched the window close up, too small to see through.

Turning from the closed exit, Ashley desperately sought a way out. There has to be one, she thought, there always is. Always. If there was, it had evaded her thankless grasp that time. The office continued to gather around her. It remained mindless of her import, heedless to her wishes. She wanted to cry, but there was no room for tears. All six sides of the room were against her, relentlessly crushing her into a fleshy little ball.

Resolute, Ashley dug deep into herself for a last gasp of her own energy. The iota of strength that might free her from her terminal prison. She knew she had to have it; she was better than the insignificant little office. After much searching and rationalization, she found it. With great effort she inflated her shrunken, once perfect chest and tensed what remained of her body for a final effort. This is it, she thought. It's just a setback. I can overcome it, on my own. She pushed in all directions, alone against her past.

The walls closed another callous inch, ignoring her heroic final effort.

"This isn't fair!" she gasped, "This can't happen to me. I have too much to live for."

Her office walls finished joining on the flat sides.

Lou 4

"Now," Lou said over his shoulder to his attentive third level calculus class, "I'll just jot this next equation on the board. Start solving it immediately. You'll have fifteen minutes to work through it."

He picked a foot long stick of chalk from the aluminum tray that formed the base of the clean blackboard. He began to etch his complex equation on the slate. Before he finished half the first numeral, a seven, the chalk split. The snap startled him, and he dropped both halves. The class snickered behind him. He ignored them, retrieved a fresh length of chalk, smaller than the first, from the tray. He managed to scribe the 'minus' sign and part of the next digit, a one, before the stick squealed and shattered to dust in his hand.

"Shit!" he exclaimed. The class laughed. He turned around. They sat in orderly, quiet rows, hands folded on their desks, attentive.

"That's better," he said, "Make believe I never said that."

He turned back to the blackboard, picked up another piece of chalk, shorter than his pinky. He finished the equation:

$$7-1=$$

The class moaned. Lou had predicted their response, and turned to face his anguished college students. He raised his hands to preempt their cries of foul.

"Okay, okay, I know this is a tough one. How about I walk you through the problem and then give you a simpler one?" His class, mostly seniors, voiced their appreciation for his offer. He turned back to the board, picked up a fresh piece of chalk, about the length of his thumbnail, and looked at his equation. He contemplated a solution for a moment without writing anything.

He racked his brain, embarrassed that he was having difficulty solving his own equation.

"I guess it is a little tough," he sighed. His class laughed. They thought he was joking. How could a mathematician of his caliber not know the solution to a problem he presented, no matter how difficult? He allowed the misguided mirth. Besides, the solution came to him at the moment of their reaction.

"Of course," he said under his breath. He positioned the sliver of chalk near the board. It liquefied and dripped back into the tray before he could indicate the answer. He picked up the final bit of chalk, barely visible, and made a final effort to mark the elusive slate. His fingers managed to finish forming the numeral '5' before the chalk disappeared. It's just as well, Lou thought, five doesn't look right anyway, even though it's the only solution I can come up with; best not to confuse the students. He turned back to the class, clapped his hands together.

"Okay, kids, how about we work from the text for a while?" The class nodded, removing their books from boxes of their favorite sugar cereal. He crossed the checked tile floor to his desk. He hated his classroom desk. Fashioned in the old accountant's style, its work surface was fully five feet off the floor. The desk was all right, he decided. It was the stool, or rather the perch, that he hated. I put up with it for ten years, he thought, I guess I can wait one more day for them to replace this setup.

He put his foot on the lowest rung of the stool, started his ascension. The rung snapped under his weight. He fell, slamming his chin on the stool's round wooden seat. The class laughed. He stood, rubbing his chin as if it smarted, and turned the stool. He stepped on the lowest rung, broke it, hit his chin again. The class roared. He rotated the errant stool once more, repeated the accident. Not interested in a third round, Lou kicked the stool, shattering it into splinters that floated in the air like a fog. The students cheered.

Lou stood behind his desk, admiring the cover of the sole textbook piled on it. A beautiful plate of a South American rain forest lagoon adorned its cover. He opened the magazine to the feature story, and was shocked to find that someone had torn its pages out. He studied the quiet class, searched their innocent eyes for the culprit. He didn't find one.

"Now who did this?" he demanded, hoping to weed out the guilty party, "Who swiped my pictures of Lake Titicaca!" Not one of the students confessed. Lou believed them. He realized that none of them could have taken his article, the one he needed most to teach calculus. He considered the wet little girl in the front row with bloody bits of paper stuck in her scythe-length teeth, but decided she was too short.

His suspicious scan shifted over to an unexpected figure squatting in the corner near the door. Lou examined the leather-clad girl carefully. She certainly wasn't a student, judging by her apparent junior high school age, and the fact that his seating chart did not indicate a desk near the door.

"Hey," he said, "You in the corner." The girl ignored him, her hardened brown eyes fixed on the front row of his class. His honor students. Lou sensed her hatred for his four brightest pupils. Her hands gripped the edges of her desk tightly enough to press ridges into its Formica finish. Her legs were twitching under the desk. They were compressed steel springs set to launch her at the four helpless nerds.

Lou wondered what her argument with his honor students could have been. They sat attentively at their desks, each with his pocket protector and stiff white shirt. They posed no threat to her, but the pretty young girl appeared ready to strike. Perhaps they suspected her of ripping out his pages, and she knew it. Though he knew that assumption to be wrong, Lou found himself pointing an accusing index finger at her, and finishing his sentence.

"You! Look at me!" he shouted. His class gasped at his surly character change. The girl in the corner released the desk, stood. She looked at him. The cold steel veil over her eyes retracted, revealing teary hope. He shrugged off the wave of sympathy his soul urged him to feel, and continued to speak alien words.

"You did it, didn't you?" he demanded.

"Me?" the girl asked meekly.

"Yeah, you," Lou said, "You took my pictures of Lake Titicaca, didn't you?" The girl reacted oddly to his words; disbelief and anguish twisted her frail features. She stepped forward.

"No, I didn't," she said, "They did. And you know it!" Lou traced her trembling finger's direction to the front row, to his honor students.

"They did it? How could these fine boys ever commit such a heinous act? No, miss, you did it." Lou heard his accusation, but felt a growing sense of disbelief in its veracity.

"No," she said. She was right, but Lou couldn't back down. He stepped toward the suspect. The four honor students lined up behind him. Each removed a pen from his pocket, clicked it, and released it. With the second set of clicks, louder and more disturbing than the first, Lou sensed that circumstances were changing. He was closer to the young woman and recognized her. It was Gloria, and his real honor students lay bound in a corner near the window, eyes wide as they moaned through cloth gags.

The imposters had successfully duped Lou. He was too late to make a change, to stop their advance. The four crooks were completing another click. The black tile under her feet was dissolving. He leaned forward, thrust out his hand.

"Gloria! No!" he shouted. Gloria said nothing. She appeared empty, even dead as she fell into the black space that opened at her feet. Lou's knees buckled as he watched, at the prompting of another click, the floor repair itself. The desk in the corner was gone. The imposters, jeering, returned to their seats. Lou wanted to unleash his anger at their hideous behavior, but by the time he fully faced the young girl with scythian teeth in the front row he had forgotten why he was mad. He returned to his desk, smiled at his well-disciplined students, and slammed his calculus text shut. The class leapt to their feet, applauded, and jumped out the closed windows to get started on their recess.

Lou pushed back on his recliner, pleased to be at the end of another long day. He pulled the TV remote from its handy pouch in the chair's arm, pointed it at the TV. He looked forward to a wasted night in front of the tube, maybe falling asleep to a comforting Dragnet rerun. He clicked the mechanical remote control. The TV came to life, filling his den with its warm white glow.

The show he watched was unfamiliar to him. It involved a fat man and little else, since the fat man's bloated form filled the screen. He was wearing a cooking apron, and was waving at him from the other side of the screen. The actor's ability to make him feel like the center of attention impressed Lou. He also thought he recognized the rotund actor, but couldn't recall his name.

"Well, it's not what I had in mind for tonight anyway," he said, clicking the remote. The channel changed, but the fat man still filled the screen, pounding. He clicked again. The channel changed once more and, once more, the obese actor was frantically waving, this time in black and white.

"What the hell?" Lou said. He clicked the remote again. The same boring show was on. Disappointed, Lou shut off the TV and tossed the useless remote into the fire that crackled cheerfully on the stone hearth. The remote began to emit a death rattle as it melted in the fire. Lou didn't care. After all, it was just a remote.

"That's a hell of an attitude, mister," Alice said over her shoulder. Lou glanced in the direction of her sharp voice. Alice was kneeling by the fire, fishing out the damaged remote with her bare hands. Lou watched with respect as she pulled the remote to her bosom, holding it close, comforting it, healing it. Lou was touched. Alice turned her attention to Lou. She was not pleased.

"Why did you do that mister? What's wrong with you?"

"Alice. It's just a clicker," Lou explained.

"Just a..." Alice said, shocked, "How can you say that?"

"I...I don't know how I can say anything. Why isn't it just a clicker?"

"Dammit," Alice said impatiently, "Look!"

She pointed the remote at the TV and clicked. A new show was on. An action-adventure starring two very familiar silhouettes. They were at the top of a highway billboard. The male actor was positioned atop the sign, leaning over its edge. He clung to a paper doll, which swung loosely beside the cigarette ad, bumping occasionally into the oversized lit cigarette that jutted from the flat sign. The butt singed the doll. The female lead was hanging on to the doll's paper leg, desperate not to lose her grip. A rip had formed at the doll's shoulder.

"Why don't they just let go?" Lou asked, "They're only a foot off the ground."

"It's a big foot," Alice snapped, "And it could be that no one's there to tell them that, 'cause some people'd rather not know. They'd rather let things burn."

Lou was about to acquiesce, but his classroom blackboard encouraged him to continue doing nothing. Pointing to his equation, he leaned forward with confidence and shut off the TV. The plastic knob broke off in his hand after the picture tube went black. He pocketed it, spoke to Alice.

"This is all nonsense, Alice. Look at the board. It still has the right answer: Seven minus one equals five. Everything's fine. It's only a movie." He settled into his easy chair. He was not prepared for Alice to backhand him out of his chair. He was on his knees rubbing his neck before he realized what she had done.

"What?" he exclaimed, "What did I do?"

"You know what you did! Pay attention, man! Seven minus one equals six!"

"You know. I think you're right," Lou said meekly. He sat on the floor, with Alice standing over him, hands on her hips. He didn't fear her, or feel anger at her brutality. Instead, he saw what it was about: seven minus one = six, not five. That meant something, something that rushed blood to his head, made him dizzy, almost conscious. He reached for the remote, still nestled in the breast pocket of Alice's faded overalls. Alice turned away before he could retrieve it, her attention absorbed by Lou's dead fern. Lou was confused, unable to fathom Alice's new attitude about their grim situation.

"Alice," he implored, "You're right. Seven minus one equals six, not five. Give me the clicker so I can fix that."

Alice ignored him, preoccupied by her leaf-by-leaf inspection of his dead fern. Lou stood, reached for the remote. Alice moved again, picking up the fern before he could snatch the important little machine. Alice, silent, put the fern on the TV and rolled both through his viscous blackboard, into the dark stain that had spread on his kitchen wall.

"Alice," Lou called after her, "Wait. I can fix it! Really!" His pleas were wasted. Alice was gone, his TV and fern went with her, and the fire was out. He sat on the arm of his broken easychair, not wishing the exposed rusty springs in its cushion to snag him. He put his chin in his hands. He silently studied the growing black stain on his wall. He wondered where it had come from.

"Must be a leak in the roof," he guessed aloud.

He spotted a chalk mark on the edge of the stain, near the top. The mark was familiar, but since the inky blotch had removed the rest of it, Lou was unable to tell what the mark represented. He suspected an equation, but doubted that since he made it a rule not to bring his work home with him. He stood, crossed the bare wood floor to the dark spot. He tried to touch it and was mildly surprised when his probing fingers passed into the spot, disappeared. The stain wasn't a stain at all. It was an opening. An opening into a crude black tunnel. The new knowledge telegraphed by his missing fingers struck him as profound. He pulled his hand out, stepped away from the wall. He wanted to go back to bed, but didn't.

"I should be in there," he said aloud.

"Should be in there, should be in, should be, should," the opening echoed, tempting him to enter the strange passage.

"Hell, it probably just leads into the kitchen," he said.

"Hell, it probably just, hell, it prob, hell it, hell," the hole responded. Lou didn't like the tone of the echo, so he kept his thoughts to himself. He wasn't terribly interested in joking about the damage to his house, anyway. He was busy fighting a need to explore the dark hallway.

"Need to explore, need to, need," the passage echoed.

"Hey," Lou said, annoyed, "I didn't say that!"

The hall remained silent.

"That's better," Lou said. He wished he could get into his kitchen for a flashlight, but the opening had grown over the kitchen door, blocking normal entry. Maybe this leads to the kitchen, he thought, I can pick up a light when I pass by. He stepped into the dark tunnel.

"Maybe not," he heard his voice echo as he finished his step. It didn't end on the dirty linoleum of his kitchen. It didn't end at all. He tumbled through hazy sunshine, down toward a smoking lava pit a thousand feet below. Land rushed by him as he fell, confirming that he was in the crater of an active volcano.

"Fine," Lou said.

It was an odd volcano, Lou noted. Its conical walls were adorned with lush, green grass and shrubbery that flourished in the sulfurous mist. A path led from the edge of the crater far above, spiraling down the wall until it met the lava pool toward which Lou was hurtling. Many people were trudging the worn path, each following it alone, and down. No one walked up. Lou, planning to choose an upward route once he reached the path, hoped he wouldn't disturb any of the solemn hikers.

Though the seething lava pool rushed at him, he felt no fear. He thought about the odd reaction for a minute before he realized why he had no cause for panic: he had left a potpie in his oven, so there was no way he could actually fall into the pit. He was, however, concerned about the young man who was finishing the final spiral on the lonely path. The well-dressed athlete was steps away from the pit, and apparently not stopping. Lou shifted his weight. His action swung the rope ladder he clung to over to the path, now a ledge barely an arm's length above the lava. He dropped to the ledge, behind Phillip, who was oblivious to his presence. The big man strode down the shallow spiral, shoulders high, gait easy. Lou sensed that he was not going to stop.

"Hey," Lou said to Phillip's back, "Where are you going?"

Phillip continued walking. Lou tapped him on the shoulder, but Phillip ignored him. Lou tapped harder. The urge to stop Phillip from finishing the spiral consumed him.

"Hey, fella," Lou shouted in the content man's ear, "You listening to me?"

Phillip took no notice. His gait didn't change. The spiral had only one turn left. Lou could feel the heat from the lava pool bubbling inches from his ankles. He tried to stop Phillip with force, by tugging on his arm, then tackling his knees. Phillip's powerful legs brushed Lou off without alarming their master.

His bravery multiplying with each step Phillip took toward completion of the spiral, Lou took a chance by swinging on the rope ladder that hung beside him out over the lava. He arced over the center of the small hot pool, swung back to the dirt path. He landed on his feet in front of Phillip. He faced the man, barely older than his own students, for the first time. Phillip's dark face was smooth, unlined. He was smiling slightly, an easy smile that elicited one from Lou. Lou stepped backwards, keeping pace with

Phillip's still unchanged descent.   He forgot his self-imposed mission, its importance clouded by a flood of empathy that warmed his bones and told him that the lava wasn't worse than a hot bath, to some.

Lou was complacent about his misadventure until his left shoe contacted the edge of the lava pool.   His rubber sole vaporized, exposing his bare heel to searing heat.   Lou remembered suddenly where he was and what he was supposed to be doing.   He waved both hands at Phillip, who strolled calmly along the path.   He was across the red pit, a few paces from the path's end, and Lou.   He started toward Phillip to make one last attempt to influence the self-possessed young man.

Lou had covered a few hundred yards before it occurred to him that Phillip was no closer.   He understood why people chose not to walk up the path.   With this understanding in mind, he continued his steady pace.   His perseverance inspired a burst of speed that shot him across the remaining distance in less than a minute.   He had feared the journey might have taken hours.

Lou wasted no breath on Phillip.   Instead, he lowered his shoulder and barreled into the man's waist.   He connected with bone-crunching force.   Unfortunately, the bones Lou crunched were his own as he bounced harmlessly off the determined man. Phillip trod over Lou's prone body without changing his pace.

"Fine," Lou shouted at Phillip's back, "If that's how you're going to be, then, fine.   Be happy, I don't care."   He snatched the rope ladder with exaggerated style, and hopped on.   Thumb on his nose, hand open, he waved good-bye to Phillip.   He hoped the man would cease his good mood long enough to realize the destination of the path he relentlessly strolled.   He figured that would not happen until Phillip's big toe touched the lava.   But it will happen, Lou told himself, it has to.

He scaled the last rung of the aluminum painting ladder, climbed over the gutter onto his lightly sloped roof.   He peered back over the edge, intrigued by the great distance he had covered. Two stories was quite a height, from above, he thought.   He surveyed the green-shingled roof, not clear about what he was to do.   Plenty of shingles were missing, but he had neither the required tools nor knowledge with him to effect repairs.   He checked his hands to see if he was carrying tar or a hammer, but they were empty except for his tattered leather brief case.

He did notice numerous items of debris: Frisbees, playground balls, an arrow, three balsa planes. He recognized them all, and admonished himself for not coming up to the roof earlier in life.

One toy that he did not recognize lay at his feet, glittering in the noon sun. Careful not to lose his balance on the loose shingles, he bent down and picked it up. He held it close, examined it, tried to remember it.

It was a tin toy submarine, old but in fair shape. The wind up key was still positioned in the sub's flank. Lou smiled, touched the key. It was frozen. Lou could not let go before that cold jumped to his fingers, filtered into his body. It gripped him, filling him with a funereal sense of loss. The tiny sub was dead, left to rust on his roof, its fine craftsmanship and detail wasted.

His hand shook as he pulled the toy near. He didn't know what a closer inspection would portend. He squinted, pushed his nose right against its hull. On closer inspection, he was shocked at what he saw.

Nothing. There was nothing there but a tin sub, and not even his, or so he remembered. It was an empty toy, bereft of amusement, barren. No clockwork existed inside, ever. No wonder it's on the roof, he thought.

"It definitely couldn't have been mine," he announced.

He tossed the rusty sub over the peak of his roof. It would fly on into his neighbor's yard, no longer a part of his life. He wasn't able to listen for its landing, however, as the energy he exerted to throw the sub worked both ways, tossing him over the edge of his roof.

As he watched the rungs of the ladder whip by, he hoped he had placed it on the side with the pool.

Gloria 4

The hardwood bench earned its name. Its flat surfaces pressed unnaturally against Gloria's round surfaces. It reminded her of a church pew, though they provided their nominal support for an hour at a time, not weeks. She shifted her weight onto the rail that separated her from the sanctuary of the courtroom for relief, wriggling in her space to maintain blood flow. She had performed the ritual countless times before, and was actually getting used to the awful bench. Figures, she thought, just in time for the end of this thing.

She performed her second ritual of surveying the courtroom. First, the Judge's bench, raised high above all the lesser furnishings in the courtroom. The Judge, one Beaufort Pierpont III, old, wrinkled, bald, mean, and fair, sat hunched at his bench, making notes. Always making notes. The courtroom's ugly chandeliers reflected on his shiny scalp. Gloria fixed her hair. She wondered what extra information he could have been entering into those black notebooks during the two-month trial. It was, after all, an open and shut case. The Jury saw it as that, the people in the gallery saw it as that, and so did her family. The four boys were guilty, period. Still Judge Beaufort Pierpont III took volumes of notes. Black notebooks were stacked to the ceiling behind him, each filled with his mysterious scribblings.

The Jury box slid into view. Worn, solid, and empty, its contents had been a high point for Gloria during the nightmare. The twelve jurors, out deliberating, had been a blessing. They saw right through her attackers', the accused, testimony. She had sensed during closing arguments that a definite confusion had risen among the outstanding citizens in the box. They seemed to be asking themselves why the rapists deserved a trial. The box was empty for just fifteen minutes and she expected that it would be occupied again very soon.

She turned her head to the attractive young man sitting at the table in front of her, just over the rail. Jake Iscariot, the energetic prosecuting attorney. He had been wonderful for her. He had believed and supported her from the beginning. He presented all the chilling evidence against the boys, and made her feel less guilty about her unseemly position as victim at the trial. He felt her glance, rotated his swivel chair to face her, as he did every morning for two months. He flashed a smile, rested a small soft hand on hers, which was still on the rail.

"It'll all be over soon, Gloria," he said. Gloria knew he was right.

"Thank God," she said, "I'm not sure how much more I can take. These chairs hurt." She forced a smile, drawing one from Jake as well. She continued, "I'll miss you when this is over, Jake."

"No, you won't," he teased before turning back to his papers.

She continued her scan across the aisle to the long defendants' table. Slouched at its end, as usual, was their public defendant. A tired old fellow in a cheap suit, unable to mask his dejection over the expected loss. Good, Gloria thought, after what he said about me. Beyond the lawyer, however, her attackers sat in a straight row, clean cut and confident. They wore the best in suits; their hair was washed, combed. They had even managed to scrub the ugly adolescent blemishes from their once mottled faces. Familiar with her routine, they turned to her in synchronized motion. All four of the beasts met her eyes at once. When they cracked evil grins, their faces resumed the horrid forms they had that night in the high school basement.

Gloria clenched her fists, bit her lip. She remembered that she had screamed once during the display, a month ago, only to discover that she was alone in witnessing it. Avoiding embarrassment, Gloria smiled sweetly at the sick boys. Why not, she thought, at least I have reason to smile.

She finished her daily survey, avoiding a glance behind her at the crowded gallery. She had to leave the throng of spectators packing the room out of her sight and mind. Their empty eye sockets disturbed her. Instead, she squeezed her mother's hand. Her mother, who had ridden through this with her from the start, tried to smile, but something haunted her. Gloria was about to ask about it when an unseen movement drew her attention to the Judge's bench.

He had raised his head, still writing. The bailiff was handing him a slip of paper. The Judge took the paper and nodded his head without reading it. Gloria suspected it was the verdict. The bailiff confirmed her belief by opening the side door that led to the Jury room. The denim and leather clad Jury strutted into the courtroom, jabbering, giving each other hi-fives, pushing bad haircuts out of their bloodshot eyes. They slumped into the twelve seats in the box. While Gloria rubbed her hands, eager to finish the nightmare, she noticed that something was wrong with them. She gasped vocally.

The Jury was no longer a cordial gathering of twelve honest ladies and gentlemen. Gloria jumped to her feet, knocking the massive bench and its occupants to the floor behind her.

The jurors who had entered to return a verdict were truly the peers of the accused. Twelve greasy, raunchy high school boys occupied seats still warm from good peoples' behinds. They each turned and acknowledged her horrified attention with cocky sophomoric faces that rivaled the evil boys at the long table just over the rail. Those boys stood quietly, their staged sincerity broken by an occasional titter. Gloria attempted to call attention to the Jury change, but words could not exit her choked throat, and the Judge ignored her frantic waves. The prosecutor, Jake, didn't seem to notice the switch. She tapped his shoulder, but he did not turn. The Judge put down his pen.

"Mister Foreman," he asked in official tones, "Has the Jury reached a verdict?" The foreman, a drug addict from the freshman class, stood.

"Fuckin' 'A' we have," the little bastard in the front corner of the box proclaimed. He balled a piece of paper and tossing it to the Judge. Judge Pierpont good-naturedly caught the ball. He flattened it on his desk. Gloria found her voice.

"Good God," she exclaimed, "You're not going to read that?" The Judge glared at her, pounded his bony fist on his desk. He removed his oval wire-rimmed glasses, cleaned them with a corner of his robe as he regarded her with little pleasure. More tittering sounded off to Gloria's right.

"Young lady," he said, leaning toward her, "How dare you! This is a sacred trust of our, your constitution. The Jury has presented..."

"The Jury?" Gloria interrupted. She pointed a shaking finger at the motley crew, fidgeting in their seats, picking their noses, "That's not the Jury. Your honor, that's more of them!" She remembered the prosecutor, who was quietly shuffling a stack of paper.

"Tell him!" she shouted at Jake, poking his shoulder harder. The prosecutor grabbed her finger, faced her. His eyes were missing, their sockets black and hollow, like the gallery's.

"Don't poke," he said, his voice void of emotion.

"No!" Gloria shouted. She turned back to the Judge, who read the slip of paper, smiled again, and tossed it back to the foreman.

"Please announce your verdict, Mister Foreman," Judge Beaufort Pierpont III instructed.

"We the Jury," the foreman read slowly.

"Wait!" Gloria shouted, hurtling the high wood rail. She landed erect on the prosecutor's table, at eye level with his honor.

"Restrain her," the Judge ordered. Two bailiffs, a couple of thugs from the hockey team, grabbed her crotch and breasts, pulled her to the cement floor.

"...find the defendants not guilty," the foreman finished. The gallery, all empty-eyed teenage boys, cheered. The Judge rapped his gavel.

"Case dismissed," he said, opening his black book to record more notes. The courtroom went wild.

Gloria shrugged off her handlers, rushed the bench. She climbed its high paneled wall and squatted on the Judge's desk, stepping on his latest notebook. She tore his pen from his hand, grabbed the Judge by his robe. She shook the misguided jurist.

"What do you mean, 'case dismissed?'"

Judge Beaufort Pierpont III theatrically removed her hands from his robe. He regarded her silently, his eyes now missing as well. A drop of blood betrayed the freshness of their removal. He pounded his fist, cracking the wood and smashing his ancient hand.

"Just what I said, you filthy bitch," he screamed, "Those fine boys are not at fault."

"Not at fault," Gloria repeated, shaking, "Not at fault?" She noticed that the Judge's tirade and perhaps her efforts had torn off some pieces of the Judge's loose old skin, revealing an acne encrusted adolescent visage that jeered beneath.

Gloria stepped back away from the bench, into the middle of the sanctuary. She spun around, away from the giggling monster in important robes, looked back at the courtroom and gallery. The hellish place was peopled exclusively with eyeless snickering adolescents.

Only the tired defense attorney remained unchanged. His gray eyes still occupied their sockets, but they glared at her spitefully, as though she had done something personally wrong to him. The assailants still had their eyes as well. Eyes that probed her, silently insulted her. They were shrugging, palms up. Then they clutched their sides, laughed uproariously. The courtroom, including the Judge, and Jake, echoed and amplified the humiliating hysteria. Her mother had left.

The defense attorney alone abstained from the vicious outburst. Gloria studied the old man in his worn corduroy suit. Something in his eyes looked familiar, beyond the face she had studied and hated over the past several weeks. His gray eyes shone beneath his anger, their depths telegraphing concern, hope, wisdom, honor, all the things denied her in the courtroom. When she noticed that he was speaking to her, her anger again clouded the truths that swirled in his eyes.

"Didn't you?" he demanded, his mismatched voice echoing in the silent courtroom.

"Me?" Gloria asked, poking her chest with her finger.

"Yeah, you," the lawyer said, "You took pictures of caca!" Gloria didn't know about the crime he was talking about, or what harm there was in photographing shit, but she did know that the man's clients were the guilty parties. They must have been. They committed every other crime charged, even if she were the only one left that subscribed to that truth. She pointed at the group.

"No I didn't," she declared, "They did it and you know it." The man followed her gesture to his clients. They had lowered their heads, donning airs of meek innocence.

"These fine boys? Commit such a heinous act? No, miss. You did it."

"No," Gloria said. The man's eyes suddenly shed once more their thin veil of anger. They flashed again, revealed the man's true feeling, his trust in her. He stepped closer to her, shocked at his earlier behavior, put out his hand. My God, Gloria thought, someone believes me! He can bring back the real Jury! He might change everything! She reached to him, but saw that the boys had paced forward with him, behind his back. They were looking over her shoulder, at the Judge. Then they held their fists straight out, thumbs pointed down. She forced her unwilling attention to the Judge. A puss-faced pubescent worm of a boy sat in the Judge's seat of honor. Bits of loose wrinkled skin still clung to his face. He had both hands on a steel lever, best resembling a truck's gearshift lever. Giggling uncontrollably, he pulled it.

Gloria lifted her head from the safe solitude of her tear-stained pillow at the sound of her family shuffling into her bedroom. Her father, mother, and two brothers surrounded her pink canopy bed. She rolled over, happy to have their attention. Sadly, they were not attending her, but her bed. Her father had a tape measure, and her mother helped him stretch it to the other side of the bed. They were sizing it up for a move out of her room.

She noticed then that all her other furniture, her dresser, her dollhouse, and her toys had been removed from her room. Only a few unused moving cartons, a bare bulb, and the bed remained.

"I guess this is it," her mother said, exhausted by the activity, "It's such a tragedy that this had to happen."

"Yeah," Bernie, her youngest brother said, "I believed her story, right to the end."

"That's because it was true," Gloria snapped. They didn't hear.

Tommy, her other brother, just a year younger than her and her dearest friend, sniffled a bit as he slowly nodded his agreement with his brother.

"Serves her right," her father said, stern, "After what she did, and the trouble she caused those fine boys, and this family. Serves her right. Now let's get this bed down to the curb."

"Dad, no," Gloria pleaded, "It's not true, it was all wrong." She gave up. No one was listening to her.

Her brothers each lifted an end of the bed, toted it down the stairs to the edge of the well-trimmed front yard. She remembered cutting the grass a week earlier. Her father had playfully squirted her with the hose he was using to wash the minivan.

The rest of her things, her life, were already piled unceremoniously at the curb, near the trash cans. Gloria crawled under her covers, uselessly willing the nightmare to end.

A garbage truck rumbled to a stop near her. The man that hangs off the back jumped off, studied her belongings, her bed, her. He held up both palms in front of him, shook his head.

"Sorry sir, can't take this stuff," he said to Gloria's father, "It's too big, won't never fit. Besides it'd be all wrong to take." Her father lowered his head, put his hand on the sanitation worker's shoulder. He mumbled something, and the garbage man's harsh expression softened. He pulled off his dirty cap, wrung it in his dirty hands.

"In that case," he said, "I'll do what I can to make it fit. You'll need to help me load it, though. Can't do it by myself. Union rules, you know." Her father argued for a short time about the trash man's duties and taxpayer dollars, but submitted to the quiet urges of her mother. Her mother was concerned about the attention the exchange was drawing from the neighbors.

Gloria's family joined the garbage man in loading her things. The bed was last, and she went with it, into the rank, filthy bowel of the truck. The truck lurched into motion. The last Gloria saw of her family was their dark silhouettes against the brightly lit house. Her mother and Bernie, bless him, were waving.

Gloria pulled her blankets over her head, waited, then pulled them down again. She was still afloat in the small shifting sea of trash in the vibrating garbage truck. There was one change, however: she was not alone anymore. An attractive woman in a tacky expensive gown and real pearls had joined her.

The woman sat, stiff, at the edge of her bed. She was gazing out the back of the truck, staring dreamily at where she had been. Curious about what the woman watched so carefully, Gloria sat up, peered over the rim of the garbage truck. They were driving through the maze of man-made mountains that formed the landfills of Staten Island. Gloria saw nothing unusual, or even worth viewing. She wished to question the woman's interest, but chose to keep her misgivings to herself. The woman's stone visage seemed ill equipped for a response. Gloria lay back down in her pink bed. She tucked the satin covers under her chin, and waited for her ride to end.

The woman suddenly jerked up from Gloria's bed, lifted to the mouth of the truck by a large male hand that gripped her wrist. Gloria, sensing an unusual chance for an early end to her journey, grabbed one of the woman's cold hard calves. She hoped to be lifted with the woman toward the daylight that beckoned beyond the truck's opening. The woman had cleared the sticky rim of the container, pulling Gloria along with her. She had enough time to see that they were rolling down a cobbled city street, lined with shops, before the woman's arm ripped free, tossing them both back into the innards of the truck.

Gloria landed in her bed. The woman sailed past her, into the sea of reeking trash. She watched the woman sink, disappearing beneath disgusting refuse without a struggle.

Gloria fluffed her pillow.

"I should've known you can't change things, not even when they're wrong."

The truck squealed to a stop. With a whir of machinery, the rear end of the container flipped up, revealing its payload to the empty desert outside. Gloria squinted in the harsh light that invaded the truck's confines. A deafening clatter sounded behind her, and Gloria braced herself, prepared for the slimy wall to push her out. It did, shoveling both Gloria and her things out onto the desert sand. The truck moved away, its engine echoing the laughter of the courtroom and Judge that sent her there.

She sat on the dune, under a bright noonday sun, alone. The blowing sand had already covered most of the material elements of her childhood. She rolled out of the bed before the sand, the elements, consumed it too. The dune was soft, the sun overhead warm. She sat back, rested, sifted sand between her toes.

T ed 4

He perched on the narrow stone ridge atop a high, high red brick wall. He leaned forward carefully, keeping his pudgy fingers gripped tight around the thin concrete ridge of his improvised seat. The ground was far below, a dizzying distance away. He whistled at the spectacle, impressed that he was able to handle the height without the usual vertigo. He leaned further, watched pedestrians far below.

"What do you know?" he observed, "They really do look like ants."

"Those are ants," his companion announced. He leaned back, turned to face the stuffed teddy bear seated beside him. His bear, since his earliest memories. His warm fuzzy friend. His annoying companion who had the nerve to finish a trite joke. He cast Dexter Bear a glare, indicating his dissatisfaction with its comment. He then looked again at the sidewalk below his swinging shoes (clad in very expensive sneakers, of course).

"Yeah," he said, after further review, "I suppose they are."

"I'm sorry Ted," the bear said, sincere, "I didn't mean to anger you. I couldn't resist."

"S'all right."

"Good. I wouldn't want to do anything to damage your self esteem."

"Huh?" he asked absently, not wishing for a reply.

"A bad self image could be most destructive to a man in your important position, Ted. You know that."

"Sure, sure," he said, rocking, dangerously close to shifting his weight off the wall. He wanted to watch the ants.

"I don't care what you say, Dex, they sure look like people to me."

"I imagine that they would, Ted. After all, people are very important to you. Or, I should say that you are very important to them. They need you."

"I'm hungry. You hungry?"

"I don't think so, Ted," the bear said. It leaned forward as well, trying to face him. Its little cloth mouth started working again. He watched it move, enjoyed its cute little arm and belly movements. Then, bored, he looked up and down the busy street.

"Is Bob's Deli open?" he asked, "I'm hungry. You hungry?" He couldn't locate Bob's Deli. It should have been on the corner next door to the Dry Cleaner's, but the shop at that address was vacant. Unfamiliar.

"No, Ted, I'm still not hungry. As I was saying, you must broadcast your importance. Shout the people's need for your unique services loud enough to bounce off the bank across the street and into your head. Can you do that, Ted?"

"Do what?" he asked politely. His bear made the climb up over the gelatinous mass of his thigh to sit in his lap. It tapped him with a felt paw.

"Ted. Ted, look at me."

He looked. The happy little bear was nestled in the canyon between his legs, waving at him. He smiled. Patted the bear's worn fur.

"That's my Dexter," he said, "Always looking for attention. You hungry? I am."

"No, Ted. That's not it, anyway. You know I can't look for attention."

"You can't even talk."

"True," it said, head low, "But today I can, because I'm tired of all these incorrect opinions about you. People should understand what you're here for."

"I'm here to eat," he chimed, "You know where that Deli's gone to? Where's the food when you need it?"

"It'll turn up, Ted," the bear said, wiggling its ears, "Now let's go through this one more time..."

"Sure wish we weren't on this high wall."

"It's not so high. We climbed up it, didn't we?"

"I suppose, but that was when I still had my strength. You sure those aren't ants down there?"

"I'm not sure about anything anymore, Ted," Dexter Bear said, his little arms folded, "But I am certainly not saying another word about you or your work if you don't care to listen."

He heard the little bear, but had difficulty concentrating on words that competed with his rumbling stomach.   The plush critter's button eyes glared at him.

"Ted!" it shouted over the groans of his stomach. His jaw dropped at his old friend's nasty tones.

"Well, Dexter, if you're going to be that way about it..." He released his grip on the edge of the wall, balancing himself long enough to snatch the bear in his hands and shove him in his mouth. Dexter the Bear said no more.

He chewed vigorously; glad to have something between his teeth at last.   Happily Dexter was mostly synthetic, so much chewing was required. This took his mind off his angry appetite.

In his zealous feasting, he had forgotten to close his hands back on the edge of his perch.   His mastication had started a teetering motion that he had not noticed earlier. When he did, it was too late for corrective action. He was falling over the wall, and all his efforts to steady himself; flailing arms, wide eyes, kicking feet, were no help. He swallowed Dexter, not wishing to lose his only friend in the fall.

His descent to the sidewalk below was short, allowing him only enough time to chide himself for thinking about all the king's horses and all the king's men before he bounced off the concrete, flattening hundreds of ants.

"They are ants," he declared.   He bounced down the sidewalk, working off the momentum of his fall. He had no need to worry, as his ambulance was waiting for him at the corner, back door open. It slammed shut behind him after he bounced into the 'service' compartment.

He sat up, shook his head. He was careful not to shake too hard, however; he hadn't examined his body yet for cracks.

"I don't even want to know who it'll take to put me back together again," he said as he began a lengthy inspection. In time he found that he survived the fall unharmed. It still was a fall, though, so he decided to get a checkup soon, and never to ride a bicycle again.

He rolled forward in the confining space to a squatting position. He waddled halfway down the narrow aisle of his ambulance before he noticed something was wrong. He stopped, listening for strange noises, sniffing for smoke. He sensed nothing, started forward again. He was at the small hatch that opened on the cab and ready to wriggle through to the driver's seat when he noticed the problem. He spun around to confirm his suspicion.

The momentum from his action shook the van as usual, but without the accompanying rattle or loose equipment, without the tinkle of glass bottles. He sat down with a squishy thump.

The ambulance was empty again, reduced by some bureaucratic oaf to a hollow rental van, with white painted walls and a corrugated floor. His shelves, his expensive wood paneling, all his equipment, bottles, and linens had been removed. The front divider was missing. A standard, torn, van seat replaced the special heavy-duty high backed driver's seat he had installed. There was no passenger seat. Or dashboard.

"Or light and siren switches," he shouted, pounding the roof, "Not my lights, too! Why does this have to happen to me? One missed call, that's all it was!"

The glove compartment door popped open, allowing a manila file folder to slip free. It drifted to his feet like a dead leaf from a tree. He picked it up. He opened it.

It was the patient's file. The one that expired during his nap. He closed the folder. No need to read that file; he was the blundering intern who wrote it. He threw it into the back of the van. It burst apart mid-flight, layering the cargo area floor with white litter.

"A deadly storm indeed," he heard himself say. He sat in the lone seat, ignoring the protest song of old cushion springs. He rested his elbow on his knee, his chins in his palm. He looked out the opaque passenger window.

"It was just one guy," he said aloud, hoping the returning echo of worn words would comfort him, "An old guy, at that. They didn't need to take everything away."

That included his ambulance. Ten years later and some bureaucratic do-gooder-fool had to take his equipment. Another blind action to prevent him from helping, from saving lives. He punched the dash. The weight of his falling fist dislodged it. It fell to the steel floor, collapsing noisily into a cloud of dust. Junk. His ambulance was junk.

"Have to make the best of it, though," he said, "Do what I can to help." He spun in his seat to face forward. He retrieved the steering wheel from the floor, stuck the thin metal column back in its place. He realized then that he had no key for this van, only for his ambulance and Pinto. Neither fit. Time to leave, he thought, to find the right vehicle. My ambulance.

"People need me," he pronounced. There was no echo.

He tried the door latch, but it broke off in his hand. He saw that the passenger side had no latch. No door. Only glass. He stood, careful not to bang his head on the clear roof. The van had crystallized. He could see through every panel, even the floor. Even the windows. Reluctantly, he looked out.

People, many people, noonday rush people, plied the city street outside.   Hundreds, maybe thousands of pedestrians swarmed. Every one of them, every man, woman, and child among them, turned toward the clear truck as they passed. He waved greeting to them until he noticed that they each shook their heads in disapproval. He wanted desperately to escape, but was unwilling to break the glass. He could cut himself. He needed help. He needed someone else's help, from the outside.

"Don't they owe me that?" he asked aloud.

He spotted one man, with a familiar woman standing at his shoulder, seated on a bench across the sidewalk. Beyond the river of disapproval. He waved both arms at the man, even chanced pounding lightly on the thick glass. The man noticed him, but did not jump up to assist him, as he had expected. Instead, the man shook his head too, and aimed a spatula at him.

The woman behind the man reacted angrily to the man's strange behavior. She leaned forward to whisper in the man's ear, but she was too late. The man had already flipped the spatula, causing the thick pancake to tumble off, onto the sidewalk.

The man and woman vanished behind the crowd. The pancake was trampled. The glass was tinting, darkening to opaque at the far corners first. The blackness worked its way quickly to each panel's center, obscuring everything. He thought he would appreciate that event, but he did not. The blackness did not stop at the walls of his box. It moved toward its center, obscuring, all, including him.

He had no time to consider the crisis, or to mourn the usual lack of options. All was black, switched off. He could see nothing. But he could still smell. And taste.

A familiar odor filled his nostrils. A sickly sweet, tempting smell, accompanied by the taste of the liquid that flowed into his nose, transporting the scent. He opened his mouth. Viscous warm lard flowed in. Liquid fat. He was suspended, no, he decided, sinking in a vat of warm lard. Probably drowning. He wasn't panicked, wasn't even concerned. Indeed, he felt good. After all, he was drowning in his favorite thing, and for the first time in his life he was sinking.

Sinking.

He sang himself the lullaby mother used to sing.

Alice 4

Alice flipped the door latch of Ed's truck and stumbled out onto the soft grass of the fallow field. She leaned on her elbows in the moist ground, scowled into the cab of the old truck. Ed was leaning across the seat, watching her. His rugged young face shifted expressions, alternating between concern and anger. Frustration, Alice thought. She kicked the door of his beloved '59 Chevy pickup closed. They weren't married yet. Hell, they'd only dated a few times. She wasn't ready yet.

"When, Alice?" Ed asked, voice deep, fists clenched, "When do you think you will be?"

She didn't answer. The fine print on her diploma consumed her. Her PhD in biology. It had faded, become illegible. She turned to Ed, who was still in his truck. He was clear, handsome, and so readable. He was waiting for her to get back in so he could start. Otherwise, he'd start without her. He'd leave her behind with only her PhD for food, for company. She was 25 -- an old maid. He was young, eager, and filled his truck (and blue jeans) well. Besides, each time she glanced in the battered side-view mirror to fix her hair a wrinkled old crone glowered back, slowly shaking her head.

Alice reverently folded the diploma. She wanted to stow it in her hip pocket, but her polyester slacks were bunched around her ankles. Alice had no other pockets, so she tore the parchment up, threw it in the air. She watched as it shredded into smaller and smaller pieces, then settled like snow on the gently blowing grass.

Ed extended his unwashed hand to her. It was a silent, sincere, pleasant invitation. Alice forced a coy grin in response. She accepted, touching her fingers to his palm. Ed's hand locked tight around hers. Alice squealed as her feet left the warm ground. Ed set her firmly on the hard steel seat of their John Deere. He pushed the starter for her, placed her hand on the steering wheel. It was cold.

"Ed, honey," Alice said, "This isn't what I had in mind."

Ed brought his head, his unshaven face, in close to her. Very close. Their noses touched. It was difficult for her to focus on his brown eyes. Alice wasn't fond of that sort of intimacy. She backed off. He followed, flashed his date-winning smile. Ed did have good teeth.

"Alice, it's harvest time. Now, you know that we all have to put in a hard day at harvest time."

"Yeah Ed," Alice conceded, "I guess I do know that."

"Good girl," Ed said, slapping her thigh. He hopped off the tractor, returned to his '59 Chevy pickup. He pulled onto the dirt access road, and sped away. A plume of disrupted dust punctuated his hasty exit. He waved his Stetson out the open window. The young blond woman in the passenger seat waved as well, her fresh manicure glimmering in the sun. Alice studied her own hand. Most of her fingernails were either gone or bruised black. Her frayed knuckles seemed excessively large.

"God," she sighed, fixing her bandanna, "How long has it been since I did my nails?" She allowed the subtle amusement of her quip to lift her spirits long enough to restart the tractor.

She felt like she had just shut it off. Her body aches insisted that she had recently dismounted the rumbling beast after a long day of manhandling it. She rubbed her tired hands. The grueling work at harvest time seemed never to end. She depressed the drive clutch, forced the old tractor into gear. The vibrating shifter's kick should have knocked her off the tractor, but she was used to it, able to manhandle the unruly rod. After the tractor lurched forward, she set to starting the harvesting machine that hung from its front end. The reaper's rusting start lever budged only after the mightiest of tugs. When it finally broke loose, the handle slapped at her, connecting squarely with her forehead. Alice shrugged off the pain: it was, after all, harvest time.

An iron yoke held the harvesting machine a substantial distance ahead of the tractor. It rode in plain sight, its activity easily monitored from Alice's position at the rear of the tractor. Its steady electric hum was barely audible above the rattle of the tractor's ancient diesel. She watched carefully as the machine's three forked appendages worked their way into two appropriately spaced rows of corn. The thickly padded tines on the gathering arms gently closed on the babies that sprouted from the tall green stalks. Alice watched alertly as the fork gently squeezed a ripe pod until it squirt a giggling baby from its juicy core. The baby tumbled over Alice's head and landed precisely in the center of the quilted sheet metal chute behind her. The painted green tunnel guided the baby into the fancy carriage that trailed the tractor. She had just enough time to confirm that the baby was lined up properly before the next one plopped into the chute. The nerve-wracking hours spent watching fresh babies somersault overhead toward the safety of the carriage were a difficult time for Alice. The infants that screamed or cried during the trip disturbed her. She knew rationally that the system was safe, but she couldn't help herself. Especially when the afternoon sun was low, and she had to step up the pace to harvest one last row before supper.

She spotted a figure, a shadow of a man, in the dim light. It was blocking her path. Her final row. She suspected her tired eyes were tricking her, and had already dismissed the man hunched over a row of young plants with a watering can as an illusion until she was nearly on top of him. Then she recognized him. She swore, floored the clutch and brake pedals at the same time. She had been moving at a fair clip, and the man was closer than she thought. She absently shut down the harvester, realizing too late that it was capable of plucking the man as well, and could have saved some time.

"Always the hard way," she said as she strained on the hand brake. The tractor skidded to a stop a few feet from the man, who had taken no notice of her. She let it idle while she watched him with quiet respect. He was administering a sip of cola to each of the four babies on the stalk before him. His gentle manner warmed her. The babies were too young for picking. They needed the sweet soda, and Alice forgave the man for trespassing, endangering her and himself. He was doing a good thing for her crop. That was rare.

As if cynically tuned to Alice's thoughts, the man suddenly stood up straight. His calm, well-mannered visage contorted to a grimace of anger. He was angry at the babies. Of all things, Alice thought, the babies! She climbed down from the idling tractor.

The man seemed ready to trample the sprouts, and she would have none of that on her farm. She stepped toward the man, prepared for anything.

Instead of projecting his impatience on the babies, the man chose to punish the plastic watering can he had recently valued. He wound up and released like a slow-pitch softballer, launching the can toward the tractor.

Alice tried to catch the projectile, but it slipped through her outstretched hands, landing in the tractor's exposed engine compartment. The idling machinery threatened to digest the small can.

"That's a hell of an attitude, mister," Alice said. She verified that the man was not exacting any judgment on the babies before she stuck a hand in after the watering can.

It had disappeared into the engine compartment. Alice reached her arm in until her shoulder contacted the tractor's high cowl. She felt around the clattering jungle of grimy iron and cracked rubber until she located the unusual plastic texture of the watering can. She extracted it. She sighed with relief when she saw that its only damage was a small crack in the spout. It still contained soda. She carefully wrapped the spout with a length of electrical tape she happened to be carrying. It wasn't a perfect repair, but it would hold. She faced the thoughtless stranger.

"Why did you do that, mister?" she asked, pointing the watering can at the babies that he had abandoned. They were trying to free themselves from their husks. Two were almost out. Alice felt a knot in her stomach, along with the warmth of blood in her cheeks from her growing ire. The man, normally the quintessence of reliability, was ignoring the babies' plight. He was aware that they weren't ready for picking yet. He stared directly at them, passively letting one fall out, dead on the ground. He did acknowledge her heated question however.

"Alice," he said, shrugging, "It's just a kick."

"Just a..." Alice stammered, shocked that the man had such a response in him. Hoping she misunderstood, she continued, "How can you say that?" His brow furrowed; question puzzled him.

"I don't know anything," he said, sincere, "Why isn't it just a clicker?"

Oh my, Alice thought, something really is wrong. Her trepidation could not, however, supplant her anger. She pointed the injured spout at the immature stalks he had forsaken.

"Dammit," she snapped, "Look!"

He obligingly watched the struggling infants. One had cleared its husk and was about to fall. Two others recognized their danger. They clutched each other in a desperate struggle to stay on their stalks. The man pointed to them.

"Why don't they go?" he asked, puzzled, "They're a foot off the ground."

"It's a big foot," Alice lectured, "And it could be that maybe no one's there to tell them that. 'Cause some people would rather not know. They'd rather let things burn." Alice had no idea from what dark crevice that stream of consciousness had erupted, or what its point was, but she could see her words were drawing the desired effect. The man was pensive. She relaxed and bent to tending the falling babies. Their discussion to that point had prevented her required attention. She might still have time to fix the damage and finish her row before sundown. Unfortunately, her first step past the man was interrupted when he spoke.

"Nonsense." he said, pointing to the stalk, "Look, it still has the right answer." He settled smugly into a battered easy chair. He was nodding his head, comforted by his dangerous conclusion. His eyes were half closed when he spoke again.

"Everything's fine, it's only a movie."

Alice shook off her shock. This is wrong, she, thought, totally wrong. She cocked the watering can high overhead and brought it down on the man. She knocked him out of his comfortable chair, and kicked it behind her tractor before he could return to it. He had fallen to his knees between her and the babies. He was confused again, but hardly submissive.

"What?" he shouted, holding up a protective forearm, "What'd I do?"

"You know what you did," Alice explained, "Pay attention, man! 7-1 = 6. Six!" She waited an eternity for him to comprehend. Finally, he sat back in the dirt, scratching his head.

"You know," he said, "I think you're right." Alice wanted to cheer her success, but she had no time to celebrate. The babies needed tending. She stepped past the man fluidly, bent down and inspected the damaged crops.

One was beyond saving, she noted sadly. Can't mourn the dead when there're still lives to save, she thought, checking the others. One was almost out of its husk, probably too far gone to save. The two that worked together seemed healthy. Maybe if I put them in water, she thought, they'll be fine. A fourth, a big one, was still in its husk, snoring. She stopped, recounted.

"Funny," she said, "I would've sworn there were six. Two must've run off. Hope the crows don't get them." She was right, of course. All stalks foster seven babies. It was an irrevocable natural law. That was why she knew the man's equation was wrong. She had little time to pursue the mystery. The sun was setting, and there was still a row to be finished. She kicked aside the dead baby and gathered up the three threatened infants in her arms. She left the fat one. It was strong, fine, and would survive the machine. She tossed the three into the pram, made a mental note to see to them later.

Alice kept her eyes shut as she reached into her mailbox. Her hand met a thick wad of mail that she promptly removed. She eagerly sifted through it, looking for a piece addressed to her. Most of it was for her father. No surprise there; it was his house. The rest was junk. She replaced it, not interested in walking it up the long driveway while Ed waited for her in his pickup.

After she lifted the door of the rusty rural mailbox closed, she spotted an envelope in the long grass at the base of the mailbox's wooden post. Assuming it dropped out unnoticed, she bent down and picked it up. She almost put the official-looking envelope back in the mailbox without noticing that it had her name on it. She gently turned it to admire the important seal embossed on the back. She couldn't read the return address, but the postal markings indicated it was from Massachusetts. A tremor of delight drifted through her. She sprinted to Ed's truck.

"Ed!" she shouted, waving the unopened letter, "Look! A letter from the East Coast! Somebody must have heard!"

Ed leaned toward the open passenger window. She could see him raise his eyebrows in the shadows of the cab.

"What's the East Coast?" he asked. Alice stopped running.

"You know," she explained, "Massachusetts. Boston. Where all that important research is happening! They wrote back."

"That's great," Ed said, "Where's Massachusetts, Boston?"

Alice stopped a few feet from the truck. Though Ed's question was sincere, and relevant, she didn't answer him. She couldn't.

She heard a baby crying. She looked over the bed of Ed's '59 Chevy pickup truck to the cornfield that stretched to the horizon. She looked at Ed. He was smiling, supportive, lighting a cigarette with the truck's electric lighter.

She reached out silently. He handed her the lighter. The small chrome can glowed orange inside, like a tiny version of the burners on her rich Aunt May's electric stove. She touched it to the corner of the envelope addressed to her.

A small yellow flame was born, consumed the envelope, and died. Alice was left with a pile of gray ashes in her unharmed palm. A scorched embossed seal rested in the center of the pile. She dropped the dust, wiped her hands clean on the tall wet grass she sat in. She lifted her head to her fiancée, who smiled down at her from the open passenger door. She laughed at herself for falling out, but wished, as she brushed cold midnight dirt from her bare ass, that Ed would just once get a motel room. Or better doors.

Ed pulled her back in, sat her beside him, and resumed fondling her and nibbling her neck. She absently watched over his shoulder while he performed his routine. She studied the moonlit cornfield as it swayed in the light fall breeze. She listened to the distant cries of unharvested babies.

"No, Ed, I don't know where Massachusetts, Boston is."

He didn't hear her.

Howard 4

Howard dove into the glass booth. He slammed the folding door shut behind him to shed light on the payphone. He lifted the cold receiver, listened for a dial tone. The familiar buzz comforted him, helped diminish his panic, his feeling of helplessness. Howard immediately started to dial '911', but made little progress. His finger punched the '9' button with ease, but he couldn't find the '1' button. It wasn't in its proper position.

He inspected the rest of the dial. All the buttons were in their places. The dial had twelve steel buttons, as always, in four rows of three, Howard noted. But it had no '1'. When he poked the button in the top left corner, he touched only 2's or 4's, never 1's.

Howard pulled the phone from its steel frame, shook it over his head. He thrust it back into place, tried again to dial '911'. Still no '1'. Howard punched the phone, freeing its cache of pennies.

"I knew it," he shouted, "I knew not to bring in the Police. They told me not to." He slid to the floor of the booth, head in his hands. The phone hung, dark and quiet, above him. It dropped a penny on his head, reminding him.

"I should have listened, Claire," Howard said to the closed door, "I should've. But how could I know? How could I have predicted this?"

The clatter of metal against metal outside the booth disrupted his dramatic moment of self-pity. He sought its source, annoyed.

An antique paddy wagon idled outside the booth, cluttered with Keystone Kops. Six of them sat in or clung to the cab, with three more gathered behind it, fumbling with the wagon's rear doors. Howard took notice of the Kops behind the wagon too late.

By the time he registered what it was they fumbled with, Claire was secured in the back of the grainy black and white image.

Howard bumped his head on the payphone as he stood, dislodging it. The clatter of its fall drew the Kops' attention. They spotted him, put their hands on their helmets and jumped up and down.

Tinny piano music played as the Kops on the cab spied Howard. The paddy wagon sped from the curve, leaving the three rear Kops behind. They ran after the zigzagging wagon, grabbed at the rear door handles.

They managed to get their ride, but the doors flew open, revealing Claire. She was chained inside, in white face, clutching her bosom. Howard shook his fist at the old film.

He tore the phone off the glass wall, lobbed it after the wagon. He had to strike it before it reached the end of the block. The phone missed its mark, succeeding only in flattening one Kop.

The wagon stopped and backed over the victim. Two Kops in the cab plucked their fallen comrade from the dirt road. The wagon accelerated away, disappearing around a corner.

Howard took up the chase, paralleling the movie screen until he spotted an alley across the street. He knew the alley, turned into it, away from the frantic piano music. Away from the square black and white moving image.

The alley ended at a brick wall, adorned with a rusting fire escape. Howard leapt without hesitation to the first platform. He scaled the iron steps one flight at a time, reaching the roof in twenty counted strides.

Howard crossed the roof on his toes, wary of the boiling tar. A bottomless fissure separated the roof's far end, where he needed to be, from him. The abyss was deep, but not terribly wide. Howard instinctively stepped back, nearly mired in sticky tar that he thought he had left behind. He shook off the black goo and ran forward, accelerating toward the gap. It was less than a foot wide at the spot he aimed for, but he was determined to traverse it, regardless of what might happen to him. This was his only shot, and he had to take it. He reached the crack, closed his eyes, and jumped.

He landed safely on the other side of the tiny slit in the tar, onto the hard slate of the roof. He skidded along its surface until the low wall that marked the edge of the roof cancelled his momentum.

He leaned over the wall, peered at the street far below. As expected, he spotted the battered yellow panel van turning onto the street almost directly below him. He removed his leather belt.

"Damn, damn, damn," he said, "I should've known I could have done this alone." He prayed he wasn't too late; that calling the cops hadn't left Claire's rescue beyond his reach.

Howard slipped the end of his belt into the brass buckle, fashioning a loop. He swung his improvised lasso over his head for a revolution or two before casting it after the escaping van. The loop caught its radio antenna on his first attempt.

Howard tugged his end. The belt held fast, forcing the truck to stop. He hopped over the wall onto the street, behind the stalled van. The rear doors were open. He reached into the dark interior, groped for his wife.

He found Claire's wrist, closed his hand on it, tight. He pulled. Her waxen arm emerged from the wagon readily enough, but the rest of her was stubborn. Howard felt her tug back.

"Claire, why?" he asked, "You're not supposed to fight me." But fight his wife of ten years did. She resisted his efforts, remained hidden within the panel van. Howard was too close. He was unwilling, unable to release her. He tugged harder.

His final strained yank produced a pop in the hidden cargo area, followed by the sound of tearing sheets. Something gave, and Claire's head emerged from the dirty open doors. Her pallid visage bore a puzzled expression, but otherwise she looked fine. He tugged harder. She stayed put.

"Claire," Howard pleaded, "Really, time's short. You've got to stop fighting me. I can't hold this van, or your wrist, much longer."

"Fighting you?" Claire asked pleasantly, "Is that what I'm doing? I think not."

"But dear, you won't come out. I'm pulling as hard as I can."

"I know, Howard, every bone in my body will vouch for that," Claire quipped. Then, her brow furrowed, she asked, "My wrist?"

"Yeah, I'm holding your wrist, see?"

"Oh Howard. I thought you had my leg!"

"Your..." Howard couldn't finish. The passenger side door of the van had opened, and a police officer stepped out. Howard, still clutching Claire's wrist, turned his attention to the lawman.

The uniformed cop approached casually, twirling a billy-club in one hand and pair of hedge clippers in the other.

Howard could not judge the officer's reaction to his belt in one hand and Claire's wrist in the other, as the pantyhose stretched over his head distorted the cop's features.

The cop stopped a few inches from Howard, still twirling his baton. Howard maintained his grips, though he had allowed Claire's head to disappear into the van again. He smiled at the cop, presenting the best nonchalant posture he could muster.

"Evening officer," he said, nervous, "Everything okay?"

"Now who should be asking that question, Mr. Barlowe?" the cop lisped through fine nylon mesh, "Me, or you?"

Howard gulped. Guilt ran its chilly fingers down his back, weakening him. He would not let go, however, of either of his prizes.

"Excuse me, officer?" he asked, his fraying nerves trashing his expected smooth delivery.

"Sorry, Barlowe," the cop said, shaking his head, "I can't excuse you. Not after what you've done." The uniformed criminal tested his shears, snapping them open and closed.

"What do you mean?" Howard asked innocently. He knew the answer, but hoped the cop was bluffing. Howard's sweating palms threatened his grips, but he maintained them. The cop didn't notice.

"You know what I mean!" the officer shouted, his spit moistening the stocking, "You called me, you idiot!"

"It was the right thing to do," Howard tried.

"Wrong," the cop said, "They told you what to do, didn't they?"

"But..."

"No 'buts' about it, fella," the cop said, setting the blades of his shears on either side of Howard's taut belt. The only anchor he had left.

"No, please," Howard said quietly.

"Howard," he heard from inside the van, "Tell me you didn't."

Howard's grip on his wife's wrist loosened.

"I can't do that, Claire," Howard whispered through his constricted throat, "I thought it was right."

"Oh   Howard,"   Claire   said.   Her   remorse   was overwhelming.

Howard let her wrist slide free.

The cop's shears, still poised, still threatening, became Howard's new target. He knew if he could reach those closing blades, deflect them somehow, he could change everything. He could reverse the pattern. He reached.

"Oh, Howard," the cop whined, brutally mimicking Claire, "You fool. You know it's too late. You are too late."

The blades snapped together, separating Howard's belt. He fell, still gripping his useless half of belt, into the gutter, splashing into a storm drain. The cop unwrapped the other end from the van's antenna.

"You'll never learn Barlowe," the stocking clad head said, tossing him the other half of his belt, "You'll never listen."

"No..." Howard said, raising a hand to the officer.

"I didn't think so," the cop said. He got back into the van, shut the door. A moment later a stocking and an officer's cap was tossed through the open window at him.   Howard heard the criminal's raucous laughter over the roar of the van's engine as it pulled slowly from the curb.

The last thing Howard saw from his position in the cold shallow stream was Claire. She crouched on the floor of the van, watching him. She was shaking her head very slowly. Before he could speak, cry out, scream or beg, the doors slammed shut. The van was gone. The street, bathed in dim predawn light, was deserted, emptied of all worthwhile life.

Howard stood, replaced his belt in the loops of his fine businessman's suit, buckled it. Claire had chosen the suit. When his emotions formed a fist, he felt the mild pressure of a foreign object in his palm. He opened his hand, inspected its contents.

Howard's knees buckled. He dropped to the cobbles once more. In his callused, quivering hand was a small metal chip.

A chromed silver metal chip. Square, about the size of a thimble. Very solid. There was an inscription on its slightly concave surface. A single character. A numeral:

"1"

Phillip 4

Run, don't stop. Attack the smooth gray path. Swing steel sinewy arms to assist in acceleration. Race up the gentle slope of the smooth gray path. Look down at pumping legs that convert extreme effort into a slow, steady gait. Pump arms harder, push legs with added fuss. Watch as herculean movement crumbles into indifferent stride up the curved path. Cease furious pumping, watch easy stride continue along the smooth gray path. Stop walking, smile at the legs that plod steadily on, up the smooth gray path. Forget running, leave haste behind, at the bottom of the path, where it belonged.

Look forward, up. See what is ahead. The smooth gray path is more than a path, it is a road. A spiral, wrapped tight around a dark granite cone that pierces the white clouds gathered overhead. The path coils rest against the hill. Beside it. Perhaps its builder was unwilling to cut into the granite cone. Perhaps the builder could not. Disregard distracting tangents, look back at the path, its perfect, easy incline, its extreme narrowness. See how it disappears every few feet, around the cone. See no option; no but to walk straight up, no room for turning around. Laugh, say:

"Turn around? Why?"

Don't wait for a response. The path, the granite hill, the sky, all are empty. All are free of disturbance, void of harassment. Filled with blissful singularity.

Hazard a disrespectful glance up. Through the clouds to the pinnacle. Green awaits up there, and blue. Smile. Not the usual green. Not the taboo blue. This green lives, breathes, invites warm touch. Blue remains unseen, but felt. Liquid cleansing, a clear pool of comfort, surrounded by green, at the pinnacle.

At the top. The top of the smooth gray path. The spiraling gray path that allows movement in one direction only. No forks, no unexpected bend. No signs. No exits. Laugh, say:

"It's about goddam time."

Try to run. Pump legs, arms. Breathe deep, hard. Employ every muscle, every grain of energy, every misguided task, every broken dream. Shudder under the pressure of a lifetime of regiment, discipline. Feel the forces converge. Feel strong wind sting cheeks, draw tears from wide eyes. Imagine the waiting pool, at the pinnacle, spiraling closer at an impossible rate. Look down. See legs walking at a steady, easy pace. Remember. Say:

"Oh."

Stop trying to hurry, again. Look down, see legs maintain their steady gait. Say:

"No sense rushing now."

Look back down the path. See clouds. Heavy, dark clouds, roiling with black mist, hiding thunder, spitting sharp lightning. Busy black clouds, not like the clean white puffs just overhead. Sigh. Say:

"Yet they..."

Never finish sentence. Find thought interrupted, stolen by a man. A bright, colorful man, glowing on the smooth gray path, in the still gray air. The man has an arm wrapped around a steadily pacing ankle. He hangs on tight, looking up with grim, tired eyes that reflect dark, roiling clouds, forgotten lightning.

The man cannot be shaken off or helped up. Steady pace controls all activity on the smooth gray path. The man, still clinging, is alone. The man, still clinging, can't help.

The man has changed. Bright colors have faded. Anger has supplanted grim intent once admired. Try, oddly, to stop. Center every fiber, every wish, every dream, years of discipline, on one single pause. Need to pause. To stop. To meet the angry man. To apologize to the angry man.

Look down.

See powerful legs pumping, continuing their steady pace up the smooth gray path. See the man shout unheard words. Watch the man let go. Watch him fall into the granite cone, sink through its opaque wall, shouting unheard words. Feel the energy employed to stop follow the man into the cone, away. Gone forever.

Look back.

Notice white clouds billow behind, gathering neatly around the granite mountains, obscuring it. Obscuring the path. Look ahead, up the spiral path. Smile, say:

"Finally."

One more turn awaits. One more gentle curve before meeting the clear blue pool, surrounded by soft healthy grass. Not sod, not turf, but grass. One more turn on the smooth, wide gray path. Unaided legs make the turn, but the pool, the fresh, cool pool, is obscured. Someone stands before it, on the flat gray path. Not colorful, not grim. Not the man. Another.

Father.

Unaided, legs cease their steady gait. The path is cold, slippery, unwilling to support static feet, but those well conditioned, powerful legs have stopped pumping. Stopped their tireless labors. Stopped because of Father. Father, who faces away, faces the pool. Father stands at the edge, leaning in at the waist. His fedora perches on his head, pipe hangs loose from his dry lips. His hands, both of them, clasp his member. He pisses in the clear, cool blue water.

Watch, helpless, as the yellow cloud spreads through the clear blue pool. See Father laugh, his head tilted over his shoulder. His pipe falls out. Also into the once clear blue pool. Watch as he finishes up, shaking twice before zipping; his often quoted rule. Watch him turn, present his back to the fouled pool.

"I told you boy," hear him say, "I said this place isn't for you. Wasn't for your mother, and it isn't for you."

Spit at Father, say:

"You ruined her pool too, didn't you?"

"I can't deny that, boy. Can't deny that."

Say nothing more. Picture him, for an instant, pissing in mother's pool. Feel knees bend, thighs flex. Feel power surge to well-conditioned legs. Feel them move.

See Father's face fall, hear his cackle end at the insistence of large, strong hands that press his chest. Savor his stumble, his pathetic struggle to stay erect. Watch him fall backward, arms

flailing.   Find entertainment in his plunge into the fouled pool.
Laugh.

Laugh loud. Laugh clean. Feel the laughter inside as well.
The first time. Pick up Father's hat from the soft green grass.
Toss it into the hissing pool. Stop laughing, slowly. Feel the
elation degrade to mild euphoria. Enjoy the moment, don't fear its
passing again.

Sit.   Sit on the soft green grass.   Watch the steam rise,
offering white texture to the clear gray sky. Notice the gray path is
gone. Sit, and wait.

Wait for the steam to clear, for the hot fog to lift. Lift off
the clear blue pool. The clear, waiting blue pool.

Lou 5

Untouched work fully entombed the metal desk that dominated Lou's cramped office. A three-foot tower of yellowing papers swayed in his sagging 'in' box. His 'out' box was empty, save for a thick layer of dust. His desk's brown Formica surface was lost beneath a sea of notes, equations, spilled coffee. He could spend a month just organizing the officious melee. Lou smiled, clasped his hands behind his head and leaned back in his squeaky leather chair.

He was content.

He should have been bothered by the clutter, perhaps annoyed at his stereotypical disorganization, but not that day. The noisy overhead steam pipes were quiet. The boiler room was gone. The walls were missing.

Some thoughtful bureaucrat had finally done a good thing in arranging to locate his office in the lovely meadow. Tall green grass, yellow and blue wildflowers, bees, and songbirds surrounded him. The only troublesome detail left was his door, which was still open to the dreary basement hall of the Science Building. Lou balled a piece of his latest theorem notes and tossed it lightly at the door. The smoky impact forced the oak door shut. Indeed, the slam was solid enough to make the door disappear. Distant green hills and blue skies filled its empty frame. Now, Lou thought, now I can get back to work.

He had lost track of his work, and was unsure about what formula it was on which he was working. His notes were no help. The numbers had faded, replaced on the loose leaf by his favorite childhood storybook. He flipped through the pages, enjoying the book until the brightly colored monsters ran away, leaving behind empty pictures. Lou shut the book, grateful for the reminder to return to work.

He tapped his calculator keypad, hoping it would cure his temporary number block, but it too was uncooperative. The green LED figures hopped off the calculator's display and danced away as fast as he could punch them up. He gave up after he had produced enough figures for them to organize an energetic football game. Fine, Lou thought, now I'll be fired for playing with my numbers. He shut the calculator off and started erasing the gaming digits with a tissue.

He had rubbed out more than half of the frisky numbers when the survivors sensed their peril. As a group they sprang out of Lou's office through the open window that hung suspended in the blue sky.

"Hey now!" Lou shouted. Not wishing to suffer the consequences of misplaced figures, Lou dove through the window after them. He landed in the front car of a roller coaster that was poised at the peak of the first hill. He looked behind him, saw the track disappear in the mist far below. The chattering chain drive disengaged, and Lou turned to see where he was headed.

He couldn't tell. The car was poised at the top of a vast maze of coaster tracks. Layer upon hazy pink layer of track unfolded beneath him, twisting endlessly toward an unseen destination far below. Probably ends in China, Lou thought, or Hell. He tightened his grip on the rubber coaming, not amused by the length of the imminent ride.

The last car passed over the crest of the hill above him. Fellow riders screamed with delight, put their hands in the air. They didn't notice that the roller coaster had not accelerated. It crawled down the steep slope, slower than the pace set during the long ride up. This is silly, Lou thought. He stood, and a smartly uniformed operator standing in the rigging nearby immediately spotted his infraction. He could not hear the kid, but understood the attendant's ire. Embarrassed, Lou stepped out of the coaster.

It roared overhead after he fell onto a greasy wooden service platform below the track. The platform vibrated as the coaster accelerated rapidly down the first steep decline. It disappeared around a bend and immediately emerged a mile below, traveling at an impossible rate, its passengers screaming in terror. Figures, he thought as he climbed a white steel stairway to a locked door floating in the air above him. He had to hold the handrail tight, since the steps had no risers to connect them. They swayed a bit, hindering his passage over the fiery abyss.

The steel door swung off its hinges before he reached it, allowing him to pass through without needing to produce a solution to its black liquid deadbolt. He stepped out onto a wide steel girder, the most recently set piece of an unfinished skyscraper. The same blue sky and greenery surrounded him, but the former was much too close, too dark.

Lou teetered on the girder, the footing precarious at that height, until he spotted two figures standing nearby. He steadied naturally at the sight of them, then relaxed completely when he recognized the duo. Dressed in black lab smocks (some untidy bloodstains marred the man's), they each acknowledged his intrusion with animosity. Intrusion, Lou thought, now why would I think that? He waved to them, addressed them by name.

"Howard, Gloria. What the hell are you guys doing here?"

Gloria and Howard stared, silently sharing an expression of confusion. Lou rolled his eyes, tried again, "Gloria, Howard," he said, "What the hell are you doing here?" Gloria and Howard acknowledged with mild surprise.

"What about you?" they asked in unison, gesturing to him, "This is my building, not yours."

"I had a feeling about that," Lou said, "Well come on, walk with me. I think we all need to think."

Not waiting for an answer, Lou stepped off the girder, landing softly on the fresh concrete floor a few feet below. He paused to see that Gloria and Howard walked at his sides down the pleasant hallway that wound, sans walls, through the construction site. He casually tried to determine what sort of building was being erected around him. When he passed unprotected operating rooms manned with busy surgeons, it looked like a hospital; when he spotted an airliner tail jutting through the floor he guessed an airport; the cranes and unmarked machinery to his left drew his assumption that a factory was being assembled. He thought to ask Gloria and Howard, but found he was not interested in their answers. Some conversation would be nice though, he thought.

"So," he asked, "Either of you know what's going up here?"

"No," they responded as a unit, "Nothing new I know of, 'cept you? Are you up?"

Lou stopped, allowing the pair to pass him. They stopped, too, and were waiting for an answer.

"No," Lou said, checking his watch, "Won't be up for quite some time. Days, maybe."

The pair, puzzled by his answer, regarded him with suspicion. Their impressive ability to mimic each other fascinated Lou. He didn't think they had it in them. Maybe they don't, he thought. Lou focused on the space between the pair, forcing his eyes to cross. Gloria and Howard merged, forming a single shape. A different shape. Blonde. Tan. A woman.

Alice. And she looked pissed.

The shock brought his focus back, returning Gloria and Howard to their original positions.

"Oh," Lou said.

Gloria and Howard stared at him, passive. Lou, wise to the charade, chose to play the game presented him instead of doing the focus thing again. He didn't like the focus thing, though he couldn't remember its result.

He resumed his quick pace along the gravel path. Anxious to return to his desk, he disregarded the lush greenery of the park around him. Supple waves of manicured meadows splashed in yellow evening sunlight rolled away in all directions, spotted by the occasional stand of trees, or perhaps a farmhouse. Fauna abounded: deer, horses, squirrels and toads were everywhere.

"You're doing a great job ignoring it all, mister," Gloria/Howard said, invading his reverie. Lou, startled, noticed that he was lying in a soft patch of red moss. He mumbled a terse response, stood and started walking again. Anxious to get to his office. Gloria/Howard matched his pace, walking with him, running with him, crawling with him. Lou gave up trying to shake them, looked instead for a place to hide.

"So," Lou said, passing the time, "What brings you to this fine place?"

"Claire." "The subway."

They both spoke at once, but said two different things. They began to fade immediately. It looked to Lou like it hurt. He wagged his index finger at them as their images merged into one.

"That'll teach you to pretend," Lou teased. Their images continued to merge until they formed a dull grey slash that marred the scenic horizon. Then, with a resounding thunderclap and a fancy puff of smoke, they disappeared. Lou waved smoke from his face, waited for the rest to clear before returning to his desk. The smoke wouldn't completely dissipate, threatening to make him late. He couldn't allow that, so he inhaled deeply, drawing the warm fog into his lungs, out of the way.

He was pleasantly surprised to find himself back on the nature trail, once more enjoying the greenery on his way back to work. He stepped lightly down the gravel path, consumed with pleasure, and scanned the close verdant horizon. He was satisfied in the simple, complete environment. At the same moment he found himself wishing verbally it would never end, his left foot sank deep into a disturbing material that was not gravel. Lou stopped. It felt like a person. A woman. To verify his assumption, he looked down.

It was a woman. It was Alice, lying in a depression in the path with Lou's foot embedded in her abdomen. Deep enough to fully conceal his hi-tops. He tried to pull it out, but it was planted firmly. She must be tense, he thought, her stomach muscles won't relax. Impressive muscles, too. Lou searched for something to say to the stricken woman. He wanted to comment on her fine unclad appearance, the way her struggling chest heaved in such a comely manner, but the warm blood dripping into his shoe influenced his words.

"Boy," he said, "I'll bet that hurts a lot."

"Only when I laugh," Alice responded, "Ha ha."

Lou chuckled at her trite response, noticing that she conveyed no amusement at her own joke. She stayed calm, though, considering her condition. Lou was puzzled. It was, he thought, a rare and very strange predicament they shared. Alice interrupted, stabbing him with her clear blue eyes.

"When you're through pondering the obvious, you want to get your foot off my ovaries?"

"Sure Alice."

"I'd appreciate that."

Lou obediently raised his foot. It came up readily, but brought Alice along. He tried standing on her, pushing into her white pelvis with his right foot for leverage. The effort produced slight torsion on Alice's part, but his foot remained encased in her flesh. Alice didn't like the second tactic, told him so.

"Enough!" she screamed.

"Listen," Lou said, "You've got to lighten up or I'll never get it out."

"Lighten up? You're the one on me... In me!"

"True, but we still need to work together."

"Fine," Alice mumbled, "Why don't you untie your shoe and pull your foot out? It'll take half the pain away and might free your shoe."

"Untie it?"

"Yes, mister," she said, sardonic, "Can you do that?"

"Well I suppose, but I'd hate to be out one shoe. I just bought these, you know."

"Mister, if you're not outta me in five seconds you won't need two shoes! Now untie it!"

"Okay, okay. Sheesh, nobody can take a joke anymore."

Lou bent over, reaching his fingers into the cavity his foot had formed. He found some strings, tried to pull them apart. Alice's body convulsed.

"Those are not shoe laces!" she shrieked. Lou let go. Something twanged.

"Oh. Sorry."

"It's all right. I have enough kids."

Lou dug in again, found more string. He gave an experimental tug, and got no response from Alice. Relieved, he yanked a length of lace out. He examined it, tentative, hoping it wasn't that time of the month for her. He sighed. It was a bloodied shoelace.

"Here we go," he said, triumphant.

"Thank God," Alice said.

Lou extracted his foot, leaving his shoe and sweat sock inside her. He stepped off Alice, admired her as she stood. Beautiful, and so strong, with sharp tan lines above her knees, elbows, and chest.

"You seem okay, except for the hole," he said.   Alice smiled at his remark. An honest smile. Lou was relieved. He took her hands, looked her up and down for any other signs of damage. She actually did seem undamaged, aside from the bloody cannon ball crater in her midriff, with a sock hanging from it. She lowered her head, subtly examining her damage. Her face was flushed when she looked up at him. She released his hands. Slowly, as if it pained her to do so. Lou was touched.

"Listen mister," she said, pointing to a nearby restroom, "Why don't you let me go in there and freshen up a bit? I'll be right out."

"Good idea," Lou responded, nodding. He walked her to the door, which she closed behind her. It was a western movie saloon door, with swinging panels that cleared the floor by a couple of feet. Lou resisted the urge to peek underneath by leaning against the concrete wall of the facility, and talking through the door.

"Everything coming out okay?" he asked, eyes fixed on the center of the door.

"Fine," her response drifted out, "It should be out in a minute."

True to her word, Lou's sneaker and sock both appeared over the top of the door, clean. They dropped to the gravel path. Lou picked them up, pulled them on. He fumbled with the fleshy laces until he fastened a tight knot.

"There," he shouted over his shoulder, "All fixed. And I'll bet you are as well." He stood, still politely looking away, waited for a response. There was none. Lou turned to the large, dirty glass doors. He opened one a crack.

"Alice? You fall in?"

Still no answer.

"Now come on," he said through the crack, "This isn't fair. Answer me!"

More empty silence.

Angry, Lou burst through the doors and into the Woolworth's store. The store was busy, but Alice wasn't a customer. To be sure she had left, he browsed the aisles, trying to ignore the unique Woolworth's aroma that permeated his shopping. He gave up, forgetting exactly what it was he had come in for. He got on the checkout line to pay for the item he failed to find.

He waited patiently for the hamster at the register to service the customers ahead of him. It was a long wait. The hamster was doing fine, but the parakeet next to it was slowing the process. The clumsy bird couldn't get its beak around a bottle of Listerine. Lou didn't mind the wait. After all, Woolworth's was probably the only department store left with hamsters and parakeets.

When his turn came, Lou handed $10.95 to the smiling rodent for the pair of shoelaces he was purchasing.

"Bit steep for shoelaces, don't you think?" Lou asked good-naturedly. The hamster nodded, inspecting the laces.

"I suppose it is, sir," it said, "But I only ring the register. You'll have to bring it up with the manager if you've got a problem."

"Could be mismarked," the parakeet chimed in, "Could be mismarked."

"The manager?" Lou said, "Okay."

"Sorry sir," the hamster apologized, "The manager's been out since 1962. Don't think he'll be back soon."

"Could be mismarked," the parakeet offered, "Could be mismarked."

"You don't? Well I guess I'll take them as is," Lou said, "It's probably the right price anyway."

"Good sir," the hamster said, smiling again, "That'll be $11.50."

"I just gave you $10.95."

"I forgot to ring in tax, sir."

"Blame the Governor," the parakeet said, "Blame the Governor."

"Fine. Here," Lou said, handing over the rest. He had to pay the sum with pennies, but the hamster accepted it cheerfully, stowing the heavy paper sack in its cheek. The parakeet had no trouble bagging Lou's shoelaces. It nudged the bag across the counter.

"Thank you sir," the hamster said, "Have a nice day. Next."

"Have a nice day," the parakeet said, "Have a nice day."

Lou nodded to them both and left, carrying his bag of shoelaces in both arms through the broken automatic door. The bag was heavy, so he donated it to the Salvation Army volunteer outside. The soldier thanked him, turned and ran away with the bag, abandoning his pot of money and bell. Lou, angered by such blatant disrespect for charity, kicked over the pot. He waded through the puddle of change, crossed the street to the Science Building.

His office was thankfully on the ground floor, not in its usual basement location. He crossed the well-groomed lawn in the lobby, stepped up a flowery knoll to his desk. He was excited to be back from lunch, to return to work.

He plopped down in his chair, but didn't find the usual tattered leather comfort of his old office mate. Instead, he found Phillip. Occupying his chair.

Lou jumped off Phillip, startled at the man's unrequested, unrequired, presence. He landed awkwardly on the clear blotter on his desk, but did his best to make it appear as if he meant to land like that. His efforts were wasted, as Phillip was unaware of Lou. Lou cleared his throat.

"Do you have an appointment, son?" Lou asked, admiring his stern delivery. Phillip, however, was either unimpressed or didn't hear him.

"I said, 'Do you have an appointment,'" Lou shouted. His voice lifted him off his desk. On the way down, Lou noticed the clean green blotter again. He didn't remember a blotter. Where are all my papers? He thought, how can I enjoy this glorious afternoon without any papers? He glanced at the blue sky, fluffy clouds, green grass, and wished again for his work. When he landed gently on the desk, he remembered Phillip.

"Perhaps you know, son," he said, "Do you? Do you know where all my stuff is?" Phillip was oblivious. Lou wondered why he didn't reach out and touch the big young man. Phillip answered his private query immediately. Lou noticed that the troubled young man had a gun in his hands. A revolver. A big one, too, probably a forty-five or even a forty-eight. Phillip was playing with the gun, opening and closing the chamber. Checking that a single bullet was there. Snapping it home, spinning it.

Phillip hefted the gun. He aimed it at arm's length, almost touching Lou, checked the chamber. Picked up a picture on the desk, checked the chamber. Put the picture down, picked up a football, and checked the chamber. Aimed the gun at the newspaper on Lou's desk. Cocked it. Rubbed the barrel on his cheek...

"Wait a minute!" Lou cried, "I know what you're up to and don't even think about it. Not at my desk! I don't have tenure."

Lou's shouts went unheeded. He was powerless, forced to watch the strong young man in the expensive suit put a rusty gun to his head, prepare to pull the trigger. Lou couldn't understand why he didn't reach forward and grab the gun.

"C'mon now, Phillip. You know this isn't right," Lou said in a halfhearted soothing tone. Phillip hesitated, looked up. Lou felt his adrenaline crescendo. Phillip appeared to hear him. The young man looked at him, eyes unfocused, gun poised at his chin. He licked dry lips, spoke softly.

"You know," he said, calm, clear, "This isn't right." Phillip squeezed the trigger.

The percussion from the blast tossed Lou like a ball from his desk. He rolled down the hill, buried his head in tall grass until he counted to ten, then looked up. A mushroom cloud had formed on the other side of the hill.

Lou was glad he had the sense to count to ten. The others, now empty grey husks littering the green hillside, were not as sensible. Or lucky. Lou stood on the hillside, shaking his fist at the cloud. He took one step uphill and started shouting at the disbursing white cloud.

"How could you do this? Look what you did to these people! And God knows what'll come of this, what with all the trigger happy people in the world!"

Lou was in a rage. Smoke rose from his clenched fist. He wanted to shout more at the scenic sunset, but the hill interrupted.

"Yeah," it rumbled, vibrating Lou's ankles, "What he said."

Lou calmed down. He looked at the knoll, trying to spot the voice. It spoke again, verifying its source.

"I can't believe that fool did that, mister. All those people. And me. Look at me! And I'm supposed to be..."

"Here to help." Lou finished. He stepped down to level ground, faced the small hill, and continued, "That's what you're trained for, isn't it?"

"Well yes, yes it is. How did you know?" it said. It was the hill. Lou stepped back again, putting some room between himself and the talking mound of dirt. Fine, Lou thought, my first time talking to the scenery and apparently we've already met. He tilted his head up, in anthropomorphic deference to the hill's anatomy, and answered:

"We must have met before, sir. Do you come to this park often?" Lou asked, smacking his forehead at his stupid question. What difference would that make, he thought, I've never been here before.

"Me neither," the hill responded, ignorant of the fact that Lou was thinking, not speaking.

"I was thinking, not speaking."

"Oh, sorry."

"It's okay. Listen, Ted - it is Ted?"

"Yes, but how..."

"I don't know. But anyway, we've never been properly introduced, and you seem to need that."

"Yes I do, mister, yes I do! I'm Ted. Ted Pantagone," Ted said, delighted. Before continuing, he extended a bus-sized rock outcrop to Lou, "And you are?"

"I'm L..." Lou was unable to finish. Ted's friendly gesture hooked Lou in his armpit and swept him into the air. The upswing of Ted's handshake launched Lou from the atmosphere.

As he gained altitude, he was able to move against the G-force of escape velocity and look down in time to enjoy the stunning panorama that unfolded beneath him. He lost sight of Ted, still going through the motions of a handshake, quickly. He hurtled away from Earth, wisely remembering to hold his breath.

Lou was able to move more freely once in orbit. With his cheeks still full, he tried successfully to navigate with simple sidestroke motions. He paddled about for a few thousand miles then said:

"Wait a minute, I shouldn't be able to do this, space is a vacuum. There is no real molecular medium to move through.

"Or talk through. But I can hear what I said. Uh oh, that means I can breath too. This is weird." He stopped muttering to himself and took a deep breath. What filled his lungs tasted like a vacuum, but he was forced to accept the circumstances and keep breathing.

Lou looked down at the cloudless globe spinning majestically beneath him. He wished he had brought a camera to celebrate the rare moment. He fished around in his pants pockets anyway, got excited when he felt something metal at the bottom of his left front pocket. He turned the pocket out, accidentally setting himself spinning. He blew firmly in the opposite direction, stopping the rotation. The item from his pocket was floating a foot away. He inspected it.

It wasn't a camera. It was a penny. Shiny, six inches wide, freshly minted. A less familiar profile had replaced Lincoln's head. The new image was smiling, as if pleased to be pressed into the lowly coin. Lou smiled, rubbed the penny twice before he flipped it into the Pacific, currently passing beneath him. It landed with a small splash, wetting his shoes, and sank to the bottom. Without a camera to record it, Lou turned from the Earth and searched for his desk once more. It was, after all, time for work.

It was a simple task to spot his desk in the empty space around him. His office orbited the moon, as cluttered as he had left it. He rubbed his hands, excited by the voluminous projects awaiting him. He sidestroked over, checked for phone messages (none), and sat down to work.

A piece of lightly burnt parchment caught his attention first. It was new to the pile, resting on top. He picked it up, examined it. It was blank, save for six short rows of hieroglyphics. He couldn't make out the writing, but did note that the second and fifth lines were scratched out, in ballpoint pen.

Lou's heart became leaden. He gently replaced the document. Uninterested in the rest of the piles, he stood, left his office. He walked down the basement hall of the old building, up the stairs and outside onto the green lawn of its quad. He sat on the bench at the quad's center, under a shade tree.

No more work, he thought. No more work for now.

Gloria 5

Gloria skipped along empty halls, delighted to tour alone the most exciting building she knew. The Natural History Museum was a wonderland, a place to visit all the things she could never have. She rounded a corner, sliding gracefully on the polished marble floor. She noticed that the ubiquitous guards had abandoned their posts. Capitalizing on their absence, she darted to the nearest stairwell. As she had hoped, the wide banister was smooth, cleared of the marble ridges used to discourage sliding. She threw herself on the rail, careful not to lose any speed earned by her run down the hall.

She rode down four flights, careening around corners, accelerating, accelerating, accelerating. Her joy was total until the banister ended, superseded by a mild concern for her wellbeing. She was moving too fast to stop once she hit the polished floor. She landed on her feet, and glided with her soft-soled shoes straight through the empty main entrance hall and into the gallery that displayed the herd of elephants Teddy Roosevelt shot. Gloria knew that she would be unable to avoid them. She attempted to skate around them, but her destination was unaffected by her efforts.

She hopped safely over the rail protecting the elephants from bubble gum and curious children but, having no control once airborne, she slammed square into the lead elephant's trunk. She fell to the gravel floor, dazed and unaware that the angered elephant had reared and was poised to drop its stuffed tonnage on her. Gloria came to when she heard its angry bellow, and ducked out of the way just as a dusty umbrella stand foot thumped on the spot her head had occupied. She looked up, saw one of the elephant's rage-filled glass eyes, and ran out of the room.

Once across the threshold and in the comparative safety of the barren entry hall, Gloria checked over her shoulder. As she feared, the elephant still pursued her. She spotted the rest of the herd behind the angry leader. They were trumpeting support as they joined the chase.

Gloria skidded to a stop, pausing to think. She thought about where she was in the big building, and where she could run. Not much to think about, really - it was a big building. Big rooms, every doorway proudly built large enough for an elephant to pass through.

The thundering herd distracted her. She abandoned strategy, choosing instead to rely on her physical attributes. They hadn't failed her yet. Her legs took over, moving with powerful strides to the Hall of Ocean life. She dove through the doors, out across the small landing, over the rail and into the soft blue water. It was only simulated water, harmless, but the elephants didn't know that. They balked at the doorway, piling into each other. The lead elephant was not interested in a swim, and Gloria suspected that he feared the presence of the blue whale that floated placidly in the center of the room. Gloria patted the whale's urethane flank as she swam to the mezzanine level of the room. The whale whistled a polite response. Unsure if simulated water was safe to breathe, she exited before she was ready to. She stepped onto the empty floor of an unfamiliar hallway, leaving the elephants' angry trumpeting behind.

She walked into the Hall of Dinosaurs, her heels echoing off the walls of the huge chamber. This was her favorite chamber, and she was pleased that she had remembered to wear an evening gown for the occasion.

The brontosaur towered over her, looking majestic in its old tail-heavy pose. Its long neck sagged a bit under the weight of a chrome steel leash attached to its collar. It seem to accept the burden, however, as it was wagging that great tail vigorously. It cast brown eye sockets lovingly at the source of the leash, hidden from Gloria by its bulk. Curious, Gloria walked around the beast, following fist-sized links to the great bony hand that securely gripped a giant leather strap.

The hand was part of an exhibit she had not seen before. It was a human skeleton, twice the height of the brontosaur. Its carefully assembled bones also appeared brown and ancient. As with all fossils, the skeleton seemed to be smiling down at her. Gloria smiled back, waved. The human skeleton returned her greeting, and the brontosaur wagged its massive tail playfully. At a gentle shake of the leash, the brontosaur lowered its head to the floor, offering Gloria a stairway to its back.

She accepted readily, clambering up the long neck with a child's honest glee. The well-trained dinosaur held still until Gloria was nestled safely between its shoulder blades. Since she couldn't wrap her hands around the big bones securely, she wedged herself in as snugly as possible. She trusted the dinosaur, so she was not concerned for her safety.

Seeing that she was settled, the human lumbered forward. The brontosaur playfully joined it, running in circles around its master, who deftly kept the chain from fouling on its fossil legs. The brontosaur cavorted like a giant puppy on its first walk of the day. It pushed its head forward, testing the length of the leash. Then the excited exhibit was ready for a walk. It tugged the leash, pulling its master along behind it.

The human skeleton tried to control it, but the dinosaur was too large. It had its own agenda, and pursued it, ignoring its master's insistent tugs on the leash. It galloped through the hall, dragging its powerless master behind. Gloria cheered, slapped a stony shoulder blade in encouragement. This is it, she thought, this is it!

Her terrific joy dissipated when Gloria spotted the fossil's apparent destination. It was speeding toward the exit, innocent of the dreadful fact that it was too large to pass through the double doors. Gloria's mood swung to fear for the great dead animal. She ignored any threat to herself, wishing only to save the brontosaur bones. She tried to stop it, screaming frantic warnings. Its empty ear cavities did not register her pleas. She tried pulling back on its giant shoulder blades to slow the happy fossil, but they were too large for her to influence. She could not prevent the disaster.

Gloria looked to her left, intending to beseech the master's aid. One glance discouraged her. The human skeleton was already fully taxed. It hauled in the leash, but since it couldn't dig its hard round heels into the floor, it slid helplessly behind its charge. Its huge skull shook violently, jaws creaking open and closed in an attempt to issue a warning. The brontosaur didn't heed the leash or the mute command. Gloria felt a little better about her own failure. If its giant master couldn't control it, then her efforts, no matter how valiant, would be useless. There was a greater force at work. The beast, after millions of years of stasis, just wanted to run. Gloria understood, even as the chamber wall loomed a few short yards away.

As its head, far in front of the group, passed through the doorway, the dinosaur skeleton finally realized that the small opening could not accommodate its bulk. It backpedaled furiously, but the polished floor guaranteed its doom. The dinosaur's body slammed into the doorframe with a sickening crunch.

The beast's inertia pulled its bones, Gloria, and the human skeleton through the doorway. Only Gloria passed through in one piece. The two mammoth skeletons were now one pile of shredded bloody bones. Gloria sighed, rubbing the back of her hand across her forehead. She wished to reassemble the friendly pair, but she couldn't tell whose bone was whose, and so much blood coated the ivory mass that she didn't want to try. The only two bones she could identify were the skulls. The brontosaur's skull had landed in the center of the Hall of Meteorites, displacing the Ahnighito meteorite. The huge rock was lying on the floor beside the skull. Gloria wondered how long the floor would support its mass. The human skull, however, was the fossil that promised trouble. It had passed into the Hall of Minerals and Gems, and had crashed through one of the displays. Alarms clattered, but the steel door that protected the room had not dropped. Gloria saw her chance and ran in. She put her weight against the bloody surface of the human skull, slid it out of her way.

The broken case contained the precious gems collection. She had read that the rocks displayed were fakes, but she had to have them anyway. Hell, she thought, this is the Museum; gotta get what you can! With gloved hands, she plucked the stones, starting with the largest canary diamond, from their displays. She shoved them into her leather loot pouch. She hefted the Star of India before stowing it. It felt real. Looked real.

"It is," she said, "I don't believe it. All those years the lyin' bastards said they were fake. This can't really be happening!" She stifled her exclamations when she heard hurried footsteps over the clatter of the alarms. She ducked behind the bloody skull, checked the entrance. Guards had swarmed into the outer room, and were inspecting the damage wrought by the errant paleontology display.   Their engrossed study of the damage provided Gloria the opportunity to pluck the Eagle diamond from its wire nest before trying to sneak past them. She progressed well, holding one of the bronto's shoulder blades in front of her to conceal her movement. She crossed the room unseen, and was past the door, safe. Then she recognized one of the guards. She froze. The shoulder blade fell to the ground, shattered.

The guard snapped his unwashed face toward her. He broke into a lipless smile, shouted, "Hey! It's the bitch! The bitch from the boiler room!"

"Yeah," their leader, responded, stepping closer, "Let's do her again!"

Gloria was not interested in providing them the opportunity to 'do' her again. She picked up a rib lying near her feet, swung it like a baseball bat. The bone, being an ancient fossil, crumbled under the stress. Gloria dropped the butt of the empty threat, and ran. The ghouls gave chase.

She slid around a corner, almost passing the long central corridor of the museum. She dug her heels in, gained enough purchase to stop the slide and make the turn. She skated down the hall, accelerating away from the chattering scum that piled up on the floor behind her. She saw that their lack of control was only a temporary boon. Her pursuers picked themselves up and gave chase again, each of them panting and salivating in his own special way. She turned away, to concentrate on her own escape.

The silhouette of a man appeared at the far end of the hall. Assuming potential salvation in anyone in the museum, even a guard, she risked the treasure stowed in her pouch and headed straight for him. As she approached, the figure clarified. Gloria mimicked the brontosaur bones' response to the small door when she recognized the man, and the shiny floor provided an identical response.

Her father smiled at her, eyes closed under his tilted black fedora. He put his hands out, catching her shoulders, stopping her. His lined face bore friendly concern.

"Dad," Gloria said, her heart racing, "I'm in trouble. Those kids are back! You must help me!"

"Excuse me miss," her father said, "Do I know you?"

"No!"

"I thought not," he said, still pleasant. He still had her shoulders clamped in his fists, preventing Gloria from moving.

"Dad, it's me. Gloria! Now isn't the time for fun!"

"Sorry miss. Can't place that name. Maybe you have me confused with someone else?"

Gloria could wait no longer. She bent her legs and sprang into the air, over her father. She kicked him on the way down, creating a black hole in his head. She didn't care, and only looked back to see if the boys were still after her. They were, but her father stood stupidly between her and them, black emptiness oozing from his head.

The adolescent rape gang, still out of control, slid as a group into her father, forcing the same carnage as the dinosaur crash: flesh, bones and blood everywhere. Not one entire assailant remained to chase her. Her father had inadvertently helped after all. Gloria skated on, enjoying the ride through the empty museum until she skidded into the Hall of Late Mammals, bumped into an unexpected glass wall, fell down.

She rose unsteadily to her feet. The floor was no longer slick, but she felt an inexplicable flash of vertigo. She surveyed the hall. She was alone again. Nothing was broken, the stuffed moose behind the glass didn't move. The wind-up travel clock on the floor had stopped, silencing the alarms. Gloria shook off the feeling and resumed her solitary tour of the museum.

She didn't get far. Around the corner from the moose diorama, she encountered a man, teetering on the low rail in front of the grizzly bear display. A familiar man, though she couldn't remember his name. She did know, however, that he had interrupted her tour, her hard won peace, and that he didn't belong there. This was not unusual, Gloria surmised, from the look of him. She folded her arms and spread her heels in a pose of defiance. The man spoke. His mouth moved for a few seconds, but Gloria heard nothing. She waited, confused and a little angry at the man's petulance.

"Gloria," he said when finally audible, "What the hell are you doing here?"   He sounded amiable enough, but Gloria wouldn't allow him to soften her.

"Me? What about you? And how do you know my name? What are you doing here? This is my building today! You can come tomorrow!"

"I had a feeling about that," the man said, genuinely apologetic.   Gloria decided to allow him a chance to redeem himself. Besides, she thought, the museum is a place for showing people things, not for solitary viewing.

"Well come on," the man said, stepping from his perch to the floor, "Walk with me."

"Where?" Gloria asked.   The man ignored her, began to walk.

"I think we all need to think," he said after a few quiet paces down the empty hall.

"That's not an answer," Gloria said. He ignored her again. Uncharacteristically, she didn't mind, and followed along at his side. In time the man spoke.

"So, you know what's going up here?"

"You speak in riddles, mister," Gloria answered, "Up? Here? Nothing new that I know of - most of these critters were shot decades ago, I guess. Nothing except you. Are you up? You know, on something?"

The man paused, seriously considering her sarcasm.

"No," he said, checking his bare wrist, "Won't be up for quite some time. Days, maybe."

Gloria wondered about her acceptance of him while the man remained still, pensive. She grew anxious when he suddenly stared at her, through her. Then he crossed his eyes. She was confused by the gesture, and agitated at the response it elicited from her. While his eyes remained crossed, Gloria felt heavier, older. Her hair felt a little different on her neck. Curly; it felt curly. The man uncrossed his eyes as suddenly as he had crossed them. He stepped back, shaken.

"Oh," he said, rubbing the bridge of his small nose.

The man began walking again, winding swiftly through the exhibits. He looked straight ahead, focusing on nothing. Gloria tried stopping for a better look, or running ahead to show the stranger her favorite dioramas, but he was intently uninterested. Gloria tired of the man wasting her time, and chose to confront him.   She stepped in front of him, but failed to break his concentration or stride.   Enough is enough, she thought as she stuck her foot in front of the man.

He tripped, fell gracefully into a glass display case depicting life underground. She stood over him, saw that his eyes had come back into focus.

"You're doing a great job ruining my day here, bud. I can't believe you can walk through this awesome place, ignoring it all, God!"

The man acknowledged her presence with an unexpected expression of fear. Without answering, he stood up and ran down the hall. Gloria didn't bother to follow: the hall he toured led right back to where she stood.   She waited patiently, arms folded, wondering who had stolen the zebra's stripes.

"Well," she said aloud, "At least I know now that zebras are really black with white stripes."

The man returned. He was on his hands and knees, and crawled to a stop at the spot from which he had rushed. He stood, brushed off his jeans. He had changed, once again appearing nonchalant, calm. He put his hands in his pockets. Smiled.

"So," he said conversationally, "What brings you to this fine place?"

"You ask a lot of strange questions, mister," Gloria said, "But if you must know, I took the..."

"Claire," a voice boomed inside her.

"...subway." She clutched her abdomen from the pain of the unspoken name. She felt it pushing against the walls of her stomach. She doubled over, trying to remember what she had for lunch, and why it had said 'Claire.' She felt her highly toned diaphragm begin to rip from the pressure of 'Claire.' The man watched in fascination as she backed away. He was saying something, something about pretending. She couldn't hear him clearly over the wind from his wagging index finger. Gloria tried to lean into that wind, but, weak from the utterance of 'Claire' inside her, she was unable to keep her balance. The invisible fist of air punched her off her feet and shot her like a projectile into a painted background. She stood quickly, wary of the strange, paper environment.

She was in a wooded glen, resembling pictures she had seen of the Pacific Northwest. They were not normal woods. The trees and rocks were all two dimensional, and had lost their luster. Even the green leaves and grass were dirty, faded. Gloria connected the scenery to recent memory, and to a small family of moose standing all too still in the distance. She realized that she was inside the painted background of the moose diorama. A stuffed squirrel gathered oil painted nuts at her feet. Gloria picked up the stiff creature, pet its wiry fur.

"I always said I really wanted to get into this museum," she said, "Might as well enjoy it." She verified that her pouch of jewels was still with her, surveyed her flat surroundings once more, and then set off to explore. She was in no hurry to leave the exhibit, just yet.

Howard 5

"Should've used the money machine," Howard said, "Of course, my safe deposit box would never fit through the little slot." He waited with the rest of the regular bank customers, winding slowly through the rope corral.

It was a busy day at the bank. He felt like he was waiting on line for a Disney World attraction. He wondered if the bank wasn't giving cash away, or if indeed he had gotten on the wrong line again.

He watched the faces pass with each trip down the long stretch of the corral. Empty, tired faces of people waiting were the norm, with but one exception.

Claire.

She was moving with the line about one chute length ahead of him. He was shuffling at the same pace, so they were destined to pass within a few feet of each other shortly. He paced with the flow impatiently until he was passing Claire. She wasn't looking.

"Claire," he said, as though he was hailing an old acquaintance. She looked up, smiled. Good God, she looked up and smiled.

The line quickly dragged them beyond the realm of polite conversation. While waiting for the next pass, Howard pictured her. Except for a missing arm and suppurated left cheek, she looked good.

They each rounded their respective ends, beginning the trek back to the center again. In anticipation, Howard groped for something witty to say. The moment arrived before he found suitable words. Claire smiled (he assumed it was a smile - it was hard to tell with no lips for reference).

"Howard," she lisped pleasantly.

"Claire," he responded, "You look good."

"I know I don't, but thanks."

"You'll be home later, dear?"

"Of course, Howard; just as soon as I'm done here."

"What's you're transaction? I'd be glad to make it for you." Howard offered. They had nearly passed again. Howard leaned backwards, stretching to prolong contact. His delay fouled the continuity of the line, disturbing other waiters.

"Silly," Claire said over her shoulder, "I don't need money. I'm here for the roller coaster. See you at dinner, say... 8:00?"

Howard was unable to respond, as the line had shuffled him away from her again. That was okay, though. Dinner was always at eight. Claire knew that.

His beautiful wife had rounded her last turn in the corral. His final image of her came at the moment she presented her ticket to the uniformed attendant manning the roller coaster entry.

He didn't mind. He would see her later. He found Claire, she found him, and all was well. Even the line shortened.

He heard "Next!" shouted from a window far away. Having expecting his wait to be longer, he was surprised that the teller referred to him. He lifted his head, put a thumb to his chest.

"Me?" he called to the distant window. The teller was leaning out over her high counter so he could see her, but he still couldn't make out her face.

"Yeah you!" she shouted, her strong tenor yell made Howard jump, "You're next."

"Okay, I'm coming," he said, jogging to the window. The teller smiled at him.

"May I help you?" she asked pleasantly.

"Of course you can," Howard quipped, "Why else would I be here?" She tossed him a look of mild annoyance. Howard figured she'd heard it before.

"You might've been on line for the roller coaster."

"Yes, I suppose I might've. But I'm not. I'm here to get into my safe deposit box."

"Must be a big box. Have you brought your card and key?"

"No, I haven't."

"That's fine. Follow me sir," the teller said, walking away from her window. Before she disappeared, Howard climbed through the window, caught up to her.

The teller, a petite grey haired woman in a flannel nightgown, strode briskly, forcing Howard to take longer steps. She led him to the back door of the bank and into a dirty alley.

Across the alley, flanked by full trash dumpsters, was the worn entrance to a Chinese apothecary. She led him into it. A bell chimed when the wooden door opened.

An old oriental man, complete with black robe and wispy beard, manned the shop. He was sitting at a high accountant's desk, busily working figures with a quill pen. The bell alerted him.

"Did he bring his card and key?" the shopkeeper asked in perfect English.

"No," the teller responded cheerfully.

"Then how will we know which drawer is his?"

"It's right there, silly," she said, pointing to a top row drawer of the apothecary cabinet that lined the wall behind the shopkeeper. Faded Chinese symbols adorned the face of each drawer.

The shopkeeper followed the teller's pointing finger, smiled and nodded.

"So it is," he said, "So it is." He climbed off his stool, walked half the length of his narrow store to a stepladder that rode on rails mounted high on the wall. He positioned the ladder under the drawer (top row, second from left), and climbed.

"Don't know why these boxes are always on the top row," he said as he slid the long wooden drawer out of the cabinet. He tossed it down to the teller, who gracefully caught the steel safety deposit box. She cradled it in her arms, looked up at Howard.

"No key, right?"

"Right. Sorry."

"No problem. But I'd best get it started for you."

"Thanks."

The teller wrapped manicured fingers under the lid on the locked box. She gritted her teeth and bent the end of the lid back. She smiled.

"There. Now let me take you to a private booth."

She left the stainless steel and marble vault, gesturing for him to follow. Howard did, into one of the Port-O-Potties lining the wide marble hallway. She set the box across the seat.

"I'll leave you alone now. Just turn off the 'occupied' sign when you want me to come back."

"Okay. Thanks."

"No problem, sir," the woman said, her small black eyes and high cheeks set in perfect sincerity. She left, flipping the lever on her way out.

Howard took the extra precaution of sliding the flimsy privacy bolt home before he lowered his pants. He picked up the box, sat on the seat, and rested its cold mass on his bare thighs.

He pulled it open, with some difficulty. He appreciated the teller's wisdom in starting it for him. He dropped the loose lid between his legs, allowing it to splash into the tank below.

The box's contents were mixed: stacks of cash, some stock certificates, the kids' birth certificates, deeds, Claire's good jewelry...

"Wait a minute. I don't have any kids."

He removed two slips of official paper, each adorned with an embossed seal. Two names filled the appropriate blanks: Nick and Nathan. On closer examination, he saw they were postdated two and four years, respectively.

He held them for a moment, waiting for the obvious figments of his imagination to dissolve. His pause allowed the ink on the painfully permanent documents to darken. He held them in his shaking hand, still not convinced. He rechecked the name of the mother.

Claire.

"Claire, but how? I know she's fine now, but fine enough for kids?" Howard asked as he wiped and stood up.

"This is great," he said, emptying the remaining contents of the box into the holding tank, "This means I was right from square one. Claire's okay, or she'll get better. The whole meat counter thing was a hoax. Nick and Nathan prove it."

Howard tossed the box down the hole, his excitement adding power to his drop, resulting in holding tank water splashing up through the hole, engulfing him.

The fetid cologne did not dampen his spirit. He could stink now, because he had his sons' birth certificates in his hand. He proudly read them again, or at least made an attempt. Some sewage had landed on them, obscuring the print.

Shaking his head, Howard unwound a wad of toilet paper, finishing the roll. He wiped the shit off the birth certificates. He also wiped off the words. The papers were blank, reduced by his foolish splashing and wiping to useless sheets of legal paper.

"No!" Howard cried, feeling the weight of what he had done bend his bones. He let the two sheets slip from his trembling hands, watched them dissolve to mist before hitting the stained floor.

Howard's pain shifted to rage. Rage at his own mistake, at starting over again, and for losing two sons and a wife just because he couldn't put up with a little shit. He burst from the stall, breaking its dead bolt.

He crossed the executive washroom in one stride, ignoring a row of his blue-suited vice-presidents preening themselves at the sinks. He stormed down his quiet, tastefully carpeted hall to his office. He crashed through the plaster wall at the point where his door should have been, into his office.

He started to cross the office. His heart was racing, his breath heavy, and he needed to sit down. A man balancing carefully on his massive antique desk disrupted his charge.

He tore off his tie and projected the best glare he could manage at the good man. Before he could verbally express his anger, the man addressed him. His words were garbled, irritating. Howard was ready to call security when the stranger became rational.

"Howard," he said, his voice soothing, "What the hell are you doing here?" Not all that soothing, Howard thought.

"Me? What am I doing here?" Howard asked. He found it easy to maintain his patience with the man as he continued, "What about you, mister? I own this place. This is my building. My only space left. I don't want it to be yours."

The man looked down on him, grey eyes bathed in moist empathy. Or dancing with amusement. He spoke soft words once more:

"I had a feeling about that."

Howard melted. He was unable to sustain his stern posture. He wanted to hug the man.

"Well come on," the man said, "Walk with me. I think we all need to think." Howard wondered at the man's odd tense, but passed it off as eccentric behavior. He stepped back to give the man room to hop from the desk.

The man hit the floor walking, headed straight out the hole in the wall. Howard followed obediently, happy to assist the man on a tour of his building. The stranger strolled at an easy gait through the Barlowe building.

The man made short order of the executive suites, ignoring Howard's gestures and handy facts about his building. Howard followed the hurried tourist into the elevator, then out onto the 27th floor, without pushing a button.

The tour proved unrewarding on that floor as well. The man simply cruised the main hall, ignoring stated points of interest, then re-entered the elevator. Once more, without doors closing, the man exited onto the 26th floor.

Howard followed along, finding himself becoming less tour guide than security guard. He wanted to trust the man, but something was amiss about his exploration of Howard's building.

The man changed his pattern on the eighth floor - in the personnel department. He stopped short, allowing Howard to pass by. Howard turned. The man, still sporting an amicable grin, spoke.

"So," He asked in a conversational tone, "You know what's going up here?"

"Nope," Howard answered, "Nothing new that I know of. And I would know, since I put it up in the first place. Except, is there something you know? Is that why you're here? Are you up to something?"

"No," the man said, "Won't be for quite some time. Days, maybe."

Howard puzzled over that response while the man continued to stand in one spot, concentrating through Howard on a spot behind him. His stomach churned in apprehension at the new position the man adopted.

The man was still, silent, and cross-eyed. Howard felt light, small, fidgety. The sensation continued in concert with his roiling stomach until the man uncrossed his tired grey eyes.

"Oh," the man said, uneasy.   He shook the feeling, reverting back to his earlier, easy calm before resuming his tour. Howard followed again, obliging and watchful.

The renewed stroll had changed.   The man stopped observing. He walked quietly, as though with blinders on, through Howard's tastefully decorated floors.

They followed the same hallway, elevator, new floor pattern to the basement. Howard didn't remember passing through the bottom eight floors.

In the well-lit, dry basement, the man adopted a new pattern. His tour became a search. A blind search. Blind enough to send him, and Howard, through two sets of cinder block walls. Finally, completely disoriented and quite nervous, the man fell backwards onto a stack of discarded PC monitors.

"That's it," Howard said, "I've had enough.   You're not going to have me doing this tour guide bit all day. I've better things to do. Besides, you're doing a great job ignoring it all, mister."

The man, startled by Howard's statement, jumped to his feet and tried to run away. Howard did not sense the danger the man thought he was in, but stayed with him just in case.

The new pace was invigorating. Good exercise, Howard thought. They ran, walked, and even crawled. Howard liked crawling the best. He hadn't had a good crawl in years.

In time, the man either tired or lost interest, and stopped. Howard stopped too.   The man faked his earlier amicable expression, his eyes betraying his true fears.

"So," the man spoke in a strained casual tone, "What brings you to this fine place?"

"Claire," Howard said, not hearing his automatic response to a simple question. Instead, he felt echoes of another unspoken sentence twist his ribcage. His gasp of pain obscured the words, words that were not his.

The man was backing away, rapidly. He wagged his index finger at Howard, uttered an unheard reprimand. Howard fell back onto the Port-O-Potty seat, the snapshots at his side launching into the air from his impact.

He scrabbled for the photos as they fluttered down from the ceiling. Two pictures. Two boys. His sons.

He stood, snatched at the airborne photos but missed, allowing them to fall through the seat into the holding tank. Howard stuck his head in the hole, watched them tumble into the shadowy chamber. Small splashes sounded the end of their journey. His eyes watered from the stench. He was forced to look away.

"Damn," he said, pulling up his pants. He heard Claire's broken voice through the plastic door, summoning him. He unlatched and swung open the door. Claire was there, or at least most of her was. She waved; he waved.

He didn't want to leave the Port-O-Potty, or its contents. Claire spoke again, drawing him. Threatening another exit.

"Howard," she slurred, "There you are. My ride's over now. Let's go home."

Howard had never imagined a sentence could feel so good. He stepped out of the Port-O-Potty, back into the shining vault. He heard a splash.

Behind him. Beneath him. Two splashes. Sounds of struggle, of gasping for air. He turned, stepped back into the stall. Looked in the hole.

His sons were splashing in the holding tank below. Desperately struggling to keep their heads above sludge. The plastic door slammed shut behind him.

Howard pushed it open. Claire waited, arm outstretched, lipless face glowing. The door closed. He peered down the hole. The boys were tiring. He pushed the door open again. Claire was further away, more disintegrated.

"Howard," she whispered, "I have to go. Come with me, now. Or never." Howard caved in and forced a reluctant foot out the door.

"Dad!" a panicked cry sounded from below. Howard paused. Claire didn't.

"This is it Howard. Please. Come with me. I need you here. With me." Howard obeyed, moved his rear foot.

"Dad! Help!" his son shouted, Nathan perhaps. With no more thought for Claire, Howard turned, slammed the Port-O-Potty door and dove through the seat. Into the sludge to rescue his unborn sons.

Alice 5

Alice was impressed by the highly polished hardwood floor. Every piece of parquet shined brightly, bringing out the best in the wood. They exploded in a pattern of concentric circles so intricate that Alice could not view it all at once. Its depth, its heady complexity, astonished her, and the story she knew it tried to tell saddened her. The walls, however, failed to impress her: they were little more than blank wallboard, unbroken by windows or doors. Still, the small room was brightly lit and that floor was fascinating.

Three small objects littering the floor at the center of the pattern constituted the room's decor. Alice squatted, wishing to admire something other than the floor in the dreary place. The first object to draw her was a shard of glass. It reflected cold grey light onto her freshly shaved thighs. The dismal glimmer evoked a shiver in Alice. A forgotten moment of horror tapped at the back of her head, seeking entry. Alice put her thumb and forefinger against the glass and plinked the dark memento away. Once out of sight, Alice felt at ease, and hopeful once more for an aesthetically appealing item.

A limp rag doll lay folded near the center blocks of the pattern. Alice knelt close, poked it with her fingernail. It seemed harmless enough. She gently straightened its back, freeing it from the humiliating fate of a life with its head between its legs. Too much of that around, Alice thought. She rotated the soft doll, eager to enjoy its friendly painted smile and button eyes.

She got neither. The doll finished the turn itself, snapping around to face Alice. It stood, lifted its head toward her. Bloody red eyes inspected her with unbridled malice. Two rows of long, narrow yellow teeth gnashed at the opening of a black maw. The dolly was pointing a small stuffed finger at Alice. Yet another distant, unwanted memory threatened to surface. Avoiding it, and seeing no value in keeping the doll around, Alice backhanded it sharply. The doll chirped in surprise, threw its stuffed arms in the air and ran away. It ducked into a rat hole that adorned an untrimmed corner. Alice sighed. She hardly considered the third item, a dusty jar of mustard. She ignored its arms and legs, its raspy growl. She turned away from it, headed back to bed.

She padded across the dark bedroom, careful not to wake Ed. He'd had a hard day. Always a hard day. She lifted the blankets, slid between the sheets to rub up against him. When she did, his jeans and t-shirt abraded her bare skin.

"Now what?" she asked aloud. She climbed over the man in her bed and lay on his other side, to get a look at his face.

The face wasn't Ed's. It was the stranger, the man who had made a career of invading her world. In another time or place, Alice may have been pleased at the situation, but her night was not going well. His intrusion into her bedroom, into Ed's spot on the bed, was not welcome. On top of that, the bastard had his eyes crossed! I don't need this, Alice thought. With minimal effort, she forced herself to consciousness. She awoke. Ed snored quietly in bed beside her. She rubbed his back, found no cloth, and pulled her hand away, careful not to wake him.

`She put her hands up behind her head, between soft hair and soft pillow. She lay with her eyes open, relaxing in the serenity of the quiet evening. Ed had left his reading light on again, so Alice could clearly see the ceiling moving above her.

It was breathing, flexing in and out in a steady, relaxed motion. Alice blinked her eyes, assuming they were tricking her, but was wrong. The ceiling was alive, and had taken an interest in her. Organic plaster stretched its stucco belly down toward her. She evaded its attack by rolling to the edge of her bed. The lithe plaster followed, threatening to smother her. Its adjustments were silent, with an alarming level of mobility for a ceiling. Alice jumped from the bed to the floor, wondering why it didn't go after Ed. The floor offered no refuge. The ceiling followed her to it, reached for her. With nowhere else to run, Alice gave up, prayed for the ceiling to leave her alone. When it was an inch from her face, and she was certain all was lost, she felt a tug on her wrist.

"...Alice," Ed was saying, his familiar voice calming her, "It's all right. It was just a dream. Wake up."

Alice woke up. She was sitting straight up in bed. No lights were on. She could see Ed's silhouette in the moonlight. It was him this time. The ceiling had ceased its attack.

"No," she said, gasping, "It was real. I was awake. The ceiling was moving."

"The what?"

"The ceiling. Didn't you see it? It came after me!"

"It did, huh?" Ed said patiently, "The ceiling's fine, dear. At least it is now. Why don't you try to go back to sleep?" His words made sense, but Alice was still nervous. She let Ed hold her tightly until she heard the steady breath of his slumber. Still wide-awake, she gently broke his embrace and rolled over to switch on the light at her side of the bed.

The bed, between her and her nightstand, was a black emptiness surrounded by moonlit gossamer sheets. Unable to reverse her momentum, Alice fell into the cold abyss.

She fell a very short distance, landed on her back in something soft, cool, unseen. She could not see out of the darkness, but felt she could reach the light at her nightstand. She felt the table but the lamp was out of reach. She tried unsuccessfully to stretch for it. Something held her fast to the bottom of the darkness. Undaunted, Alice reached a little further, waved her free arm about for her lamp. She bumped it, but was still unable to reach the switch below the bulb. She found the cord and pulled the lamp over. It fell into her hand, the switch nudging her finger. She pushed it. Daylight spread over her, and her visitor.

It was him. That bastard interloper, and he had pinned her deep in her bed, holding her firmly with his boot. She assumed it was a hiking boot, from the shape of its pain, but she couldn't see it. It was buried deep in her, pressed against the front of her spine. Alice thought that pressure should have hurt much more than it did. At first, she suspected that she was in shock, but when she moved, she found her nervous system was in perfect condition. Every nerve, every fiber of her body exploded at her slightest wriggle.

She tried to lie still. She looked at the man standing above her. He was regarding her with a wry smile. As if he were guilty of some clever mischief. Alice wanted to throw the lamp at him, but flexing her fingers brought stars. The man spoke to her. She could feel the vibration of his voice on her ribs.

"Boy," he said, mildly concerned, "I'll bet that hurts a lot."

"Only when I laugh," Alice lied, "Ha, ha." She did her best to hide her pain from the man. He had enough of his own. She felt relieved when he smiled, released a small, honest laugh. She felt relieved, but her body felt like it was digesting a bag of glass from the vibration of his amusement.

He became quiet, lost in thought as he stood silently in her. Alice didn't mind his reverie, since he wasn't moving. However, he was still imbedded in her belly, and that situation needed immediate attention. She groped for a voice that wouldn't wreck her or sound too demanding.

"When you're through pondering the obvious," she said, slowly, carefully. It sill hurt. She finished, "You want to get your shoe out of my belly?" He snapped from his thoughts, looked down at her as if she had just appeared. He smiled.

"Sure Alice," he said. Ow, ow, ow, Alice thought.

"I appreciate that," she said.

The man raised his foot, succeeding only in hoisting her up from the bed. Alice couldn't quietly endure the ripping, tearing electric shock of such movement. She cried out in pain, grabbed his shin. He responded by standing on her, putting all his weight between her hips for leverage, and pulling again.

"Enough!" she shrieked, holding him with both hands, trying to push him away. He held his ground, or whatever, and his boot didn't budge. He did, however, stop moving long enough to frown down at her. She wondered where Ed was through all this. Probably asleep.

"Listen," the man said, still calm, "You've got to lighten up or I'll never get it out." Alice would have laughed if she could; a 200 pound man was fondling her insides with his foot, and he told her to lighten up.

"Lighten up?" she asked, curbing her natural sarcasm, "You're the one on me!" When she shouted, knives turned near her lungs.

"In me!" she added.

"True," the man said, nonplussed, "But we still need to work together." Alice was at a loss, unable to imagine how she was to contribute to the fine new team the man proposed. He had, happily in one respect, stopped trying on his own, though, so she knew she had to think of something. She thought hard until the next spasm, and then had a brainstorm.

"Fine," she said, trying not to move her mouth when she spoke, "Why don't you untie your shoe and pull your foot out? It'll take half the pain away, and might free up the shoe."

"Untie it?" the man asked, doubtful. Oh, come on, Alice thought.

"Yes, mister," she said, containing her frustrations for her own sake, "Can you do that?"

"Well," the man said, rubbing his chin, "I suppose. But I'd hate to be out one shoe. I just bought these, you know." Alice was milking the last reserves of her patience with the man.

"Mister," she breathed through her teeth, "If you're not outta me in five seconds you won't need two shoes! Now untie it!"

"Okay, okay," the man said, "Sheesh. Nobody can take a joke anymore." He bent down to his shoe, mindless about tempering his movements. He shoved his hands deep into her abdomen. As his fingers entered, Alice questioned the sense of her suggestion. She regretted it when he started groping around. And forgot it when he grasped a tube near her pelvis. She forgot everything, except how to scream.

"Those are not shoelaces!" she informed him. The man reacted instantly, letting go of his catch. Her body vibrated in pain for an eternity.

"Oh," was all he offered, "Sorry."

"It's all right," Alice sighed, "I got enough kids."

"Shall I try again?"

"Please," Alice said, shocked by her consent.

The man dug in again, rooted around. The second effort brought only major pain; bearable. In time, he stopped moving and looked at her, smiling slyly.

"Here we go," he said, setting about untying his shoe.

She felt his wrists move inside her as they worked the laces. She noticed he wasn't wearing a watch.

"Thank God," Alice said, wondering why she hadn't passed out from the pain. The man suddenly pulled his hands free, rose to his feet, pulled his bare foot free (big foot, Alice thought, big foot), and stepped off her. He continued to stand on her bed, regarding her. Surveying his damage, she thought. And where the hell is Ed? This guy could be standing inside him, and he still wouldn't wake up.

"You seem okay," the man said, "'cept for the hole." Alice smiled, unable to stay angry at the man. She didn't know what it was about him. Maybe the absence of pain softened her. She let the man take her by the hands, help her out of bed. He examined her from head to toe. Alice hoped he was looking for more damage. She took his cue and passed a careful glance at her midsection. She tried to make it look casual, but the sight of a hiking boot jutting from her belly shook her. She felt her face flush with embarrassment. Well, she thought, at least it doesn't hurt and there's not too much blood, but it sure is ugly.

She pulled her hands slowly from the man's, in an effort to attract as little attention to the shoe in her abdomen as possible. She wanted to turn away, but that would imply that the boot bothered her; she couldn't have that. She looked into the man's grey eyes, held them. She forgot her original intent to hold his gaze after she fell into its depths. She gathered herself, sought some sensible excuse to turn away.

"Listen mister," she said, nodding towards her bathroom door, "Why don't you let me go in there and freshen up a bit? I'll be right out."

"Good idea," the man said brightly. He was pleased with her decision and walked her across her bedroom to the door. Alice stepped in quickly, shut and latched the louvered door behind her. She set to work immediately. She tried first to remove the shoe by simply pulling it. She bent both arms inward, got a good grip on it, but the boot wouldn't budge. Alice sighed; she didn't have enough leverage to pull. She tried rubbing against a wall to scrape it out. This failed too, and the wall was cold. Soft soap didn't work either.

"Everything coming out okay?" the man called from the bedroom. Alice snapped her head up, checked the door to be certain he wasn't coming in to help.

"Fine," she shouted back, "It should be out in a minute." Her response reminded Alice of another item she periodically removed from near the shoe's current location. Experimentally she felt around the hole for the lace the man untied. She found it, slid her fingers to its tip and removed it.

Without hesitation, she crossed to the towel rack, threw the towels to the floor. She carefully tied the shoelace to the chrome rod, tested it. Then she squatted and backed away from the rack. The shoelace tightened. The boot began to slide out of her abdomen. It came out slowly, painlessly. She felt her insides closing in around the vacuum the boot created as it exited. Then, with a champagne cork pop, it was out, swinging from the towel rack. It was clean. And it was a high-top sneaker.

"Funny. I was sure it was a hiking boot," Alice said. She untied it, walked to the door and cracked it. The man was still there, waiting. She tossed him his sneaker.

She was about to close the door when she felt an odd wriggling sensation in the hole. Worried, she looked down for the first time since the man held her hands. She sighed with relief, pulled out the clean sweat sock she had forgotten to remove. She tossed it out the door.

"There," she heard the man say, "All fixed." She closed the door, stepped into the shower.

Sunlight filtered through the bathroom's stained glass window, flashing a rainbow on Alice's slick body as she rinsed shampoo suds from her hair. She turned off the water, ending the warm flow. As she reached through the plastic curtain for a towel, she remembered in full the sneaker dream. She automatically shot a glance and a hand to her flat, white, intact belly. She shook her head, laughed at herself.

"God," she said, "The dreams I've been having lately. I must lay off the Mexican food."

She pulled on her bathrobe, went into the bedroom to start her day. Her chores. Ed was still under the covers, asleep.

Everyone's asleep, Alice thought, tightening her terrycloth belt. Just me. I'm up. Always up first.

"Hey Ed, this isn't fair," she said to her husband. She playfully grabbed her pillow, cold already, and threw it at him. He didn't react. He was a light sleeper, so she knew he was awake. Ed always woke up at the slightest noise.

"Oh, no, you don't. If I'm up, you're up. I don't care if it is Sunday." She tossed her pillow again, causing a stir. The blankets rustled, Ed rolled over to face her. Most of his covers came off, revealing his chubby middle-aged body. Chubby but powerful, Alice thought. His head was still covered.

"Get up, Ed. Face the day. It's gorgeous out!" Kneeling on the sheets, she reached down and pulled the remaining covers from Ed's head. His face was yellow, pasty.

"Jeez Ed, you must've had a wild time last night, too. I don't care. Wake up." She shook his shoulders. Ed opened his eyes.

Alice jumped off the bed. She stood a safe distance from him and stared, masking her revulsion. Rather than revealing his baby blues, Ed's eyelids uncovered two pools of blackened dry blood. Alice panicked.

"Ed! What happened?" she asked, hand on her mouth.

"Why, nothing, dear." Ed said. He smiled, displaying two rows of razor edged yellow teeth. Ed's head became a rag doll's. A horrid, threatening rag doll.

"No!" Alice shrieked, "Not more!" She ran for the bathroom, pulled open the door. A woman, or what was left of a woman, prevented her entry. The mutilated corpse reached out a gangrenous arm to Alice. The other arm, a rotted stump, flapped uselessly at her. The cadaver smiled permanently through an exposed jawbone. Alice gagged, turned, and leapt through the bedroom window into darkness.

She landed on her face on a surface she didn't recognize: a few inches of hard, splintered floor followed by a foot of loose stones, then more wood. It was too dark to find any resolution in her surroundings. She concentrated on the darkness, denying its cloak, and her world brightened to steel dawn. She wished once more for darkness.

The cuff of her jeans leg, frayed from years of barefoot living, was caught on a spike. Alice stood on a railroad tie, trapped in the path of an approaching train. An odd train, the first passenger train without a roof she had ever seen. Filled with screaming passengers, it was moving toward her at high velocity. Alice tugged at her pants. She couldn't loosen them or rip them. Her belt buckle was jammed, preventing their removal. Her back against the concrete wall that spanned the tracks, she could do little more than wait for the train to hit her, crushing her into the wall. She wondered what it would feel like.

"Probably not good."

Deciding to avoid the answer, Alice bent to the soft fill to remove the railroad spike. It slid effortlessly from its position by the rail. She held the rusty object near her eyes for a moment, shaking her head. When she saw the train coming into focus behind the spike, she remembered her plight and ran for cover. It was a big train, and a big wall. That told her that a big bang was imminent.

She scanned the area. Though attractive in a pastoral sort of way, the local terrain was flat, offering nothing in the way of shelter from the coming blast. She was ready to give up when she spotted a small hill lumbering away from the track. She chased after it, catching up to it in short order. As she dropped to safety behind it, she noticed a small crowd of sightseers at its summit. She tried to warn them, but went unheeded.

The train hit. Its impact with the wall filled the air with a brilliant white flash. The people on the hill screamed in tormented surprise while they could. The flash illuminated their bones, burned off their clothes, their skin. The shock wave from the crash tore their remains loose, mingled them with other debris in the terrible wind. Alice shook her head violently, vanquishing the pitiful image.

She snapped awake, stifled her screams, and cautiously surveyed her surroundings. The morning sun sent soft yellow streams through the windows. Her bedroom was warm, bright; correct. She felt the bulge next to her, then looked. Her husband faced her, still sleeping peacefully. He was warm. He was correct.

"Now if only you'd be bright," she whispered, pushing a lock of his hair into place. She stretched, cast a glance at the clock radio. The brass hands read 10:30.

"Omigosh," Alice said, sitting up, "I overslept. Ed, it's time to get up. Lots to do today."

She stood, crossed the cold floor to the bathroom, wrapping her flimsy nightgown tight. Ed groaned behind her, indicating that he might also be rising soon. She hoped he would sleep a while longer; she needed some quality time in the bathroom.

Alice closed the louvered door behind her, absently pressing home the courtesy lock. She remembered portions of the previous night's dreams, and looked forward to a long hot shower to rinse away their sticky residue. She stretched her foot across the blue tile floor to the scatter rug in front of the sink, sparing her feet one extra chill. She then stepped over to the rug in front of the toilet. She sat, peed, stood, and stepped to the rug in front of the tub. She reached behind the shower curtain, felt for the spigots. She found them, and set the water to the right temperature. She turned, stepping back to the scatter rug in front of the sink. She laid her hands on the cold porcelain and leaned toward the mirror for a close look at how much older she was that day.

The bathroom reflected clearly in the mirror. Alice did not. She wasn't included in its image. She wasn't in her bathroom. Alice backed away, stepping on the concentric circle tile pattern of the cold blue floor. She peeked once more into the empty mirror, folded her arms, and waited.

Waited to wake up.

T ed 5

He was careful not to serve another ace. Instead, he tossed the red tennis ball overhead and lightly batted it over the net. The striking, athletic woman across the net still could not return the powerful serve. He wished he could remember her name. The admiration in her eyes when he drove home the set-winning volley suggested she was more than a casual acquaintance.

He hopped the net gracefully, took her hand. She wrapped her arms around his slim waist. The scent of her perspiration excited him. He, of course, didn't sweat. She looked up at him, eyes wide.

"Ted, you're wonderful. We must do this more often."

"Do this?" he asked, winking. She grinned.

"Ted, you know I'm not that kind of girl. But for you, I could change."

He kissed her tanned forehead lightly, walked through the chain link gate, shutting it behind him. He hopped on his Harley Lowrider. He pulled the heavy motorcycle off its stand with style, dropped his sunglasses onto his nose. He checked over his shoulder to see that the babe in black leather had joined him. She was settling onto the small rear seat. He waited until her pale arms wrapped around him, each of her hands grabbing one of his denim thighs, before he let out the clutch, twisted the throttle.

The Harley leapt to life, vibrated with power. He heard the girl behind him squeal with delight as he accelerated down the empty two-lane highway. He felt the girl press against his back. Her lips brushed his ear.

"I don't know which makes me hotter," she said, licking his earlobe as she spoke, "The hot bike or the hot dude bustin' it." He knew. He said nothing, maintaining his cool persona. He rode on, letting the hog speak for him. He smiled when he spotted gridlocked traffic ahead. He didn't bother slowing. Hell, his brakes weren't connected anyway. He drove the bike at speed between the snarled rows of cars, missing door handles by inches. One rude driver opened a door to stop his progress. The hog didn't even shudder when it snapped the car door off its hinges, into the air. He flipped the fat driver the bird as he passed. His heroics earned him an extra squeeze from his wickedly amorous passenger. He took his success in stride, hardly batting an eyelid under his dark glasses.

He turned into the park, off the crowded city street, gliding uphill easily on his neon rollerblades. The tall redhead at his side was panting in her effort to keep up. He decided to ease his pace. He took her hands in his, spun her around him, then he spun around her. He tilted his head backward, left his eyes open to soak in blue sky and green trees as they spun crazily overhead. He breathed in the fresh air deeply. He could feel it fill his lungs with life. Lungs that expanded without a wheeze. His iron legs moved him painlessly. The woman, a hard-bodied redhead in a thong bikini, couldn't keep her eyes or hands off him. He remembered that he hadn't thought about food in years. He smiled.

Life was perfect.

The woman did not smile back. She had broken her adoring stare to follow an object that moved behind him. When he turned to look, the wheels fell off his skates. He watched as all eight bright green wheels rolled down the asphalt path, over a quaint stone footbridge, and into the grill of an approaching tractor-trailer.

"Now that's not right," he said aloud as the semi barreled down the scenic trail, scattering without discretion joggers, skaters, and nannies with baby carriages. The truck's white trailer had an oval logo painted on it; its yellow paint was old and faded, unreadable.

Three women had gathered around him: a blond in wet tennis attire, a raven-haired tough girl in leather, and a tall redhead wearing more skates than clothes. They clutched him frantically, gesturing at the approaching disaster.

"Ted," they pleaded in a single voice, "Ted you've got to save us from that truck! It'll kill us all!"

He paced on the path, flexed his muscles, groaned in a manly way, but all his tools were useless. He could not stop the truck, already starting over the bridge, but he was afforded a moment to think. The truck, not quite fitting through the centuries-old stone walls, was slowly plowing them off the bridge into the stream below. It made a horrible racket, summoning louder squeals of panic from the girls.

He surveyed their wide blue, green, and brown eyes. He longed to prevent their imminent doom. He decided to hide them behind his perfect body, sparing them at least. He gathered the girls around close, but as a group they were simply too wide to conceal. He was confused, sure that they should have been able to comfortably stand behind him and be safely eclipsed from anything. Stand behind his slim, healthy body. His slim body. Tan. Slim. Strong. Slim. He snapped his fingers, remembering.

"Wait a minute," he shouted, "I'm fat!"

The girls cheered.

"Yeah, I'm huge. I'm a pig! I got a gut that could fend off a battleship. Hang on there, girls, help is on its way!"

The girls cheered.

He loosened his belt, let out his belly. He remained thin, his abdomen rippled. He tried breathing in deeply, succeeded only in enjoying more fine fresh air. The semi was over the bridge, spinning its wheels in preparation for a final charge up the garden path. Desperate, he ran in circles, searching for a solution to his crisis. He skidded to a halt and slapped his forehead when he spotted that solution idling right beside him. A candy apple and nut wagon, with a smiling Italian holding a bag of cashews.

"Of course!" he exclaimed.

The girls cheered.

He dug into his spandex bicycle shorts for a coin, handed it to the vendor. He then wrapped his highly conditioned arms around the cart, picked it up over his head. Pausing first to relish the moment, he dropped the cart and, accidentally, the smiling Italian into his mouth. The semi was close, blaring its air horn, grinding gears.

He stepped in front of the truck an instant too late, allowing it to crush three strange women into him before it disintegrated against his belly. The remains of the truck burst into flames, promising no survivors. He had to assume that, of course, since his bulk blocked most of the wreckage. He wished the driver had lived so he could sit on him for making him fat again.

He felt a stir between his thighs. Someone was pushing through his legs, away from the wreck. He looked down. A man's head poked out below the rim his stomach. The man was looking cautiously at something in front of him. The semi and the beautiful women were a vague memory, so he doubted the man was rubbernecking. The man crawled through his thighs, looking shaken, emotionally disturbed about something. The man turned, looked up at his shoulders, turned away, and began to rant.

"How could you do this?" the man shouted at the broken stone bridge, "Look what you did to all those people!"

He understood what the man was shouting about, and the man was right. The nerve of that banana trucker, he thought, making me fat again. The man was still shouting, so he let the guy finish before he spoke.

"God knows what will come of this, what with all the trigger happy people in the world!" The statement's meaning eluded him, but he went along with it. His anger at being hungry again had swollen along with him.

"Yeah!" he shouted at the bridge, "What he said!" The bridge didn't seem to care, but the man took notice.

The thin stranger ceased the tirade, turned back to him, offered a puzzled, then bemused expression. He felt a vacuum forming, decided to fill it before the guy wandered off.

"I can't believe that fool did that, mister. All those people. And me. Look at me! I'm supposed to be..."

"Here to help?" the man finished for him. It wasn't what he had in mind, but the man, still speaking, had a point.

"That's what you're trained for, isn't it?"

He looked again at the man, but was unable to identify him. He would certainly have remembered those eyes... Not that it mattered: the man knew him, treated him amiably, and that was very, very important to him. He played along, tentative.

"Well, yes," he said, "Yes it is. How did you know?" The man sighed, appeared introspective but still quite interested in him. The man was careful to look him in the eye when he spoke.

"We must have met before, sir," the man said.

Sir!

"Do you come to this park often?" his new friend asked, striking his forehead, "What difference would that make. I've never been here before."

"Me neither," he said. His response startled the man.

"I was thinking, not talking."

"Oh. Sorry," he said, looking away. He should have noticed that the man's lips had stopped moving. The man passed off his embarrassment with a shrug.

"It's okay. Listen Ted,"

Ted? Yes, Ted. How many times had he heard that name, and only now this man provides it with a definition. Ted was thunderstruck, frozen by the significance of the moment. The man hesitated.

"It is 'Ted'?" he asked hesitantly.

"Yes," Ted said, "But how?"

"I don't know," the man said, smiling like he did, "But anyway, we've never been properly introduced. And you seem to need that."

Ted shook his head, deciding that he must be dreaming. Someone wanted to meet him, in the most sincere manner. Ted responded immediately.

"Yes I do mister," he squealed, unable to control his enthusiasm, "Yes I do! I'm Ted. Ted Pantagone." Pantagone. Now where did that come from? It sounded right, so he didn't correct himself. He did remember proper decorum, however, and presented his hand.

"And you are?" Ted asked, taking the man's hand, engulfing him from finger to shoulder.

"I'm..." the man started to say, but he didn't finish, as he abruptly jumped from Ted's grasp into the oak tree branches above, out of sight.

"Fine," Ted said, "I try to be friendly and the guy takes off like a rocket! Guess he had somewhere to be."

Ted didn't mind, really. After all, he thought, what would they have discussed after introductions? Food? He probably never met the man.

"Guy probably just made a lucky guess."

He let the man and the image of him slip from his mind, from his memory. He heard distant thunder, and was scanning the blue sky for a storm when the sound came again, much closer. He put his palms on his belly felt it moving, demanding attention.

"I'd best see to that right away," he said aloud. He expertly turned the cart around the tile corner, into his favorite aisle. He whistled a forgotten tune, searching surreptitiously for opened packages of cookies to sample.

Phillip 5

I sit here, on the floor of a bathroom. It's not mine, of course. Nothing is. Never was. I've had enough, I can tell. I can tell because I sit here, in a bathroom. On my own. Evading no one. Signing nothing, honoring my wishes only. It feels good, except the floor. The floor is cold. And I have no wish. Only a conclusion.

I slide onto a scatter rug. It's warm. A football, the football, official NFL, rolls from the sink to the floor. Partially deflated, it doesn't bounce when it lands near my knee. It does rock back and forth, presenting its logo. Still seducing me. Even now. I pick it up, unafraid, now. I heft it, toss it back and forth in my hand. I smile. It is just a ball. Just a goddamn ball. My life, twenty-two years, spent chasing it, dreaming it, wanting it, and here it is. A deflated, unimpressive ball. Still, if I had no father, I could have caught it.

Father. Master, planner, owner. I crush the ball, crush it because of him. In one hand I enclose it. Make a fist. It's gone. Thoughts of my father are not. A picture slides from the sink. Eight by ten. Black and white. A portrait. Father, Mother, me.

Mother stands behind Father, slightly. She always did. Always will. Taught me to catch, Mother did. Father beat her for that, occasionally. We're all young. I'm a happy child, eyes bright. But Mother, Mother knows. A tear rolls from her thin cheek. It moistens the photo. I set this photo down picture against the floor, in deference to Mother.

A printout, the green and white kind, thumps to the floor beside me. Impressive in its mass. A thousand pages, easy. I check. Last page says not one but two thousand. Just what the world needs: more pages that I thought. I flip through the pages, expecting the same numbers again. Numbers, poison, same thing. Father likes numbers...expected me to, as well.

They are different this time. No, not different, not really. Same numbers, same indicators, but arranged all wrong. Almost random; no columns, no headings. Father would be upset. I flip the photo. He is. I flip it back. I flip the pages, fast. The numbers are no longer random. Or numbers. They are pixels, moved by the flipping numbers into action. Into pictures. I flip faster. My life races across green stripes: childhood, my last dog; high school, no time for Harriet; college, Ivy League, football pays the bills; Wall Street, the market. All there. I stop looking, sorrowful at my own clichéd inventions. I lift the top page, crumple it into a ball, and throw it into the blue water.

Still attached, the rest of the ream flows in, a thin green snake blindly following itself to its own destruction. The last sheet flips through the air, swirls into the toilet. Without standing, I pull the silver handle. The noise of the turbulent flush hurts my ears, but the racket ceases soon enough.

Funny, I thought it would have felt better. The football, gone. The information, gone. Father, face down. Face down, but perhaps not gone. I retrieve the photo. Turn it to face me, one more time.

Mother is gone. I am gone. Father remains. Father. Father and his pipe. It is lit. Smoke fills my eyes, draws a tear. Father laughs at my weakness. From the picture he looks at me. Regards me with contempt, or empathy. I can't tell. He speaks.

"I always been proud of you boy," he says.

"I know you mean that, Father," I responded, bile rising in my throat.

"Always doin' the right thing."

"Yes sir."

"Always. That's my Phillip."

"Father?"

"Son?"

"What's wrong with football?"

"Don't you know, boy?" he says, only now removing the horrid pipe from his mouth, "Don't you know?"

"No, Father, I don't."

"Your Mother, boy, your Mother," he exclaims, thin lips parting to reveal straight brown teeth. He cackles.

"Mother?"

"Yes, sir. Always was," he cackles on. The sound is more deafening than the toilet. Ignoring his protests, I roll the photo into a tube, silencing him. One last time.

I lay the tube on blue tile, study it. Round, smooth, reflecting the wet tile's cold blue sheen. I tap its hard surface, roll it away, then back. I admire its solid clicks across the uneven tile. I pick it up, heft it in my fingers. It feels heavy. It feels good. I insert my index finger into one end. I make a fist with the remaining finger, thumb in the air. It feels right.

I peer into the tube. It is dark in there, but I know what it contains. Father is in there. Mother, too, against her wishes. And me. I am in there too. Surrounded by all of them: agents, teachers, coaches, superiors. No friends are in there. Not one. I remember no friends.

Light from the bare fluorescent over the sink casts a shimmering image in there. Father's trophy case. Filled with the symbols of my achievements. Packed in tight, my past, achievements only, is ready to perform once more.

I point my finger away from me. The room, the strange clean bathroom, comes back into view. I open my fist, leaving the index finger inserted in the photo. The room, the bathroom, is cleaner. But wrong. I wish to close my fist, but a shadow in the mirror high over the sink distracts me. As I crane my neck to see, the rolled up photo slips off my finger. As I fight the urge to dive after the paper tube, I see the image begin to come into focus. It is a man, I think. A man, looking down at me from his place high above, behind the glass. Behind my own reflection.

The man nods, senses that I have again dropped the photo. I understand, but when I reclaim the tube, the man again fades into shadows. I insert my finger, and his fair image disappears. But me, I am warm. I make a fist, thumb high. The image is a misty shadow. I understand, unmake my fist, remove my finger. The image is redefined. I see it through a haze, shower steam on the mirror, but I see he, the man, understands. I lay the paper tube in front of me once more. The man, his reflection, becomes agitated. I touch the tube. I find words. I wish to make them matter.

"You know this isn't right," I say, not interested in a response. They are my words, not his to use. I pick up the tube for the last time. The man, his image, the mirror fades from view. I insert my finger, and the bathroom walls fade to white. Clean grout lines disappear. This, this is right.

I pull back my thumb, the high one. It stretches easily back nearly to my wrist. I look once more into the tube. They are all still there: Father, Mother, me, the trophies, teachers, coaches, superiors, achievements. All together in one thin layer. The layer that lines the tube. It is a weak layer. The paper provides the strength. The plain white paper. Paper I rolled.

There are no friendships in the tube. No love sandwiched between my forefinger and cellulose liner. That, above all, makes the tube right.

I wish to look no more. I rub the paper tube down my unshaved cheek. It stops under my chin. I see nothing now. No darkness, no light, no blue. Just white. Right white.

I close my eyes, for the first time in 22 years I see. I stretch my middle finger away from the others, point it out straight. I curl its tip. I squeeze it back to the fist in one smooth motion.

Lou 6

Lou fumbled with the can opener. His repeated attempts to position its small tongue on the lip of his beer can met with consistent failure. He shook his head in consternation. It should have worked the first time. It was a new opener, with an especially sharp triangular point that glistened in the sunlight. Lou grunted with pleasure when the tongue finally caught and allowed the point to pierce the tin can. His small victory came at a price, however. Foam sprayed liberally from the unsealed can, saturating the green indoor/outdoor carpet that protected his porch's ancient wooden planks. He verified that the rug was unstained, and finished cutting the triangular hole in this can with his metal opener. He removed the corroded instrument, tilted the can to his mouth. He wrapped his lips around the edge of the can, ready for the flow of ice-cold beer.

His thirst was not sated. No beer emerged. Lou pulled the full can from his mouth. He peered into the small tear he had made and glimpsed a swirling golden liquid. He shook the can, turned it upside down, rolled it on the floor, but it did not pour. Before he threw the errant container against a wall, Lou remembered what he was opening. He sighed loudly and retrieved the can opener from his pocket. He hooked it on and popped a little air hole on the can, halfway around the rim from the drinking hole. He tilted it back and drank the smooth cool beverage.

"Funny," he said, "It tastes like regular beer." He shrugged and reclined on the padded lounge chair. His raised feet framed the bay in the near distance. He spotted his boat bobbing on the clear burgundy tinted surface. Lou smiled. He hadn't realized that he lived on the Red Sea.

He wondered if there was any oil in the yard. Might be worth a look, he thought, as he selected a manual on oil drilling from the stack of journals spread loosely on a wrought iron table to his left. He finished his beer, and returned to the plastic spigot in the side of the cooler on his right for more. He refilled the can, wondering if it was kosher to drink beer near the Red Sea. Who cares, he thought. He sank into vinyl-wrapped luxury of his lounge chair, looking forward to a blissfully dull afternoon watching the sailboat regatta in the red bay. It was a good race, too: two boats had already sunk and a third was on fire. A rap on the screened door stole his rare moment of peace.

Lou hoisted himself to his feet. He trotted across the creaking porch to the door. Unable to recognize the visitors, he hesitated before he unhooked the thin metal hasp. The best he could make out of his unexpected company was four shadows lurking behind the screen. This bothered him, since the midday sun was flooding the neighborhood with cloudless, shadow-free light. He was about to walk away when he heard Ted addressing him through the wire mesh.

"As long as you don't drive," Ted said.

"Huh?" Lou asked.

"You can drink as long as you don't drive," Ted repeated. Lou remembered the beer in his hand.

"Oh, yeah," he said, "Thanks." He sipped his beer. It had become warm and sandy. Lou spat out the bitter brew and headed back to the cooler for more.

"Hey, wait a second!" he heard Alice shout, "Where are you going?"

Uh oh, Lou thought. He couldn't decide whether his unease rose from Alice's terse question, or from the broken cooler that oozed thick amber slime. For cleanliness' sake he chose to ignore the beer. He returned to the latched screened door. He opened his mouth to speak, but a manicured tan hand that burst through the screen interrupted his intended cautious platitude. A well-muscled female arm followed the hand in from the shadows. The hand opened wide, then clamped its callused fingers on his face, and pulled Lou through the screen.

Lou picked up his spilling bottle of beer from the cockpit floor before it stained the fiberglass. He placed it carefully back into the plastic cup holder that swung from gimbals on the chromed rail.

"Yep," he said conversationally, "Can't be too careful about these things."

"Whaddya mean 'careful'?" Gloria screamed from her perch on the boom that swung limply overhead, "You'd better start being real careful, bub, or we all cooked!"

"Cook?" Ted asked, turning his globular head from its endless sweep of the forward horizon, "Someone's cooking?"

"No, Ted, no one's cooking. Sorry, but this galley stove doesn't work. Alcohol, you know. The owner insists it works, but I'll be damned if I can get it going."

Lou paused, noticing that no one in the group was paying attention. They were all fixated on the empty, placid red horizon. Their expression ran the gamut of Gloria's near panic to Howard's distant, sullen interest. Lou stood, mindful of the boat's steep healing attitude, and scanned the empty horizon.

"What?" he asked, "What do you see?"

No one answered.

"Fine," he said, "If that's how you're going to be, I'll just mind my own business too.

"Anyway, like I was saying, the stove doesn't work, the depth sounder's out, and there's only two usable sails, but the radio's in perfect shape. Got me... what the hell are you guys looking at!"

"You tell us," Alice said, fire in her blue eyes, "You're the one driving this thing!" she was pointing off the starboard bow. Lou followed her finger (a piece of metal screening dangled from it) to the granite reef toward which they were headed.

"That's not there," Lou said confidently as he studied the low, dark contours of the menacing breakers, "I've been sailing here all my life. I know every inch of these waters, and those rocks aren't there."

"That's real reassuring, mister," Gloria growled from above his head. Lou had never seen a black leather bikini before. It looked right on her.

"Thanks," he said. Gloria dropped to the slanted deck in front of him. She landed softly on her feet.

"You've got impressive sea-legs Gloria," he said.

"Watch your mouth, mister," Gloria snarled, "And watch where you're going, too."

"Don't worry. I know what I'm doing."

"He is the one who's supposed to know," Howard stated from his seat at the bow.

"Thanks for the input," Alice snapped, "Now go back to looking, if you don't mind." Howard obliged. Alice stood behind Lou; put her palms against his temples. She forced his head to look at the rocks, then said, "Look over there."

He did, and noticed what his passengers had been observing. A boulder, higher than the mast, loomed just off the starboard bow. From its conical shape, Lou determined that it was the peak of a stone mountain hidden beneath the surface. The setting sun reflected yellow on its wet face. Red water lapped its steep walls in a steady, calm rhythm. The color and sound combinations soothed him subliminally.

"It's pretty," Lou observed.

"Pretty!" Gloria shouted, "Do something asshole, before we're all struck by the 'beauty of the moment' permanently!"

"Yeah," Ted said.

"Shut up Ted," everybody said, including Lou.

"Okay, okay," Lou said. Time to take control, he thought. He adopted his best commanding tone.

"Everyone below deck!" he shouted. The group complied, in an orderly fashion. Howard was first, dramatically exiting the cockpit for the relative safety of the cabin below. Ted was next, and got stuck in the narrow companionway. Alice and Gloria, each manning a cheek, were able to shove Ted through quickly. Alice, the last one in the cockpit, eyed Lou with matronly concern.

"You sure you don't want me to stay up here with you? I've never been on one of these things..."

Lou smiled gently, shook his head, "It's all right Alice. It's best if I stay up here alone. I can cover more. Thanks, though."

Alice shrugged and went below decks with the others. Lou took a long draw of beer, carefully placed the bottle in its holder, and followed her down the companionway.

He settled into the thick leather cushions of the sectional couch. Gloria shared the couch with him. She was listening with interest to Howard, who lounged in a matching easy chair on the far side of the glass coffee table. He had to shout to be heard, and though Gloria apparently followed his speech, Lou was unable to decipher his gibberish. He sipped his tea, watched Ted browsing the munchies at the bar. Alice was admiring the mountain view through the glass wall. Howard's content voice finally poked into Lou's realm of comprehension.

"I mean we just have to let him run the ship."

"Ship?" Alice shouted from the picture window. Lou looked past her. He could not avoid the impolite gesture. The mountain scenery was too breathtaking to ignore: the trees, the rocks, the setting sun that warmed the largest of the peaks with its golden rays. Lou found the vista irresistible. And painful. Wait a minute, he thought, counting on his fingers: sunset, yellow light, a conical mountain. Alice caught on first. She turned from the window. She ran to him, grabbed him by his tuxedo lapels.

"Hey!" she exclaimed, eyes wide, "You're not supposed to be in here! You should be outside steering!"

Lou stood, started for the antique double doors that led to the exit.

"Yeah," Gloria said, confused, "Aren't you outside?"

"Lou!" Alice said.

Lou ignored them all and broke through the locked doors. When they slammed behind him, shaking the plastic bulkhead, Lou spotted the hatch to the cockpit. The rock had eclipsed the yellow sun, but the resulting golden corona shed enough light in the cabin to illuminate the small wood-framed opening at the top of four varnished steps. He scrambled down the companionway toward it, but the hatch didn't grow. He ran faster, covering miles of thin carpeting and plastic walls. Exhausted, he had to stop. There was no chance that he would be able to reach the narrow hatch before the rock struck the boat. But he didn't surrender. Instead, he pushed harder, diving through the hatch inches in front of the rock that crashed through the bulkhead behind him.

Lou landed on his chest on a resilient purple surface. He slid for an eternity before easing to a stop in front of four pairs of wet shoes. Sandals, work boots, stiletto heels and untied tennis shoes greeted him. Disinclined to talk to footwear, he did not return the pleasantry.

He sat up, looked around uneasily. The only visible landscape was the familiar wearers of the shoes, none of whom seemed interested in helping him to his feet. He sighed, rubbed his eyes, stretched, and stood by himself on the odd surface. Though mirror smooth, it was not slippery. Though diamond hard, it gave a little. Lou scratched his head.

"This isn't right," he said.

"Nope," Alice responded, arms folded across her naked chest, "Not right at all."

"I guess," Lou said, handing her a t-shirt. She accepted it silently.

"Feels right to me, but why are we here?" Gloria asked.

"Got me," Lou said, "I hoped you could tell me."

"How's that?" Howard asked, "The lady here says that you brought us here."

"I didn't hear that," Ted said.

"I did?" Lou asked, "How?"

"Aren't you supposed to tell us that, Lou?" Alice asked.

There was something distinctly different in her manner of speech, Lou noticed, but he was unable to identify the change. He touched the sleeve of her t-shirt. It was light blue, very dirty, and "Frank's Pizza" was sewn to its front in crude block letters.

"Nice shirt," he said, "Where'd you get it?"

"You serious?" Alice asked.

"He's going to be a lot of help," Gloria whispered.

"Someone needs help?" Ted asked.

"What's the problem?" Lou asked, "I was kidding!"

"Oh, that's a relief," Alice said.

"I know where you got the shirt," Lou said, touching the letter 'r,' "You got it from Frank's pizza."

"Oh, Lou," Alice said, slapping his hand away.

"Now what?" Gloria asked.

"How about we all go over to my place for a beer?" Lou suggested, pointing to his back porch. It stood alone on the empty purple plain, with just a hint of lawn spread before it and the dotted outline of his ramshackle rented house behind it. The group, except Ted, followed his gesture. They each gasped or stepped back in their own way when they saw his porch. Alice put her hands on her hips, shook her head. Gloria touched Lou's hand in a quiet gesture of supreme affection and appreciation. Howard, head lowered, was mumbling to himself.

"Got any lemonade?" Ted asked.

"Of course. And cookies."

"Lou," Alice said. She stepped between him and his house. Her slim shoulders were squared, stretched tight, as if she were unwilling to present her back to his porch. Eye contact with him had taken priority, however. And boy, can she make eye contact, Lou thought. Alice continued, "How long have you known that was there?"

"It feels like forever sometimes," Lou said, "I don't know, ten years? Fifteen?"

The fiery woman, his dearest and most trusted friend that day, did not take his sincere bit of trivia well. Her face slackened and she stepped experimentally onto the tall grass of his backyard. She was disturbed, confused, as though everything he said was wrong, or there was a fact he had left out.

"I'm sorry Alice," Lou said quietly, "I didn't realize how important my old porch and pretzels are to you."

"You have pretzels too?" Ted said, rubbing his white robed belly. The poor man, Lou thought. He felt small arms wrap around him from behind him. He looked down to see two pale, bangled hands meet on his chest. He felt the pressure of a thin warm body against his back.

"I think it's wonderful, mister," Gloria breathed softly into the Lou's ear, "You've done a great thing offering it to us. It's been so long since I thanked anyone for anything, I've forgotten how to do it right."

"Call me Lou, Gloria. And come in. That's thanks enough." Gloria squeezed him, kissed his ear, and then came around to his side, nuzzling her head against his shoulder. She pushed her long raven hair over his arm. It was cool, soft. She returned his smile.

Lou was about to start toward his porch when Alice again stood toe-to-toe with him, blocking his path. She was not smiling. She was not smiling so well that Lou abandoned his. Her glare loosened his knees. He waited for her to speak, but she just continued glaring.

"What!" he cried.

"Can't you see?" she asked, her tone measured, controlled.

"See what?" Lou asked. I'll bet that was the wrong question, he thought.

"See what?" Alice rolled her eyes, confirming Lou's thought, "Those. What about those?"

Alice neither turned nor pointed, but he looked down to his left. Two empty life preservers dimpled the surface of the plain. He recognized them as the vests that were missing from the boat's locker. They were wet, torn, very used. Lou's heart sank as he studied the empty little vessels; his failure led to their broken condition. He was responsible. He had forgotten. Their weight must be enormous, he thought, to dent the surface like that. He left his head lowered, tightened his grip on Gloria. Lou's dry throat scratched the words he was able to muster.

"Oh, those," he mumbled.

"Yeah, those," Alice said, softening noticeably. She stepped aside, to Lou's left, near Ted. Lou bunched his thighs, urged them to move. When they did, his protesting knees creaked to life, allowing his heavy feet to inch over to the depression. He bent low, picked up the vests in one hand. They were still warm. His parched throat reminded him about his porch.

"Anyone for beer?" he asked cheerfully.

"And pretzels," Ted added, "You said pretzels." Ted's outburst drew laughter from the group. Forced, perhaps overdone laughter, but it did effectively lower their shared tension. Lou slung the jackets over his shoulder, crossed his scraggly lawn to his screen door. The screen was torn inexplicably. Lou stopped on the top of his unpainted porch stair, unsure about the condition of the inside of his house. The telltale screen could have been a subtle harbinger of a real disaster inside. The neighborhood had changed over the years. He rubbed his chin while his four guests waited silently around him. Gloria noticed the rend in the screen, but said nothing.

"Why don't you folks wait here for a second while I go in and make sure the place is tidied up?"

"Something wrong mister?" Gloria asked, "Lou?"

Her warmth calmed him. He manufactured a smile, removed his arm from her shoulder.

"No, Gloria, nothing at all. I'll be right back."

"You sure?" Alice asked

"Everything is fine, Alice. I just want to make sure it's not too messy in there. I'm a bit of a pig you know."

"Lou,"

"Yes Alice."

"Make damn sure you come back."

"Yes Alice," Lou said. Wishing no more discussion, or another request for food from Ted, Lou opened the screened door, stepped up onto the indoor/outdoor carpet. The door squealed closed on rusty springs. Lou crossed the porch, lifted the lip of his plastic cooler. A full case of his favorite brew lay packed in fresh ice, awaiting his weekend consumption. He closed the lid, and was poised to sit down when he heard four sharp raps on the porch door. He sighed wearily, wondering who could be bothering him in such an obtrusive, demanding manner. He walked across the floor, kicking aside two dusty life jackets tossed casually on the floor.

"Those should be on the boat," he said aloud. He shot a glance to the quiet bay. His sailboat bobbed lazily at its mooring. He stopped at the screened door, put his hand on the metal latch, but didn't bother to open it. The concrete steps to the street, weed covered from disuse (he generally entered and left by the kitchen door), were unoccupied. So was his yard, and the street. It was the off-season, and the summer people were months away.

"Must be those damn kids again," Lou said, "This neighborhood sure has changed over the years."

He settled back into his cushioned lounge chair, twisted the cap off a fresh bottle of beer. The sun was setting, its golden glow tinting the green bay a glorious violet shade. Lou sipped his beer. He loved afternoons like this. Quiet. No responsibilities.

No responsibilities.

The porch door drew his attention again. From his chair, he examined its screen. It was in good shape: still silver, spread taut on its frame. He sighed with relief, sat back, and wondered why he cared so much for a screen.

T ed 6

"Now that's not right," he said to the status chart of patient #147, "How could patient #147 be having a party? He's in a coma, or dead, or something. He's certainly in no shape for fun."

He plucked the clipboard from the frame of bed #147, took a closer look at it. It wasn't for patient #147. It was addressed to him.

"To someone named Ted, anyway," he said.

He read on. It said that he was invited not to a party, but a picnic.

"A picnic. That's much better. Food's there."

He was overjoyed to hold his first invitation to anything. Tears of happiness flowed freely down his face. They converged to form warm salt rivers that coursed between his cheeks and nose. The torrent of his joy spilled onto the embossed invitation, obliterating the writing; erasing the name of the host; washing clean the picnic's address.

He stopped the tears and wiped the paper with the hem of his white smock. He was too late. A final examination of the clipboard confirmed that it was just that - a clipboard for the stiff in bed #147. The depressing chart shunned his attention. He slammed it back on its hook.

He kicked open the double steel doors, left the recovery room in a practiced huff. He almost had his scene ruined by the doors as they swung back on him. He made it through before they slapped him and paced the striped hallway floor to the elevator bank. He pushed the 'down' button on the wall.

"I should have known," he mumbled while he waited with his arms folded, "Why I even imagine that someone would invite me, I haven't a clue. Dammit, it isn't fair!"

He wanted to continue ranting, maybe stamp his foot, bang his fist into his palm, but the elevator doors opened, and he had to step inside. In his lingering preoccupation with anger, he forgot to check that the elevator was actually there before stepping aboard. It wasn't.

He plummeted down the fieldstone shaft, windmilling his hands for a purchase. He didn't panic. He couldn't see the bottom of the shaft (he couldn't see below his belly in the best of circumstances), so it presented no immediate danger. Also, he was able to grasp the cables that slapped at him like friendly strands of black spaghetti. The cables were greased, limiting his effort to stop, but they slowed him enough to allow time to look up at the round opening of the well.

Above his head, out of reach, the sky formed a perfect blue disk broken only by the blond head of the woman that watched him fall away from her. She was annoyed at him. When he raised a hand to help explain his predicament, the woman touched his index finger. He crooked it around her small palm and held tight. She didn't slow his fall. Instead, she tumbled into the well with him. Landing first, he set the half-dressed woman on her knees on the clammy rock floor of the cavern. Her breasts shimmied when she hit. He liked that, but knew he shouldn't enjoy it. Mother always said she never enjoy such things. To be sure, he didn't enjoy it; he picked her up and dropped her on her knees again. Ashamed, he tried to look away from the rare bounty, but couldn't. Embarrassed, he explained his voyeurism:

"It's okay, lady," he said gently, "I'm a doctor."

"No you're not," the woman glared at him, "You're an asshole."

He stepped back, more annoyed than hurt. The bitch, he thought, she might as well have called me fat! But then, she may be right.

"I suppose I am," he conceded, "So?"

"So?" she said, her thumbs hooked in the waistband of her cutoff shorts, "So come with me, Ted. I'll show you a way out."

"A way out?" he asked, confused by her sudden charity, "You mean to the picnic?"

"Yes, Ted," the woman smiled, wiggling her raised middle finger, "C'mon."

He followed. She chose one of the round sewer tunnels that branched out of the cavern from countless random locations, entered its dark mouth without hesitation. How could I not follow her, he thought, not only is she nice to me, and she's taking me to a picnic, but look at that ass!

She stopped, put a hand on her hip, turned, and smiled.

"Well thanks, Ted," she said. She resumed her quick stride down the tunnel.

"How?" he started before waving off the thought, "Oh, never mind." The woman ignored him.

They twisted and turned through the brick sewer tunnels. He wondered at the woman's ability to ferret her way through the maze. Then he wondered about her ability to ferret her way through the maze. Finally, after a half dozen more apparently haphazard turns, he wondered if she had an ability to ferret her way through the maze. He was about to ask about it when they exited the round tunnel system, stepping into a brightly lit blind alley.

It was a disgusting alley, rife with trash, slime, and derelicts. He was, however, happy to be out of the sewer and one step closer to the picnic. He waited patiently while the woman conversed with two bums cowering in a dumpster. He ignored their brief conversation, wishing she would start moving again, until the woman addressed him.

"You see anything, Ted?" she asked, shading her eyes as she studied the back wall of the alley. He was confused, but played along. She was undoubtedly working some social gambit to get the uninvited bums to ask them to come along to the picnic.

"No," he said, playfully sniffing the air, "I smell a barbecue, though. Let's check it out."

After he said his part, the conversation eluded him. He grew impatient waiting for them to work out the details, but also knew that he couldn't leave. The woman was his guide; he had to wait. Finally she spoke.

"Time!" she said, agitated, "We gotta go."

He was thrilled. He felt saliva run in his mouth.

"We're getting barbecue?" he asked. The woman ignored him and walked through a small previously overlooked doorway in the back alley wall. He followed, anxious not to lose sight of the woman or the fruit and pretzels she may bear. He learned quickly that he had made the right decision in keeping up. The door opened on a lovely New England wharf bathed in golden afternoon sunshine.

The woman stopped a few paces ahead of him. She stood beside a curious craft moored to the freshly planked wharf. It was long, sat low in the water. A thick layer of topsoil carpeted its beamy deck. Tulips sprouted from the dirt; thousands of them, bright and festive.

The woman was pounding on the door of the barge's tiny pilothouse. The captain of the fancy ship was clearly visible inside, but the surly sailor seemed loath to address her commotion.

Finally the captain rose and shuffled to the door, taking a sip from a beer can during the short trip. This must be the place, he thought. The man, dressed in Bermuda shorts and a t-shirt, a bit woozy, who might have already started the party without them, held up a finger and peered through the plastic window.

"We'd love to join you, mister," he said brightly, "And we'll even pick some tulips on the way. We'll ride with you as long as you don't drive this thing." He crossed his arms. He felt that was fair. The woman looked at him, stunned by his statement. The man inside eyed him suspiciously as well, but heard him.

"What exactly are you saying Ted?" the woman asked. He was honored that she had taken his idle statement seriously.

"I just said that you can drink as long as you don't drive," he repeated as best he could.

"Drive?" she asked.

"I guess that wouldn't make sense here, huh?" he kidded.

"I guess," she said, not amused. The man inside saluted, though, by raising a beer to him. Then the captain walked away, below decks.

"Hey," the woman shouted through the closed door, "Where are you going?" she didn't wait for a response. She boarded the barge without asking. She must be invited, he thought. He followed her on board, as did the two bums from the alley. Hoboes, judging by their attire. They gathered around the locked pilothouse. The drunken sailor had reappeared. The more attractive of the two bums, perhaps a woman, perched on the roof of the shabby pilothouse, appearing agitated. He glanced at the other two members of his new group, who were also grim. He feared something might be amiss, but since he wasn't privy to their muted conversation, he felt it socially improper to care. He tried to listen, however, to catch any chance that occurred to join in. He wanted to participate; they might ask for an invitation otherwise. The small woman above him was speaking. She was shaking her fist at the captain.

"You'd better start to cook!" she shouted. Her terse words encouraged him.

"Cook? Someone's cooking?" he asked. This is what I'm here for, he thought. Unfortunately, the man's head was slowly shaking behind the dirty glass. He feared that the unheard words the captain spoke were not in his favor. He chose to ignore the small group, hoping they would reciprocate, forestalling the inevitable discovery that he had no invitation. He took to sniffing tulips and admiring the sun setting over the bulwarks.

"Pretty?" the small woman shouted.

"Yeah," he agreed politely.

"Shut up Ted!" he heard everyone shout at him, including the man inside.

Oops, he thought, there goes my anonymity. He tried to regain it by shrinking away from the group gathered on the sunny suburban sidewalk. He feared that if he bothered them again they would take away his ticket for sure. He hid behind a mailbox, began to plan his method of surreptitiously following the three to the picnic. He was growing impatient of their inactivity, however, and peeked around the box to see what was keeping them.

They had gathered around a body lying prone on the sidewalk. The still body of a man. They were watching the body, but didn't appear to be administering any aid to it. His expertise was needed. He debated the decision to help for a moment before he stepped toward the circle. A stricken body was more important to him than a picnic. For the moment, anyway.

When he was in earshot of the group's conversation, he was still unable to hear their animated discussion. Their postures and gestures ran the gamut of emotion from the loving, funereal respect paid by the small dark woman to the half-hearted interest of the big man to the obvious disdain expressed by the weathered blond. The small woman kicked the body without noticing that it moved. He did, and his heart leapt. He stepped more quickly toward the group, heard the big man speak but couldn't catch the words.

"I'm sorry, sir," he interjected politely, "But what did you say?" The man ignored him. He stepped closer, glad to be part of the conversation. If not a participant, at least he could witness it. He surmised that the man stirring to consciousness at their feet was responsible for his acceptance by the group. He liked the groggy fellow.

The man sat up, looked around, particularly at the bare-breasted blond woman. He wondered if that woman caught a lot of colds. The man, hand on head, spoke in a bewildered tone.

"This isn't right,"

"Nope," the blond woman responded, jiggling a bit, "Not right at all."

"I guess," the man sighed, carefully wrapping a surgical smock over her shoulders. The blond woman seemed to appreciate the gesture. He wished he had thought of it. It was an aid he should have administered. He had already begun to indulge in a round of self-pity before he noticed that the group had resumed its exchange and he had again been left out.

"Hey, wait," he said, holding up his hand, "I didn't hear that. Tell me again."

"How?" the man asked. With no response available, he just bowed his head. Pity parties aren't such a bad thing, he thought. He had almost allowed the group to fade from view when he thought he heard a heartfelt plea for assistance by the small woman. He raised his head, the group snapped back into focus in time for him to hear them.

"Help!" she said. He reacted immediately, truly professionally.

"Hold on there folks," he said, as though he had just arrived on the scene, "I get the impression that someone here needs my help."

The thin man in the center of the group looked agitated.

"What's the problem? I was kidding," the man said.

He backed off, embarrassed by his outburst. Now they'll never take me, he thought. He was proven wrong again when the man suddenly smiled and spoke up.

"How about we all go over to my place for a beer?" the man suggested, pointing across a perfect lawn to the split-level ranch in the distance. His stomach growled at the mention of any nourishment, but beer was a bad thing, an alcoholic thing.

"Got any lemonade?" he asked, risking impropriety. The man smiled.

"Of course. And cookies."

"And pretzels?" he pressed, "Do you have pretzels too?"

The man was oddly distracted by the two women. They quietly discussed some private and very serious matter amongst themselves. He was dying to invade their conversation but opted against speaking. He was much too close to the picnic to anger anyone now. Joining the big man, he waited quietly until the man, the potential host, broke from the huddle with the women and hoisted two large bags of tortilla chips over his shoulder.

"And pretzels," he called to the man's back, "You said pretzels!"

The group burst into spontaneous laughter. A bit too loud, perhaps. He suspected that they laughed at him, but chose to believe that they were simply happy to have him along. He liked to realize impressions like that now and then. It kept him going.

The man hopped up the concrete stoop of his house, with the two women close behind. Once inside, the man callously turned and shut the door behind him.

He walked off the elevator and started across the busy lobby. Always so crowded on Saturday night, he thought. He stepped up his pace as he passed by the glass wall of the hospital gift shop. He didn't want Gertrude, still at the register at this ungodly hour, to notice him. Gertrude had a thing for him, always talked to him.

Normally that would be okay, but tonight was different. Tonight he had an odd craving for lemonade and pretzels, outside. Gertrude wasn't outside, and she didn't serve lemonade or pretzels.

Gloria 6

Though the basement was a mess, Gloria couldn't resist abandoning her broom to join the rats that hunched over a low table, engrossed in a board game. The pieces were too small for Gloria to determine what they played.

"Definitely not Mousetrap," she said. One of the rats, a light brown one with blue eyes, shook its head at her. She poked its belly with her forefinger, eliciting a giggle from the tiny creature. The other rodents mocked it, laughed merrily at the sissy giggling. Embarrassed, the blue-eyed rat flipped the game board, creating a brief rainbow of flying plastic tokens.

Gloria wanted to join the minor mayhem that ensued, but the creaking door at the top of the crude cellar stairs interrupted the excitement of the moment. She snatched her broom to avoid being caught idling by Mrs. Fleischman. Gloria didn't understand her own apprehension. She had volunteered to clean the basement.

Mrs. Fleischman's wrinkled stockings did not appear at the narrow angle were the top of the wooden stairs left the ceiling. Instead, four pairs of untied Reeboks shuffled down.

It was them.

Gloria should have been terrified. Those were the rules. The bright florescent lights of the clean dry basement helped her discard the usual regimented emotions. She stood in front of the ping-pong table, facing the stairs. She loosened her soft pink cotton shirt, her new denim slacks. No sense shredding perfectly good clothes, she thought.

Her tormenters rounded the bottom step side by side, like skaters executing a whip. They stopped when they all faced her, checked each other's rusty flies for smooth operation, and then moved in. They sneered and spat as they approached, but Gloria did not hear their abuse. She attributed that blessing to the bright lights. Or maybe the rats, she thought, the rats are much too polite to hear such words. Whatever the reason, the attackers' stifled remarks made it much easier for Gloria to hop up on the table and peel off her jeans.

"Hello shitheads," she said, leaning back on her elbows and spreading her legs, "Come on in."

The adolescent nightmares circled her, continuing their muted taunts without noticing her feigned acceptance of their evil intent. As always, the gang's small leader initiated the festivities, dropping his pants first. His stooges held her arms and legs to control her. Their grimaces of strained concentration made Gloria think that she must have been putting up quite a struggle.

"Not this time," she said aloud, heedless of the lads' interpretation. They didn't hear her. When the leader fumbled his way into her, Gloria felt nothing but a need to act. She snatched a cigarette that hung loose from the lipless mouth of one of the sweating leader's cohorts. He didn't notice. She took a deep drag of the wimpy menthol butt, fanning the ember at its tip to a hot orange glow. With no hesitation or even thought, Gloria touched the tip to the gnarled, greasy mat of hair on the leader's head. The ember started a small flame in the high-octane snake pit immediately.

"You should have used the flame retardant stuff, buddy," Gloria quipped as the monster's head burst into flames. The sweaty boy continued pumping, unaware of his plight or his pain, ignorant of the flames as they spread down his equally well-fueled back.

Gloria would have savored the fireball between her thighs, but her pubic hair was being singed. She whipped her hips back, forcing the boy out before he torched her as well. She was successful, but had to cross her legs to keep him from angrily re-entering. The flames had to engulf his hands for him to notice that he was about to be a charred husk. Even then, he passed a desperate moment trying to snuff out his hands, mindless of the rest of his body. When the fire reached his groin, the boy understood his fate, and the pain. Gloria felt pleasure tempered with suppressed pity as the boy began to scream. Acknowledging her own risk, she smothered the small flames in her crotch and climbed over the ping-pong net to safely watch events unfold.

The surprised boy turned to his wary friends for assistance. He shouted at them. The three had their palms outstretched, futilely deflecting his advance. They wanted a new leader. When the leader's spent body crumpled to the floor, his three assistants, too close, burst into flame. They did not share his poise, however, and ran around the nave, igniting anything they touched. The entire church was ablaze before the third attacker fell in an orange pile of embers.

Gloria sat up in her pew. The flames were closing rapidly. She was the only thing or person not already engulfed. The congregation wailed in harmonized agony around her. She heard their pain clearly. Especially the pastor, whose anguished cries from the pulpit were amplified by the glowing microphone before him.

Gloria jumped to the top of the wooden pew, flailed her arms a bit to adjusted her balance, and skipped along the wooden ridges to the open doors at the back of the church. She tumbled through the vestibule to the hot asphalt street outside. She landed painfully on her shoulder, and continued her roll to douse any flames that may have found her. There were none. She skillfully finished her roll on her feet in time to look back at the sleepy country town at the moment of its incineration. Gloria swallowed hard as the whole street roared to fiery life. Torched people ran aimlessly in all directions, spreading more flames.

"Now I've done it," Gloria said, "Now I've really done it." She spotted a bus stop enclosure nearby. It was but three glass walls and a plastic bench, but Gloria sensed sanctuary. She ran the three or four steps to it, sat on the bench. She silently watched the town burn from her safe haven, waiting for the flames, or guilt, to consume her. She stayed cool, however, and noticed her inability to mourn the dead or dying as they staggered blindly past the metal frame of the bus stop.

"They would have done the same to me, given the chance," she mumbled.

"Huh?"

Gloria sprang to her feet, noticing for the first time that a man, a very large man in a polyester business suit, shared the bench with her. His haunted eyes looked past her to the flames that had surrounded the bus stop.

"Nothing," Gloria said, regrouping quickly, "Just thinking out loud."

"Oh," the man said. He turned to her, "Maybe we should think of a way out of this mess out loud, too."

"I thought you were nicer than that, bub."

"Howard."

"Huh?"

"Not 'bub'. Howard."

"Oh, sorry. I'm Gloria."

"Pleased to meet you, and yes, I am nicer than that. It's just all those rocks and concrete blocking my way, maybe ruining every..."

"Rocks? Concrete? What are you talking about?" Gloria asked. Flames licked the bus stop on all sides. Gloria wondered if the three glass walls were as impervious as she had presumed. They had begun to buckle, emitting a low groan as they changed shape. The big man beside her, Howard, mimicked the noise.

"Why are you doing that?" she asked.

"Doing what?" he meant it.

"Never mind. Hey, what's that?" Gloria pointed to a dark shape she spotted across the field of fire. A silhouette in flux, it shifted from a man to a building then back before towering flames blocked it again. Howard didn't look in the indicated direction, but did respond.

"I see it," he said, sulking, "Saw it before, too, but it's no use. We can't get to it, and it won't help us much even if we do."

"What the hell are you talking about Howard? It's not there. It's over there! See! It appeared again. Looked like a house this time."

"Well, wherever it is, and especially if it's not there we should leave it be. Stay put."

"Stay put?" Gloria said, not sure whether her blood boiled from the heat or from her impatience with Howard. She saw the man-shape through the flames again. It, he, was sipping from a shiny aluminum can that reflected the mad flames. Gloria had to get to him. She put both hands around Howard's wrist, tugged. She might as well have tried uprooting an oak with her hands. She looked back at the black silhouette, unmistakably a house, and then at the stubborn, good man at her side. I can't leave Howard here, she thought, not in this weather. She relaxed her grip, felt better about herself for staying. It was right. The flames will probably only hurt for a second, she thought. The black silhouette of a man disappeared again, and eclipsed by two new images.

These shapes were clearer, constant. A beach ball rolled lazily toward the bus stop, propelled by a solemn child. As they grew, the new shapes defined themselves as two adults. They entered the bus stop. First in was a thin, attractive blond woman perhaps ten years Gloria's senior. Behind her loomed a grotesquely obese man in surgical garb. The woman, who Gloria respectfully named Alice, seemed to be guiding the fat man. She is a determined woman, Gloria noted. The fat man remained a mystery, however, one that she was happy not to solve. She addressed Alice.

"Thank God you're here! I found a way out of all this. But I think it's too late to get to it."

"You did, did you," Alice said, rudely condescending. Then she brightened, "Wait. You're Gloria, aren't you? And that man staring into space...Henry?"

"Howard, but that's not important now."

"It's not?"

"No. I found a way out of here."

"Through that?" Alice said, disbelieving her.

"Well," Gloria said, "I didn't think of that part yet. But I know where we have to go."

"Oh?" Alice asked sincerely, "Where?"

"There!" Gloria pointed again to the black silhouette of a bus, "If we can get to that, we'll be safe. The driver knows how to put out the fires."

"He does?" Alice asked, shading her eyes as she obliged Gloria by looking in the right direction, "I don't see anything. You see anything Ted?"

"No," the fat man said, not looking, "I smell a barbecue, though. Let's check it out."

"It's there!" Gloria shouted, "He's there! Right in front of us. What the hell's going on here?" Gloria felt panic invade her already unsteady frame. The flames were closer. Burning neighbors beat their fists on the softening glass walls. It was time to go.

"It's time to go!" Gloria repeated aloud. She was not concerned about her fear's exposure. She grabbed Alice's wrist, tried to drag her along. She wrenched her shoulder, but her effort fostered no success. Alice was nearly as immobile as Howard. Gloria didn't even consider moving Ted.

"Time?" Alice asked. Misunderstanding Gloria's frantic gesture, she contemplated the face of her watch. Alice's face tightened from slack calm control to wide-eyed surprise. Her eyes closed halfway. Her jaw remained stiff. She nodded her head.

"Yeah," she said quietly, "You're right. We gotta go." With no further preparation, she walked into the fire.

"We getting barbecue?" Ted asked, following her out of the enclosure. Ted walked a few paces behind Alice through the searing heat without melting. Mindless of their improbable progress, Gloria had lost interest in hiking across the inferno. She began to hope that the bus stop could withstand the heat, the pressure of the burning souls. It might be safe to remain.

"Wait," she called after them, "Don't you think we should think this through first?" Alice ignored her, or couldn't hear her plea over the roar of countless hungry tongues of flame.

The glass walls started to bend inward. Come on walls, she urged silently, hang in there. She felt a sudden need to follow Alice, to stay together. Howard apparently did as well. He looked at Gloria, perhaps for the first time, and spoke.

"Oh good," he said pleasantly, "We can go now." He left, following Alice into the flames.

"Oh, no," Gloria sighed. Well, she thought, at least they're headed in the right direction. Her legs began moving before she had made her decision to follow. She stepped into the flames, willing them to stay clear. She caught up to Howard, hooked her finger into one of his belt loops, and hid behind his heavy frame. He won't burn, Gloria thought. None of us can. After all, we are heading in the right direction.

"Aren't we?" she asked aloud. No one answered. She hoped they were okay, but didn't risk a peak over Howard's shoulder. Her attention was occupied exclusively by the flaming people that swarmed the group as it zigzagged through town.

Her burning neighbors were still alive, and felt the flame. The fingers of their agony reached further than their out-stretched arms to paralyze Gloria. Her forward motion continued, for Howard dragged her behind him after her knees gave out. Gloria could do little more than stare at the engulfed crowd, pity them, and thank all that is good she wasn't one of them.

"No," she said softly, "You can't be alive anymore. You have to be dead."

The sad creatures all shook their blackened heads at once, rolling lidless eyes. They circled in close. One touched her, its melted flesh frosting her bare arm.

Gloria shrieked, remembered how to use her limbs. She jumped to her feet, and continued up, over Howard's broad back, onto his shoulders. She spotted the English double-decker crashing through a garage door at the insistence of Alice's hand, which tugged its grill. The bus was close, and so was the hell-struck horde, so Gloria took a chance and jumped to the safety of the open top deck of the bus. She was the first passenger to board. The conductor smiled at her from the bottom of the steel stairwell.

"Yep," he said, "Can't be too careful about these things."

Gloria peered over the metal wall of the bus. A group of burning bodies had gathered below. They attempted to block the entry of Alice, Howard, and Ted, but the trio passed through the smoky pile and into the bus unscathed. Gloria surveyed the horizon from her safe position. Fire raged as far as she could see, in all directions. The mood of the fire had changed. Burning people walked, drove cars, or rode bicycles on the busy streets below, unaware of their immolation.

Gloria was aware. She could feel the heat, smell the charred flesh. She was astounded that the conductor, the worldly man in uniform below her, did not acknowledge the disaster. It was wrong to confront him, but he deserved an awakening.

"What the hell do you mean by 'careful'?" she called down to him, "You had better start being real careful, bub, or else we're all going to be cooked in this fire."

The man ignored her, walked down the narrow aisle to the front of the bus and sat in the driver's seat. Gloria was able to watch his progress through the vehicle because her deck's aisle lacked floorboards.

The bus drove smoothly with high and dusty velocity over the dirt path that dissected the endless green prairie. Gloria lifted her head high, letting the cool breeze blow her long hair straight back behind her. It felt good to be there, alone atop the speeding bus, fresh air blowing clean, hard. She was as close to peace and ease with herself as she'd been in a long time. She glanced at her companions below, expecting to see them sharing her delight. They did not.

Alice was anxiously staring at the horizon. Howard surveyed it calmly, but the vanishing point of the straight road intrigued him more. Ted was picking his nose and munching the bounty of his efforts. Gloria looked down the road and found herself enraptured by it finale as well.

Though faded by distance, a burning city marked the dirt road's end. Flames and black smoke rose high in the sky. Gloria's euphoria surrendered to panic once more. They were speeding straight for a fire that would surely engulf them all. The man at the wheel did nothing to slow the bus.

"What are you looking at?" he asked loudly. Alice said something Gloria could not hear, pointing toward the burning city. The driver followed her finger, but shook his head.

"That's not there," he said adamantly. Gloria rubbed her eyes in disbelief.

"That's real reassuring mister," she shouted down, "What with us careening to our deaths and all." She hopped between the rows of seats, landing on her feet in the first level aisle. The driver smiled when she landed.

"You've got some impressive legs, Gloria," he said.

"Watch your mouth, mister," Gloria snarled, secretly pleased by the honest complement. It had been so long. She was mildly self-conscious of her bare legs, and puzzled by her smoking crotch. She had no time for vanity, though, and finished her sentence, "And watch where you're going, too. You do know where you're going, don't you?"

"Don't worry," the man said. Gloria obliged, sensing reason to trust the driver. Her short-lived complacence was disrupted when she caught the man admiring the alarmingly close disaster.

"Pretty," he said, invoking horror and death with a single word. Gloria felt the heat of the city again.

"Pretty! I'll shove something pretty right up your ass if you don't do something! Pretty! What an asshole! And you'd better be quick, before we're all struck by the beauty of the moment permanently!"

"Yeah," Ted said.

"Shut up Ted," Gloria finished, folding her arms. It hurt her that she was forced to lose all respect for the man just moments before her death.

He did consider her speech, and said finally, "Okay, okay. Everyone below deck!"

Gloria didn't understand, but the bus had stopped and that was message enough. She rushed to the narrow open door, but Ted had beaten her and, of course, got stuck. She was ready to dig explosives from her black bag, but Alice interceded before that extreme was required and helped her push Ted through.

Howard filled the red vinyl booth bench across from her as well as his words filled the small diner. Gloria listened attentively to the proud man. She wished his stories of conquest, love, and loss made it past her hair. She understood nothing he said.

The man, grey eyes calm, cheerful in an odd way, sat beside him. She took little notice of him while she struggled with Howard's muted noble speech.

The waitress, Alice, stopped at the Formica table to drop off their coffee, and noticed the man at the booth. She dropped the coffee, grabbed his t-shirt, and started yelling.

"Hey! You're not here! You're outside!"

Gloria wondered why Alice was so frantic about the location of the man, or why she thought he was outside. Or why Alice was a waitress. Gloria sensed higher aspirations in the angry woman.

The man, his shoulders sagging, reluctantly stood and tried to leave. He seemed to be wrestling not only with Alice but also with a need to remain in the diner. Probably to pay for lunch. Gloria wished she understood. Though Alice silenced his mild protests, Gloria couldn't help agreeing with him, feeling strongly for his side.

"Yeah," she said. When he glanced at his only supporter, Gloria was able to remember him completely. Alice was right. He was, for some long forgotten but vital reason, out in the parking lot. She tugged on her lower lip, tried to picture him in two places, like Padre Pio.

"But aren't you outside?" she asked.

The man didn't answer. He shook off Alice's iron grip and left the busy diner with severe determination. Alice started after him. She didn't make it to the door before the diner started rocking. Its violent movement knocked Alice to the worn floor, and urged Gloria to her feet. She wished to scramble out the door, but it was gone, replaced by a smooth convex steel wall. Gloria ran along it, probed its polished curved surface for an opening. She found one all too soon.

The opening wasn't a doorway, but a rend in the steel. Fire sprayed through it, engulfing the railroad terminal's patrons with its fury. Gloria remembered its source, and sat on the hot stone floor to watch, stunned. Innocent strangers ran aimlessly, arms waving, trying to shake off the orange flames. None fell to the floor, none died.

The crack in the wall widened, encircling the terminal hallway. Unable to withstand the pressure, the venerable old building broke into two pieces. The one she was not in fell away, leaving an open wall of access for the roaming fire.

Gloria felt her skin begin to melt. She lifted her hand, watched with curiosity as the silver jewelry on her wrists and fingers turned to liquid and bubbled to the red floor. It didn't hurt. Physical pain was for travelers, Gloria decided. She got the other kind. Her body too exhausted to run, her soul too beaten to care, Gloria sat and waited to finish melting. She wished it were a dream so she could wake up.

A burning child stopped in front of her. Flames had reformed every part of her body and licked the rim of every orifice, but the child was still able to smile. She gave Gloria her doll, and pointed with an odd circular gesture over her shoulder. Gloria took the smoking doll and turned.

She sensed the change before it struck. It was him. The man. She felt his love, his mantle of responsibility, his depth approach before she could see him. When he did appear, it was an awesome entrance indeed. He rode the apex of a green vortex that swept the burning landscape aside. He slid to a stop right in front of her, on his face. He lay still between ancient tombstones in the quiet cemetery, surrounded by Alice, Howard, Ted, and herself. Alice had mislaid her blouse again. Gloria remembered that she had completely forgotten about the burning, and the man on the ground was responsible for that act of supreme kindness. That man. That dead man who had sacrificed all for them.

"Lou," she said. The formation of the name in her mouth sent a shiver through her.

"Huh?" Howard asked. He didn't appear as relaxed as Gloria felt. Nor did Alice. She couldn't tell with Ted. Maybe they didn't like old cemeteries.

"He brought us here," Gloria said, gently nudging Lou with her pointed leather boot.

"Don't be so upset about it, kid," Alice said, "You're breaking my heart."

"What?" Gloria asked, wondering how Alice could be sardonic at such an important moment.

"I said..."

"Wait," Howard interrupted, "I think he moved."

"What'd you say?" Ted asked. Lou had begun to move. His meager motion released a tremor in Gloria's spine. He rolled over, sat up, rubbing his eyes. He looked around him.

"This isn't right," he said.

"Nope," Alice said, "Not right at all."

"I guess," Lou said. He handed Alice a small rag, which she draped over her bare shoulders.

"Feels right to me, but where are we?" Gloria asked. Lou regarded her with fresh interest. He was still puzzled, but pleased by her attention.

"Got me," he said, shrugging, "I hoped you could tell me."

"How's that?" Howard asked, "The lady here says that you brought us here." Gloria clapped. The lady!

"I didn't hear that," Ted said.

"I did?" Lou asked, "How?" Lou's ignorance confused Gloria. She was unable to focus on him, and missed his heated debate with Alice. She watched them argue, and was mortally hurt when he reached out and unconscionably caressed Alice's left breast. Something was wrong, Gloria was sure of it. She fought off the instinct. She chose to be comforted by Lou's fading aura of heroism while he argued with Alice. They were both good people, she knew. They would come to terms. She thought she'd try to speed up their reconciliation.

"Okay now guys, that's enough. What are you fighting for now? There's no need."

The pair did stop. Lou looked at her, smiled, and came into full focus. Then he spoke, saying nothing. He was pointing to a beautiful marble mausoleum set atop a perfect round knoll. The setting sun colored it soft amber. He was inviting them to join him there. Gloria felt great affection for the giving man. She reached out and touched him lightly on the back of his other hand.

She scolded herself for presenting such a tiny gesture to the rare being before her. She put her arms around him from behind, laid her hands flat on his chest. She stood on her toes to get her chin on his shoulder, whispered in his ear.

"I think it's wonderful, mister. You've done a great thing offering it to us. I'm sorry if I'm doing this wrong, but it's been so long since I thanked anyone other than Ian for anything. I'm afraid I might have forgotten how to do it right."

Her speech, forgotten before she finished it, had its desired effect on the man. She felt him soften to her gentle kiss, and almost fainted when he gently wrapped his arm over her shoulders. She had never felt more secure.

"Call me Lou, Gloria," he said softly, "That's thanks enough."

Alice still faced him, and Gloria, and she was pointing angrily at two fresh graves nearby. Gloria didn't care about their heated conversation, so she didn't listen. She wished she did, though, when she felt Lou stiffen in her arms. She wondered angrily what Alice had done to him until she saw him pick up broken tombstones lying near the fresh graves. His reverent examination of the sections of hewn granite brought tears to Gloria. He turned his head up to the group, forced a smile.

"Anyone fear?" he asked. He started up the knoll with the stones under his free arm; Gloria nestled happily under the other. The group followed them closely, treading carefully as if they were nervous about the stability of the dirt path they followed. Gloria, encased in the secure folds of the strange man called Lou, failed to understand their unease.

Lou stopped suddenly, causing Howard, Alice, and thankfully not Ted to bump into him as they stopped short as well. His pause startled Gloria, and she felt the anxiety escalate in her companions.

"Why don't I make sure the lace is tied up?" Lou suggested without taking his gaze off the mausoleum's front gate. Gloria really didn't care what shape his laces were in, or where he kept them. He was holding her tight again, tensely. She squeezed him back, reassuring him.

"Something wrong, mister?" she asked, he still didn't answer. She touched her lip to his ear.

"Lou?" she said softly.

"No Gloria," he responded absently, "Nothing at all." Good, Gloria thought, as Lou released her. His warmth lingered.

"You sure?" Howard asked from behind.

"No, Howard," Lou said, "I'm not." Uh, oh, Gloria thought.

"Lou," Alice spoke his name with compassion. Who'd a thought, Gloria whispered to herself.

"Yes Alice?"

"Come back."

"Yes Alice."

Lou stepped from the group, pushing open the mausoleum's iron gate. It swung slowly on its rusty iron hinges. Lou stepped into the shadows, disappeared.

"Lou! No!" Alice screamed after him, her hands outstretched. Gloria had a second to study her, to admire her strength, her mortal fear, before the iron gate slammed shut, sending Gloria into the air.

She tumbled down the dirty basement stairs, contacting each one solidly. Her momentum carried her into the center of the rats' poker game, sending corn chips everywhere. The six rats, except the blue-eyed one, glared at her as she got to her knees and clumsily tried to fix the mess she made. The blue-eyed rat touched her hand with its little paw, looked at her. She stopped fumbling.

"Don't worry, Gloria," it said, "Why don't you just go back to sweeping?"

"Sweeping," Gloria repeated, "Yes, I'll go back to sweeping." Relieved, she picked up her broom from the floor, went back to work.

Just in time, too, she thought. The cellar door creaked open at the top of the stairs. Must be Mrs. Fleischman coming down to catch me idle, Gloria thought. She wondered why that mattered as she waited for Mrs. Fleischman's wrinkled stocking to appear.

Howard 6

"Excuse me, son," Howard said, "Can you direct me to the Lost & Found department?" The young crew-cut stockboy wiped his hands on his bloodied white apron. He nodded, pointed to a steel door at the end of a narrow aisle.

Howard acknowledged the friendly gesture and headed toward the door. The aisle proved a difficult passage. Howard was bumped repeatedly by living sides of beef slung from hooks along the wall struggling to be free.

When it was within reach, Howard grabbed the long steel handle, twisted. It broke off in his hand. The door remained closed. Howard dropped the useless handle on the slick tile, checked his fingernails. They would do.

He slid those manicured nails deep into the narrow crack outlining the stainless steel door. When his fingertips finally touched cold metal, Howard bit his lip and bent his fingers backward.

"This is going to hurt," he said.

He was right. His fingertips whitened as his nails bent to right angles. Howard was able to resist the pain, the urge to release the door and go home. He was making progress.

The door groaned under his insistent pressure. His nails felt ready to break, but Howard maintained his grip until he heard the solid thunk of tumblers dropping within the door's works.

Howard's small success revitalized him. He applied more pressure to the loosened door. With a hiss of escaping stale air, the massive steel barrier swung open. Howard, sensing danger, was reluctant to enter the dark, cold, rank Lost & Found department.

He wondered who had turned off the lights, or if perhaps the fellow in charge had gone home for the day. He didn't care to wait for an answer. There were things to be lost. And found. Immediately.

He tried the light switch on the wall to his left, but, like the doorknob, it broke off in his hands. He wasn't surprised.

"Guess a guy shouldn't expect a break," he said. He squared his shoulders to the doorframe and stepped inside.

Howard admired his swift reflexes when he sidestepped a grey slab of granite that crashed to the patch of earth he recently occupied. Then he cursed his lack of foresight when he slammed headfirst into a concrete piling.

"Didn't hurt," Howard chided the rough square column of fabricated stone. He inspected the fallen granite where it lay on its side nearby.

It was about the size and shape of a casket, painstakingly polished until it reflected the yellow glaze of the noonday sun. His own reflection shone clearly, but faced away from him.

"Hey, I can see myself," he said, "Sort of."

He also spotted in the reflection another slab of similar dimensions dropping toward him from the clear blue sky. He had no time to react. Even if he did, the forest of concrete pilings barred his way.

The new granite block crashed silently into the first, splitting them both. The four pieces of wounded granite bled profusely. Dry, red, sandy blood layered the dead ground, permeated his work boots.

He looked around. He was lost in a concrete forest during a granite rainstorm. He felt his metaphor apt, as more distant blocks did resemble raindrops.

"This is not a good place for me," he said aloud. He wasn't frightened. He felt as capable as the next man of walking between the raindrops.

He did reluctantly accept his own recognition of the danger, though, and scoured the vast dull plain for cover from the heavy rain.

He found nothing. Indeed, he was ready to give up and hope for the best when a particularly large granite obelisk whooshed past his face and landed inches from his toes. "No, this is not a good place for me," he reminded himself.

Howard, driven towards more positive results, peered around the upended slab that had nearly crushed him. This third glance revealed an additional piece of trash on the littered plain: a rusting corrugated steel shed that leaned nearby. Its open door beckoned, promising refuge.

Howard didn't hesitate. He rushed to the shed, weaving cautiously between static concrete and mobile granite obstacles. He stepped into the occupied chamber, sat on a sawhorse to catch his breath.

The occupant was a handsome raven-haired young woman wrapped in black leather. She was babbling frantically, pointing in the direction from which he had come.

"Huh?" Howard asked, annoyed by his usual social clumsiness. The woman spun, her hair flowing around her, apparently startled by his presence. She settled when she saw it was him, but Howard sensed no recognition.

"Nothing," she said, in a deep feminine voice, "Just thinking out loud." Howard wondered what it was the lady thought. Probably something about the weather, he guessed. It was certainly a hot topic for him.

"So," he said, "Just thinking out loud? Maybe we should think of a way out of this mess out loud, too." The woman frowned, put a hand to her hip.

"I thought you were nicer than that, bub," she said.

"Howard."

"Huh?"

"It's not 'Bub.' My name's Howard."

"Oh, sorry," she said, "I'm Gloria."

"Pleased to meet you," Howard said, relieved to survive the opening formality, "And yes, I am nicer than that. It's just that with all those granite slabs and concrete pillars blocking my way maybe I'm beside myself. Sorry I ruined this pleasant meeting."

Gloria stared at him, her head cocked to one side, as if she were trying to comprehend some oddity about him. Howard felt insecure and wondered if he should check his face for dirt, or drool. He politely held still.

"Why are you doing that?" Gloria asked, clearly bewildered by whatever action it was that he hadn't taken.

"Doing what?"

She sighed, shook her head.

"Never mind," she said.

A phone booth attached to a concrete column fifty paces from the shed captured her attention. She grew oddly relieved, pointed to the phone.

"Hey. What's that?" she asked.

Howard didn't want to answer. He knew exactly what it was, but it was not a solution for them. He had already tried. The dangling receiver should have been sign enough that the payphone wouldn't work.

"I see it," he mumbled, "I saw it before, too many times. But don't risk your neck out there for it. It's no use."

Gloria was studying him once more, confused. She was also pointing in another direction, toward a wall of crashing granite. The slabs tumbled by the score on top of each other as she spoke.

"It's not there," she declared, "It's over there. Look this time!" This young lady's getting a mite pushy, Howard thought. He obliged her by looking to the new location her slim index finger indicated. He watched a stand of concrete pilings tumbling like dominos under the impact of numerous granite slabs until he was sure that was all she pointed to. He shook his head.

"Wherever it is you want me to look is a disaster, Gloria. Give it up. No, I think we should wait out the storm. Stay put."

A blond woman, older than Gloria but no less attractive, crossed the threshold into the shed. She was covered in lint and towed a huge pink balloon behind her.

The woman and Gloria exchanged knowing glances, touched wrists, whispered some hidden thoughts. Howard suspected they discussed him, since he heard his name mentioned twice. Then the woman left, balloon in tow.

Howard noticed immediately that the course the woman and her balloon took was clear of both concrete columns and granite rain. He also noted that that very rain had begun to fall on the shed's roof.

"Oh good," he said, relieved, "Now we can go." He followed the blond woman, politely leaving Gloria's decision to exit in her own hands. He worried about her for a moment, then diagnosed her misgivings as stage fright. She would enter on cue, he was sure.

Howard stepped to his mark near the gas footlights, swept his velvet cape over his shoulder and proudly began to recite his soliloquy:

> "Are we the bubs we sought just yesterday?
> Have they removed the radio knobs too?
> Where is the rock? I see we take the route
> We breathe. Easy my lass creep home, for
> He is the one who is supposed to know!"

He beat his chest lightly, proud of his command of the role. Hamlet was after all, his favorite character. Howard sensed that the audience loved him as well. He finished his verse.

> "Darest I speak I mean it well, we just
> Folk must have toil.
> Let him flee, who ruins The pain.
> Worship he does ungodly gain!"

He drew a breath for the next verse when a bit player jumped on stage from the wings, interrupting him. She was dressed as a tightly bodiced serving wench, but Howard couldn't place the part or the player.

Without a word, the wench wrapped her hands around a piece of scenery, a styrofoam Doric column, ripped it from its position and threw it into the audience. She then leapt into the dark audience after it. Howard attempted to upstage her with his voice.

> "Shut tight the door, lock up the gate, we see
> Too soon the beast's timeworn torment be free!"

He was ignored by all, but Howard had no opportunity to lament his failed effort. The space left by the tossed plastic pillar had not been filled in by stage. Rather, the space it had occupied was white. Blank, bright white.

Howard mistrusted the anomaly, but the stage's hot footlights blocked his planned exit. He put his arm over his head as a shield against the growing purity and stood his ground.

As if on cue itself, the brilliance yellowed, dimmed, almost disappeared. Howard kept up his guard, and was rewarded when the theater was flooded in a complete, cold flash of amber lightning. He was safe; he didn't see it.

Howard lowered his arm, surveyed the small group gathered on the huge granite boulder: two women, a fat surgeon, and a dead man. Familiar people, he thought, but I can't place them. He wondered if the blond woman knew she was topless.

The monolithic dimensions of the granite slab humbled Howard. It stretched as far as he could see, maybe farther, since the dim sun stopped working a few yards away.

It was hewn, too. Not natural. Howard was about to decide that the slab wasn't big, that he was an ant on a stepping stone, when the smaller, clothed woman spoke. He didn't hear.

"Huh?" he asked.

"He brought us here," the woman said, kicking the carcass lying prone on the cold grey stone.

"Don't be so upset about it." the blond woman snapped, "You're breaking my heart."

"What?"

While their conversation progressed, Howard quietly observed the body. He had been listening to the women intently enough earlier that he had failed to notice initially what he was watching.

The body was moving.

Its back expanded with breath, its fingers flexed. Hell, Howard thought, I think this fellow's still with us.

"I said..." the blond was saying.

"Wait," Howard interrupted. They both glanced at him, offended by his rude interruption. The fat guy kept to himself.

"I think he moved," Howard said, mindful to include melodramatic undertones for effect.

"What'd you say?" the fat man asked, rubbing his eyes. Howard, occupied by the resurrected corpse, didn't answer. He watched the man, who appeared in excellent health, roll over and observe his odd surroundings. He rubbed his eyes, too. Howard fought to keep his own balled fists from aping the motion. The man used his freshened, wide eyes again.

"This isn't right," he said casually. He stood, taller than all except Howard.

"Nope," the blond responded, "It's not right at all." She was overly serious; too cold.

"I guess," the man said, handing a baseball glove to the woman. She covered her upper privates with it.

While Howard looked away as she donned the sports equipment, he noticed the edges of the slab. All four of them at once. It was easy, since the granite sheared off into vertical cliffs on all four sides, inches from their feet.

Howard suddenly felt very large, and equally imperiled. He also felt the whole mess had something to do with the man, who could change things if he wanted to.

"Where are we?" the smaller woman asked.

"Got me," the man smiled - as if it were a joke! - "I hoped you could tell me."

Howard, his right foot already slipping off the sudden edge, did not like that response. Not at all.

"How's that?" he asked, finger in his ear. The man failed to respond. Howard spoke up, adding a supportive statement. He hoped it was true.

"The lady here says that you brought us here."

"I didn't hear that," the fat man said, still rubbing his eyes.

"S'all right big guy, I was talking to him."

"Who?"

"Uncover your eyes and you'll know."

"Oh."

Ted's distraction (hmm, Ted, Howard thought) prevented Howard from hearing the man's response. When he did look, the man was already across the thin stone bridge that arched from their slab to the next.

He was entering a telephone booth. A telephone booth with a working phone. The two women watched intently as he waved, shut the door. Ted rubbed his eyes.

When the glass door shut, it did so with a bang whose force started the slab rocking. Howard dropped to his knees, not wishing to be knocked off.

As he feared, the flimsy bridge crumbled under the vibration. Their safe passage disintegrated into bits of grey rubble that tumbled skyward. Skyward? Up?

Howard did a doubletake when he realized that the rubble had not flown up. It had fallen. Just as he was about to, seeing that he knelt on the bottom, not the top of the granite slab. The knowledge of his location forced him to drift off the slab. He began the rapid descent to the concrete columns, arranged in organized geometric order far below.

He sighed, not surprised to be part of the granite storm.

"Fine," he said, rolling his eyes.

Alice 6

Green shag rug carpeted Alice's world. Carpeted it. Ruled it. Dominated it. Was it. Horrible shag rug, from the '70s, in a shade that was consciously chosen for its resemblance to mucus. It had to have been.

The strands of the rug that stretched flat to every horizon were tall, tickling her bare ankle. She rubbed her feet against it. It was soft, she conceded. But she would not accept that it was her universe. It couldn't have been. Its panoramic presence denied her that self-assurance.

She prepared herself to walk, to cross the extra deep pile plain, but a slight rustling at her feet delayed exploration. Hands on her knees, Alice bent low to inspect the thick pile. She saw movement in the strands. Something small and alive was making its way through the carpet, away from her foot.

"My only company here is a cockroach," she said, "It figures."

On closer inspection, it didn't look like a bug. It was too pink and round. Familiarly pink, and round.

"No. It can't be."

She knelt carefully, lowered her face until her nose touched the carpet. She took a long close look at the figure that struggled in the strands.

"Son of a bitch," she said softly, not wishing to disturb the miniature fat man, "It is you."

She decided that Ted was in a jam of sorts down in the shadowy broadloom bowels, and she should give him a hand (or a fingertip in this case, she thought). She eased her thumb and forefingers together around him. Ted saw her approach and reached for her hand. He clasped her forefinger. Alice observed too late that Ted may have lost his size but he had managed to retain his mass.

She was airborne, en route to disaster before she could assess her plight. Her efforts to help the little man had worked against her. Ted had held on tight and pulled her into his world, his scale. Her anger swelled with the awful green carpet strands that expanded around her until they achieved the proportions of trees. Old, gnarled, rotted trees. The rest of the carpet enlarged with the broadloom. Dust balls blew by like tumbleweeds. Bugs, ignorant of her presence, crawled by in search of cast off skin, a patch of which she knelt in. It was moist, disgusting. She couldn't believe that Ted, still holding her finger, could be smiling. After she shook off his grip, she noticed the friendly grin was actually a blatant leer. His beady, half-buried eyes stared directly at her breasts, which were bare save for a sprinkling of bits of dust, dead skin, and one large moth larva that she brushed off quickly. This guy's disgusting, Alice thought, I didn't expect that from him. Ted made eye contact accidentally, and a red glow washed, eclipsed, his cantaloupe cheeks.

"It's okay," he said with pathetically delivered patronizing authority, "I'm a doctor."

He assumed she would believe him.

"No you're not," Alice snapped, choosing anger rather than laughter (there was, after all, a human being tucked inside all that padding), "You're an asshole!"

Ted stepped back, deeply offended. Alice worried that she might have hurt the young man into catatonic submission, but saw that he was merely regrouping in a rippled, messy sort of way. Alice, though she was pleased her nature had caused little harm, wished Ted were more in control of his expressions. And his bowels.

"I suppose I am," he said, long after she had forgotten what it was she had called him, "So?"

"So?" she repeated, thinking fast. So we've got to get the hell out of this disgusting shag rug you dragged me into, she thought, so we can find some other sucker for you to 'help'.

"So," she said aloud, "Come with me, Ted. I'll show you a way out."

"A way out?" Ted asked stupidly. The brilliant surgeon's brain at work, Alice thought.

"Yes, Ted," she said, "Now come on, let's go." She started to pick her way through the rayon forest, admiring her poise. She didn't know where she was going. Ted didn't care, however. She felt his attendance behind her. He didn't speak, but she knew he was developing a strong sense of loyalty to her. Not lewd loyalty, but abject thrall loyalty. And he paid her the highest complement of all: he admired her class. Touched, she turned back for a moment, hand on her hip, and smiled.

"Well, thanks Ted," she said. Ted's puffy cheeks reddened again, but he chose not to express any sentiment... best to maintain the omniscient thing as long as possible, she thought. She resumed her exploration of the miserable green forest.

A cockroach, big as a horse, strolled across their path. Alice remembered that it was morning and the big bug was probably on its way to the kitchen. It left a clear trail of droppings and partially chewed skin bits, so she chose to follow it. She turned off the path. Ted followed like the happy bug that he was. He seemed to sense the cockroach's motive as well: a small bead of saliva ran down his chin.

The cockroach's nasty trail led them on a crooked path through the forest, but Alice sensed that they were making progress. She cursed herself for that thought, since it caused the reliable trail to disappear. Alice, denying herself the luxury and freedom of being lost, wandered around aimlessly. Ted followed doggedly, close behind. She hoped to stumble upon some new landmark, or rugmark, as it were. Ted was oblivious to their predicament, and was disgusted when they stumbled across an overturned glass furniture caster and the two figures cowering beneath it. Alice, first checking that the massive canopy was secure, stepped underneath to greet the nervous pair: a big man and a small woman.

"Thank God you're here," the woman said, clapping her hands. She was obviously pleased to see her. Alice wanted to ask the little woman what she expected, but she continued before Alice could speak, "I found a way out of all this, but I think it's too late to get to it!"

"You did, did you?" Alice asked, wishing to trust those dark, wild eyes. Wild eyes. Wait a minute, Alice thought, I know this woman.

"You're Gloria, aren't you?" she asked. The woman didn't respond, but Alice knew she was right. This is too bizarre, she thought. She pointed to the big man, "And that man staring into space. Henry?"

"Howard," Gloria corrected, "But that's not important now."

"It's not?" Alice asked. It seemed monumental to her. So did Howard.

No," Gloria said hurriedly, "I found a way out of here!" She pointed an unsteady finger back through the rug. Alice followed her gesture, studied the gently swaying strands for a sign of a clear path. She saw only the dark forest, a couple of fist-sized rug mites, and more skin. Not very appealing. She began to appreciate the haven created by the fallen caster. Still, she desired to believe Gloria. The girl's self-confidence was invigorating.

"Through that?" Alice asked. Maybe I missed something, she thought. Gloria's face fell.

"Well," she said, disappointed, "I didn't think of that part yet." Alice was ready to settle down, introduce herself to the big man... Harry, was it? She couldn't remember... When Gloria brightened, said more, "But I know where we have to go!"

"Oh," Alice asked, her curiosity piqued, "Where?"

"There," Gloria said, pointing at the same unvacuumed jungle as before, "If we can get to that we'll be safe. The driver knows."

"He does?" Alice asked. She saw no driver, but a certain sincere passion in the woman's claim urged her to look again. She shaded her eyes, less from the dim light than to protect them from falling debris. She looked hard into the shadows, but sensed nothing unusual.

"I don't see anything," she said finally. Just to be sure, she turned to Ted, gestured to him to take a look. He thinks he's useful, she thought, maybe he'll prove it. She asked, "You see anything, Ted?"

"No," Ted said brightly, without a glance, "I smell a barbecue, though. Let's check it out!" Thanks for the input Ted, Alice thought, guess I should've known.

"He's there," Gloria shouted, "Right in front of us! Hell, it's time!"

"Time?" Alice asked. She looked at her watch, and noticed that Mickey's hands were spinning madly backward. Alice was intrigued by their movement, and delightfully surprised when Mickey looked at her and winked.

"That's right boys and girls," the familiar squeaky voice announced, "It's time to go all right. Time to go that way boys, and girls. Huh ha!"

The hands stopped spinning, both of them pointing together in a direction opposite of that Gloria had chosen. Alice nodded.

"Yeah," she said to the passive watch face, "You're right. We gotta go."

Alice left the safety of the glass wheel, walked in the direction Mickey's hands had indicated. She could see their destination in the distance. She wondered how she could have missed a landmark as large as the Playskool castle earlier.

"Must've been looking the wrong way," she said. She followed the red brick paved path, glad to be on a road that lifted her bare feet off the scummy rug.

The walk to the lowered plastic portcullis was short. She waited until the rest of the little group had reached the castle wall before she rattled the yellow bars.

The response was immediate, but not positive. A familiar man appeared, dressed in colorful paper armor. He peeked out through the bars, shook his head, and rudely turned away.

"We'd even pick tulips as long as you don't drink!" Ted shouted after the retreating figure. The man returned to the bars.

"Huh?" he said, dumfounded. Alice was too.

"What exactly are you saying, Ted?" she asked.

"I just said that you can drive," Ted said. Alice wrestled with the significant phrase while the man responded.

"Oh yeah," he said, dipping his rubber sword in an odd salute, "Thanks." He walked away.

This is wrong, Alice thought, incensed, he can't just walk away, leave us here.

Hey," she shouted, "Wait a second. Where do you think you're going?" The guard stopped again, turned back toward the gate. He said nothing, and appeared ready to leave again without lifting the portcullis. Alice, furious, would have none of that. She reached through the flimsy bars for a piece of the cruel man.

Her fingers clawed the top edge of his newspaper bodkin. She closed her hand, felt it sink into the filthy material. She backed up fast, not letting go. The man followed, helplessly crashing through the gate, destroying it.

She fished Lou out of the salt water, deposited him behind the wooden wheel of the motor yacht. He was dry, of course. Always dry. He bent right over, picked up the beer can lying beside the captain's chair. It must be his, Alice noted, remembering a vague warning from Ted about beer before they had set out. She looked at the fat man, dwarfing the forward bulwarks, with what's-his-name (Herbert?) at his side. Ted was unconcerned, his attention commanded by the rocky horizon. Alice wondered how Lou could handle the yacht with all that ballast in the bow. Must be drunk, she thought.

Lou deposited his beer in a mahogany box by his side.

"Yep," he said cheerfully, "Can't be too careful." I guess not, Alice thought, but she had to grin.

Gloria, seated above them in the flybridge, allowed no such emotion.

"Whaddya mean, 'careful?'" she shouted down, "You be careful, bub, or we're all cooked." Alice knew Gloria's trite statement was true. Something out there made her nervous. She couldn't identify the problem, even when she looked over the bow past Ted at the reef they steamed steadily toward. Though she was growing as agitated as Gloria appeared, Lou was smiling placidly as he steered the careening little ship. Careening?

"No," he was saying, "No one's cooking: sorry, the alcohol, you know. I'll be damned if I can get going."

His statement prompted Alice to refocus on the yacht's rapidly approaching destination. The granite reef rose above the bow each time the boat dipped into a trough. Alice was sure the man next to Ted could reach out and touch it. Of course, neither seemed too concerned by the looming disaster. Lou, however, had taken an interest in where he was propelling his yacht.

"Anyway," he said, trying to maintain a captainly level of calm, "What the hell are you looking at?"

"You tell us," Alice said, unwilling to shift her gaze from the wall of rock that rose high above them, "You're the one driving this thing!"

"He is the one to know," the man at the bow said, projecting nicely. Hubert? Alice thought; no, that's not right.

"Thanks for the input, Howard," Alice said. Howard, of course! She continued, "Now you can go back to looking, if you don't mind." Howard did. He probably never heard her. Alice forgot about him immediately. The reef and Lou's disinterest in it monopolized her attention. Having little recourse, and noticing that the raven-haired girl in a black bikini had failed to influence the man, she stepped behind him and pressed his head between her palms. Twisting his stubborn skull toward the reef demanded substantial effort, but she was eventually successful. Once he turned, she checked that his misty grey eyes were open. They were.

"It's about time those precious things started working again," she whispered, brushing her lips lightly over his ear, "Now look. Over there!"

He looked. Alice held him a little longer, expecting that her assistance was necessary. It wasn't. The man relaxed, smiled at what he saw, and didn't veer off.

"It's pretty," he said.

"Pretty!" Gloria shouted, banging her fist on the pilothouse roof, "Shove pretty! Do something, and be quick before we're struck by that!" Alice couldn't have said it better herself, so she didn't.

"Yeah!" the fat man at the bow called. Ted. He could have said it better.

"Shut up, Ted," she said.

"Okay," Lou said, adopting a commanding tone, "Everyone below deck!"

Alice volunteered to oversee the exodus below decks. She assumed Howard was first into the companionway, since he was no longer above deck. Ted got stuck in the narrow passage, but

Gloria helped her shove him through. Gloria followed, disappeared into the darkness below. Alice lagged behind, watched as Lou mastered the helm. He was clearly in charge, but sadly had not yet started steering.

"Hey, mister," she said, "You sure you don't want me to stay up here with you? I've never been on one of these things, but I can plow a straight furrow. The wheel looks the same. It can't be too different."

Lou glanced at her, smiled a real smile, spoke, "It's all right."

"Really, I'd love to help."

"Alice. It's best I stay up here alone. Thanks."

"You're a hero, mister," Alice said sincerely. He was. She shrugged and proceeded down the marble stairway alone, careful not to catch her spiked heels on the hem of her red sequined gown.

The ballroom was majestic, its ceiling invisible, lost in misty clouds high above the rows of crystal chandeliers, each as big as a house. Alice crossed the crowded parquet dance floor. The dancers, stepping to a finely orchestrated waltz, parted for her. The pink marble floor beyond had dozens of round tables arranged on it. Most of the places, set with Lennox and Baccarat, were empty. Probably dancing, Alice thought. A small group occupied half the wooden chairs at a table near the picture window. Alice thought she recognized the trio, as well as the man standing behind them admiring the hors d'oeuvre tray carried by a white uniformed waiter. She passed by them, enchanted by the picture window.

Picture didn't describe that window. Panorama was more appropriate. The window was of titanic proportions. If turned on its side, it could protect a football field. It was constructed of thin, air-clear glass. She was afraid to touch it, but had to, for a better look at the vista outside. A scene that was beyond the containment even of the expansive pane provided. She pressed her face and hands against the glass. It didn't break.

The mansion she visited was anchored near the top of a range of verdant mountains that rose as high as the Himalayas and flowed away under golden sunshine in wave after perfect wave to a horizon uncountable miles away. Pressing her forehead against the hard thin surface, she looked down. The land dropped away beneath her, disappearing into white puffy clouds far, far below.

"Magnificent," she said aloud.

"Dare I speak?" Alice heard a voice from the table she had ignored. A male voice, strong, filled with pomp, had risen above the sounds of the crowded ballroom. She figured he deferred to their unseen host. The man was right, of course, for all the grandeur presented demanded humility.

"Well," the man finished with a practiced vocal flourish, "We just have to let him run the ship!"

"Ship?"

Alice turned back to the table. Her chest froze. Her throat closed. She recognized them all. She remembered where she was. What those sun-drenched, lichen covered granite mountains really were. She stepped to the table, shoved the waiter aside. Without hesitating, she grabbed the grey-eyed man by his gold filigree uniform lapels and hoisted him to his feet. The host, caught partying while his yacht faced certain disaster at the other end of the marble stairs, was either amused or startled. Alice couldn't tell. She didn't care either, as she shook him vigorously.

"Hey, you're not supposed to be here. You should be outside. Steering!"

The captain shook limply in her grasp. His eyes cleared. He turned from her and sauntered toward the dance floor.

"Yeah," the small woman in a black satin gown said. Then she touched a finger to her chin, and asked, "Aren't you outside?" The captain may have agreed with them both, but he moved too slowly.

Alice could stand no more of the charade.

"Lou!" she shouted. Lou.

He heard her and reacted. He bounded up the marble stairs three at a time, reaching the landing as the old stone steps crumbled to dust behind him. He was too late.

White hot water engulfed the room, melting the dancers, the floor, and the food into a unified steaming muck. A mountain poked through the majestic window, shattering it. Shards of glass rained down on well-dressed revelers, shredding them into a pink viscous fluid. The new sauce mixed nicely into the existing knee-high stew.

Alice pulled the emergency cord under the table. She could at least protect the group that sat there. The table emitted a shrieking alarm. Its sides got bigger, enveloping the group in a cocoon of lace and muslin.

Alice scanned the empty purple sea for life. Even a seagull would have satisfied her, but there was nothing. Nothing anywhere except flat violet water, a warm sun, a makeshift log raft, and them.

Howard, Gloria, Ted, and, lying face down on the log floor, Lou. She knew them all. Always did, she assumed, since she had never met any of them. She would have remembered. Yet somehow they were all in the same boat together.

"No, we're all in the same raft," she quipped. No one heard.

She and Howard were unclothed from the waste up. No one seemed to mind, or notice. Not even Ted, who stood at the other end of the small raft. Tilting it a bit, she observed. She did notice Howard, though. Powerfully built, tan, big hands, worn but pleasant face; huge neck. He seemed like a good person but she would never truly find out - he was preoccupied with his own misguided deeds. She could tell. I can tell everything about everyone, she realized, if only I could remember what they are. Her selfish thoughts were extinguished when Gloria said something deeply heartwarming, but unheard.

"Huh?" Howard said, distantly interested. Always so distant. How did she know 'always'? Ted showed no interest at all. Of course no one had mentioned Twinkies yet. Alice concentrated on the bright young woman. She found value in Gloria's thoughts. She wished she knew why.

"He brought us here," Gloria said, reverently tapping Lou's dormant midriff with her bare toe. She was on the edge of mournful tears, honoring Lou for putting them on this raft in the middle of nowhere. No, Alice corrected. She knew Lou. He was clumsy and stupid sometimes, and he was the reason they were all on the raft. He was also, however, the reason they were there. Alice felt for the younger woman. She would understand Gloria's loss if there were a need to. She leaned forward, over Lou, who she knew was fine. She wished she could convince Gloria.

"Don't be so upset about it kid," Alice said, choking back her own emotions, "You're breaking my heart."

"What?" Gloria asked, eyeing her suspiciously.   Uh, oh, Alice thought, I butted into unwelcome territory again.   She forced a smile.

"I said," she began, but Howard, who was still staring at Lou, interrupted.

"Wait," Howard boomed, "I think he moved."

Alice was pleased to see Gloria moved to ecstatic pleasure by the surprise statement from Howard.

"What'd you say?" Ted asked.

Lou stirred, opened his eyes.   Moaning, he lifted himself up off the rough-hewn floor to a seated position in the center of the small circle of people.   He rubbed his eyes, looked around.   His surroundings puzzled him.   He tentatively stood up, achieved balance easily on the tilted raft.   The group stood around him, almost crowded him.

"This isn't right," he said.   Alice heard an audible sigh from Gloria.

"Nope," Alice responded, adopting an angry posture, "Not right at all."

"I guess," Lou said.   He absently passed an article of clothing to her.   She took and donned the simple white cotton blouse, fastened some of the buttons.

"Feels right to me," Gloria said softly, out of her trance, "But why are you here?"

"Got me," Lou said, "I hoped you could tell me."

"You brought us here," Howard informed Lou.   He should already know that, Alice thought, I knew it.   But then, she concluded, I know all things today.

"I did?" Lou asked Howard, "How?"

"Aren't you supposed to tell us that, Lou?" Alice said.   She hoped he wasn't toying with them.

Lou seemed to notice her thought.   For, instead of responsibly answering her query, he reached out and rubbed the fabric of her new sleeve between his fingers.   He never took his eyes from hers, though.

"Nice shirt.   Where'd you get it?"

"You serious?" Alice asked.

"He's going to help," Gloria said respectfully.   Alice wasn't so sure of that. She tilted her head and waited for him to recover. He stared blankly.

"What's the problem?" he asked defensively, "I was kidding."

"Oh, that's a relief," she said, not relieved.

"I know where you got this shirt," Lou said, fondling her left breast through it.

"Oh, Lou," Alice said. She was worried. That wasn't like him at all.

"How about we go over to my place for a beer and some cookies?" Lou asked, gesturing with his thumb to the quiet gray sand beach that firmly held Ted's end of the raft. Lawn chairs and an open cooler were arranged in a welcoming manner a short distance down the beach, near the water. Alice would not believe the land's entry into her watery world until she stepped off the raft and her spiked heels disappeared into the sand. She discarded the shoes, just in case, and wiggled her toes in the cool sand.

"Ok," she said, "So it's real." She was not happy that rescue from certain oblivion had come so easily, or that Lou had claimed it as his. She should have known. Knowledge made things real, and without it she had to rely on the machinations of Lou. Though better Lou than Ted, she was still annoyed. And the world, her world, remained incomplete. She faced Lou, who was still aboard the raft.

"Lou," she said firmly, "How long have you known that was there?" Lou paused for a moment, pensive.   Then his shoulders sagged.

"Feels like forever, sometimes. I don't know exactly. Ten years? Fifteen?"

His solemn response continued to echo in her long after he presented it so casually. Fifteen years, she thought, how could that be? We just met. Didn't we? When she slumped to the forgiving sand to contemplate the notion, she spotted two large pieces of flotsam bobbing in the water beside the raft. They were logs. Thin, cut recently from strong young trees. They had been part of the raft once, but the lashings had broken, and they were set adrift. She wanted to blame Lou for the painful discovery, but couldn't. Yes, he had bound the logs, and maybe his rope wasn't thick enough, but the logs were thin, slippery. No rope could have secured them permanently from drifting away. Still, the dead stumps disturbed her. Nobody on the crowded raft chose to share her sentiment. Lou wished to respond, but was still confused about her, about the lost logs.

"I'm sorry Alice," he tried, head bowed, "I didn't realize..." His statement was sincere. Alice felt her burden lifted slightly by his empathy. Maybe Lou would make things okay.

Gloria consoled him too, wrapping her thin arms around him from behind. She squeezed, whispered something that moistened his grey eyes.

"Come, Gloria," he said, "That's thanks enough." He nestled the emotional woman under his right arm. Alice could feel the comfort Gloria absorbed from him. But, when Lou stepped off the raft with Gloria, away from the logs, Alice realized that he had not empathized with her, or even understood her. Furious at his condescending callousness, she positioned herself in front of him again, blocking his path. She wanted to punch Lou for being a blockhead, but was leery of doing so. Gloria might rip her eyes out in retaliation. Instead she held her ground, glared her meanest glare. Lou grew agitated quickly. She guessed that her revelation of a truth he thought he could forget disturbed him. She was a good guesser that day.

"What!" Lou snapped. Alice didn't cringe at his display.

"Can't you see?" she asked.

"See what?"

How can he be this way? Alice thought.

"See what?" Alice squealed, struggling for control, "Those. What about those?" She kept her eyes connected with his. He'd figure out what she meant soon enough.

A little later than sooner, Lou looked down to his left. His face clouded when he recognized the logs, and his shoulders sagged under the weight of their presence. A wave of humiliation passed through Alice. What she had done devastated her. She would have killed a person who rekindled pain she had successfully repressed. Oh well, she thought, I can't take it back now.

"Oh, those," Lou said quietly, unable to look at her.

"Yeah," Alice said, "Those." He understood, and she regretted it. She allowed him room to pass her. He instead released Gloria and bent into the water to pick up the logs. He shouldered them, stepped onto the beach. The load lightened his demeanor.

"Anyone for beer?" he asked cheerfully.

"You said pretzels," Ted chimed in. Gloria and Howard burst into nervous laughter at Ted's statement. Alice joined them. She didn't understand the joke, but Lou's changed mood deeply relieved her and she needed to show it. Lou started the inevitable parade to the lawn chairs. Alice, with Gloria at her side, followed. They were not clear of the raft before Lou hesitated. He stood silently, forcing Alice to do the same, and spoke softly over his shoulder.

"Why don't you folks wait here while I go tidy up?"

Alice was suspicious. How do you tidy up a beach? Gloria paused as well, looking small again without Lou's arm around her.

"Something wrong Lou?" Gloria asked, openly concerned.

"No," Lou responded, slowly shaking his head, "Nothing at all. I'll be right back."

"Are you sure?" Alice asked.

"Everything's fine, Alice," Lou said, not looking directly at her. He always looked directly at her.

She didn't believe him.

"Lou."

"Yes, Alice?"

"Make damn sure you come back."

"Yes Alice," Lou said as he resumed his tentative pace. In his apparent caution, Lou ignored the tidal wave that had formed in the calm water near the chairs. She looked around. The others were concerned but did nothing. She was about to yell at them for their inconsiderate behavior when she saw that she was doing nothing as well.

"Lou no!" she shouted, trying to chase after him. She was too late. Lou walked into the cresting wave, and was absorbed by it without being knocked over. The wall of water turned and headed toward her, sideways down the beach. Alice could do nothing but scream while the warm water picked her up carried her in tumbling wet darkness until it deposited her on the seaweed-swathed beach.

She opened her eyes and yelped in disgust. She had fallen asleep while watching TV again, somehow wound up face down on the awful green shag rug.

She jumped to her feet, felt her hair and clothes for cockroaches. Odd thing to look for, she thought. On her way to the bathroom, she passed the cleaning lady in the hall. The young maid struggled with an unbristled broom and a foot tall pile of dust. She paused, looked up at her.

"Don't worry Gloria," Alice said automatically, hoping her face wasn't too wrinkled from the rug, "Why don't you just go back to sweeping?"

"Yes. I'll sweep," the maid said. Funny, Alice thought, even in the best years Ed said 'no' to help. She dismissed the thought as she entered the blue bathroom. She stepped up to the mirror, touched her face.

"Well, I guess I didn't have to worry about wrinkles."

There was, after all, no reflection in the mirror.

Lou 7

Lou covered his head. The sheets were cool and fresh, but useless as tools to engage in silencing his alarm. The persistent pulsating electronic buzz of his clock radio beat with undiminished volume through the thin bedclothes.

"Shut up shut up shut up!" he shouted through cotton percale, unwilling to wake up while darkness still clouded his bedroom. He surrendered, but reviewed his familiar shadowy surroundings to confirm that morning had not yet broken. The clock was lying to him.

"What the hell," he complained, "It's still night out." Nonplused by his logic, the alarm buzzed on. It must be right, he conceded, and I'm wrong. He despised the thought.

Lou reluctantly pulled an arm out from under the rich comfort of his warm blankets. He reached over his head through the cold darkness. He dropped his palm sluggishly on the top of the clock radio. Though the first slap should have been sufficient, the persistent ringing led him to repeat the motion several times. That was wrong. The alarm always submitted after the first whack. He pondered the significance, and decided that perhaps the object was not his clock at all, but something new. It felt like his clock radio, and it was in the right place...

"Son-of-a-Bitch," Lou mumbled, woefully aware that he would have to roll onto his stomach, hoist his semi-conscious body onto an elbow and investigate the source of the ringing. He hated the thought, but the nagging need to tend to the ringing won. He lifted himself until his eyes cleared the shelf of the headboard, where his clock had resided for a decade.

It had moved, replaced by a new appliance. The source of the ringing was a telephone. Not his: his was the latest model big-button touch-tone. The phone jangling insistently a few inches from his nose, eerily lit by grey wisps of dawn, was something from the 50s'...big, black, metal. An office phone with its rotary dial missing. It wasn't his phone, but it rang for him. It was his call. A wake-up call he forgot to cancel. He wrapped his lethargic fingers around the cold instrument and picked it up.

The receiver was far more massive than he had expected, even from a metal phone from the 50's. Lou's hand almost slipped off before he managed to move it, white knuckled and quivering, high enough to clear the cradle, to open the line -- to stop the ringing. That was his limit. He broke into a sweat as he strained to lift it higher, to respond to the faint female voice that spoke through the oversized earpiece.

"Hello?" she asked weakly. Her tone led Lou to believe the caller knew he was there, and that he wouldn't speak to her.

"Are you there?" the frail voice asked. Lou yearned to respond, but his effort to suspend the heavy receiver was enlisting every muscle fiber available. If he tried to speak, he would drop the phone.

"Please," the voice said, wavering, "I know you're there. Please talk to me."

The plea burrowed into his soul. Its blunt need encouraged him to overlook rationale, to follow emotional priority. To respond.

"Hel-" the receiver landed hard in the cradle of the old phone, cracking its surface, disconnecting the caller.

Lou fell back into bed, sweat flowing from every pore. He breathed deeply, tried to relax, to enjoy the warm morning sunshine that glowed through his bare window. He shook his wet head, chasing away any remnants of the dream that had already escaped his memory. He cast a furtive glance at his window again, loosely judged the time without looking at his clock. He decided arbitrarily that it was not yet time to get up, so he rolled away from the bright window. He settled in for a few more moments of brief slumber. His eyes hadn't finished closing before the ringing invaded.

Lou ducked under his sheets to escape the intrusive racket. He was mildly surprised to find that the linens also sheltered Alice and Howard. He instinctively curled up his legs to make room for the quietly chatting pair. Their distant conversation indicated that accommodation was not necessary. They had plenty of room under the multicolored tent, and didn't notice Lou hovering over them anyway. He shifted his head closer to them, quietly; for a better look at his guests, no more. They were engrossed in a game of Chutes and Ladders.

"Howard, it's your turn," Alice was saying, her tone serious.

"Yeah, I'm going," Howard responded, equally sincere, "And thanks for remembering."

"It's why I'm here, Howard," Alice said, brightening, "You know that."

"I do now," Howard said, leaning towards Alice as he spoke. The big man wanted to touch her. He moved his token instead. He looked past her and spoke again, "Thanks."

"No need for that," Alice said, "Finishing your turn is enough."

This is getting silly, Lou thought.

"Okay," he said politely, "What are you two doing in my bed?"

They didn't answer.

"Really," he said, "I want to know. And 'Chutes and Ladders?' Seriously, should you be playing that here?"

They ignored him.

"Fine," Lou said, "Enough of you then." He pulled the sheet from over his head. The real world beckoned from outside the sheets: the morning, the angry, pulsing alarm. He bent his neck, surveyed the covers that formed a smooth contour over the rest of his body, and then flattened over the rest of the bed. He tentatively lifted the sheet once more, peeked at Alice and Howard.

They played quietly at a picnic table. Howard thrust his fist in the air in spontaneous reaction to climbing a ladder. Alice smiled. Birds sang. They all ignored him. He let the sheet fall around him like a parachute. He watched it settle slowly to the bed, aware that he was fending off the inevitable. Finally, he moved to shut off the nagging alarm. His roll onto his stomach was interrupted mid-motion by his second and sadly vacant pillow. It had changed. It was pink, and much larger than he had remembered. He touched it, then pulled is finger away in surprise. It wasn't his pillow at all. It was Ted.

The fat, well meaning man lay curled into a ball at the top of his bed. Naked, sweaty, and asleep. A microphone, one of those art-deco chrome models from the 30's, was nestled in the crook of his arm. Lou warmly admired Ted's dedication. He had no idea what it was Ted was dedicated to, or why he should admire it, but Lou did. He slapped Ted's big bare ass, leaving a handprint on the sweaty flank.

"Hey Ted," he said, "That's the way to be."

Ted ignored him, didn't hear him, or just slept right through his attentions. Lou sighed and finished rolling over onto his stomach. The alarm still rang. Its clarion call was unavoidable, irresistible. He couldn't ignore it. Lou would have to heed it since he knew it was for him.

"For me," he mumbled, eyelids heavy, as he tried to find the snooze button, "For me, yes. For me now. No, I'll sleep. Just a few seconds more..." His limp hand landed not on the simulated wood of his clock radio, but on the receiver of a phone. A heavy black metal office phone from the 50's.

"Why did I know this was going to be heavy?" he asked aloud, his stubborn eyes still closed. He tried to lift the receiver high enough to stop the ringing. He felt a weight on the back of his hand. A warm, soft weight, pressing, resisting his effort to answer his call. But, he thought, the phone, the alarm, is for me. I have to get it.

"No, mister. Lou. Please. Pick it up," the weight said. Lou opened his eyes. Gloria was perched on his struggling wrist. Her smooth white legs dangled on either side of his useless arm. Her hands rested on her bent knees. Lou searched for new strength: if the ringing stopped, Gloria would be gone. He didn't want Gloria to be gone. Gloria, by the pressure of her thighs, also indicated that she wanted to stay.

He couldn't honor that desire. She was too heavy. He couldn't answer the phone with her on it. He wished it would occur to him to ask her to get off the receiver so he could stop the ringing before the phone did so itself. He hated himself for not thinking of it, but still hoped that the thin and troubled woman would take action. But then she wouldn't have been on the phone in the first place, he thought. Lou looked into Gloria's wide dark eyes. They were awash, unfocused, and tearing at the more vulnerable muscles in his chest. All she wanted from him, all her tight, struggling features told him was to pick up the phone.

But he couldn't. The frail woman was too heavy. Too much from him to bear. The phone stopped ringing.

"Oh, Lou," Gloria murmured. Her plaintive sigh echoed softly as she faded with the knell. He felt her warm weak mass drift past him, joining the shadows under the sheets.

Lou held his hand down on the snooze button of his alarm clock. He didn't wish to cancel it completely just yet. He wanted five more minutes of sleep before he got up. A few minutes of empty peace to forget the nightmare that swam behind his eyes. He had already managed to lose most of the details. Indeed the primary images of the terrible event escaped him. Yet he was haunted by a sense of loss, of love lost, life lost, haunted him. It was too much weight for him to bear at the moment. He reasoned that the despair he suffered would surely dissipate after five more minutes of blissful sleep. The world could wait. The effort required to hold his eyes shut was minimal.

"No, Lou," a familiar voice said, "Not this time."

With her words came a new pressure on his wrist. A light, firm grip that circled the limp appendage, placed it gently back on the cool smooth surface of the metal bedsheet. The attention paid him distracted him from his quiet time. Lou winched back heavy eyelids to examine the intruder.

It was Alice. She stood above him, one hand on her hip the other still touching his wrist. Her head was bowed. Fierce blue eyes targeted his, held his shifting gaze. His jeans and t-shirt hung loosely on her.

"Alice, what?" Lou asked, "Why can't I just rest a minute? I got the snooze on."

"Lou, come on," Alice said softly, shaking his wrist, "You're putting way too much into this." She couldn't mask the strain in her voice. Lou was beginning to lose focus. His eyelids closed. Alice shook harder.

"Lou," she said, shaking his wrist, agitated, "Enough already. You gotta go home."

Lou, his snooze frustrated and the disturbing dreams behind him, allowed himself the task of waking up. The effort required little more than open eyes, he knew, but the waking world was elusive and, once those heavy lids rolled out of the way, not quite what he had expected.

Instead of looking up from his fluffy clean pillows at Alice's concerned visage, he faced a fuzzy green sea. When he noticed that his nose was being crushed by that sea, he forced a second look. He focused, concentrated on his surroundings. They resolved quickly for him.

He sat at a plain metal office desk. His face rested squarely on the empty green blotter. A phone, its antique black metal receiver still cradled in his limp hand, was ringing at the corner of his desk. When he flexed to pick it up, Alice stopped him. He looked up at her.

Her blond hair arranged in an untidy knot. She wore a faded print dress that was tight in all the wrong places. She was smiling at him. Her eyes were wet. Her head shook. Her tone was severe.

"No Lou," she said, pulling his hand away from the jangling phone, "No more for now. Go home."

"Huh?" Lou asked, "Home?" He was still dazed, he decided. Half asleep. Probably enduring another dream. Alice lowered her head to his ear. Instead of raising her voice, perhaps in deference to the folks seated at the herd of metal desks around him chatting on their own phones.

"Yes Lou. Home. You've been here three shifts already. That would be enough for anyone, but you also were here every night last week. They never should have placed that ad in the yellow pages. It was too much for us; for you."

"Well," Lou said, moving his head slightly so her lips brushed his ear (she didn't retreat), "I guess I have been here a long time." His head started to clear, and he heard the phone ring again. Heard it summon him. Reaching for it, he continued, "Let me just answer this one, and I'm out of here."

Alice pulled his hand away. Before he could reach again she pushed a blinking button on the phone so it rang and was picked up at a neighboring desk by an eager, overweight man.

"No, Lou," she sighed, "I'm serious. You've lost two callers this week, and that's enough for anyone. Even you. No come on, give it a rest. I'll drive you home."

Lou smiled, shook his head.   He tried not to be too condescending when he spoke:

"It's okay, Alice. It's all just a dream. I'm waiting for the snooze right..."

"Lou!" Alice said, frustrated. Saying no more, she gripped his armpits and assisted him rather forcefully to his feet. His legs felt weak. He wanted to sit back down. The phone might ring. The snooze alarm might sound too soon if he stood.

"Alice, please. Let me stay a little longer. Just a few more minutes. It might ring again."

"I guarantee it'll ring again," Alice said, "'Tis the season. But it'll be ringing for someone else tonight. We're leaving."

"But Alice. It's all a dream. Just a dream."

"It sure is Lou. The suicide hotline is a damn nightmare, and you've endured enough of it. We all have."

Lou nodded his heavy head, fighting finally his soul's profound reluctance to face reality, to wake up. To see the ugly public room, remember the ugly calls. The losses.

"The losses," he repeated aloud.

Alice squeezed his shoulders.

"It happens Lou. We can't save them all. Now please, let's go. I'll buy you a drink."

"Yeah," Lou sighed, "Let's go. Thanks for caring Alice."

"Hey," she said brightly, "It's what I'm here for."

Also by Peter A. Luber:

Oneironauticus

ISBN: 978-0-6151-8290-2

Published by Sageous

www.ingramcontent.com/pod-product-compliance
Lightning Source LLC
Chambersburg PA
CBHW031156020726
47499CB00002B/383